On Distant Fells

-being a story of the Great War

Dr David Sutherland

1

Second edition 2014

This is an expanded and updated version of the novel
'On Distant Fells' - first published in 2003.

Published by:

Cherwell Dene

CherwellDene@aol.com

Printed and bound by Martins the Printers, Berwick-upon-Tweed
Typeset by the author and i.glasgow@icloud.com

ISBN 0 978-0-9563564-4-4

This book is dedicated to the memory of our wonderful dogs, including Simon and Tess, and all our pets (Spirit & the cats, and our rare and endangered breeds - cows, sheep, hens and ducks) past and present - who have enriched our lives.

Other Novels by the author: The Holly Blue, A Child at War, The Sower Went Forth Sowing, A Highland Story - written on glass, Dickens by Charles Dickens.

Book 1. An Unsuspecting Family

Chapter 1. On Distant Fells - one hot evening in late August 1913.

On the Top Road to the village stands an old oak tree, so gnarled and so wide, that pressed against its trunk the outstretched arms do little to embrace it.

There is a solid permanence about this tree; but the superstitious in the Dales (and there were many a century ago) always said that all manner of soldiers' ghosts wandered to and fro within its shade.

This superstition took root one summer evening when a brilliant flash of lightening streaked across the valley. With the roar like a cannon, a huge bough ripped free and crashed to the ground. It exploded into a shower of orange and red; sparks that lit up the evening sky.

It was an omen, so the villagers said, of the bitter fury and sacrifices of the war. And in the same week, just to prove their fears, four local boys (they were hardly old enough to be called men) were killed. That was in August 1916 in the horrific Battle of the Somme. At first, everyone accepted their loss as the inevitable Will of Fate. 'Now, God be thanked Who has matched us with His hour,' the Minister quoted to a stunned congregation.

But it was to be a long and bloody hour.

At the outbreak of the Great War things were very different, after all, as everyone agreed, it was a man's duty to fight for King and Country; a duty which could not be shirked. Martin Norman had felt the same.

It was in 1914, he recalled, that he stood transfixed in one of those curious, seemingly extended fractions of time and said a prayer. His mother would have been proud of her eldest son going to war. How he wished for a second that he could speak to her now. He would have asked for reassurance. But it was not to be and he suddenly collected himself as the waves slapped against the jetty; and the shouts of men and the raucous screaming gulls brought him back to reality. For a moment he let his left foot linger on the quay-side, his final tenuous link with home. And as the setting sun cut blood-red and unwholesome through the dark clouds, Martin began to climb slowly up the metal gangway of the troop ship carrying him to France.

****

It was, as he reminded himself many times later, a strange year - 1914. But the events that were to lead him to France had begun the previous summer, one Saturday evening in August 1913.

4

Dark clouds had rolled in from the east and oppressive as the air was over Compton Vale, a sharp breeze had suddenly sprung up. Now the air was cool and fresh in the meadows.

It was good news for those who were out and about. Martin was on the high fells shepherding. He paused to watch the bad weather slowly melt away; ahead a young girl hurried on, head-down and preoccupied. The Doctor, Vicar and villagers breathed a sigh of relief. For the villagers, it was their night of pleasure. They called it by the grand title – the Harvest Ball. It was not a ball in the true sense of the word, no formality; just ordinary country people enjoying a welcome break in the industry and tedium of their lives. Nothing special really, but it was to be a defining moment for some - as this narrative will tell.

This is the story of Compton Vale in Northern England, remote and beautiful; a place you would appreciate most if you walked along the Top Road to the village. Ahead the whole valley suddenly stretches into the distance to where the Pennines fade from view. And nothing disturbs, nothing can disturb, their solitude.

Such was the scene on that Saturday evening in August 1913, when the sky stretched in pallid blue. The setting sun splashed the horizon with red and gold and the fading light tinted the purple heather to a curious magenta. It was a warm and tranquil dusk.

The meeting line of sky and valley top, allowed an observer seeking the last sun's rays to see two small and silent forms resting on the grassy edge of a crag, in a spot at the transition of reds and greens and blues. Such black and white border collies are frequent workers on the fells and their presence, in itself, would not have attracted much attention. But while Sam explored the rough bracken, Sorrel was alone on a craggy promontory and intent on watching a figure in the valley below. Her gaze was unbroken.

Blue, indigo, violet went the sky in darkening hues. On distant fells the night had come to send the wild birds winging home.

Chapter 2. One pastoral night. June Norman.

At this seemingly transitional hour when the colours of dusk become muted, the shadowiness of the valley lent a diffident complexion to the hills and trees. In the increasing gloom of the valley a faint white blur was visible from the crag above. Thus Compton Vale slowly donned its coat of night and the old bell hung silently.

For the building, on approach, assumed the tower of the ancient church; sycamore, juniper and yew patrolled the graveyard's grassy hillocks, where the graves appeared untidy and neglected. The locals claimed it was originally a Bronze Age burial ground and in that they may have been true. It was a remote and somewhat desolate spot and rarely frequented apart from alternate Sundays and Holy Days. In the western corner hung a wrought iron gate which angled precariously from one of its hinges. Only minutes before it had scraped the pebble stone drive into miniature furrows. The brass-handled oak door was open, the darkness admitted that much, but the silence was absolute. In fact the building seemed to hold its breath.

Suddenly there came a sound, precise then indistinct. A man's voice, yet no minister spoke with such mock incantation... 'Dearly beloved we are gathered together here in the sight of God and in the face of this congregation, to join together...' Here the whisper faltered and died away.

No sound, no breeze, no lone bird's call had interrupted the speaker, only a sudden irrational feeling. It was a feeling of utter foolishness.

****

Sorrel, the Border collie continued to observe the scene, partly from curiosity, partly by instinct. Her gaze was unwavering, even when a grouse cackled in alarm from a patch of heather close by. The girl's broken haste, sometimes running, sometimes walking, intrigued the animal. She watched the figure hurry across the broad expanse of fell.

However, the gathering dusk did little to dispel the girl's natural beauty.

Even in this half-light, June Norman's eyes seemed to dominate her face - a sparkling brown delicately tinged with a hint of hazel. The depth and subtlety of their colour spoke her mood. Within their expression were happiness, humour, anger and sadness that could be conjured up in a second. She had long since given up trying to disguise her emotions. Her feelings were always written in her features. With her dark hair cropped boyishly short (unusual at that time), long black lashes, high cheek bones, even teeth and dimpled smile – it was a combination that added to the eagerness of her face.

Across the sparse and brittle heath grass, she ran - not pausing for a moment. Then she headed towards a narrow, winding path. It wound up the hillside, in a series of sharp curves, each one carved out by the winter torrents that sprung from the mountains beyond. Many stones were loose and uneven. So much so, that her progress at times was annoyingly slow. The larger rocks, which had been whipped loose by the intermittent raging streams, needed extra caution; and this delay only added to her impatience.

June paused to catch her breath. She surveyed the first ascent of the approaching hill; the abrupt escarpment framed against the sky. Beyond it the horizon formed a series of undulations that dipped towards the ancient drover's road, just visible beyond. Should she take the steeper and more hazardous route? It was a decision made in an instant. She knew that the drover's road followed a horizontal course to avoid the steeper ascents but it would be too slow.

So, after the briefest of considerations, she crossed a downfall of scree to join an old sheep track. It had one startling disadvantage; it ushered her towards a narrow ravine which hung almost a thousand feet above the stream below.

Whatever the tensions and resentments she had felt in the previous week, and the apparent cooling of their relationship, they were momentarily forgotten. She had to focus on the way ahead. Nothing else; because before her was one major obstacle – a towering massive rock slab cleft by a deep chasm, a gash from a primeval force.

But June was in a hurry; and love fed her impulsiveness. It is an old cliché that 'love is blind'; and in June's case, sadly true. She had tried to rationalise her thoughts during the last few days and there was a determination to act sensibly, and to hold steadfastly to her firm conclusion to end it all. But for a young girl often overwhelmed by love, this was proving to be difficult; for emotion filled her day, casting recurring shadows on her happiness from which she could not escape.

And she was hampered by one fact - she did not have

anybody to turn to for advice.

She needed help; and repeatedly felt like telling her elder sister, Mary. But should she? June could not decide, and in her indecision blundered on. Anyway, what was the use of accepting advice (she kept telling herself as an excuse), since it is never what one wants.

So, she reached the conclusion - that she alone would decide her future; but only when she got to her destination and confronted the problem. And, by inference, the quicker she arrived there, the quicker she would make up her mind. And she was late. She knew that he would be annoyed at the very least, probably angry. He was so busy and might even have gone. If so, that would be for the best, thus end the matter, once and for all. Did he love her as much as she loved him? There was always an underlying embarrassment in his manner towards her. At nineteen she did not have any experience of life, certainly not beyond Compton Vale and its confines. The more she thought about it, the more her recent disappointments turned to anger and then despair.

Now to concentrate on the mountain ahead; and as she climbed, the air became brisk and fresh. It ruffled her red dress, pushed back her hair and cooled the increasing warmth of her face. Cautiously she approached the massive rock. She was late, so late, and June knew that the shortest route was the frighteningly precarious narrow ledge that the locals called 'The Rake'. This confined slope, at the most two feet wide, was hazardous and treacherous, terminating on the brow of the hill – and now her immediate destination.

By day this route was dangerous enough; by night seemingly impossible. Only for a second did June pause to consider the danger. But anxiety made up her mind.

There was to be no turning back.

She hesitated as she approached the cleft in the mountain. The rock face seemed overwhelming in its intensity of blackness. Slowly she gained confidence in the first few steps. She pulled herself up by the short jagged promontories of rock, and the odd outcrop of bracken.

By pressing her body against the narrow granite walls she gained extra leverage. Suddenly the incline became steep, the path ill-defined and frightening. But now was not the time to look back. Her dress clung to the wet rocks as she pressed upwards; her shoes barely gripped the green, treacherous slime. Once again June hesitated. She caught her breath. Then, with a supreme effort, she scrambled up the tight cleft towards the two pinnacles of rock that led onto the summit path.

As she pushed cautiously between them, the valley suddenly appeared below, as if a window had opened on the world.

She had almost reached the top. Another pause, another deep breath, and the decision made. Her best course, she decided, was to slide down an incline onto another narrow ledge nine feet below which led to the summit.

Bracing her fall with her feet, June slithered down; and for a second she felt trapped by the final steep forty yards of ascent. The mountain shadow at this point only added to the uncertainty of her route and June could hear the rocks as they fell around her into the void.

Stopping for a moment to regain her composure, she calmly brushed back her wind-blown hair with a mud-streaked hand, looked down and gave up on her dress. It was soaking with the water that sprang from the numerous clefts in the rock face; and the red was a dark crimson. How stupid she had been in trying such a route; then shrugged her shoulders resignedly.

Cold and wet, she felt the chill mountain breeze as, without warning, the ledge turned to the right and whipped upwards. Now the wind was full in her face. June hauled herself up. She had reached the grassy ridge beyond the summit. Now was the overwhelming thrill of success. 'Across in the dark, who would have believed it?' And she laughed as she realised that she had gained at least twenty minutes by avoiding the tedious drover's road. Such time June considered, in her youthful way, she could ill-afford to lose.

Refreshed with excitement, the nineteen-year-old girl ran on. But as she approached the church June hesitated; then stopped once more to compose herself. She had to tidy her hair, wet and unruly as it was. She brushed it from her brow to reveal the eagerness of her eyes. Then she looked at her soaking dress, gave a rueful smile, and smoothed down the creases as best she could. Finally, she wiped her hands on a tuft of grass. Feeling she could do no more, June shrugged her shoulders, pursed her lips, smiled and looked up to the sky for inspiration.

For the first time that evening, indeed for the first time in days since their last argument, June felt more composed, more resolute, more determined.

With a hand that trembled slightly she grasped the brass handle and pressed her body against the heavy oak door.

To June what might have seemed impossible could yet come true.

To the man in the cold solitude of the Church darkness - what might have been true - had now become impossible.

Chapter 3. One night continued. The Matriarch and Mary.

If Martin's love for his mother knew no bounds, his other deep affection was for his grandmother; at seventy still going strong and as kindly domineering, as ever.

'Men... are... such fools!'

That was the distinctive voice of South Hadley Farm, a voice that was often heard before dawn and it even diminished the strident calls of the rooster.

South Hadley Farm was an imposing building; there was no doubt about that fact. It stood foursquare on the brow of a hill facing the valley two miles away - a twelfth century edifice with, to its left, a quadrangle of low buildings surrounding the cobbled yard. A handsome house with broad pillars, just visible amongst the rough grey stone of later years; austerely whitewashed below the tidy thatch; while four mullioned windows and a rounded arch above the front door gave a feeling of permanence.

'Why isn't he here? By the Lord, if there's anything that's better both for the figure and the soul, then let me know!' Grandma Wetherall paused once more, munching the bread and bacon sandwich, the latter crisp and hot. 'They both go together like quails in a bevy!'

A rich aroma of sizzled rashers filled the air, and rose imperceptibly to linger between the heavy oak rafters of the kitchen, darkened by ages. The well-worn shiny flagstones gave the room a functional and austere homeliness. The room was bright, angled south, and the sun's rays had enough guile to penetrate the narrow windows and defined both speakers as they sat in Windsor chairs. They faced each other before the cavernous fireplace and blackened Yorkshire range.

'What do Grandma?' The reply came after a considered pause.

'Why dancing, honey, dancing... and romance (she added slyly). You must be going to the Harvest Ball tonight! But where's John these last few day? What a man and my kin to boot!' She paused, 'Tho' the Bowes are not of the marrying sort, some folks ain't, and that may be a blessing!' She placed another streaky rasher on the upturned loaf and guillotined a generous slice off the top. With a tight Victorian bun of grey hair, a ruddy complexion, smiling blue eyes and a shawl as varied in colour as the biblical counterpart set against a black dress, the Matriarch held forth.

The young girl sitting on the floor by her side replenished the small fire with a pine log and a staccato poking of the ash. Small embers broke into a spreading glow and drifted as a fine cloud before settling back onto the blackened hearth. The glow was over in a moment. But the gentle light had reflected on the young girl's pleasant smile. Seven years older than her sister June, and the second eldest of the five children, Mary Norman's face and figure fulfilled, in many ways, the promise of her retiring farmhouse existence.

By the villagers she was considered, not maliciously, to be 'plain'. True her hair was long and simply pulled back from her narrow face, and it was, at best, an indiscriminate sandy hue. Her eyes were a greenish colour in direct sunlight, while her mouth was thinner and less distinctive than her younger sister's. Her figure was medium to slight and she stood about five foot five inches, like June.

However, there was a latent firmness and resolution in Mary's expression that commanded respect from her three brothers and everyone who bothered to get to know her. A solemn dignity was also present which often hid the sweetness in her features. In a word, some said, she could be 'tough'. Twenty-six years of age, she had assumed the qualities of leadership since her father's death several years before and the recent illness of her mother.

She replaced the poker on the hearth and stared at the small flames before sighing. 'I do wish Mother would eat more!'

The Matriarch took a deep breath. 'So she should! 'Least Dr Ashleigh says so.' The old lady pecked at her bread again. 'I don't know! If you want my advice... and how often have you heard me say that over the years... it's dripping.'

Mary laughed. 'What's dripping?'

'Well it's not that darned back yard tap for one. Why on earth doesn't Joseph fix it? '

'I have not the slightest idea,' rejoined the girl laughing at her grandmother's quizzical expression.

'Dripping! That's what us old 'uns call it, beef dripping. Fresh sirloin or ribs gives the best. Take my word for it! Let the fat settle, then go cold, skim it off in chunks, and what remains is brown and rich...nature's remedy for aught that ails.'

Mary smiled. It required little imagination on her part to visualise the brown congealed mixture in the roasting pan. How thickly it was spread on the bread, and how eagerly she tried to avoid it. 'Dr Ashleigh did recommend good food, Grandma, especially tripe, and plenty of fresh air....'

The Matriarch paused before taking a bite, pointed heavenwards with the sandwich and took a considered breath. 'Fresh air be damned! There's enough air, fresh or not, around this wheezing old farmhouse to cure a thousand ills. Take the wind from the north east. Picks up the cold and dust from the high fells and throws them in your face. And what do the hens do? Nothing! They won't lay! It's a good job they can't cough!'

Mary laughed loudly. 'But Dr Ashleigh said...'

'Mary, let me say one thing - the doctor be damned also!' There was a short silence. Grandma Wetherall chuckled in satisfaction. It was apparent that she had an inherent distrust in the locum doctor. It was instinctive. 'He's too young to know much. Why old MacKenzie doesn't come here more often is way beyond me. He delivered you all and a good job he made of it too. What's wrong with his horse? Nothing!' the Matriarch shrugged her shoulders and gave a reflex adjustment of the shawl. 'If his excuses are as lame as his nag they'll both need shooting and I'll tell him so.' She paused again to shake her head. 'But the bills, by the Lord, they'll be galloping this way by Michaelmas, or I'm as dead as a donkey.' They both laughed again and the old woman clapped her hands in mirth.

Mary smiled. She found it impossible to resist her Grandmother in such an expansive mood and waited for the next blast.

'Dr Ashleigh's a London man born and bred - a scholar no one can doubt that!' Grandma Wetherall tapped her fork on her plate for emphasis. 'But he'll never understand the Northern Dales and their folks, and they'll never warm to him in consequence. He's a bit too uppity if you ask me. I like a doctor to be friendly and look you in the eyes, which they mostly do,' - she smiled broadly and almost dropped a strip of bacon from its precarious ledge on the fork - 'except when they're rustling up the bill.'

Mary laughed, but it was an uneasy laugh and she did not reply. She was gazing at the fire. She could not be so dismissive about Dr Ashleigh. She liked him and found him attractive. In her eyes the young doctor was refined, handsome and intelligent. They were the adjectives that sprang to mind in that moment. Was it his bookish imposing manner that lifted him head and shoulders above the men in the village? Most of whom she considered boring, and plodding along a narrow path in life. Yet she was awkward in his presence, unlike June who continued in the same cheerful, diffident way whether he was around or not.

She recalled that she had liked Dr Ashleigh the first time she saw him, just over five months ago. She had watched him examine her mother's chest, first with percussion and then, impressively, with the most modern of stethoscopes, registering each dull note, wheeze and cough with a profound gravity.

At first the illness was pronounced 'a severe chill' but as the symptoms progressed and blood appeared in the sputum (what the doctor called 'haemoptysis') the diagnosis was not in doubt.

Her mother had consumption, - pulmonary tuberculosis, and the scourge of the dales; and Mrs Norman knew the outlook would be bad. Other faming families had caught the disease and some had died, for the infection spread mainly through the cows and came out in the milk.

Mary had prayed fervently since then and tried to remain positive. She knew the death of her father eight years before had left a void that Martin, the eldest, had reluctantly filled. He was always studious and reserved by nature, and college had been his aim. But the monotonous grind of hill farming had eventually dampened his enthusiasm for further learning and he now seemed loosely bonded to this life, solitary and unfulfilled.

The wall clock struck the hour and the resounding notes broke Mary's short reverie. 'What will become of us Grandma if Mother does not get better?'

The old lady sighed and wrung her hands. 'There are enough boys around the house, but marriage will break up the farm…if they all want a piece. And that's the fact! But you're all right Mary, dear! John Bowes will make you mistress of Low Green Farm one day. Yet he's slow about it! Thirty years of age, heaven help us, and still deciding.' She reflected for a moment. In the silence the ticking of the clock grew even louder and more intrusive. 'Their dairy farm is good,' she muttered, 'but men and milk, unlike wine, don't get better with time.'

Mary gave a forced smile. Almost five years had elapsed since their engagement had been announced at a harvest ball and yet she was still sewing and knitting for a seemingly eternal bottom drawer.

Click, click, click went the needles – and the years had flown by. Nothing had been ventured and even less gained, except her oak chest had filled to capacity. He was a popular figure in the villages was John Bowes; an earnest, heavy handed hill-fellow, kind in spirit but stubborn by nature. He was always described as 'a fine figure of a man' – and so he was. Standing over six foot tall and more than fourteen stones, he had hazel coloured eyes that were sometimes filled with a soulful disposition, as if reflecting on the vagaries of life. Yet within the ruddy features were a ready smile and a kind expression that made him attractive. His hair was long and fair, and it gave the distinct impression that it was about to be

18

brushed at any moment.

Mary paused. She remembered how everyone was so delighted with the engagement. No one more than Grandma Wetherall who had been born at Low Green Farm and had long hoped that one day it would be reunited with South Hadley. Her parents had been overjoyed, especially her father who had always doted on his eldest daughter.

But there was an impediment. For marriage, to John, meant leaving his home until 'his inheritance came about'. He always said that to bring a wife into the house... well, it would disrupt everything, his parents and his two sisters and 'what they were about'. And Mary understood. It was the farmers' way; and John often chided his sisters that 'they were doing little or nowt about wedlock and getting a fresh roof over their heads. So everyone wud have to wait!' he bluntly told all and sundry who inquired about the wedding day. 'And that was that!'

He was as pragmatic and resigned, as he was content to wait. So John waited and wiled away his spare time in the sheltered confines of the 'Frozen Plough' or the 'Dog and Gun'; and the last few days were no exception.

Mary looked up once more. The fire crackled and seemed to drown what was said in a half-whisper. 'Time will tell, Grandma.'

There was no disapproval in her voice, no disappointment; but that brief remark signalled the end of this discussion.

Since seventeen Mary had searched no farther than Compton Vale for her future happiness, content to work the farm's less onerous tasks. Turkeys, geese and hens were her family, the white doves that hung about the red tiled barns her own especial friends. These were the animals she truly loved above all else. The cats...well they were June's. Forever purring around the dairy floor at milking time, catching each jet aimed in their direction with mouthful bounds.

Now, her thoughts wandered for a few moments, as the Matriarch fell to silently gazing at the flickering flames. Suddenly Mary had doubts. It was irrational but the doubts suddenly seemed to grow, take on their own shape and momentum in the fire glow. Her mind raced to one conclusion after another. Was marriage worth a future in Compton Vale? She had never doubted this before. She looked across the valley and the long silent line of the fells opposite. 'Perhaps one day,' she pondered, ' Perhaps one day I'll live on a better farm... or even on a country estate somewhere milder and more fertile, perhaps in the south...'

Then the clock struck the quarter.

Since June had not arrived home, and their mother required her evening drink and medicine, Mary slowly got to her feet. She gently and lovingly squeezed the Matriarch's hand before leaving by the low-beamed kitchen door. She paused. Should she go to the dance?

If June did not come home soon, she would not go. John, no doubt, would arrive late and be overly jovial and facetious through drink, which irritated her; irritated her at times beyond measure. She flatly refused to spend a weary hour sitting alone in the Barrington Hall while he cheerfully attained this end by propping up the bar. Then she smiled to herself at the vision of Dr Ashleigh arriving, perplexed and aloof; yet she knew deep down that in the end he would probably invent some excuse for not being there.

And with that thought her fate was sealed for the night and, as it turned out, forever

Chapter 4. One night continued. Martin.

Martin Norman was not, in general appearance, a hybrid of his two sisters.

At just over six feet he stood almost seven inches taller. His hair was fair, his eyes the same blue as the Matriarch, his physique broad with muscles evenly distributed between trunk, arms and legs. He was in complete proportion.

Above all, he had a quiet disposition like his eldest sister, Mary. His reticence, his studious demeanour were often misunderstood and seemed to indicate a lack of warmth and enthusiasm, at least that was the general opinion of most farming families. However, he was not unpopular amongst the other shepherds of the dales.

Long days on the fells were his speciality, quiet periods in the company of black-faced, Swaledale or his Herdwick sheep. Forever by his side were the two companions of Sorrel and Sam. Border collies *par excellence* in every meaning of the phrase. Martin called them his shadows. Always obedient to his shrill whistle and call, they were the expert herders of the flocks that tumbled and spilled across the heather moor when down-land bound. And he loved to rest on this high land looking at the valleys below which met in a natural trefoil.

The valleys were deeply enclosed by mountains making the horizon appear foreshortened in the midday sun, so much so that each connecting ridge and individual summit was easy to identify. Noon was the time he loved best.

For lunch he would rest on some outcropped crag, gently contemplating the patchwork valley floor below, patterns etched from the varied greens of the fields, the criss-cross of the stone walls and the broken shadows of the passing clouds as they made inroads through the hills and trees.

Beside him lay the dogs, jealously and affectionately licking his hand or cheek, eager to be noticed and wanting to be fed. They were the enthusiastic supporters of every move and gesture he made, uncritical and, as such, perfect companions. Both were border collies, a breed which blended into the moorland scenery like dolphins in the waves. Their coats were of medium length and slightly wavy, the colour the traditional, glossy black on white, with a flowing tail inverting to the whitened tip. Sam had large expressive brown eyes and a broader head, but Sorrel's features had the softness of a bitch's gaze. Martin always looked at the dogs with unbound admiration and delight.

This evening found him returning from Ullock Moor, a broad, brackish expanse of cruciform heather, ling and sphagnum moss that dominated the skyline with its long, gentle undulation of two miles or more. It was sunset and the curlew's call rang plaintively across the winding ridge close to the Drover's track.

The sheep were on the high moor, compact and well.

Rarely checked at this time of year, strengthened in numbers by growing lambs, it would soon be time for the final harvest, followed by the shepherding of the multitudes to the lowland fields, where emerging shoots would be green and tender. Each field was enclosed by grey piled stones - walls that had for generations made good neighbours. Although each rough block had weathered for centuries, they would occasionally tumble with a ground swell or frost, thus making depressions that the sheep were happy to exploit.

Stopping in the gloom to watch a covey of scattered red grouse, as they skimmed low with their characteristically stiff outstretched wings and harsh revving call, Martin noticed a figure heading towards the Drover's path below. He stared for a moment, both in curiosity and surprise, when he recognised the hurrying form emerging from the dark shadow of the crag; and it was his youngest sister June. She had just left the old churchyard. As a Methodist family - a Wesleyan by creed - he wondered what on earth she was doing there. But Martin was not the sort who thought deeply about such matters, nor did he consider calling. Indeed his attention was taken by the collies chasing a foraging stoat.

It was a pity, because if he had continued to look his calm disposition would have turned to amazement; for another person, equally familiar, had suddenly appeared from within the church.

But the dogs ran on. Suddenly stopping, they crouched on the ground in their characteristic herding way, and encouraged their master onwards with echoing barks.

Now the sun had almost set. Doves, bantams and hens settled down to roost for the night, while the cows benignly chewed their cud in the blissful warmth of the dyke backs. None were disturbed by the emerging music a mile away.

An owl hooted - and that was all.

Chapter 5. One night continued. The Village Players.

Tuning an old wooden fiddle can be described, in the politest terms, as the nearest thing to the choirs of Hell.

Such an even less than encouraging sound now enlivened the Old Barrington Hall, a long low building owned by the Church but situated fortuitously, at the present time of the screeching strings, a half a mile away. It was nine pm and a small fire burned in one corner to air the hall while on the opposite side there was an elevated platform which was to contain the band - if that's what the three musicians could be called.

Currently the arbitrator of the 'musical feast' was one W. Pearson, affectionately called Willie at his work as a chimney sweep and odd-job man, but respectfully known as William while pursuing another versatile trade, namely that of the village barber, a trade he carried out at home in the company of his mother who believed that all good Christian names should be respected before God.

With fresh vigour Willie gave the instrument of torture all the undivided attention he could. The fiddle responded with more eloquent howls. 'Damn blast and hell! The bridge is all wrong!' he muttered. Then with a deft adjustment, the fiddle broke forth into more compassionate tones. 'That's more like it!' he said in an affectionate way as if addressing a child.

Sixty years old and unmarried, Willie had a weather-beaten face with a long brow that gave his features an almost indefinite appearance, and the whole was crowned by a long strand of brown hair (not yet grey) that wound forward in an enticing way greatly reminiscent of a creeping vine.

Screech went the fiddle, crunch went the cinders in

the hearth, tremble went the walls, and perspiration poured from that perpetual brow in nervous anticipation.

Now Willie's disquiet did not arise from his musical talents, or to be exact - his lack of them, but from the unexpected news that a lady was coming to the dance that night for the first time in years.

Anyone familiar with his history would recall that some forty years to the day, freshened with harvest ale, he had proposed to this lady, to the delight of his mother and the enthusiastic congratulations of all assembled in the Barrington Hall. He was at the time only an embryo violinist and sweep. But his potential and charm had proved, so it seemed, irresistible. Yet only three days later the engagement had been called off and Ivy, the lady in question, turned her favours towards an undertaker. She married shortly afterwards to raise a family some fifty miles away in another dale. But the most recent news was that she had been widowed for a year and was returning to visit her cousin in the neighbouring village that very afternoon. Rumour portended her appearance within the hour.

Each year, and undiminished by time or circumstance, Willie had marked that sad anniversary by earning the condolences of his friends, their free beer as a compensation and - despite being generally in a stupor by midnight - the fierce admonitions of his mother.

Tonight, resplendent in a masterpiece of dress, namely a shirt of mustard-check and brown, broad black trousers and waistcoat (finished to perfection with a dangling silver watch chain - his grandfather's sole memento of fifty years down the mine, apart from the severe bronchitis that killed him) Willie awaited his fate with the same composure as Nelson on the Victory's quarterdeck.

The fire and the fiddle continued to work on his brow - dab, dab, and dab went the spotted handkerchief and he sighed; the years had not diminished his love.

'A pint of Peculiar, Willie my lad, will grease the strings.' The speaker who entered the hall by a side door was a lean man of sprightly steps and sparkling eyes. His main feature was a long grey moustache, waxed close at the corners.

He carried a frothing pint of beer in one hand and an extended accordion that bounced and vocalised with every step. 'Blast me if they ain't lit the fire on a night such as this, the Reverend will have something to say'

Willie replied with a slow smile and a relocation of the vine. 'George, I'll be blowed if there's not a grand turn out tonight. And the old doctor's presenting the prizes - biggest leeks, spot dance and all that!' He turned, 'Where's Angus?' The reference was to the third member of the band, the drummer a man of strict tempo and rigid habit.

'He's not in the Plough, so maybe the Dog and Gun warms his old hide,' George reflected gazing at the fire, 'For I've seen his good lady and she says that he's been gone a fair hour.'

'A fair hour, eh; he's the man for a dram, is Angus. But it's not for the wrecking of him, such life in a seventy year old is fair grand to see,' said Willie in a tone of genuine admiration; 'and married three times afore he was forty. That takes some spirit whether it's whisky or not!'

'Aye it does, for marriage but once can be a major calamity if things ain't right! And that old baritone voice,' enthused George with a short laugh, 'it gets better and better the older he gets.'

Willie laughed and contemplated his friend. 'That's

the point, George! It's due to the old vocal cords being marinated in Glenfiddich.'

'Undoubtedly, even if the doctors'll never admit it!'

'Aye and he'll argue his age to any of the fairer sex - even today,' continued Willie at length. 'Says his father forgot to register the date of his birth for a year or more... due to there being seventeen of them and the new vicar not yet come to the village. Always reckons he's as old as his ears and a bit younger than his teeth!'

This well-worn joke still aroused some mirth amongst his fellow musicians who now chuckled long and deeply.

'On a different note, the schoolmaster states that there's trouble abrewing in Europe,' said Willie after a pause of several minutes during which time they had arranged the platform, putting chairs to one side for the expected short rest periods, then moving the drums more to the centre for added effect.

George nodded.

'I suppose it could be!' continued Willie brushing his brow and looked more earnest than before. 'But it'll never get this far, not by my reckoning anyhow. Who's heard of Compton Vale in Europe and who ever will? The only thing German about here be the clocks! And doesn't that beat all!' The violinist continued with a laugh.

'True, Willie, true!' said George laughing in unison. 'But who can tell in the vagaries of life? Anyway there's no point in being maudlin my lad, so let's have another pint for the adagio! The old squeeze box is a rar'in to go and in fine fettle for I've already taken the liberty to warm up in the Plough. So let's step next door to the aforestead, for when the pub turns out the Vicar'll be about, and the place will be aburstin'.'

'Undoubtedly a smart man, the Reverend,' retorted

Willie, 'I've know him let all and sundry into the dance free, for as many a dozen had sneaked in by the back way, then lock the doors and charge them each time they want to go out...to the pub or you-know-what.'

'Whether they could afford it or not, is another matter,' replied George with a slow shake of the head. 'Anyway, that's the workings of a learned brain, I suppose.'

'True, George, true! But he gets on well with the village though. Few have a bad word to say, and when they say it, well who listens, I ask you?' Willie considered his own rhetorical question and seemed well pleased.

'Speaks Greek and Latin,' continued George on his predetermined theme unaware of his companion's reply, 'but to whom I don't rightly know'. He gave a faint shake of the head. 'The only foreigner who sets foot in the village these last twenty years is the scissor grinder and he's gormless and has nowt to say.'

'Aye, gormless right enough until it comes to asking for the money. I always give him half and let him get on with it.' Willie beamed after this burst of business acumen. 'Maybe the gypsies know summat of the sort?' he responded with some thought.

'Bah! Some are as thick and as bad as a week-old pork pie, at least the lot that comes clod hopping through the village with their fell ponies to Breacon Fair.' George paused. 'Maybe I'm being a bit harsh when I think about it; for they're a better lot than some folks make out. Have a weird religion… they don't like to touch anyone's feet, and that's a rum un!'

'More than a rum un, George, when I come to think of it; but knowing all that Greek and Latin, the old Vicar that is - not the travellers - must be of some use,' argued Willie at length, having taken another long draught of beer and wiped the froth from his chin.

'A lot of the Church's learnin's a mystery, Willie, but it's the will of the Lord that some things the parson says cannot be understood.' He gave a quick blast on the accordion to emphasise the point. 'It makes the sermon holy like and perplexing. And, taking all us humans into consideration, the Reverend Clenham is one of the most perplexing men of all! Enough of all this, I need another drink.' He laughed, 'My throat feels like a quarryman's glove. Come on!'

So down went the fiddle next to the drums, and out went the men and the fire - at the same time.

Chapter 6. One night continued. Agnes Norman.

Agnes Norman was a kind, gentle woman; imbued with a strong sense of loyalty especially to her family. Perhaps that was her downfall. She always said she loved her husband, was grateful for all he did for her. But deep down she wondered if he really loved her at all.

To understand the life of Agnes Norman is to understand the vagaries of human existence. She was young, lonely and in love when she met a key figure in her life – a dangerous cocktail of emotions.

As she looked through the half-open window at the darkening shadows of the fells she tried not to dwell on the past. She had relived the past so many times in the early years of her marriage, those uncertain years; but the children had arrived with a monotonous regularity. They had absorbed every minute of every day, so that gradually her fears and anxiety had evaporated, only to return more vividly in recent weeks as she lay in bed and had time to ruminate and regret. So she tossed and turned and worried almost to distraction. Illness held a final cruel irony in its grasp.

That evening she sat upright against the cool pillows and gazed across the valley to where the unchanging conifers of Darling Wood ate into the hillside.

The setting sun, which bathed the front bedroom window of South Hadley Farm, shone directly onto a large oak bed with a quilt of many colours and myriads of squares. Through the window was her final view on life, seeing the sombre firs shaking in the wind, listening to the burn as it soughed and spilled in the lower fields, watching the dense population of rooks in their clerical and raucous ways; birds that arrived on Valentine's Day each year and left in the autumn. Where they went to - no one knew. They held their own secret, she reflected with a faint smile.

Agnes had seen them arrive that year.

At that time she was in bed and suffering from what was called 'a winter chill.' She had heard their calls throughout the spring and summer, the noise sometimes made imperceptible by the wind swaying and sighing through the pines close by her window; slanting trees that seemed so crushed and bent by the storms that their crowns resembled arrowheads pointing the way to Heaven.

At first she had fought against the enforced bed rest ordered by Dr Ashleigh. But lately an increasing lethargy had made her confinement more acceptable, and at times a welcome relief.

The first flapping, black chicks had plucked up courage to depart the high nests by April, a time when her cough grew dramatically worse and the first traces of blood appeared. Then when the young rooks had ventured forth across the dale in soaring loops, her weight had begun to fall and her cheeks assume a pinched and waxy hue, so that she became almost afraid to look into the mirror by her bed.

During one bout of fever, when the toxic effects were at their height, the swirling, flapping forms had assumed the appearance of a cortege of mourners, bewailing her fate, and in her fear she had pleaded for the pine trees to be felled, conscious of their spiralling roots creeping long and low beneath the foundations of the farmhouse, insinuating themselves between the cracks in the flagstone floor, crawling up the chimney breast unseen, encircling her chest and suffocating all vital organs within. She could feel her ribs being constricted one by one; and those black mourners had encouraged the strangulation with incessant cries, dancing round and round in the air with wider and wider reels.

Then a shaking chill would sweep over her body like a winter wind, and her mind would clear and focus on one of the girls sitting beside her. How comforting were the soft hands that held hers. But the bacillus pursued its relentless course, from lungs to kidneys to the lymph glands. And lumps appeared in her neck one by one as the breathlessness increased, until the open window failed to supply enough air even when the Pennine wind was in full force.

That two girls had tried their best was always on her mind. She appreciated their love and kindness and wished, how she wished, that she did not have to rely on them. She worried over the fact that neither was married, their future was not secure; and here they were nursing a mother who should have been in her prime of life. That was the

31

bitterest thought of all. She had turned to the Wesleyan minister, and he had visited her regularly, prayed in earnest and appealed to God in His mercy. She hoped it would do some good.

Agnes was deep down a realist, she tried to remain calm when the family was around but it was difficult. Alone, the darkness overtook her and a strange desperation born of helplessness overwhelmed her. She tried to make sense of a life that had not been what she expected. Then she reassured herself that everyone's life was never black and white but streaked and swirled with the greys of anxiety and despair.

One thought cut through the despair, one overruling anxiety. What of the farm when she died? Martin worked the farm without enthusiasm, she acknowledged. Martin always was more studious than the others, perhaps like his father. Russell was all humour and good nature but often slipshod in his approach to life and wonderfully fond of girls. Young Joseph...he was so unsure about his future and often idle and spoilt. Cock-fighting, shooting and the chase occupied his mind day after day even when the farming did not allow. She had always spoilt Joseph, but so had her mother – even more so at times.

She adjusted her pillow and pulled up the quilt to warm her chest.

June was as sparkling a child as she could have wished to have, but Mary... Mary would be the saviour of the farm. Soon she would marry her cousin John and the two lands could be joined as one as they were almost sixty years before. For a moment she savoured that thought and smiled.

And what of James? She had loved him in her own way, not deeply, but she had loved him. But as her husband, he had given little or no guidance about the children or life in general, always content to work stubbornly on, farming in a way that never brought in much money. She had given up berating him about his lack of ambition. She missed him though, good-natured as he was; yet at times weak and indecisive. There never was a period when she could really rely on him. And what of the Will; the Will they had agreed, after their persistent arguing? She had never agreed, and could never agree -but understood his reasoning behind the decision.

Agnes coughed and sipped from a small glass of water, resting on the small walnut table beside her. Her friends had told her about an old woman in the next dale who was a spiritualist and had powers to communicate with the dead. Could she speak to James about the Will, get his final guidance? But the more she thought about it - the more unsure she became; how could anyone communicate with the dead. And she knew the risks. What if her secret came out and the old woman told the village.

Agnes Norman lay back on her feather-down pillow and contemplated the darkening sky.

Could the farm go to Martin; who was not James Norman's son?

She continued to ponder and worry in the crowding darkness around her. Despite the summer warmth she felt alone in a curious bleakness of spirit; who could she turn to, to whom could she speak?

Suddenly her face brightened - she would write a letter to Martin, and explain the reasons for her husband's choice, the contract they had entered into before marriage.

She knew Martin would be shocked and hurt; deeply shocked no doubt. But he was always the most sensible... the most understanding. Perhaps he would forgive.

The enormity of what she was going to do, and the doubt as to whether she was doing the right thing, overwhelmed her for a moment. She began to sob uncontrollably. Yet such was her strength that she quickly composed herself in case one of the girls came upstairs. She reached towards the drawer in the Georgian cabinet, paused, and looked towards the woods beyond in a brief moment of doubt. But it was only a moment's hesitation.

Taking out a pencil she scribbled a short note to Martin, pausing between the coughing bouts that produced fresh smears of blood on her handkerchief, small crimson droplets that increased with each bout and flecked the white cotton-lace.

After she had finished writing she read the note once more. Then overcome with sadness, she shed bitter tears that flowed profusely in her perplexity and grief.

Once again Agnes reflected and composed herself. Suddenly, in a moment's desperation, she tore the note into two. Reaching forward to the open window she let the wind take the fragments from her grasp and it swirled the pieces high into the valley, dancing and hanging like larks in the night air. She watched the fragments spin into the distance and felt relieved.

For a further few seconds she contemplated, took a deep breath and resolved to change fate. Grasping the pencil firmly she wrote a short paragraph on a fresh piece of paper. She sealed this second note in an envelope and placed it in a large packet next to her husband's old will. With relief she locked the packet in her secure cabinet drawer.

Exhausted by the effort, she lay back in bed and thought; and as she thought in the gathering darkness, she awaited another long, lonely night while anxiously listening to the unseen criers of the calls of dusk.

Chapter 7. One night continued. The Vicar.

There were four professional men in the neighbourhood and the tallest by far was the Reverend Daniel Clenham, vicar of St Cuthbert's.

He stood at six feet four, physically and intellectually above the rest of the villagers. His sermons were not unduly long but continually peppered with Latin and Greek quotations like currents in a simnel cake. He avoided pomposity and although he lingered in the crowded church porch each week to receive the congratulations of the congregation, he was well aware that they, like him, were eager to go home.

His features were not unpleasing - straight greying hair with odd strands of the original black still dominating, combed neatly to the side with a parting to the left, dark blue eyes continually darting to and fro with the sharpness and concentration of a bird of prey, while his nose and ears were long, one supposes designed in proportion to his form, and yet curiously odd and out of keeping with the rest of his face.

As a blessing Martin had not inherited the ears or nose.

The mature-minded farmer James Norman had accepted the onset of pregnancy when the morning sun had heralded the morning sickness. He had proposed to Agnes and when the child was born a Wesleyan, the Reverend Clenham had been spared the final ignominy of having to baptise his own son with another man's name. Even Grandma Wetherall had remained in blissful ignorance.

Time had produced a robust and growing Norman family, with harmony all round.

The Vicar had continued on his designated path in life, had acquired a new housekeeper (once Agnes had left), eaten porridge at all times of the year for breakfast; and enjoyed dried fruit, not soaked, and the piano in the evening hours.

Tonight he was strolling through the village, contemplating a passage recently read in Greek from Homer's Iliad.

'O restless fate of pride,
That strives to learn what heaven resolves to hide,
Vain in the search, presumptuous and abhorred
Anxious to thee, and odious to the lord,
Let this suffice: the immutable decree,
No force can shake,
What is, that ought to be.'

Over the years they had been so near, such was the distance between vicarage and farm, and yet so far apart had been their conflicting spheres of life, their thoughts and their emotions. But that long held secret, Agnes's illness and the newly written note, were forces that were soon to be; and in their very being, were doomed to change some lives.

Such are the simple, hidden seeds of fate.

And still the Minister hummed his classic Brahms, tranquil in blissful reverie.

A fiddler's sound caressed the night; the new moon slumbered in the cradle of the old moon's arms, while to the left the evening star in bolder terms eclipsed its light.

Chapter 8. One night continued. The Doctor.

The shallow crescent of the moon had just begun to assert itself over Ullock Moor, with Venus still exultant in the west, poised for all appearances on the tip of Wainstone Crag like the proverbial star on the top of the Christmas tree, when a hesitant figure slowly emerged from the porch of St Cuthbert's Church.

For the second time he took a few cautious steps to the entrance of the porch. He quickly looked to left and right, making sure the way was totally clear and there was no one about. His eyes instinctively searched for the girl although he had not expected her to have hung around. He knew that his outburst had almost certainly ended their association. Yet his feelings were mixed.

The long shadow from the crag above darkened the valley at this point so that part of the churchyard was excluded from all light, and into this darkness he stepped, furtive and solitary, thoughts and emotions swirling round his mind.

He paused again and listened. There was no sound of voices, no steady human tread. He was alone and pleased. For the first time since he had begun the secret affair a feeling of relief and calmness overwhelmed him, he was suddenly free from all emotional pressure.

'The whole thing is ridiculous.' In the darkness he began to analyse his emotions. It was strange how his feelings for June oscillated between deep love to an almost calculated rejection. Tonight he felt that rejection had the final upper hand. Curiously, he found that he suddenly had no conscience. She was compellingly beautiful, with a vivacious personality - even by the standards of the dales. Yet June lacked a certain refinement. It was an instinctive opinion, but he could not put it out of his mind. An opinion which had grown over last few days; and not being totally able to analyse his thoughts to their finality, he had simply used this opinion as an excuse to end it all. She had not the class to be acceptable in his intended society, his London society. Satisfied with this trite conclusion, he shrugged his shoulders. He stepped out of the shadow and into the moonlight. The brightness seemed to purify his thoughts, and denigrate the young girl even more. His vision was now of a farm girl in a dishevelled and mud-stained dress. Sometimes her over-eagerness to please irritated, as it had done tonight. Old MacKenzie had advised him to choose well and not from the practice. 'He might be a bit old-fashioned when it comes to medicine but sometimes he knows what he's taking about. Sound advice when I consider it now,' he thought, 'sound advice.'

Dr Julian Ashleigh LRCP MRCS esquire, graduate of the University of London Medical School paused once more by the hump-backed Waggoner's Bridge and watched the water slowly circulating the rocks. 'Yes, a certain lack of class!' he said loudly; and then to give himself confidence he repeated it again.

It was a cruel image. For a second it made him wince and hesitate in his resolve to end the love affair. 'My God, it's not the appearance, the soaking clothes! But that look, like a whipped dog craving for affection when he said it was time to call it all off. Then the pleading and sobbing, and the deep emotions… so alarming and repelling.' He paused. 'Yet why am I so bloody unsure? Damn me! Who wants fawn-like devotion instead of intellect?' His mood turned to anger. 'And why is she always so late when she knows I am so busy? Haven't I told her over and over again? Surely to God she knows that it is difficult enough for me to get away from the Practice, especially when MacKenzie's away for three days.'

He gazed into the increasing solitude of the fells and

scrutinised the horizon in the fading light as a cloud brushed across the moon. For half a mile he picked his way down the stony path and around the bracken; then stopped again. He sat down beside a narrow twisting beck that suddenly rushed forward into a small waterfall. The little stream then slipped between smooth, grey stones, lapped fern-tips and splashed invisible droplets onto their leaves before disappearing into obscurity through a sharp rock cleft.

Had the darkness lifted he would have been seen to be fixed in a trance. Handsome in both a bold yet sensitive way, six foot two inches tall with fine features, a pleasant mouth that smiled encouragingly in its fullness, a firm conviction in his dark blue eyes with fairish brown waving hair spilling forward to his brow and neck in a Bohemian style.

He had what an artist might have described as the classic attraction of brooding conviction, intelligence and charm - part natural... part acquired.

He thought of their first moments together when she stopped just being another girl and started to spin her web of humour and love about him. He had never been in love before and the sensation was overwhelming at first.

Dr Ashleigh listened to the rippling water. There was a certain physical tie, a heightened sensitivity between them from the first; she seemed to transmit minute almost electrical emotions through the softness of her skin; emotions that were totally overwhelming and seemed to draw him back for more and more contact. Yet he was uneasy. His analytical mind rationalised the situation was 'fun' at first and 'absurd' now.

He got up, sighed and in twenty minutes he had reached the style by the Top Road. Without another thought he hurried on, crossing the path to South Hadley Farm. A path the labourers had used once when his great-grandfather owned the quarry. His cottage was close to the Vicarage - a comfortable parochial tied house of two bedrooms and a compact living room, rented for a year.

He stopped, reluctant to go indoors. He liked the freedom of the night air, now cooling rapidly after the hot day, the sound of the cattle in the fields never free from bellowing even at this hour, and the total relief at having made the final, irrevocable decision.

'Perhaps I loved her once,' he considered, 'in a curious way!'

With this final thought, June was dismissed from his mind. He headed for the Vicarage drive. The Reverend Clenham had just left.

'Life is much too intense at the moment! I need a break! The grouse are prime, gone is the twelfth, and ready for the gun, while the sea trout are on the run!' He reached the cottage door and pushed it open. 'Now's the time to ask MacKenzie for a few days off; that's the first thing I'll do when he gets back. I've hardly stopped in the last three moths and I'm getting fed up with the damned mundane.'

Suddenly his thoughts were broken as a hint of music carried softly on the night air. 'Good heavens, a violin in torment,' and he smiled for the first time that evening. 'The village band's in fine fettle and, as usual, not too good to miss. It's a relief that I'm not going!' He laughed at his own sarcasm. 'What did his old Grandfather say, "Women love deeper but men love longer!" Or some such rubbish.' There was a further laugh, but it was hollow and unconvincing.

With a final look to the darkening blue, he went

indoors. The stone walled cottage with its low oak beams and broad marble fireplace was welcoming. He lit the oil lamp and a golden glow suffused the room, cutting a dark shadow from the main rafter.

'What should I do?'

He had decided earlier that day to take the night calls for his partner, because Dr MacKenzie was going to the dance. 'Let me see... bacteriology! What did that eminent German scientists Koch have to say on the identification and spread of the tuberculosis (TB) bacillus. That can be the focus for tonight!'

Thus preoccupied with his studies June Norman ceased to exist - at least for the present, as the next phase will tell!

Chapter 9. The end of the first night. Russell and Joseph.

The first of the harvest dances was always a memorable affair, taking place just as the harvest was entering its full force, yet the festivities did not greatly interfere with the travail in the days ahead.

But what about those who were not there? June was in such turmoil of grief, anger and despair. She came in from her walk and went straight to bed; the Matriarch raised her eyebrows and went on stroking a cat, saying nothing.

Mary was content with her decisions and the thought of avoiding John Bowes, facetious, jovial and red-faced with too much ale, ensconced at the bar. Nor could she understand June's mood and was happy to remain in the kitchen with her own thoughts. She looked out of the small window, past the cross-bar and sash which divided the scene into distinct halves - the top one empty and dark but for the crescent moon now full high above the crag; the bottom one showed the silhouette of the outbuildings, in every way like a Victorian picture.

A barn owl flew by, silent on muffled wings like a pale ghost from the past; for some reason that silent movement compounded the emptiness and darkness around her.

Five years of knitting for her bottom draw suddenly ended in those moments. She felt a strange tingling in her spine; life had begun to take a new course. She knew that for certain. She sat slowly rocking to and fro in the old Windsor rocking chair, the slow rhythm of movement strengthening her resolve as she gazed into the night sky for further inspiration. She heard Martin crossing the cobblestone yard and the dogs barking a greeting.

Martin reached the pump and cleaned his fell boots in his usual meticulous way. He chased the dogs into the barn where they soon languished contentedly on the hay, oblivious to the hens curiously perched on the rafters above. Then he went indoors, shouted to Mary who did not reply; had a cold shower followed by a shave. He placed his work clothes to be washed, changed into a casual shirt and trousers, pulled on his favourite red slippers and decided to settle down in his bedroom to read for the night. So 'Barnaby Rudge' and the antics of Simon Tappertit and the 'prentice nights occupied his thoughts, and the dance and his day's work became the last thing on his mind as he rested in silence and solitude.

But 'The Frozen Plough' was a different scene.

Honestly described as bursting at the seams by nine (to the Landlord's unbounded delight) it was now even fuller. Men and women jostled to the bar. 'Peculiar' and 'Mild' frothed and foamed to the paved stone floor, while an odd farm dog lurked under the long wooden benches that served as extra seating around the periphery of the room. George Havelock's accordion was in full voice and bonded the revellers in one harmonious sound of laughter and delight. Smoke crept like fog on the fells, attacking the high ground of picture rails, ceilings and lights, before descending to the valley floor of tables and chairs. Arms swaying, bodies swaying, voices shouting, voices singing, feet tapping, dogs barking, laughter and shrieks of delight - all was a persuasive scene of rural happiness.

In the bar there were two people of interest to this story.

The lounge was clearly visible through the arch door in the bar. Next to a thin, shabby clerk sat two young men of twenty three and eighteen. They were the younger Norman boys - Russell and Joseph.

At first they appeared similar, both standing around five feet ten and both had dark hair that curled in a tight bunch with a parting down the middle. However, the principal difference was their eyes and consequentially their expressions. Russell's eyes were of a dark brown while Joseph's were a bluish hue. Russell's smile was generally warm and engaging, but Joseph's features were more petulant; the result of the family indulgence. Joseph's thoughts, it was generally acknowledged, almost always focused on himself

Willie Pearson ambled through, 'How are things back home?'

'Only fair,' replied Russell putting down his dominoes, 'Only fair.'

'Well let's hope that things get better soon, Russ.'

'Aye, we could do with that, Willie. The doctor's are doing their best,' he paused, 'but you know how it is.'

43

The violinist who had lost an uncle through TB did not reply for a few moments and then changed tack. 'They say my old flame Ivy be coming tonight, but I doubt it.' He waited for a response, but not getting one continued. 'Anyway I've done myself up as best I can but it's probably a bit of a waste of time, things change in forty years for better or for worse – I divn't know in my case which way it's gone.'

Russ smiled. 'You never know what may happen, Willie old son, but you've never looked one jot older to me since I was a young 'un.'

'Thanks, Russ, but I sometimes think I've been around since Adam was a lad; it gets like that as the bones get older and more ratchet like.' They both laughed. 'Anyway, I'm a half open field gate, not knowing which way to swing,' He paused as he thought for moment, 'My fondest regards and best wishes to Agnes, Russ. If Ivy does come, God willing,' he reflected, 'I'll probably wander off to discuss old times and the band'll be a fiddle short and perhaps none the worse for that.'

'If you're a fiddle short, Willie,' said Joseph laughing. 'Perhaps Russ could lend a hand.

The clerk looked up and put down his dominoes for a second. 'The Devil be damned, is he playing or not?'

'Definitely not the mouth-organ!' responded Joseph with a laugh.

'I mean dominoes!' continued the clerk.

'I know you do! And a good thing too!' said Joseph still smiling, 'you've obviously heard how my brother plays the mouth-organ.'

'Can't say yes, can't say no!' responded the clerk slowly. 'Have I Russ?

'Indubitably! Such beauty is rarely forgotten,

44

Tommy,' replied Russ with another laugh, 'indubitably… whose drop is it?'

'Talking of drops,' continued Joseph winding up to his usual excruciating pun, 'Pound to a penny, Willie doesn't see the night through without a good pumping from the yard tap by Mabel Braithwaite.'

'Well, she'll be filling the barrels with what's left, the beer gets weaker by the week!' replied Russ laughing.

'I don't know about "weeks"! But William can certainly get into a blinkin' "days" after five pints,' chortled the nervous clerk winking and rising to occasion even more.

Russ grimaced and made a mental note to silence the clerk by playing a five. Within minutes Joseph played a double four and took the kitty of ten shillings.

The fourth player scowled, a tinker by trade. 'Lucky again Joe,' he said slowly and with emphasis. 'But it'll run out one day, my lad!'

'Never!'

'Never say "never", Joe, mark my words or pigs might fly.'

'Not on our farm! But your skinny old things have a fair chance,' retorted Joseph with pleasure.

'If I thought you were a real bettin' man, Joe, 'I'd tell you how to wager a guinea or two and make ten or even twenty!' said the scrawny tinker in a black waistcoat and leggings.

'Hold hard Bert!' said Russell firmly.

'I mean it, honest to God, with the old game cocks.' Bert looked slyly round and winked.

'What your old duck against my best!'

'No Joe! Yours against a champion from Wolf Cleugh by Cranford Dale! He's a rare one! Despatched nigh on twenty birds so I've been told, and they'll give you at least four to one!'

'Do you think I could get twenty on the win?'

'Pounds?'

'No guineas!'

Bert paused for a minute. 'Leave it in my hands. I'll see what I can do!'

'Let's shake on it Bert,' said Joseph reaching across the table. 'We will meet in our big barn before the fortnight's out and before the hay's full stacked.'

'Done!'

All four raised their glasses, as the tinker shuffled off to another table. Russ looked at his brother. 'Let's reconsider it again tomorrow, Joe. We will have clear heads by then!'

'Not by much!' laughed his brother. 'Not by much!'

The tinker and Bert drifted away. Joseph smiled as he thought of the money he would win. His contemplations were broken by a seventeen year old girl who crossed the room to speak to her cousin. He smiled and winked and whispered a brief, 'Hello, Joyce.' It was Mrs Bell's niece, visiting her aunt for the weekend.

'Must be having a break from The Grange, where she works,' continued Russ. 'My, she's pretty enough though,' he stated in his professional way.

'I'll be wandering off, Russ. If she's staying up at her Aunt's house, well… she'll need walking up there. It's a dark old path beyond the Tithe Barn.' He laughed and nudged his brother.

Russ was not impressed. 'If that waspish Mrs Bell finds out you've been seeing her over recent weeks, there'll be hell to pay, and she'll have her boss, the old Doctor, after you, if my reasoning's sound.'

But Joseph, true to his natural impulsiveness was already half way across the room. 'I will walk you home, Joyce,' he said. She laughed and he laughed too.

And so the dance went on until the roosters shook off their slumbers and rose by four to herald another day. While at South Hadley Farm, the Vicarage and the Cottage all seemed at peace - some slept, some thought, some tossed uneasily between the sheets.

Thus, with their memories for a period freed, so ends one peaceful pastoral night, the last before the years of need.

Chapter 10. The Rake Maker and his son: a harvest happening.

August is a time of great bounty for country folk - hay, corn, wheat, vegetables, apples, pears, grouse, trout and all. The whole village shared in the industry and the excitement. None were spared, young or old.

From his coppice called Yaffle Spinney the rake maker, Jack Hampshire, plied his trade. At this time rake making was an art, and the products of his trade a necessity for miles around. He was well served for customers especially at harvest time.

His speciality was seasoned ash which he selected as young trees or branches with a craftsman's eye. Thus the haft (long handle) was made and then split for a foot or so at one end. Across this piece went the head, sometimes of sycamore, and at a right angle; into the head went the fine wooden teeth (called pegs or tines).

These pegs were made of the most durable wood, for they would have to stand upto years of heavy raking in the fields. Their fixation without screws or nails was an art. Each one was fitted into a moistened hole and seemingly transfixed by a natural magic as the wood dried out.

On this particular morning he stood in his shop, the door open to admit the cooler air and the cooing of the doves. Jack whistled with the sheer enjoyment of life while his fourteen-year-old son stacked some wood in a corner.

'These long handled rakes can withstand anything the Lord gives', was Jack's proud boast.

And he meant it! That day he would have to test his wares in a way he would never expect.

For in the fields of the Bowes farm the grass was down. Sliced from its undulating height of three feet or more, it had lain for two days in long, neat, parallel rows – thus dividing the length of the field into a regular striped pattern; and once partly dry, each narrow strip had been turned over and in a warming sun and with a gentle breeze it was crisp and golden. The next step was to rake it into small heaps, which eventually piled one on another. These were the half-ricks, substantial mounds of hay about five feet high. Finally as it turned into a golden brown over several days more, these half-ricks were combined into a series of stacks or pikes, each one reaching to about seven feet and solidly weighted down with a cross of string and four large stones.

On the day in question, the conversion of the smaller mounds to pikes was taking place in one field and the loading of mature pikes in another. There was a sweet scent of hay and the sounds of earnest working in the air. The three Norman boys were helping their half-cousins in the task.

The sun was high in the sky and hinting at a lazier approach to life. The partridges strutted around the edges of the fields and an occasional corncrake made its presence known by its jarring, rattling call. The cows stood or lay close to the limpid shallow waters of the burn half a mile away, but were clearly etched in the contrasting darkness of the delicious tree-shade they so eagerly sought. Grasshoppers kept up a restless chirping from the banks, while a rainbowed dragonfly hovered uncertainly in the field before its sudden dart towards the rushy banks. A few butterflies drifted expectantly around the clumps of flowers the farmers had left in their wisdom and respect for all living things.

The centre piece, as in a Constable painting, was the horse. It was a sturdy Suffolk Punch, considered by many the pride of all the dale's horses. He stood staring into the valley, composed and immobile supporting a huge wagon. It had been dragged from the large empty barn that morning. Built to carry 2-3 tons of hay, the wheels were a formidable six feet in diameter, and the planked sides rose five feet to retain the load with a panelled end to disgorge the hay, when required.

The coupling pole, the principal member of the undercarriage, was of heavy timber and linked to the front and back axle. The whole massive structure was constructed by craftsmen not only to withstand the weight of the cargo but also to balance so expertly that the sturdy chestnut Punch could drag the whole mass forward with seemingly little effort.

The belly band and girth straps were coupled to the saddle; the crupper went over the tail. Then the shafts were secured and the whole heavy harness and cart were in perfect harmony of balance and power with the majestic horse, Vulcan.

What was the task ahead? There were five large fields on the hillside facing east, four were cut but none were yet cleared of hay. However, the fresh mown grass had already changed to a burnished gold - so that the reflected sunlight looked extraordinarily bright, making the workers blink and shade hand-on-brow to seek the unloaded wagon as it climbed slowly up the lower fields. It passed through a large gap in the hedge, scattering the finches that flocked in the fatter middle reaches.

About twenty villagers were at work, the women generally with bonnets and pastel-coloured print dresses that added to the gaiety of the scene; the men with knotted handkerchiefs over their heads, coarse dark trousers and open-necked shirts; using brawny forearms to wipe perspiring swarthy faces - and occasionally sighing in the heat. Then they would rest on the shafts of their forks for a few moments and contemplate the summer luxury all around.

June raked the remaining strands of hay idly left between the half-ricks, forming neat piles which she added to the main pikes with a laugh and an occasional tickling of some bare back as she passed the younger men, the brown of their skin bleached by the sun as it poured down on the valley.

Jack Hampshire, proud of his work, also leant a hand, his son raking beside him.

Thus the day moved merrily along. The large horse swished his tail with a monotonous rhythm, effectively driving the flies in the general direction of the workers, who swatted at them in turn. There was a constant hum of activity and an occasional song.

'Lunch is served, blessed be the Lord,' called Grandma Wetherall resplendent in a large blue knotted handkerchief around her grey hair, a long white dress and high collar. The handkerchief hung as a loose triangle over her neck against the sun. 'Lunch everybody!'

There was no need to call twice. Spread out in a mouth-watering array were bacon and potato pie, steak and kidney pie, black pudding, sliced gammon, potted beef, pease-pudding, fresh crusty loaves baked that morning and still slightly warm, gooseberry tart, raspberries in cream, Eve's pudding, elderberry wine, mulled ale and tangy homemade lemonade.

The sight was greeted with an unbounded enthusiasm, heightened by the heavy work on a hot day that sharpened the already eager appetites.

George Havelock left his wall-mending a field away and joined them for lunch. With a cheery greeting he sat down next to the Matriarch who presided over the feast. 'Well...if you know of a better life than this, Grandma W., let me know and I'll be on my way!' He smiled towards the food in appreciation.

'I knew you might come, George,' she replied with a laugh, 'and I popped in some extra strong ale. A drop of the Hadley special, it'll make the coping grits (*the highest stone that tops the wall) leap up by themselves when you grab them!'

51

George laughed heartily at this perfect metaphor.

'You know, Grandma W., there's more stones round these fells than any wall in China, I'll be bound! But they're never noticed, piled there for ever and a day. People will look at them in a hundred years and not know of George Havelock. But my hand's been there, and that's for sure; an architect on the land where we all belong! There's as much work in these dales as in a thousand temples, churches and pyramids put together.'

'Bless my soul, George, if you're not the philosopher of the Vale. But I like your talk and if another piece of bacon 'n tattie pie will keep things going - all the better.'

George nodded in contentment and stretched back on the grass, the warm sun browning his face like the ripest nut. He chewed steadily and smiled.

'It's fair warm today,' she continued, 'like when I was a girl. The heat haze used to shut out the valley on a summer day; and the food, well it melted long afore the vittles reached the fields. Not that it made any difference to the eating, it soon went. Like now!' She smiled at the young Hampshire boy who grinned back through a mouthful of gooseberry tart.

'Times seemed better then, Grandma W., but were they? We forget the bad times. Why? I'll be blowed, because they strike home at their introduction very soundly. But it seems that the human spirit always keeps on hounding for better things, and if it can't find them, well it drinks and looks again with spirits refreshed. Perhaps people were better in the old days, more reliable and resolute!'

'Suppose they were, George,' she reflected, 'but there'll always be good and those that think they're good. But the Creator gave us mules and horses, George, and although the mule may slip into the horse's harness you can always tell a mule by the shape of his shoes'. (*magnet shaped rather than the round of the horse)

This last piece of wisdom brought a murmur of appreciation from the farming audience.

June laughed too, as she sat by her Grandmother's side, helping with the food and drink; her pretty pale blue dress pulled high to her knees for comfort, her dark hair dishevelled but shining in the sun; while John Bowes' two sisters cleaned the utensils and stacked them in a spare box.

And the sun moved slowly round, taking the shadow of the horse beneath its feet like a living sundial, and three-quarters of an hour onward. While John reclined on his back with knees bent and the sun beating on his ruddy face, and the two younger Norman brothers, never far apart, lounged against a wall, with legs outstretched. Joseph poured cool water over his face and neck, letting it trickle slowly down his chest, enjoying the luxury. The valley, stretched out below, seemed subdued in the summer heat. Then the church clock shook out the hour.

John Bowes stirred with the rest, slowly stood up and the respite was over.

'Well, it's back to the old grindstone. Thank you Grandma W. for the food and drink,' said George getting up, 'and your company too, it's always a delight!'

The Matriarch watched the stonemason stride away. 'The men of today,' she thought, 'well...they're just boys by comparison. George's generation was the last of the fighting men - the Boer War saw to that!'

'Everybody back to work!' cried John Bowes and his father echoed the cry.

The others arose, some quickly, some reluctantly with a long yawn and a stretching of the arms. Soon there was laughter and contented chattering as if it had never been interrupted; beads of sweat poured down the faces and bare backs as the forks and rakes rattled and scraped as before.

The horse had been quietly enjoying the first fresh hay from a nearby mound, keeping a wary eye on the workers. He slowly moved forward at the bidding and stopped, either by instinct or design, close to the next pike.

'Load 'em up boys,' sang out Russell. 'We've about forty or more to go!'

Thus the hay was piled higher and higher on the cart, pressing down the shafts which were neatly counter-balanced by the straps over the horse's flanks and back. Up and up went the dry hay, its characteristic smell filling the air with a scent that epitomised all that was beautiful in summer.

The loaded mound was now fifteen feet high.

'Whoa!'

'Steady boy, steady!'

June felt the radiant warmth on her face and body that

made her alive and vibrant. She paused for a moment unaware of the playful comments of the men close by, forever trying to attract her attention with some remark or gesture. She looked across the valley towards the church and drew a deep breath. Then she shook her head, an imperceptible movement which no one else saw.

The swallows and martins swooped from the fields to the valley floor, to the church, and then back again in minutes, chattering in their freedom to twist and turn in the warm air. She loved this merry sound of summer above all else, for it meant light nights and summer's splendours. Each year she waited for their return with increasing impatience.

Suddenly these thoughts were broken by a loud scream from one of the women next to the wagon. The coupling pole had slipped as the horse moved forward on a gentle incline.

For a moment the animal strained, heaving with all its might; and for a brief moment the wagon seemed to right itself. But the load had imperceptibly shifted. So it shook, swayed one way and then another until finally the hay broke as a giant wave. Then the tilting shafts hurled the horse to the side, flinging it huge body to the ground, so that it lay terrified, screaming with pain while the hooves flayed wildly in the air.

And the rake maker's son?

He was engulfed in this overwhelming tide of hay. For a second his head bobbed through the brown morass and then was lost in the swirling cloud of dust.

Joseph and another man threw themselves instinctively onto the horse's face restraining the lunging head in the hope of controlling the dangerously whirling hooves still caught in the straps. Martin raced forward grabbing armfuls of hay, almost appearing to swim into the crisp, brown spiky mass. 'Get the wooden forks, watch those metal spikes on the hayforks or we could spear the boy!' he yelled.

Jack Hampshire stood rooted with fear, crying, 'Oh! My God! Save him someone!'

Now all hands made haste with the fallen load and the huge wheels were speedily exposed.

One wheel lay across the boy's chest and pinned the right leg to the ground. His features had turned an alarming bluish-black, and his pale skin began to speckle with tiny cherry red haemorrhages that grew by the second, the white of his eyes suffused with blood so that all colour vanished and he became like a hideous phantom. He could not breathe. The weight of the wagon's wheel crushed down on his chest forcing the blood to his head and holding him in a vice.

'For God's sake, lift the wheel!' Someone shouted in the confusion.

'It's stuck!' was the general cry.

'Quick the rakes!' yelled Martin. In an instant a dozen rake handles were thrust under the side planks and wheels, and everyone heaved in unison.

There was a brief moment when the wagon seemed to move, a second of relief.

Then snap went the first rake.

Snap went the second and then the third.

The remaining nine began to bend alarmingly and just as it seemed they were about to break too, the wheel slowly moved a few inches upwards, poised ready to crash down again.

Summoned by the cries and screams George Havelock came running from the wall, 'Stones! Bring coping stones. Hurry, jack up the wheel and the coupling shaft.' Such was the authority in his voice that the women and the few men who were not supporting the rakes quickly obeyed. Eager hands, alarmed faces and perspiring bodies raced to the half-built wall, tearing off the top stones and scattering the rubble as they went.

'Hold his head or he'll swallow his tongue!' yelled Grandma Wetherall, bending over the boy.

June ran forward and sat down, cradling the boy's head in her lap. 'Sshh, all will soon be well!' She spoke calmly but her heart beat wildly, and her hands trembled as she supported his neck and chin as best she knew how.

The boy gave a suppressed groan and lay limp and pale. But his groans were overshadowed by the horse screaming in pain.

The front leg's gone,' someone shouted in the confusion. 'It's broken.'

'No it hasn't,' cried Russell abruptly. 'Quickly, give me a knife! Cut the traces!'

A man darted forwards and began slashing at the leather but in his panic several cuts appeared in the animal's flesh around the straps. Blood spurted out into the man's face and over his hands. With a huge swivel of its great frame, however, the animal leaped to its feet scattering the red-flecked hay. It limped forward for a few yards and then stood unsure as to what to do next.

But the stacked stones were producing a reprieve and the wheel moved inch by inch away from the trapped form. Colour began to return to the boy's cheeks and his breathing became more regular.

'Get the doctor, quickly!' was the cry. But Martin was already running down the field towards the village.

'Drag him out,' beseeched his father.

'We can't!' said June, her eyes moist with tears. 'Look at the broken metal on the rim; it has gone straight through his leg!'

'He's spiked to the ground,' muttered Russell.

'By the Lord, mercy upon us, it's right out the other side of the calf. We'll have to wait for help,' cried Grandma Wetherall. Then she shook her head slowly. 'I hope it's the young one, for old MacKenzie can't handle this!'

Thus a subdued crowd waited for one of the doctors to arrive.

Chapter 11. The doctor arrives.

Dr Ashleigh mounted, bag in hand, within a minute of Martin's arrival - and was, in an instant, galloping across the Top Road.

He paused briefly to leap a ditch, then a fence in turn, the excited animal fresh and bounding. He raced up the field to the hushed crowd.

He did not notice June until he had dismounted and was standing by the boy's side. But he gave only briefest of glances in her direction. Bending over the pale, almost lifeless figure, he rapidly examined the wound - gently teasing back the pink fat and crimson muscle. 'It's not life-threatening, if we act quickly,' he shouted. There was a collective sigh of relief. Out came the modern stethoscope, and he listened intently. 'Air entry good... chest movement... normal... heart sounds... normal.' He ran his fingers over the chest wall looking for a deformed rib or escaping air bubbling and collecting under the skin. He looked up. 'No broken ribs either.' The group murmured in concerned appreciation and Jack Hampshire mopped his brow with relief.

Cautiously crawling under the wagon, the young doctor felt the pulses in the lower leg to see if they were sound. 'Little blood lost, thank goodness!' he muttered. Then he inspected the metal rim as it spiked through the calf. He moved the limb slowly to the side, and after a moment's contemplation, decided on the line of release. The boy groaned with pain as the metal momentarily sawed into his flesh. June held him tightly as she could, her head resting on the side of the wagon. She was alarmed to see fresh blood suddenly squirting from a small muscle artery; and tiny droplets momentarily bathed her hands and face. She watched Dr Ashleigh reach for his black Gladstone bag and saw him take off his dark jacket and roll up his shirt sleeves. Then opening the bag, he took out a large corrugated green bottle with a glass stopper. The distinctive sickly smell of chloroform drifted into the air.

Turning to June, he asked, 'you can help by dripping this liquid onto the cloth. One drop every ten seconds; please avoid the eyes!' Without waiting for a reply he turned to Russell, 'and you keep shouting out the seconds.'

Rolling up a thick pad of meshed cotton he gently placed it over the boy's nose and mouth. 'Hold it firmly and press down,' he said to June, and bending to the boy he said, 'Do not be at all afraid of the strange smell. We'll soon have you better!'

The terrified boy squeezed June's hand, his palm cold and clammy. Then, at the doctor's command, drips of chloroform began; each drop falling to the rhythm of the count. June held the bottle as steadily as she could; trembling slightly. With each drop the pungent vapour distilled into the air. There was not a sound from the onlookers.

Suddenly, with only the slightest of struggles, the boy's breathing began to slow second by second; and in less than a minute was deep and regular; eyelids flickered for a moment and then closed

'Hold the count steady please and let the drops fall!' The doctor said brusquely and taking out a large bottle of sterilising carbolic mixture, he washed his hands - the liquid feeling cool in the hot air and the sharp bleach smell mingling with the sweetness of the anaesthetic.

Dr Ashleigh observed the breathing for a few moments. Satisfied, he took out a long barber's knife and a short, sharp-pointed scalpel. Quickly he freed the entangled clothing with the knife; and conscious of what would happen next, some of the workers looked away. With a deft flick of the scalpel the wound edges were opened. Through the gap the silver-red flesh bulged. So quick and pure was the movement that only a few trickles of blood appeared.

The entry track was now clear.

With another few strokes of the blade, the spike was released from the muscles. The bone was undamaged and just visible in the base of the wound. Grasping the metal spike he lifted it up, clear of the flesh. 'Gently pull the boy back someone!' Someone did and the unconscious form was soon laid on a mound of soft hay.

The next step was to carefully pack the wound with antiseptic gauze. 'We will not be closing the wound Mr Hampshire,' he remarked looking up, 'for fear of tetanus or anthrax or some such infection. With luck, it will heal in a few days!'

The father nodded in mute agreement and

astonishment. He watched the doctor bind a light dressing around the leg and secured a wooden splint along the length of the limb with another bandage; and finally the chloroform soaked gauze was removed from the pale face and, by degrees, the boy came round.

June felt faint with both the smell of chloroform and the harrowing experience and tears rolled down her cheeks in relief. While the admiring crowd rushed forward to congratulate Dr Ashleigh. 'I can never thank you enough!' Jack Hampshire said trembling as he held the doctor's arm for a few moments with tears also bathing his face.

The doctor smiled. 'I will visit him tomorrow,' was the sole reply. He packed his bag and said no more.

June looked up. She tried to catch his attention. But Julian Ashleigh did not glance in her direction. Then, mounting his horse, with a fixed expression, he rode slowly down the field and into the distance.

Chapter 12. A visitor calls on the doctor.

Two weeks after the haymaking incident Dr Ashleigh completed his calls on the Hampshire cottage. The wound had healed and the power was returning to the leg, there were no signs of infection and he declared that all would be well within the next few days.

Word had spread around the Vale and admiration knew no bounds. The doctor, who had previously been accepted with diffidence and his modern ways looked on with scepticism, could hardly have been more in demand. Several farmers' wives vowed that their next child, if a boy, would be called Julian.

If June's love needed any re-awakening, the harvest

incident should have been the spur. She was self-conscious when the matter was discussed. She wondered if she had been too proud in the past; then wondered if she had been too forward in her approach. And she was conscious that her love had changed, taken a turn towards pure admiration; and with that admiration there came a feeling of her own worthlessness. A degree of inadequacy which was unsettling; and she felt that the best wishes and gratitude of the villagers would only deflect and detract his interest in her. Thus came a feeling of jealousy to add to the mix of emotions.

June had pondered for hours over the last few days. She realised that she could very easily fall into the old trap of utter devotion. So, in her inexperience, she decided that there was nothing else to do but avoid him in future – at least, not to meet him alone again under any circumstance.

Yet, a week later, after much indecision, her curiosity took over. She had to wander down to the stile in the field by the Top Road. At first June felt annoyed with her indecision, but little by little she was drawn out of curiosity. So in time she came to look in the familiar hiding place.

To her surprise, there was a note hidden below the large coping stone.

For a second she paused. Picking up the note, she scrutinised the outside of the envelope, afraid of its contents. Plucking up courage, she tore the letter open. It simply said, 'I miss you!'

Three short words in the handwriting she knew so well. She tried to think calmly and objectively. 'To begin again,' she thought, 'will bring another rejection, sooner than later it means I will be hurt.' She spoke in half-whisper as if to console herself. 'I know him only too well.' In this reverie of indecision June thought she heard a brief pattering of stone on stone. She looked round anxiously. Was it footsteps behind the wall? Her heart seemed to miss a beat. She listened but there was nothing more. Cautiously she looked over. Standing there was an old ewe rubbing its loose fleece against the stones. 'I am fool to think he would come and a bigger fool to think he'd change. The outcome is bound to be the same.'

So June tossed the paper to one side, watched it tumble in the wind, unwanted, and set off on her mission up the valley.

The summer days moved on.

Over the following two weeks Julian had waited for a reply. Many times he deliberately passed the stile, at first in expectation. Then in time expectation gave rise only to a faint hope. There was always a furtive searching, followed by annoyance and despair in equal swirl. But there was no note. Irritated, he felt uncomfortable by his repeated searching; and the rejection made him more determined than ever - a determination to speak to her face to face. However, as in many situations in life he was hamstrung by one weakness, one flaw in the argument –and that was her distain; because indifference is almost impossible to overcome. How could he force the issue? He was unable to think of an excuse to visit the farm. For in a fit of pique he had handed their calls to Dr MacKenzie and the older doctor, eager to retain his former popularity in light of the haymaking incident, had begun regular house visits once more.

So Julian hung around the environs of the Top Road as much as he dared without sparking the villagers' curiosity. Thus he remained in a state of emotional distraction, which taxed his temper.

At first, he consoled himself that she must be busy. But as the days passed, his anxiousness turned to anger and added to these complex emotions, was the certainty that he was being increasingly slighted.

One afternoon he had returned home in a sombre mood bordering on annoyance, believing that the affair with June had gone forever. He would work on his research, he decided, and just as he began to concentrate on the task in hand (never easy during the last week or two) there was a gentle knocking on the door.

Quickly smartening his appearance by flattening his hair and adjusting his shirt collar and jacket, Julian strode to the door feeling distinctly nervous. He knew it was June. 'How would she react after the awkwardness of the last meeting?'

As he opened the door for the first time, he felt that he was losing his composure and was conscious of his heart beating rapidly.

Such was his haste that he did not have time to consider the female figure, blurred though visible through the small pebble-glass pane.

'Good afternoon, Dr Ashleigh. I have come on behalf of the village to bring you some small tokens of their gratitude.'

The speaker was not June Norman, but her sister Mary. She entered the house without bidding.

While he stood back politely, his face for once expressionless.

Chapter 13. A meeting with the doctor.

Mary was armed, figuratively speaking, with two strings to her bow.

First, she had just reason for being there - namely the bearer of gifts.

Second, she was indoctrinated by the wisdom of the Matriarch - namely that men can rarely differentiate between flattery and truth.

She sat down in a broad, soft leather armchair close to the window, at the doctor's request. She faced him with a smile. 'I am sorry for the sudden intrusion...' she began politely and in a soft voice.

'Not at all!' Dr Ashleigh interrupted quickly and somewhat abruptly, although trying to hide his disappointment. 'I do hope that nothing serious and unexpected has...'

Mary hastily interjected. 'Oh! No! Mother is as well as can be expected and June has almost recovered from the shock of the last couple of weeks.'

He looked beyond Mary and out of the window. 'I was meaning to call and see if June was well, to see if that alarming experience had caused any emotional upset, nightmares...' He paused for a second's contemplation. 'Perhaps a sedative would have been in order...' His voice tailed off once more and he looked blankly at the wood beyond.

'She is her old self again, nothing worries June for too long!'

This was exactly the news the doctor did not like to hear and he sat down in the opposite corner and folded his hands without reply.

Mary did not seem to notice. 'The purpose of my visit is to bring these tokens of appreciation from everyone in the village. Their wholehearted gratitude is expressed by these gifts.' She smiled and touched her hair, brushing it back self-consciously.

The doctor nodded, half-smiled and waited.

'George and the villagers have sent gifts which I have left outside, they're very heavy you see and the two boys who carried them here vanished once we had reached the front door.' She smiled again. 'Jack Hampshire has also crafted something he hopes you will like!'

Dr Ashleigh seized the opportunity to get up. 'I'm looking forward to seeing them!' It was a half-hearted reply. He walked to the door and Mary followed. Outside on the porch three objects were clearly visible. One by one he carried them into the room. His mood lightened.

The first was a finely cut marble slab, a door plaque, roughly eighteen by twelve inches, which read "Dr Julian Ashleigh, Doctor of Medicine - Eternally Grateful Are The People of Compton Vale". The plaque was beautifully inscribed in gold Gothic letters which seemed to glow in the bright afternoon light like dragonfly's wings. George had crafted it with care.

The other two gifts were bound as one, bookends of ten inches in height and stoutly based, carved with the serpent and staff of life, the emblem of the medical profession since Hippocratic times. Made and carved from the finest mature oak, lovingly sculptured by Jack Hampshire.

The doctor took a deep breath and laughed, his blue eyes moving from gift to gift. 'Well! This is unexpected but quite delightful and I must say I am quite overwhelmed. Please convey my gratitude to everyone. In fact it's hard to think of the right words other than to say I cannot thank them enough,' There was a brief pause. 'I will call tomorrow to see George and Jack and tell them what wonderful gifts they truly are!'

Mary, noting his spontaneity, laughed also. 'Your

books will look magnificent on the Victorian writing desk, don't you think?'

He nodded in agreement. Picking up six books he stacked them between the bookends and stood back admiringly.

Mary stepped forward and rearranged them in a smooth gradation. 'There, how's that!'

'What it needs is a woman's touch, I suppose!' Although he spoke laughingly, he said it without any conviction.

'In this cottage?' Mary seized on the remark.

'No!' he added hastily, 'it is far too small for two. Perhaps; when I have a bigger dwelling...my own practice... I will consider a housekeeper.' He said the last word with emphasis but the visitor kept to her task.

'Here?' said Mary swiftly and blushing with embarrassment at her inquisitiveness, 'in a practice in the Dale?'

'Perhaps... perhaps not, who can tell!' He continued to gaze at the books. 'I have some plans to finalise but it will probably be nearer my home... in London.'

There was a lull in the conversation. Mary folded her hands and sat down, the doctor undecided for a moment sat down also, but to his discomfort Mary got up again.

'I am quite forgetting the time. I must be going.'

'Would you like to stay for tea... Darjeeling or Earl Grey?'

'Thank you, but no! Grandma is preparing one of her gargantuan feasts for the boys' supper and I must return to help,' she paused and gently stroked one of the bookends. She continued in a nervous exploration of the surface for a few seconds. 'You read a great deal, Dr Ashleigh'.

'To improve my knowledge, little fiction... I'm afraid.'

'It must be satisfying to have such knowledge at your fingertips, an insight into all the physical and emotional expressions of human nature...'

'I fear medical knowledge is often wanting when it comes to both, especially emotional. The mind is so little explored apart from Freud and Jung. Why we love one thing and not another is the Creator's mystery.' He spoke in a reflective way. 'Anyway...'

But Mary interjected, 'Perhaps it is better so! Maybe emotions come and go, untapped and unexplored, then wane with age, unfulfilled.'

'If it's an aegis thing, then we should ask your Grandmother or if unfulfilled, then Willie Pearson.'

They both laughed. For once Julian looked earnestly at her face, making a slow but gentle contact with her eyes, noting the long lashes and the greenish colour around the pupils dilated with suppressed excitement. He hastily returned to his former theme, 'I am looking into what we call grandly "Zoonoses"; or put simply, the transfer of disease from animals to man.'

'Such as tuberculosis?'

'Yes! And anthrax, farcy and the like!'

'Are you on the way to becoming an expert,' she asked with a smile and a faint toss of the head.

'I doubt it,' was the straight reply. At the conclusion of this brief remark there was a silence. He was lost in his thoughts, she in hers. 'Most research rises but little above mediocrity, we all jostle at the same mediocre level.'

Mary ignored his pessimism either subconsciously or by design. 'Are there any breakthroughs forthcoming, any new treatments?' She spoke earnestly, for once gazing boldly into his face without realising it.

'Of course Pasteur has shown the value of vaccination

for example in rabies. There is one famous case. He cured a bitten man by killing the mad beast and injecting an extract of the dog's brain into the patient to produce a defensive immunity against the disease.' For once the Doctor spoke with enthusiasm, not lost on Mary.

She decided to continue the theme. 'What about tuberculosis? Is there any hope?'

'Yes, Koch, the eminent German scientist, has identified the organism, however, currently there is no vaccination or similar treatment, I'm afraid. The whole field is a bit ambiguous at present, although progress is being made all the time.'

'Oh!' Mary was silent for a moment. 'What about the work you were...'

'It's shown nothing so far,' he hurriedly interjected, 'other than one might be able to identify the cows that carry the disease and they could be culled. These are the conclusions I am working for.'

Mary was still eager to flatter. 'That will not make you the most popular man in the dales, Dr Ashleigh.'

'I suppose not! They both laughed and he took her hand. 'Thank you and the villagers for their kindness; it has been a memorable day.'

'And for me too!' Mary stood up and walked to the door.

'Good afternoon. Miss Norman,' he said formally.

'Good day, Dr Ashleigh,' she replied demurely.

She walked up the drive in the cooling September afternoon air. The latest hatch of swallows practised aerial manoeuvres overhead. Cabbage white and peacock butterflies searched the dying buddleia blossoms.

'Give my regards to June,' he called after her.

But Mary did not hear. Wrapped in a cloak of thoughts

she walked briskly on, past the vicarage. 'It's strange how Grandma can be so wrong about him,' she mused, 'and at her age! One day I'll tell her so! And that's for certain!'

Chapter 14. The tinker's return.

The Suffolk Punch, Vulcan, had made a rapid recovery with ten days of rest and good food. He paced around the large barn, the floor full of deep straw trampled flat, stopping occasionally to pick up loose fragments or to gaze abstractedly at the far corner wall, sometimes idly shifting from one hoof to another as he did in the field while awaiting orders.

He snorted in exasperation.

Work had ceased for a few days, the Norman fields being all carted in, and the final cut of the emerging second grass was not yet a reality.

But the horse was disturbed by the arrival of Joseph.

The youngest Norman opened the gate and proceeded directly to the horse. Grabbing the mane, he led the animal out of the barn and into the paddock close by. Looking towards the Top Road in the distance, Joseph scanned the approaching path but in vain. The tinker and his new-found adversary had not yet appeared.

He walked over to a small side room used for storing meal and grain and carried out a cage, placing it on the barn floor. Within the confines of the bars stood a magnificent gamecock idly scratching the sawdust, tail and wing feathers had been clipped in the characteristic cut so often seen in Victorian prints. The stubby feathers gave the bird a squat but more robust figure. His red comb flopped languidly to one side; his orange eye looked sharply towards the young farmer. As a mentor of death he was a fine specimen and unduly proud. Joseph rubbed his hands in eager anticipation. They were slightly moist with apprehension of the unknown factor - the opponent's bird. But he was confident, if not overconfident. He expected Russell at any minute.

Martin was out dipping sheep with other shepherds; the animals were being thrown into a shallow pond filled with the chemical that cleansed them of ticks and lice Most of the animals raced out in anguish. But a few swam around too unsure or too dumb to clamber out. Sorrel and Sam watched the scene of endless splashing and clambering, with a profound interest that border collies reserve for all matters appertaining to sheep.

The girls had walked into the village to visit friends. June was pleased to get the fresh air to relieve a slight headache and Mary was secretly hoping that she might meet the young doctor; so they walked largely in silence.

Joseph lounged against a wall and watched Vulcan wandering and chuntering to himself. It was a supremely warm day and the thought of the money he would win buoyed his spirits.

He slowly reached into his pocket and sat down on a small mound of straw. A few sparrows hopped round in the chaff, while a hen or two gazed hopefully through the barn gate.

With a precise motion of the hands he extracted a gleaming pair of objects from his pocket. He looked on them with admiration.

They were a set of spurs, sharpened by the scissor grinder in razor perfection, with an edge so keen, he had been told, that it could split a hair. The long curves resembled miniature sabres.

He rubbed them softly against his shirt, enhancing the gleam in the afternoon light. The metal flashed and sparkled a set of fine rainbow hues which merged into a point of dazzling brightness.

Suddenly a loud whistle attracted his attention. The tinker, sniffing deeply as was his custom and clad in an old black suit, bagging at the knees but supported beneath by two stout pieces of brown string, suddenly appeared from behind the dovecot wall. He whistled again.

Joseph leapt up like a shot hare and half-vaulted the gate.

'Joey boy, we're here... bird and all' He pointed to a thick-set, rusty haired man with a long bushy beard of about forty but who could have passed for a decade older. 'Here's Ginger Hawkins acome to see you and the fowl. We calls this champion Red Devil on account of his shine. Look at 'im. But it's still two-to-one... that's right Ginger, ain't it?'

The rusty haired man being a man of few words and almost no intellect grunted and put out his hand. 'Maybe we'll shake on't. But let's see thy bird furst!'

Joseph beckoned them towards the cage on the barn

floor. Without his brother he suddenly felt less confident than he had been in the "Plough". There was a latent aggression in the men's attitude, and a demeaning smirk between them.

For the stranger's bird had the powerful look of a champion. It had a glossy plumage, black breasted with a dark almost blood-red overlay, the fine muscle of chest and wing were hard set.

The young farmer rubbed his moist hands and took another look at the "Devil". To his horror he noticed that the comb and wattles had been removed, thus denying an easy hold by its opponent. He was about to protest when Hawkins spoke again.

'Thine's a good 'un, Norman, thus I think evens would be a fairer bet!' The ginger man stroked his beard.

'It's two-to-one or the fight's off!' replied the boy firmly. 'Thine's been dubbed!'

The tinker standing hard by, sniffed and smiled simultaneously. 'That's what we reckoned, Ginge, two-to-one under the circumstances!'

Joseph welcomed the support and the tinker slapped the boy on the back and laughed.

The red-haired man scratched his balding brow and cursed. 'I'm not a chap to bloody-well argue, heaven forbid Bert, with a boy over a bloody tenner.' He emphasised the word 'boy' and smiled at the tinker. 'Okay! It's two-to-one and ten pounds bet to the nail!'

'Done!' replied Joseph, still listening for his brother.

'Spurs of course!'

'Yes, spurs!'

'Our old devil'll despatch your bird in a bloody minute or I'll be damned to Hell,' said Hawkins with a coarse, confident laugh. The tinker smiled and winked at the boy and slyly shook his head as if to doubt the fact. Joseph felt his confidence returning.

The two avian antagonists were prepared in each corner of the barn. The razor sharp weapons were strapped to the feet with great care so as not to draw blood from the owner's hands. By now the birds had given up their relaxed pose and were eyeing the other with increasing anger and intense hate. Suddenly there was a series of challenging calls that echoed around the barn.

'Aren't we waiting until Russ's here?' asked Joseph somewhat nervously.

'Damn and blast, I'm not acradling this object of death forever,' retorted Hawkins. 'He's as tense as a spring and ready to fire at any moment.'

'If he's not here in a minute, the fight begins,' said the tinker abruptly and suddenly losing his good nature. There was an uneasy silence for a minute.

Joseph strained his ears for any sound of Russell.

'We're forgetting something, gentlemen,' said Bert, 'the money! It's only fair that an independent honest fellow like me holds the purse, so it's ten pound a head.' The money was handed to the tinker who slipped it into a pouch in his top pocket and gave it an affectionate pat. 'If it's a draw, how about me anursing it until the next match?' sniggered Bert.

'Blast me if you wouldn't evaporate like a fell fog in May and the money too!' cursed Hawkins. 'But we've waited long enough! So it's now or never, or we'll go with a small fee for the inconvenience,' he added with a brandishing of the fist.

Joseph had hung on for as long as he dared. He reluctantly opened the cage door and took out his bird. 'There's no room for being a coward now,' he whispered against the bird's neck feeling the softness of the feathers against his lips, 'get stuck in boy and rip him to bits!'

The bird showed no response to this plea. Already with its head erect, the eyes were firmly fixed on the other bird, the pupils small and round and unflinching. Its adversary to the death responded with a threatening call.

Both birds were thrown down, and landed stiffly on the floor in the centre of the barn.

At first nothing happened. They simply looked at each other, searching out each other's weaknesses. The men held their breath and waited. Slowly, almost hesitantly the larger reddish bird of Hawkins stepped forward a pace. It then stood its ground, neck arched and feathers gently swelling with pent up rage.

The smaller brownish fighting cock had left Joseph's grasp confident on its own territory. It approached the adversary with stealth, its neck getting more and more rigid. Blood pumped into the comb, which became a fiery red, and stood directly upwards. Slowly it edged forward, took one pace to the side, moved in a slight circle - then forward again, with head held low, its hawk-like beak directed towards the opponent.

Both froze.

Suddenly a dart by the brown bird, a parry, a flapping of wings, a forward flurry with both birds spinning round in a maze of feathers. A cry! The large bird had the other by the head feathers, then the wattle, then the lower eyelid which it stretched out into a bloodshot film. But only for a few seconds! The smaller one leapt vertically with a broad sweep of the spurs. A gash appeared on the side of the Devil's head, blood spurted onto his wing, making the feathers even redder, the neck angled to one side.

'Stop the fight!' yelled the tinker, 'a spur's loose!'

Hawkins darted forward and grabbed his bird, giving a violent kick on Joseph's bird which squawked and lay on its side.

'There's nothing wrong with the spur and you've bloody well winded my bird,' shouted the boy with rage.

'Call me a liar and I'll wring your blasted neck!'

'Call him a liar and I'll wring two foul necks, and one will be yours!' said Russell approaching with a sudden brisk run and scrambling over the gate.

Hawkins was taken by surprise and scowled. But Russell's strong right hand gripped him by the shirt collar and held him like a vice. The farmer stared at him for a few moments and realising the futility of his anger he slowly relaxed his hold. 'Put your bird in its cage and be off!'

The red-haired man quickly locked the cage door and hurried towards the gate. 'Where's Bert, or I'll be damned, and where's the money!'

The brothers looked round.

The tinker had gone; vanished by the side door of the corn room; and it was to be some time before they were to see him again.

However, it is an absolute fact, never denied, that a red-haired man was seen enjoying a few free drinks with a jovial tinker, later that evening, in a wayside tavern - somewhere in the confines of Cranford Dale.

Chapter 15. The letter begins its journey.

It was a bright September day. The mountain ash was resplendent with clusters of red berries along the fell side, and the last lingering dog roses shone out from the hedgerows like delicate pink or white lanterns. Many of these bushes added to the wayside colours with plump spiky hips, ripened to perfection. Departing swallows and emerging fieldfares from Arctic climes were to be seen for a short time together in the fields. The evening air became crisper yet, chilling the fresh cut meadows, and causing opalescent delicate cobwebs to glint and gleam as thousands of tiny jewels suspended on each tuft of grass; invisible droplets by day, they had been changed into something tangible by the night. Small clumps of sheep's wool mimicked the webs as they waved on grassy hillocks or barbed wire, and the passing shepherd bathed his morning brow with their refreshing dew. Then after throwing down the wool, the dogs took up the game, snatching mouthfuls and entangling short threads of irritation around their front teeth. With a half-shuffling head-down gait they would drag the side of the jaw across the grass while trying to dislodge the spikes of wool, and Martin would laugh.

The dogs were in their final rehearsal for the Saturday Annual Show; agricultural in design, with horseracing and sheepdog trials as the climax.

Martin took the collies by an invisible bond of sound and understanding - round, down, forward, down, slow, advance and quickly forward, crouch, then pen!

Sam and Sorrel loved this game most of all.

The sheep bleated with confusion and exasperation, being split, turned and compacted at will, in sevens, sixes and fives, then flocked again.

The bitch, four years old, was the farmer's first choice and she knew it. In idle moments she leapt and licked his hand, bounding with her paws against his chest, all anticipation and excitement. Then by turn she was flat on the ground, belly uppermost, and waiting for a congratulatory pat, while panting happily.

Meanwhile at South Hadley Farm June played on the kitchen floor with the two tabby kittens - Tamster and Katy - throwing small pieces of paper crushed into inch wide balls. The kittens scattered them all over the stone floor, using both forepaws as miniature bats. June laughed and clapped her hands, kissing each one in turn as they rushed back to her knees.

In the kitchen Grandma Wetherall rolled the pastry - firm, greyish white and an inch thick. Flattening the dough to a rounded foot in diameter she adroitly flipped the whole onto a pie dish of comparable size that contained chopped steak and kidneys, with a generous layer of sliced potatoes above. A small funnel of porcelain marked the centre of the dish and the whole pastry settled down around the funnel which appeared through the apex like the pole of a circus tent. Snip went the scissors and the crust took up its permanent position to be crimped by a Sheffield fork at the edges.

The old Yorkshire range was in full force. The oven door was almost glowing hot, but still as black as a raven. In went the pie and soon a delicious smell filled the air.

Upstairs Mary sat in a chair and read to her mother an extract from the weekly "Illustrated News". Her mother looked weary and pale as she lay in bed, propped upright against three pillows, the patchwork quilt canopy being pulled well back.

Mary had often thought of the meeting with the doctor a few days before and, as she read, she had an abstract background thought that by degrees crystallised into a strong desire to see him again. But what excuse could she invent?

Luckily for her, it was not long in coming.

'Look mother, how beautiful are these villages in the South. The thatch is different from ours. Here's Woodstock in Oxfordshire. What a magnificent palace is there! They say the eminent politician Mr Churchill was born in it, but it really belongs to the Duke of Marlborough. The designer Vanbrugh built a tiny house in a bridge so that he could live in the grounds but the first Duchess threw him out. What gratitude!'

Her mother looked at the page. 'Living is gentler in the South, Mary! I used to visit your cousins near Windsor when I was young, but it was almost a three day journey by train and coach then, and I only went a couple of times. But it is gentler, no doubt! Maybe in the next visitation I will be born there, away from these scattered Pennine storms,' she replied wearily

Mary glanced out of the bedroom window and across the valley, deep in thought for a minute. The valley side sloped gently at first and then more steeply to Scarth Wood, then across Iris Force Burn to the Darling Hill plantation of firs opposite. A lark appeared framed in one small pane of the window for a moment hanging between earth and sky. The clouds were heavy and broken into long floccules of white and grey.

The silence was broken by her mother. 'Mary, I have an errand... something to deliver,' she said cautiously.

'Yes, Mother!'

'A letter!'

The girl waited.

'It is stamped personal and is to be delivered...' then Agnes Norman paused, '...to the Reverend Clenham.'

Mary looked surprised. 'But...'

'Not to the Wesleyan minister Mary, that will follow, but to the Reverend Clenham,' she continued emphatically, noticing the puzzlement written on the girl's face.

But her mother had misread the look, for Mary was lost in thought. This was the opportunity she needed to call at the Tithe Cottage next to the Vicarage and see Dr Ashleigh. Putting down the magazine she took the white envelope from her mother's hand which had been retrieved from the Georgian drawers close by the bed.

So Mary brushed her hair to give it a shine, placed a ribbon of blue at the back for added effect, and with her dark dress devoid of the customary white apron, commenced her mission.

Needless to say, she little realised what the letter contained or the profound effects therein.

Chapter 16. Sorrel learns a lesson.

The annual show, pronounced modestly on the bills as "The Oldest in the World" had begun as a medieval goose fair.

One late September weekend, just after the harvest, was given over to the festivities and 'The Dog and Gun' and 'The Frozen Plough' braced themselves for the deluge; beer was delivered by the barrel load and the brewers and draymen worked themselves into a frantic perspiration. Gypsies came from all around, forming untidy camps on the outskirts of the villages. They traded heavy-footed feathery-legged fell ponies, pegs, utensils and brooms. Tinkers, tinmen, weavers, besom makers and fortune-tellers (all authentic and of unrivalled ability and fame) made Compton Vale their Mecca.

On the designated day stalls, marquees and tents appeared in Chapel End Meadow as if by magic, like mushrooms springing up overnight at the behest of a shower; and they were soon packed to capacity with fruit, vegetables, flowers, breads, cakes, confectionery and a whole host of household fare.

Wooden pens were erected to receive a cacophony of cows, goats, pigs, sheep, horses, dogs and donkeys, and much more. Farmers and their wives feverishly groomed, washed, combed and pampered their animals - short-horn bulls bellowed in admiration of their sleek, shiny girth; black and white saddle back pigs stood in grunty clumps with their backs to the admiring throng, preferring to eat and go home. Emden geese waddled with broad paunches; while white leg-horn and the recently introduced Rhode Island Red hens clucked in bewilderment from their cages.

In fact Compton Vale was alive and blooming.

Entries and visitors came from every nearby dale including Cranford and Christmas Common; and soon the trickle of visitors and competitors began to increase in numbers. Families greeting relatives and old friends; children with hoops, brothers and sisters chasing to and fro, all waiting for the fun rides of suggy boats, slides and roundabouts to open.

Then more long human streams moving towards the show ground; couples arm-in-arm, dressed in their Sunday best, waistcoats of dazzling hues, watch-chains, parasols of every colour; walking stick in farmers' hands, carved with sheep-horn handles some bought at the fair decades before. Old farmers limping on arthritic hips, young ones bouncing with a brisk step so often used to clear the heather and bracken in the fells; some with wives, some wives alone, some husbands on their own, each one remembering in their special way of how it used to be.

The smell of animals, hay, cut grass, straw, lavender water and perfumes, food and ale - all added to the sensation of movement, bustle and noise that would live in their memories forever.

Now to the beer tent!

How it burst at the seams! Already full by eleven it was barely able to accommodate Sydney, a small farmer with his large dog. The animal's sagacity led him straight there and it was equally confident in its ability to lead his master home in as straight a course as the ultimate effects of 'Tanglefoot' beer would allow.

While in the main arena the horse racers came from every quarter and aroused a great deal of interest and betting for just over an hour. But everyone was waiting excitedly for the main event.

The sheepdog trials were, without doubt, the climax to the fair; and they began in the early afternoon. Almost five thousand faces watched in eager expectation. Compton Vale had not won the event for six years and hopes were high this year. Rival banter and sincere betting were the order of the day.

The sheep were released in fives on a familiar course. About seventy were penned in the far corner of the arena and they waited patiently with only an occasional resigned bleat to disturb their monotony.

The twin dog trials were the prelude to the single dog event. These trials were few in number and soon over, the cup going to Cranford Dale.

Then the interest and excitement rose even higher as the single dog championship began.

By this stage the sheep were becoming somewhat unpredictable in front of the large crowd, regularly scattering in all directions. Changed at intervals by late afternoon they were becoming even more fractious, weary and difficult to control.

Martin stood with the other competitors, twenty-two in number. Sorrel sat by his side.

Slowly the sun moved across the sky and began to cast shadows, long shadows, from the highest tents. Simpson from Cranford Dale was favourite and for good reason, having won the doubles earlier. He set a fast pace - his dog, Grip, being fourth to go.

All competitors watched Grip in profound admiration and some trepidation. For the dog was almost faultless in its herding, - controlled and determined. Into the pen went the sheep; and there were no penalty points!

The locals tried to keep up their spirits with friendly banter as the event progressed. But no one else seemed to approach Simpson's ability or Grip's excellence. So the betting began to slow down over the minutes and then ceased.

The villagers pinned their hopes on John Bowes. At first he did well, but his dog failed with the final penning of the sheep as they took up a stubborn stance in front of the last gate before scattering. This scene was greeted with cries of anguish and dismay.

So, one by one the competition moved on without anyone challenging the leader; and the bookies continued to look benevolent. 'Eight-to-one, Norman!' cried a bookie trying to raise more money, 'eight-to-one on the local boy in his first big event with only five to go!' Angus, George and company all shuffled nervously, having secretly bet on others and lost.

'Eight-to-one, come on gentlemen, where's your sporting instincts? Eight-to-one on Norman!'

Joseph darted forward. 'Damn me if I can't back my

flesh and blood, who will? Here's a pound!'

Russell had wanted to split this bet at first, and then suddenly changed his mind. 'You're right Joe, here's a pound from me too, squire!'

The Bookie's voluminous waist bag swallowed the money like a hungry trout presented with mayflies.

Away from the noise and in the shadow of the competitors' tent, Martin waited patiently, the twenty-second to compete as luck would have it! He hadn't wanted to be last, but was resigned to his bad fortune, keeping up his spirits with an occasional comforting word to his dog.

Sorrel, unconcerned, lay a few yards away on a grassy, heathery knoll, gently panting in the warmth of the day, ears back and eyes alert. Sometimes glancing inquisitively at her master, she seemed oblivious to the tension in the crowd.

The supporters of the Simpson camp from Cranford Dale could hardly contain their joy as numbers eighteen, nineteen and twenty failed. Twenty-one was Brian Havelock, George's son, and a keen competitor from the Vale. He was considered the last great chance for success.

The dog began with an erratic sweep and the sheep diverged. Time was lost and the locals groaned. No further bets were placed and the bookies began to clean their slates for the last time. To them the event was over.

However, for those uncritical observers of dogs who believe that most canine behaviour is instinctive and for the vast mass of spectators whose gazes were fixed on the ring, one important point was missed. Sorrel had a clear view of the ring from a small heather outcrop and had been intently watching for several hours.

Another fact was not in doubt.

She had learnt her lesson.

The ability to record every detail, every twist and run, had been watched by those bright brown eyes and was recorded in that alert brain.

Thus Sorrel felt confident of victory long before she entered the ring.

Now the crowd held its breath.

'Number twenty-two!' The Marshall's voice echoed around the arena. 'Number twenty-two!'

The five sheep were let loose at the far end of the field as Martin and his dog entered through a side gate and walked to the centre post where the shepherd had to stand.

He paused to gather his breath and compose himself. He was briefly aware of a blur of people around him, their fixed gaze, and the blue sky above the distant horizon. He felt both elated and nervous at the same time. For a second he feared no sound would be forthcoming.

The excitement was tangible in the air. Ten thousand eyes watched and waited.

Then a sharp whistle which Sorrel read in an instant. In fact she had made up her mind beforehand. The sound was the signal, but the result was at her discretion.

It was a long four hundred yard curve to the left on the gather, wide of the outermost ewe. That animal paused and spun towards the flock.

The dog seemed to break step in full flight and the sheep, although stubborn, were alarmed but just enough to turn as a flock.

Through the first gates, then the second in a three hundred yard fetch and into the centre ring ran the sheep. They stopped truculent and resentful, bunching together with a snorting and a stamping of feet. The dog waited, spreading her paws firmly on the hard ground, seemingly transfixed in an unyielding stance. Purposefully she eased towards them. Suddenly the sheep were off again and gathering pace.

But Sorrel was after them in a flash, swerving and altering speed at each command, feeling totally in control. Her paws were like springs on the firm earth and the ground whizzed by.

Another turn and the sheep were on their way towards the pen, between the third pair of gates, but still stubbornly unsure. The crowd groaned inwardly but not a sound was heard.

The judges continued staring at their watches.

Another sheep broke loose but to the dog it was now a simple routine. The animal was put in place in a second, compact with the others.

'Steady girl...easy now!'

Instantly the black and white Border collie stopped, head low and faced the sheep.

Five thousand people breathed as one.

Only thirty seconds left, and still the shepherd waited.

Another whistle and the dog glided imperceptibly

forward. She fixed the flock with the strong-eye of concentration.

Once again the sheep paused, standing defiantly together and the one by one they began to give way, slowly to move back. But Sorrel was patient; knowing that she could not press the sheep too closely or they would panic and scatter once more.

So she lay down - in total silence!

Then like an arrow she was off. With a broad agile sweep the dog drove the flock in a tight mass, heads bobbing, that moved as one into the pen.

Martin slammed the gate shut and threw up his hands with joy.

The collie bounded round his heels with excitement.

A blue mist etched the horizon.

All was well in Compton Vale. Ten seconds in hand...and no faults! Russell and Joseph jumped for joy as the crowd went wild with delight. The brothers hugged each other, sixteen pounds taken - and more to follow when they caught up with the tinker, as that day of judgement must surely come.

Chapter 17. Two drinks... and a third.

'If that dog could fiddle,' enthused Willie amid a tumultuous din in the 'Frozen Plough 'I'd give way to him in the band!' The landlord laughed, even his opinion of dogs had risen markedly that afternoon.

'She's too good for thee, William,' cheered a tall, thin man who helped the aforesaid with his sweep's brushes, 'more of a symphonic type!'

'Dang me if that's not true. I'll drink to that! Stick another two on the slate, Landlord.' Two more pints appeared on the bar.

'The way Martin controlled that dog was uncanny, such a quiet lad, but smart,' replied a third man, who although penniless after the day's frivolities, surveyed the two drinks with a professional zeal.

'And one for Samuel,' said Willie with a nod of the head and a slight slide of the hair, still arranged in a long vine.

'He'll be a grand farmer when his time comes to own South Hadley,' continued the third man, Samuel. 'But, what of the other two boys?'

'They've got time to learn a trade like me, if they have a mind,' stated the apprentice sweep of thirty years, 'but the girls - well Mary's half way taken already and June's time will come, for she's pretty enough!'

'They don't look much, I mean the boys,' said Willie correcting himself so as to give no offence in his good humoured way, 'I mean they're not asearching for jobs...or womenfolk either!'

'Ay! Forever playin' and gamblin', the pair of them if the truth be known!' stated Samuel wiping the froth from his mouth and putting down a half-empty glass.

'I'll tell you what! The farm can't support all three, James Norman knew that much,' continued Willie emphatically. His voice dropped, 'By the way how's Agnes, Samuel?'

'Only fair to middling, Willie I'm afraid. Least that's what I heard when up that way a week back! The doctors go a lot but Mary said that her mother is still pretty poorly.'

They all gazed solemnly down for a few seconds.

'She was a fine woman,' said Willie inadvertently speaking in the past tense. 'June's her double, as beautiful and as wilful.'

The landlord joined them, whisky in hand. He leaned over the bar in that professional manner becoming of his trade and whispered hoarsely. 'I've heard, mark you, mark me,' he glanced around, 'that the young Norman was taken for ten pounds by the tinker and Ginger Hawkins, those renegades from Cranford Dale. This is how it happened!'

But his whispers were lost in the undiminished din of human voices. However, what transpired will become apparent in the next chapter.

Chapter 18. The drummer, and more.

Angus was not a tall man, in fact he was five feet, and a drummer of Scottish descent, although none of these facts have anything in common as far as medical science is concerned.

He was three times married by forty, and considered shrewd and careful with his money. He was a man who could, it is said, peel an orange in his pocket or crack a nut silently, if he did not like the company. He lived comfortably in a small cottage that reminded him of his Highland upbringing and generally took life as he found it. His briskness added an ardent vitality and warmth to his face and manner. Generally he was kind by nature, marginally hidden by an obvious brusqueness to hide his embarrassment.

Tonight he sat in the 'Dog and Gun', bigger by far than the 'Plough'.

It was an old coaching house with a long table at one end and a carved oak bar at the other. A huge mirror gave a continuous view of the barman's back, which interested no one, but when the weaver's daughter served at the weekend, she was greatly appreciated; it was often remarked, from both perspectives. Angus sat with his faithful companion - not a dog, he was no animal lover with seven children to support - but a double malt. 'There's much pleasure n' sae little scolding to be gained from such company,' he mused looking at the drink, 'for marriage has taught me that a' men have their faults that come to light sae soon after their wedding, but are undetected before - such a rare curiosity o' nature!'

Having called in at the 'Plough' for a few moments earlier he had walked deep in thought to the 'Dog and Gun'. His brief period of solitude and philosophy was interrupted by the appearance of a red bush of whiskers and the faithful helper - the tinker in black. Neither seemed abashed in the present company. Both smiled and strode towards the bar. Angus stared for a second and then hailed them cheerfully. 'Guid men from Cranford's fair dale, my deepest commiserations on thy failure at the dog trial today! Let me buy you a drink!'

The two men started, for a second they were under the impression the statement was directed at someone else for Angus rarely spent his money in such a lavish way.

Two additional chairs were brought forth and Angus got up to greet them, 'What's the old fool want?' whispered the tinker jerking his elbow into his friend's side and then rubbing the side of his nose with his sleeve. He was about to remark something to the affect that Angus was up to no good when Ginger Hawkins spoke. 'No hard feelings, Angus, old man,' he said in a condescending tone. 'Are you feelin' well?' he added hastily, still amazed by the offer.

'Quite well, thank you!' said Angus in a controlled voice and smiling. 'And your good selves?' They both nodded.

''Twas a close one tho', there's no denying it,' added the tinker. 'Any dog could have won.' He flourished his hand expansively and gazed down at the half-empty glass.

'Aye, it were. But what about a celebratory dram?' asked Angus calling over to the bar. 'Two whiskies please,' he said warmly to the barmaid, imparting an impressive and seductive glance that had served him well several decades before.

The drinks were pulled and put down.

'To the bark o' the dog that beat you,' shouted Angus, clapping the tinker exuberantly on the back, 'and better luck a' the next time!'

All concurred and within ten minutes another round appeared by mutual consent.

'I have avoided most o' the troubles in life,' continued Angus reflectively, 'by sticking to whisky and women. In that order!'

The three cheered.

'A little whisky'll make the flames of love leap high,' stated the tinker with emphasis.

'Aye, but too much man...and the fire gans oot!' Angus laughed.

'That's my philosophy on life and love too.' roared Ginger, vaguely wondering why everyone around him was laughing.

They were a few minutes of earnest drinking and reflection and nothing was said. Then the tinker solemnly filled his pipe from one of his two old leather pouches in his top pocket.

'If that's not the finest tobacco pouch I've seen in years,' enthused Angus taking it from the tinker's hand.

'Have a pipe!' said Bert flushed with the whisky.

'No! I dinna partake, thank you kindly,' replied Angus

slipping the pouch back into the tinker's top pocket and giving it a pat. 'Anyway friends, I must be awa, awa to meet my luv, who's like a red, red rose that's something sprung in June,' he sang out cheerily forgetting the words. 'Sae adieu and better luck the next time!' he continued in his normal voice, walking towards the door. He paused and smiling said, 'You ken that lightning rarely strikes twice! That's a fact!' With this final philosophical commentary on life, he left the room.

After a short journey, he stopped at his house to collect his wife. They walked arm-in-arm to the 'Frozen Plough'.

'Well?' said Willie at length as his two friends had settled comfortably in one corner of the bar.

'Well to you,' said Angus in turn.

'Nothing new?' responded Willie.

'No! Nothing's new!' he laughed.

'Something's a brew,' replied his wife joined in the laughter.

'That's good and true!' Willie continued the lyricism to its finality.

'The hands of a drummer are nimble hands!' said Angus reflectively, reaching for a glass of ale and handing it to his wife.

''Tis true since Adam was a lad!' said Willie picking up his drink. 'Take a dram from me Angus, it will keep the fingers forever flexible!'

Russell and Joseph Norman, who were sitting on chairs near the hearth playing dominoes, looked up. Angus walked over and gave them an expansive hug, 'Luck's been with you both today!' he laughed. 'It's hard to fault when it's in this mood!'

'Good luck Angus, rarely strikes twice,' replied

Russell, 'but I'm hoping it will for Joseph and me in the next few days!'

Angus concurred with a chuckle and returned to his wife and friend.

As they reached the outskirts of the village, Ginger Hawkins roared with laughter. He could hardly contain himself and it took several minutes before he could speak and, as he did, he had to wipe the tears from his eyes. 'You should have seen your face when I telled you that the old goat had takin' your money pouch Bert, it was fair fun to see! But I whipped it back from his coat pocket when he was finishing his drink and popped the money into my wallet for safety. The old Scotch goat will be acursin' his bad luck tonight.'

Sometime later, however, Russell said with great surprise, 'What's this in my top pocket, Joe. Here's ten pounds for goodness sake. How ever did it get there?'

But Angus, the drummer with nimble hands, had long since left for home, pleased with his day's work; and what the red bearded man expostulated when he found that his wallet had gone instead was never recorded, although the tinker felt the full blast of his fury, and to tell the truth - that may be a blessing.

******

Meanwhile, Joseph had slipped away and headed for Prospect Row.

It was there that Mrs Bell (Doctor Mackenzie's waspish housekeeper) lived in a neat terraced house which by its very shelter forfeited a magnificent view of the valley. For much of the broad panorama of pleasant pasture was concealed; while a greater part of the fells, woods and twisting burn were also obscured from the good lady's view by a clump of pine and laurel trees, and most of all by a wooden barn (half filled with damp hay) that had seen the trees sprout from saplings and the burn change track a dozen times.

The tithe barn had once belonged to the church, strategically placed in a central position in the Vale amongst the most fertile reaches of this land. It had witnessed most things in its long active life of over two hundred years and had latterly succumbed to mute decay. Hidden down a narrow path of thistle, bindweed and nettle profusion, surrounded by birch and close-branched hawthorn, it was seldom noticed and rarely visited. It was a secret haven to the rats and mice and owls - a neglected solitude unto itself.

Tonight it served for another scene.

And, Mrs Bell pulled her thin fingers though her hair, the regular bun being released so that the dark locks hung loosely round her back, accentuating the very peaks of her forehead, cheeks and nose. She looked impatient and muttered towards the clock. Near ten, and Joyce had not yet come. Her niece had been expected earlier, and the kettle was continually boiling away to self-destruction. She moved the shiny copper from the warm coals and hung it on a cross-bar so that it continued to hiss but in a more compassionate and docile tone.

'Where was Joyce?' Mrs Bell looked out towards the last lingering glow of twilight that made the trees more statuesque and beautiful by an accentuation of their blackness. The embracing hills cut across the impending gloom while the tithe barn seemed even more shabby and alone.

But it wasn't; that fact Mrs Bell did not know; but her niece did. For Joyce Cartmell who had lost her mother two years previously, had left The Grange, where she lived and worked, just over three hours before. At first she had loitered around the village green, taking the bye ways when anyone approached, and skirting round the back of the Barrington Hall to avoid 'The Frozen Plough'.

She was seventeen, not furtive or shy by design, just the current circumstances. Her dark green skirt reached in an uncompromising fashion to her ankles and seemed to tug at every step, as if determined to impede her progress up the hill. A grey shawl was pulled firmly over her head so that the face was largely excluded from the remaining light, and beneath it the purple woollen jumper was almost hidden from view. She paused for a minute and looked towards the terraced houses of Prospect Row on the crest of the hill; their grey stone facing and black slate tiles looked gloomy and foreboding, except where an odd oil lamp or fire-glow broke through the narrow paned windows. She could not see her aunt's house for the trees and wished deep in her heart that she was not going there.

Joyce climbed the hill slowly and sighed, feeling slightly faint and ill at ease. She paused once more to sit on the bank by the narrow path as it deliberately and steadfastly pulled its way up the incline. The colours were fading in the western sky, and the hills and outcrops had begun their transition to the purpling blues of dusk. The stars were just breaking through; and as she sat and gazed, she thought that the stars seemed to tremble in the twilight haze.

She knew nothing of stars.

In fact, she concluded she new nothing much of anything; except she would always love Joseph, 'Always.' The finality of this resolve gave her hope as she laboured up the hill; her plump, normally cheerful form stopping once more as she collected her thoughts. Would he come?

The barn was just under a half a mile ahead and she scanned the building, now almost a black silhouette in the gloom. But the young farmer was there, sitting on a broken wooden plank that triangulated somewhat awkwardly from the inner side of the rotting door to the ground. Her lips quivered for a second as she saw him. Joseph waved and she hurried forward and into his arms.

'Why, Joyce, you're a bit out of breath and a bit pale, to my way of thinking. Have they been working you hard up at the Grange.'

'No, not a bit, my love,'; she just held him close and looked up into his broad face and light blue eyes, 'I've got two days off this month and have come all this way to see you.' She caught her breath. 'I've got something to say…' She stopped again. 'My, it's a harsh walk from yonder Dale, near twelve miles and I'm fair whacked.'

'What's the matter?' Joseph held her close. He pulled back the grey shawl to reveal her dark curling hair and intense brown eyes. Then he reached forward to kiss her, but she continued hastily, 'I'm fair whacked I am, and a bit sickly!'

Joseph looked at her with suspicion, a sudden thought made him pause. There was an uneasy silence. Joyce broke the silence. She spoke softly against the side of his face. 'I've got to speak to you about something before you go.'

He did not comment.

'I'm pregnant!' She said the words almost abstractly in her desperation. 'And you're to blame, Joseph Norman, with your constant demands.'

'Me, why has it to be me? I'm only eighteen and know nothing about women.'

'You seem to know enough! Anyway I'm only seventeen, unless you've forgotten.'

He did not answer and looked away, relaxing his hold.

'You can't tell yet, it doesn't show.' She replied innocently.

He could hardly bring himself to reply. 'It will afore long. Anyway, what have I got to do with it? It…'

But she broke in, 'By the Lord, everything, don't you understand!' There was another uneasy silence. 'What should I do next? I'm afraid, Joseph, afraid.'

Joseph stared into the distance as if seeking some answers from the darkness that crowded in. 'Oh, God! I don't know; how should I know! If you've got to see Dr MacKenzie, then see him you must. It's a bloody worry, I can tell you! But I am so young and what would my mother say? She'll flay me alive, Joyce, and I can't do it… not at eighteen.' His voice quavered with misery.

'Can't do what?' She turned angrily to confront him.

'Don't talk so loudly, Joyce.' He continued in a subdued voice. 'I can't get married…' and suddenly brightening as an escape opened up, 'I've put my name down for the military! The family has decided that there's no future on the farm for me, and the army offers me the best life. There's trouble ahead, some say and the army needs men.' Although it had only been the vaguest of ideas, Joseph seized the excuse with both hands; in his mind, one lie was as good as another.

'Aye they do that, real men who will accept their responsibilities.'

Joseph did reply. Joyce waited for a few moments. 'So…I'm on my own, with only a whining aunt…and a drunken father who couldn't care less.' She gave him a pitying look and strode off, quickly climbing the path. For a moment, Joseph thought she would turn back and he hesitated, wondering whether to follow. He was about to

97

shout, 'What are you going to do?' but the words stuck in his throat. So with a resigned, somewhat disinterested, shrug of the shoulders, and without another word, he hurried off in the opposite direction, lost in darkness and in thought. Thoughts that oscillated to and fro but, by en large, reflected on his own cleverness in avoiding the pitfall of parenthood and the fact that he might, just might, think about joining the army, if push came to shove, and Joyce was determined to 'trap' him.

Mrs Bell put down the kettle and surveyed the girl when she entered and sat down. Her voice showed no emotion, the tone was hard and uncompromising. 'So that's the case is it? Well it's not the first time in this dale nor will it be the last. And if it's who I think it is - at least you'll get away from that disgraceful boy. Dr MacKenzie always cautions against a wild tongue and a gabby mouth. So I'll keep my counsel and it's best you do…and get away from the village, as well. I will sort it out with our family. I have a sister-in-law whose husband's in the church.' She paused. 'They live near Lincoln. You can go there. Dr MacKenzie will make arrangements and I'll tell the owners of the Grange that you've got another situation. So that's settled, our Joyce, and may the Lord guide you through the years ahead.'

Outside the pine trees gently sifted the evening breeze. It was the only sound that evening.

Chapter 19. 'Sleep, it is a gentle thing.'

The death of Agnes Norman occurred one evening in September when the fine weather had broken and a mist cloaked the high fells. The valley seemed in repose, the village was silent and no bird or animal called.

She closed her eyes that night as usual, unaware that the long evolutionary spiral which had created her over millions of years had ceased, and that a biological reversal back to primordial atoms had begun.

She always thought before she slept, read her bible a little, blew out the candle light.

She always slightly opened the window so that a cold draught fanned her cheek before she fell asleep, thus cooling her fevered skin.

She thought, she slept, she died.

There were no recriminations, no final regrets, no chronicling of past happiness or misfortunes.

She had often wondered what the Divine Creator might say, what penance she might have to pay, what James would look like - strong and virile as when they met, middle aged in the caring years while anxious to make ends meet as a hill farmer, or perhaps as an old man, ageing as she had.

Being a Wesleyan there had been no confession and no mass.

There had been no response to her letter. No visit! She had hoped for more. Why had he not come to see her?

Still all would be well when she departed. She had a deep rooted confidence in Daniel Clenham. He would help her! He would sort out the Will!

And James? Well, he would understand in his kind and loving way.

Thus, as usual she fell asleep, so simply.

There were no sounds on the high ground that night, only drifting mist. The valley was subdued, and perhaps - by coincidence - mourned another departed soul.

Chapter 20. A New Year's visitor.

Just over four months had elapsed.

Now winter's silence gripped the fells. Early frost and intermittent hail had driven the sheep from the outcrops, crags and steep hillsides so that Martin and Russell had brought the flocks down early in October, before St Luke's summer (*a mild spell around this saint's day in mid-October), when the autumn reds and oranges were at their height.

Many of the ewes were now heavy with lamb and fed fresh hay and turnips in the low lying meadows near Scarth Wood, where the fir trees gave shelter from the north winds.

In the grip of winter, the plough was really frozen.

The black clouds of the morning had been shredded for a brief period and then been compressed into black smudges of the eastern horizon before melting away and leaving a liquid blue. The trees were frosted and caught the weak sunlight.

The night before the winter's storm had broken with unmitigated fury and high winds had lashed the hills and mountains, while the piled snow of the dyke back lay soft at first and then, in the chill blast, set as hard as steel. Even the deer, driven by the pangs of hunger, crept closer and closer to the village.

The horses lunged in the farmyards and the pond, once brimming over, was diamond hard but for an area where Joseph had broken through the ice, an area popular with the perplexed ducks and geese. Sparrows huddled in damp eaves, cheeping in the byres and barns, robins fought in the shade of the garden laurels and on window ledges where the crumbs were plentiful; and the cats stalked the adventurous mice as they scrambled around the granary after spilt grain. Breath rose in steaming clouds over the hogs, while cows stood chewing a docile cud, resigned to a long and patient wait indoors, warming the byres with their body heat.

June had suffered agonies of sorrow for three unbearable weeks after her mother's death, hardly able to concentrate on her daily tasks, eyes moist or weeping in intervals of grief, made worse by the recognition or touch of a familiar object - shoes, brooch, rings or shawl and much, much more.

Mary had suffered imperceptibly by comparison, and while June's sorrow had begun to mollify recently, her sister's had begun to deepen. For Mary the days suddenly became tedious and without meaning, all purpose evaporated, the Matriarch's anecdotes failed to amuse. She now felt that nothing bound her to the dales. But as to her future, she could not plan at present, try as she may. Mary viewed life with indifference, the greyness of Compton Vale that morning only added to her unease.

Apart from the day she had delivered the letter, she had not seen Dr Ashleigh. Dr MacKenzie had certified the cause of death and had attended the funeral. She later learned that the younger doctor had been away on a vacation in London.

As Mary pondered her life nothing became certain, she did not quite know which way to turn. She had written to her distant cousin in Windsor to see what that area had to offer, and had also applied to a large estate in Oxfordshire for a post as a nanny/governess, emphasising her rural background, her educational abilities and her expertise with animals especially horses. So far she had no response.

She folded the aired sheets she had recently washed and placed them in a large Jacobean carved box which had been in the family for generations. She glanced out of the landing window across the valley. An earlier light drizzle had suspended wisps of fog in the fields but in the gloom she saw a figure approaching, pausing for a moment by the second stile.

At first the mistiness hid the outline. But as the silhouette took shape, she recognised the approaching man to be the Reverend Clenham, head low beneath a broad trilby hat. Once she would have questioned his reasons for coming in such weather, even his reasons for coming at all for she could not recall the last time he had visited. This time she simply shrugged and went on with her tasks.

Within ten minutes there was a loud knock on the door. Mary hurried downstairs and welcomed the minister in. She found it difficult to greet him with a smile but tried her best.

He noticed the strained expression, and removed his

hat. 'It's Almighty cold, is it not?' She gave a faint smile and ushered him into the front room. He had not visited for so many years and yet the room had an instant vividness in the morning light. He was surprised at how much he could remember of the details of that last visit, so many years ago. Agnes had looked as strained and nervous then as Mary did now.

He took a seat on the large settee and accepted a cup of tea and a ginger biscuit from the Matriarch who had heard the knock and had immediately recognised the familiar voice.

Having just prepared a pot of tea for herself, she was more than happy to oblige. She greeted him with a smile (for she always enjoyed the Vicar's company - she knew not why). After a few words she wandered back into the kitchen to finish washing the pots.

Mary stood for a few moments and seeing that Grandma Wetherall did not want to return and join them, she sat down opposite the Vicar. It was an uneasy silence.

'I'm sorry to trouble you, and extend my deepest sympathy at your sad loss,' he said slowly and with feeling, 'but I have called... with some curious circumstantial details...I suppose... at your mother's request.'

Mary looked at him carefully.

She was inquisitive but at the same time afraid as to what he would say. She fidgeted a little and then clasped her hands to remain calm. She did not reply.

'You delivered a letter, you will recall, a few months ago!'

Mary inclined her head and smiled faintly. 'Yes! I remember!'

'Your mother used to work in the Vicarage,' he began slowly, 'however; I must confess I was surprised to hear from her again!' He stopped for a minute thinking of the right way to explain it. He continued after a considered pause when he held the cup inches from his lips, 'She was always kind to me, you know.'

Mary waited. She knew of the Reverend Clenham's circuitous sermons; the ponderous way he sometimes took to reach the point. 'I do not know if you are aware of the contents of that letter?

'Mother never told anyone,' she replied quietly.

'It was about the Will.'

'The Will... the Will in the hands of the solicitors, Morgan and Peters?'

'Yes!'

'What about the Will! Is there any problem?' her voice trembled slightly with anxiety.

'Perhaps so!' replied the Vicar after taking another sip of tea.

Mary continued to look him in the face. 'What problem?'

There was another pause. 'I must be candid! But according to the letter I received, the farm does not pass to the eldest son!'

'What!'

'I repeat, not to Martin, but to Russell.'

Mary gazed at him in astonishment. 'Surely not! Why so?'

'It was your father's request and your mother upheld it. That is the straightforward fact of the case.'

'At his request... I do not believe it!'

'I must repeat that it was at his request. I'm not sure why,' he said slowly and with deliberation, 'but that was what I was told.'

'By who?' Mary did not pause for a reply but continued nervously, 'Surely there is some mistake?'

The Vicar paused and sipped his tea, relieved that these unpalatable facts had come into the open. 'None really, I'm afraid. None at all!' he said with a sigh.

Mary gazed at the fire. Her heart beat wildly and she tried not to show her emotions.

'There is another slight, well perhaps not so slight, problem,' he continued after a short pause.

Mary remained silent and gazed at the fire.

'There may be a letter, a note of some description, in your mother's hand, which revokes the Will. In essence, makes your father's Will invalid; or at least not acceptable in its present form!'

'What makes you think that?'

'Something she once said in a private moment,' replied Reverend Clenham slightly evasively. 'It was a long while back, there's no point in going into it all, but I did mean to come and see her…she asked, you know… but I sort of dallied,' he tailed off. There was another uneasy silence broken by the ticking of the clock and a sudden blaze of logs that sent the sparks hissing.

Mary looked up. 'Are you saying there is another Will or a caveat?' She stumbled a little over her response, perplexed by the thread of the argument.

'Perhaps! But I'm not saying there is! I'm not saying that I'm acquainted with one, not at all. But this is the question, there could be another Will not witnessed, if so where is it?'

'If there is, well, that alters everything. It's a different story entirely. I'll go and see at once.' The vicar sat composed as Mary rose and hurried upstairs, calling him to follow. She went straight to the Georgian drawers next to the bed.

She opened the writing box, spilled the contents of the

drawers onto the bed. She examined the documents one by one and then hurried downstairs. 'There's no other Will or letter.' She stated emphatically.

When the Reverend Clenham walked slowly down the path from South Hadley farm, the mist hung over the valley and only a pale primrose glow affected the sky. The sun was cloaked over for the day, and by a perversity of nature resembled the moon.

He shook his head. Something was wrong.

'But what and why?' he took a deep breath and surveyed the valley hoping for inspiration and an answer. 'God works in mysterious ways, his parishioners often remarked, but when man intervenes, the results are even more irrational, more disastrous.'

He looked up at the sky, 'and that is something I know for certain!'

Chapter 21. The clock stops, but only for a few seconds.

The path sloped gently for half a mile towards the first stile, the air was chilled and quiet as befitted a January day. There seemed little movement in the Vale, no energy for change.

Nature slept.

Preoccupied the Vicar had just placed his foot on the first rung of the stile when he saw a figure approaching in the adjoining field, two dogs leading him on. He greeted Martin. The shepherd waved back cheerfully.

'Just visiting,' Rev. Clenham began brightly, 'I like to think everyone in the Parish is part of my flock, if you do not mind the comparison.' He laughed and Martin smiled. The clergyman continued, standing on the top rung of the stile. 'A raw day!'

'It is that!' responded Martin.

The Vicar paused and felt instinctively that he had ascended into the pulpit and had a natural inclination to preach. 'Martin,' he began in earnest, 'your mother once worked for me, many years ago.' He hesitated. 'She recently wrote a small letter, the contents of which I have described to Mary.' He stopped abruptly.

Martin waited for the clergyman to continue, descend, or both. The minister maintained his lofty stance. The dogs grew impatient and jumped onto the wall, standing immobile like sculptured ornaments for a few seconds in the frosty air. Reverend Clenham seemed to be choosing his words carefully and Martin watched his thoughtful expression with interest. Then he descended with a bold leap, which made the shepherd smile.

'It's of no importance at the present, Martin, perhaps some other time!' With that final remark he walked away into the damp gloom.

Martin remained astonished for a moment and then gave a resigned shrug of the shoulders. With a whistle to the dogs, he set off towards the farmhouse. Smoke curled and hung around the chimney pots in the misty air giving it a bluish hue. The two dogs raced ahead and bounded into the warm straw of the outhouse kennel and then out again in the excitement of being home. They briefly paused to lap from a small stone trough, ice-free, beneath the backyard tap, before chasing the kittens from their winter refuge and comfort in the hay.

Martin scraped his boots clean and gently wiped them with handfuls of dry straw. He entered the kitchen. Joseph sighed and grimaced, idly polishing some brasses and silver under the stern direction of Grandma Wetherall's gaze. Mary read by the fire in the next room, hardly deeming to look up as her brother entered. The wall-clock ticked away, pendulum aglow in the firelight, as usual.

He warmed his hands before the fire, crouching down so that the blaze threw brightness across his cheeks and accentuated his eyes and mouth. 'The Vicar's a rum one, there's no mistake,' he said at length.

Mary looked up, her face paler and more serious than usual. 'He just left! Did you meet him?'

'Yes, at the Top Road stile.'

'What did he say?'

Martin smiled. 'Nothing much; whatever he says is often beyond the reach of mortal man.'

Mary scrutinised her brother, watching the firelight flickering shadows in his face.

'What was he doing here? I suppose paying his condolences.' Martin continued gazing at the fire. It was a seminal moment is his life, although he did not know it at the time and Mary remained silent.

'It is very curious. He said that Mother wrote to him. But why, he didn't say!' Martin continued to warm his hands, gently rubbing them in the glow as the circulation returned and his fingers tingled.

Mary collected herself. 'It's about the Will!'

Martin looked up. 'The Will, in the name of the Lord, what does he know about the Will?'

Mary remained calm. 'I don't know! But I'm hoping everything will be clear once we have visited the solicitors.'

'So do I! We'll soon see, I suppose.'

She looked across the Vale towards the mountains now fringed with powdered snow, apart from the gullies where it lay deep and compact. Patches of blue sky were just showing through.

Martin stood up. 'The clock's stopped,' he said casually and walked to the corner. He opened the glass front and retrieved the brass key; and slowly counted the number of turns to tighten the spring.

Mary continued to gaze at the bare trees in the distance and the soft blue behind them; she plucked up courage. 'Martin,' she began cautiously and in a subdued voice, 'what of the Will? I mean the money. If there was enough you could study, apply to one of the local colleges. You have all the qualifications and it was Mother's wish...'

'Mother's wish,' he interjected brusquely, 'was for me to look after you all, to takes father's place in the running of the farm. There was no other choice at the time. I asked, but there was no other option.'

Mary was annoyed by his outburst. Her mother's memory brooked no contradictions.

Noticing her expression, Martin suddenly felt contrite at this outburst of pent up emotion. 'Come Mary! Whatever the Minister had to say, and I have no idea what he said, seems to be coming between us, and there's no need for that! I'm sorry!'

Mary took hold of his outstretched hand. She paused for a moment. 'The Reverend Clenham meant well by coming here, Martin. And what transpired made me think that, if true, you would have the chance to continue your studies; that was all!'

He shrugged his shoulders. 'I don't understand what his coming here has to do with my studying, either now or in the future. Nor do I understand for one moment where all this is leading to.' He tapped the pendulum, setting it in motion again. The familiar tick-tock, tick-tock, tick-tock rang out around the room.

To Mary it was a curiously soothing sound and gave her confidence. 'The farm has been left to Russell!' she blurted out.

Martin looked at her in blank astonishment.

There was a blanching of his face and a hardening of his expression. 'So that's what you have been trying to tell me!' He went silent, standing, looking at the clock, seeing his pale face staring back from the glass. Mary would have felt happier, more relieved if there had been a sudden outburst of anger, some harsh words.

But he continued in silence. Then turning said calmly. 'All the years of hard work and sacrifice; years and years.' There was bitterness in his voice. He sat down on the Windsor chair and gently rocked to and fro for a moment. 'Well! Thy Will be done, as they say, or the Vicar says. But it does nowt for me now. What shall I do?' he said without looking up.

'Let us move South, Martin. I'm fed up here and you could begin your studies there, with so many fine Universities to choose from...' she said brightly.

But the shepherd looked into the blazing fire in considered disbelief. He did not reply, if indeed he heard what she said. 'What about the dogs and the sheep? We have the best flock around, due to my efforts. Years and years of work.' He repeated. Now he could hardly suppress his tears. 'My future was on these moors, my days on the fells, any future prosperity is bound up with this countryside... until today!' he stopped for a moment to get a grip on his feelings. 'Whatever will become of me now?'

She said nothing.

He looked into the dejected face of his sister. 'Whatever will become of me now?'

Chapter 22. News of the young doctor.

Morgan and Peters was a fine firm, but a brisk firm, with brisk partners. Not standing on ceremony they announced the Will based on the wishes of James Norman from a decade before, and adhered to by his wife.

The junior partner, who was entrusted with the deed, looked over his glasses and through them in turn, briskly opened the Will and Testament, waited for Grandma Wetherall to resettle herself (being too hot by the coal fire) and announced the contents. "The farm to Agnes in her lifetime, and then to my second son, Russell."

The Matriarch grew warmer by degrees, her face darkening with each syllable, but she said nothing, commented nought in the carriage home and dined in solitude that evening.

June did not know whether to congratulate Russell or cry. Russell looked abashed at first and nervously placed his arm around Martin's shoulder. After a brief pause, Martin returned the warmth and shook hands.

Joseph considered his sudden wealth of two hundred pounds that each of the children had inherited and he was determined to quadruple his amount by the autumn on the basis of his luck at gambling and the certainty of his racing tips. 'I always have that lucky streak, when the chips are down,' he thought and rubbed his hands in expectation. Joyce was far from his mind and so was any responsibility – another lucky break.

But South Hadley Farm was colder than cold that night, the very draught down the chimney or past the velvet curtains seemed to be of an intensity not felt for many years.

June sat playing with two of the cats who had sneaked

in for warmth. 'Mary,' she said at length, 'I have some news from the village today.'

Mary walked in from the kitchen.

'About Doctor Ashleigh!' she continued. Mary blushed slightly and tried to collect herself. 'He's leaving the village to return to London for his studies.'

Mary felt herself going redder in a strange mixture of apprehension and surprise. 'When did you hear that?'

'Today! Weren't you listening? It's common gossip! He's to continue his research into tuberculosis, so they say! Anyway, he's definitely leaving!'

'When?'

'In the spring!'

Mary looked at June for a second hoping for more information while wishing it was not true. But her unflinching gaze had no effect on her sister. 'I will certainly miss him! He was marvellous with Mother!'

'We know Mary, we know,' said June curtly. 'And I don't want to hurt any family feelings, but personally I have changed my mind. I used to like him a lot,' she looked down at the cats for a second, 'but taking everything into consideration I think Grandma was right! He seemed well enough at first, good mannered and handsome, yet in many ways he's too uppity for the dales' folk!'

'That's nonsense June!' Mary replied brusquely. 'I'll never believe that! He's never rude or condescending...and always a gentleman!'

'I'm not going to argue Mary, and I've said he's good mannered. But it's my opinion that there's a harder, less caring side.' June reflected for a moment. 'Perhaps it is part of a doctor's make-up to stand aloof when needs must!'

'I never agreed with Grandma, June, and I cannot agree with you!' Mary turned and walked into the kitchen without another word.

June resumed stroking her tabby cat. 'Well, that's me told Katy. Mary certainly likes Julian, I'll be thinking. Anyway, so what!'

She smiled and patted the soft, rounded head. 'If humans had your eyes and instinctive wisdom Katy kitten,' she whispered, 'what manner of things could we see and feel, and guard against!' she added quickly. 'We can live a life of ease in this old farm, although a little more money would be more than welcome.'

She thought of the doctor as he was and how he had become. Always present in her mind's eye like the mountains opposite, she mused, but equally aloof and unobtainable. She had not seen him for several weeks, and did not expect to see him. It was deliberate. She had avoided his known-routes, and had only once (when driven by a strong inner compulsion) checked their familiar hiding-place underneath the large coping stone close to the stile.

Within moments of finding nothing there, she had felt annoyed with herself; indeed angry at giving in to an irrational urge to meet him again. She felt weak and vacillating, so unlike her normal self. Apart from the anger, there had been no feeling of longing, no thoughts of marriage.

That was the final disappointment. 'No longing, no future!' She repeated the phrase in a whisper three times, as if seeking some sort of consolation.

The kitten Katy clicked the girl's red jumper and June frowned and scolded. The second cat stopped grooming, unsure of the direction of the reprimand. 'The finest people are like cats,' she whispered to the kitten and picked it up, we don't want to be dogs, do we; so obvious in our love and so easily commanded? No! To succeed Katy, I have to be like you, confident of affection but sparing in return.'

June thought of the future for a moment. Still cuddling the kitten against her cheeks she continued, 'One can never hold the future Katy; it is a reflection in a stream. The present is tangible and can be moulded. The past is gone beyond reproach. So many people, with so much wisdom, dwell on the future and the past. It's like the weather, it can never be altered. So let us keep to the present Katy and life can be managed with some success.'

She then cuddled the second cat; it had bounded onto her knees before settling down on the long woollen black skirt. She kissed it on its broad forehead, the animal's ears slowly flattening in bliss, its orange coloured eyes closing momentarily with a long, deep purr of satisfaction. 'There Tam, we will decide the future later, but you can decide the present now! What shall we do?'

The cats arched their backs and meowed expectantly.

'More milk and cream, did I hear? Dear me, I sound like Alice in Wonderland talking to her cat, don't I? A vicar wrote that book you know,' she said confidently to herself. 'I wonder, what would the Reverend Clenham write?'

But by the vicarage fire the minister had picked up his pen, held for a minute then put it down. He crumpled the scrap of paper which read, 'Dear Martin...' and formed a small ball.

With no cats to throw it to, he simply lobbed it onto the flames, and ate some dried fruit in a reflective mood.

Chapter 23. The paths cross - the first incident.

Next morning it rained, and the water dripped from the stone walls, pooling and forming rivulets in the sparse grass and streaking the bark of the pine trees close to the house. Mary donned her warmest dark coat, her longest woollen blue dress, stout shoes and set off down the path not long after the winter sunrise.

The chilliness of the air caused small clouds of breath to hang around her head, like mist on the high crags, and to follow her in slow, easy columns as she hurried across the fields. She heard the lonely raven's croak in the distance and saw a buzzard circling high. She feared for the doves, but hurried on. The sheep bleated for food as she walked past and when she looked back she saw Russell and Joseph emerging from the large byre with hay.

She would miss the seasons in the North, their distinctiveness, she thought; the first flowering autumn crocuses planted on her mother's grave - yes, she would miss them if she left.

But she had to go. And to go, she had to see two people. For once there was a recklessness that cut through her controlled exterior. She was conscious of her mission and the consequences. She had never been afraid of the consequences, she told herself, as she set off, and now was no time to change.

The ground was firm with frost when she left the path, climbing a wall as a short cut to Low Green Farm. In the crisp morning air her face reddened and her lips numbed. She pulled her coat more tightly and felt no remorse for what she had to do.

She had wasted years; that was the only salient fact in her mind. A letter had arrived offering a post in

Oxfordshire with a doctor's family in Deddington. The household sounded delightful and she had accepted by return, telling no one.

As she walked on she saw John heading towards her with a long wave and a broad smile. She waved back.

The farmer hurried forward scooping the girl in his arms and planting an affectionate kiss on her half-turned face. 'Why, Mary, so soon! Up with the larks and twice as pretty!'

'Like the larks, John, but less full of song!'

John Bowes paused to contemplate the remark. 'Why so, Mary?'

The girl was a Norman, through and through, and not afraid to speak out. 'I'm leaving, John!'

'Leaving?' he gasped, then in a half-whisper, 'for how long?'

'Some time!'

'Some time? A month?'

'Longer!'

'Longer?'

'Yes! More than a month or two, John.'

He remained silent and looked imploringly into her face.

'It may be a year or two!' she had not the heart to spell out the whole truth at that moment. 'I'm so unsure at present John, what with Mother's death and the upheaval on the farm.' She paused for a moment and took his hand. 'Two years, John, if all is well! His silence made her continue. 'I know you are the kindest, sweetest man imaginable and easily hurt. And I don't mean to hurt you...not for one moment.' Her sentence suddenly ended as she gazed at the dumbstruck farmer, his hands held half-out towards her waist, but not daring to touch in his disbelief.

'Can I say something Mary?' he asked hesitantly.

'What, John?'

'You're making a mistake.' He spoke abruptly and turned slightly away, as if unsure of his brashness. Then he rudely added, 'A bloody mistake, Mary, and I hesitate to speak to you in this way.'

'You may think so John, but I'm not making a mistake,' she replied slowly without looking into his face.

'I can't help but think you are. Still, why should you pay any attention t'me if you're already of a mind?'

'Mother's death has affected me, more than I can say.' she felt it was a valid reason and used it to good effect.

The farmer stepped back and shook his head. 'We'll just have to be a bit patient then, won't we! But two years is a long while in these changing times.'

'I'm sorry John.'

'Are you?' he spoke hesitantly and without any expression in his voice or face. His feelings went beyond grief or stubbornness. He tried to imagine the future without her.

'I will return to Compton Vale one day, never fear! Perhaps sooner than you think! I have been offered a job in Oxfordshire as a nanny and probably will not like the place at all - you know how the South is...'

'I could hardly know, Mary, I've never been beyond York, you ken that! I'm not a worldly man.' He smiled for an instant, 'Suppose I could travel though; see you from time to time.'

Mary was not expecting that response and felt some discomfort at the thought of John arriving in Oxford. She felt ashamed at thinking so, and let go of his hand undecided, as to what to say next.

He returned to his former point. 'But why leave,

Mary, why leave?' he moved closer to her for a moment and then stepped back.

'I can only say I'm sorry John and I've given you the reason as far as I can understand.'

'Aye, you have!' He shrugged his broad shoulders. 'So there's no reason for me to go on about it, is there?'

There was a pause. 'I suppose not.'

'It's fair hard for me to understand, Mary, and what I'll do without you, I don't know.' He tried to smile.

'Oh, John! You know how I feel about you...and always will.'

'Aye, I do that! But when you've been brought up in the Dale, well, everyone knows that an engagement broken...means there's a fault on one side or t'other; and they'll all blame me, I know that!'

She looked into his solemn face, once so radiant and smiling, now cold and crestfallen.

'They won't John; tell them I've gone away for a short time because I've been given a Governess appointment.'

He paused. 'Aye, I'll do that but it'll not make any difference with some of the gossiping busy-bodies in the village.'

They looked at each other, their emotions in a state of limbo.

'Well, I'll be on my way, there's a morning's work to be done.' He gave a faint sigh.

She could not even bring herself to say goodbye and reaching up kissed him on the lips, lingering for a second as in the past, and then turning abruptly she climbed the stile and was gone.

John said later it was the only occasion in his life he really cried as he kept repeating softly, 'Please don't go Mary'.

But at the time he would only admit to standing with his back against the icy wall for twenty minutes and watching the hazy mist through even hazier eyes; and the only expression of his anger was a faint shaking of the head, like a tethered bull.

Mary did not look back.

She never saw John Bowes again.

Chapter 24. The paths cross - the second incident.

Mary continued towards the church on her second mission. The first episode was closed forever.

The tithe cottage was her object, Dr Ashleigh her intended meeting. She was undecided what to say, but had made up her mind to be forthright.

The view from the cottage was so familiar in every aspect to the young doctor, so engrossed in his studies that he rarely gazed out in a comprehensive way. Thus it was with some strange twist of fortune, as he was shaving that morning in a back room, that he had made up his mind to visit South Hadley Farm.

He too had decided to be decisive in love. Having poured out the warm shaving water from the basin into a jug and having just wiped his face with a hot towel to remove the last traces of soap, he looked up. The view was towards the farm and the Top Road.

Framed in one corner-square of the small window was the hurrying figure of Mary and the young doctor acted instantly, his heart beating with joy.

With a sudden impulse he ran downstairs, almost slipping on a rug, grabbed his coat, jumped on his horse which was already saddled for the journey, and using a short-bridle spun the animal round in a tight circle.

Ignoring the driveway, he cantered into the vicarage garden by the side gate.

This astonishing event was not seen by the Reverend Clenham who was visiting a sick parishioner. Undaunted the doctor leapt the evergreen cypress hedge at the back of the house and then raced over the burial ground. He cleared a three-foot stone wall, then a ditch, then a four-foot gate - and was across the steep fields and onto the Top Road in a minute.

Mary arrived five minutes later, composed herself, knocked on the door, and waited.

And she waited for some while – there was no answer.

For Dr Ashleigh having galloped along the road out of view of the girl turned the horse at the wooden sign which read "South Hadley Farm". He cut across the fields, taking each stone wall with exuberant leaps. The animal sprang gazelle-like in its enthusiasm.

He too stopped to compose himself. He knew June could be alone, at least away from her sister, for some while.

Unlike the church incident, this time the roles were reversed. He was out of breath and flustered. He was well aware that this time he had to choose his words carefully and, above all, remain calm; and luck was with him.

June had just left the farm and was crossing the main field with a supply of eggs for the village shop. She looked up and saw the doctor. Her first impulse was to hurry on. But the wind blew back the hood on her coat and, as she tried to adjust it, a clip caught in her hair. In that moment as she paused to untangle it, the doctor approached at a steady pace. In exasperation she threw back her head, hair and hood in one gesture.

Thus she exposed her dark, shining locks, now longer and gently curling at the ends. She had never looked as lovely, he thought, as he reigned in his horse.

June said 'Oh, it's you.' But her voice lacked conviction.

Julian said nothing. He would have liked to say something, but waited. As he dismounted, however, his face broke into a smile that was both warm and reassuring. 'I haven't seen you for so long, June!' He laughed, his features displaying every form of pleasure. 'Have you been avoiding me?'

She was accustomed to his change of moods but as he laughed in such a delightful and overwhelmingly warm way, she suddenly felt confident and laughed too.

'Why do you laugh so?' he asked still smiling.

'On impulse! But I don't know why… considering all you've said... and done.'

He bypassed this remark. 'Well, isn't it true?' he said, 'You have been avoiding me.'

'Yes!

'Nothing more than "yes" June.' He paused, 'Why so monosyllabic?'

June glanced at him in temporary exasperation at his usual lecturing. 'Yes, Julian, if you want me to continue, I have been avoiding you. Loving you comes easily to me in one respect, but then there's the soul-searching…,' her voice trailed away.

He ignored the last remark and continued on his theme. 'I do not suppose you could consider that it's your fault, that I've not seen you?' he inquired

June did not answer for a moment. 'I did avoid you at first, I will admit as much, and would have done so now- but what about you? You have had a hundred opportunities to put things right. I felt as if I was being used, nothing more, nothing less. That's the annoying bit.'

The fact that she had come to accept their separation without a qualm irritated Julian but once again he controlled his emotions. 'Don't pout June,' he said with a shallow laugh and trying to change the subject, 'it's for the doves, not you!'

'Now I'm pouting?' For a moment she felt uncomfortable in his presence as she did on the night of the church meeting. She waited for him to speak, noting the expression on his face.

But he misunderstood her look, reasoning that it was out of devotion and continued sublimely. 'No, I do not wish to irritate, I am sorry! Say you still love me June, and all will be well!' He began to move closer.

She stepped back, feeling awkward. 'If that's the answer to all ills, then I still love you.'

He reached forward to kiss her. She moved to one side and ran around the horse, gazing at the doctor over its broad back. 'Now's the time to have our Vulcan between us Julian, I certainly would feel safer.' However, for the first time she laughed in a spontaneous way and he immediately felt that there was excitement and encouragement in the laugh.

Julian's response was to look amused; and the half-smile was also annoying. Then in the next moment, he appeared so crest-fallen that, for some odd reason, it made her feel ashamed of her manner towards him. To June's inexperienced reasoning, he seemed so vulnerable.

Pre-occupied, he did not notice this response and continued, 'I have forgiven you June.'

'Have you now!'

'I have!'

'And what have you forgiven?'

'Your peevishness and your stubbornness; it is all forgotten!'

'Well that's something to be grateful for! But forgotten, by you or by me?' She responded sarcastically.

'By both of us,' the doctor replied.

'For a moment you had me worried.' Once again her tone was one of irony.

He looked surprised. 'I would hope it is all forgotten.'

'Julian, don't hope… it's not forgotten by me!'

It was his turn to check his annoyance. Her composure was the annoying factor. He bit his lip. 'For God's sake June, surely it is all forgotten and forgiven?'

She paused for a moment. 'Yes! It is all forgiven. And if you have any doubt in your mind I'll tell you, once and for all, that I still love you Julian, perhaps forever.'

June expected him to respond - how she did not know. But Julian just stared at her in a way that made it impossible to judge his emotions.

She gazed at him even more keenly. Not for the first time she doubted his love. 'I have another question. You are going away, I hear?' She spoke in a matter of fact voice.

'I am!'

'Now, you're almost monosyllabic, but no matter… we're not going down that track again. You must really want to stay here, mustn't you?'

He ignored her sarcasm. 'If you are annoyed June - so be it! But it is only for two or three years until I finish my postgraduate studies.'

She continued her unflinching gaze. She began to see a different man from the one she loved. 'You want to move on, fulfil your ambitions…who can blame you.

But what are the chances of us meeting again- with you in London? Slim, no doubt!'

'No!' he replied, 'I thought you would say that, and it is just not true. The future will soon be here, you know.'

'There's one thing I do know and that is the future is never the present Julian, I've often thought of that! Who knows what might happen in the next year or two. Anything! You may become an eminent doctor in the South. You have always talked of the culture there and the sophisticated ladies. You have always made certain that I know how much you admire their fine fashion, their manners and demeanour.'

Now Julian felt angry and slighted. He stepped forward. 'June, I have had enough! Please do not talk like this again. I came here in a manner of forgiveness and... it is one argument or opinion after another. If you can't just say you will wait for me, I'll be gone and that's the end of the argument!'

She was taken aback by the brusqueness, the finality of it all. Suddenly she felt vulnerable. 'I do love you, Julian, really I do! But I will not wait like Mary, for years and years. One in the Norman family in such a situation is quite enough!'

'This is different, just say you will wait... and nothing else.'

She smiled but said nothing and started to walk away.

'Stay a second, June.'

'Only a second?'

'I said 'stay' because there's a sleepy wasp that has alighted on your hair.' As he reached forward and brushed off the imaginary insect, he touched her shoulders. As the mist from their breath curled about their faces, Julian put his arms around her. Gently pushing back her hair, he kissed the soft cheeks and then the lips by slow degrees. June could not resist.

Suddenly she collected herself. 'We can only see, Julian, only see!'

'You will wait?'

'Yes, I will wait!'

He kissed her once more and held her close for a minute. 'I may leave the Vale for a short time, it's important to me. But, rest assured, I will always be here in mind and spirit. One day soon I'll return and we will spend our future together. You will see!'

June did not reply, she thought, 'Will we?', but felt numbed by the turn of events, unsure of her feelings and even less sure of his sincerity and candour.

When Julian left, he felt at peace, even exhilarated. No mariner of old, no Captain Cook, had his route more firmly charted, his mind so resolute, his future determined – or so he believed.

But June's sadness was one of rejection bordering on despair, her love souring to a sudden dislike. She placed her back against the stone wall and wept. She had held back the pent up emotions for as long as she could. Now the tears that flowed misted the fields for a moment. He was part of the future and not the present, and to her mind... the future did not exist.

Chapter 25. Two strangers visit Cranford Dale.

The February snow had fallen deeply, two feet or more, giving a uniformity to the Dale and causing sheep to stamp cold feet and snort in exasperation for the hay. Hogs grunted in the myriad of sties around the dales; women besomed steps and paths with short, sharp movements and miniature flurries of snow; while men dug deep trenches from house to the main road piling the snow eight feet high in parts and producing secondary valleys and canyons of a firm whiteness. The trees were of crystal, bent and still. The few birds that could be seen, hopped forlornly and in hope of some morsel to come.

On the day in question this bright, white uniformity two figures were seen approaching, not black and white like the border collies of the introduction, but almost totally black - hair, face, body, clothes and all. Theirs was a contrast of contrasts!

The taller person spoke. 'Ay! 'tis done!'

'Ay! 'tis done!' echoed a familiar voice.

The fact that God worked in mysterious ways the prerogative of the Reverend Clenham and here, according to the two strange figures in Cranford Dale, was living proof - if proof was needed. For the familiar voice, heavily disguised, belonged to none other that the previously mentioned William Pearson - barber, violinist and sweep. And the taller man, who had deemed to break the silence, was his apprentice of thirty years.

'It were a rum do, W'llm,' he continued after a few more long strides that tinged the snow with black. His walk was lugubrious like his talk.

Aye, it were,' replied the master, deep in thought.

'Tis amazing what a smokin' chimbly'll bring,' he went on.

William nodded and was about to say, 'Have you now!'

'Lumps of soot as big as George's rubble for the dyke hearting!'

Willie smiled at this allusion to his dear friend.

'But never an address.'

'Ay, that's so!'

'What an address, what an address!' chortled the apprentice.

'Well you don't have to keep agoing on all the time, like a parrot with croup. It'll fair get on my nerves, it will!'

'Just think of the luck, W'llm.'

'Suppose so,' replied the sweep after pausing for a moment. 'You're right, old boy! What a find, indeed. It fair made my day!' he continued enthusiastically and brightening up. 'I had a lucky notion when we come to Cranford that something would happen. And it proved true!' he wiped his black brow with the back of his coat sleeve; for the walking was brisk and the brushes heavy.

Now, nothing plays more havoc in country domesticity than a smoking chimney. All friendship and joviality of the hearth evaporates, for no lover can be more capricious than a fire at this time. Dense smoke can billow back into the room with every whim of the wind; walls darken, eyes run and faces become streaked with vertical lines of black

Willie had been summoned through an acquaintance to someone who had recently moved to Cranford. This friend of this acquaintance was having trouble. When they arrived the room was filled with bellowing smoke from an essential fire, for the February cold would have struck deeply into the pipes of the attic and walls, bursting them with a monotonous regularity as they thawed.

Willie had knocked politely, shaken the snow from his boots, then knocked the apprentice by way of an encore to remind him to do the same, before striding manfully into the room.

Soon the fire was doused and the soot allowed to cool

(which it did rapidly) and the brushes were thrust up the chimney amongst a small hail of stones from the chimney breast. Then before conjuring up a small avalanche of soot a broad cloth had been securely draped over the chimney front so that none of the grime could escape.

'Is everything all right there?' the sweep called. The apprentice, who was consigned to the cold outdoors, chattered 'Yes!'

'Speak up!'

'Yes!' bellowed the assistant.

William went through the familiar routine. Up and down went the brush, the chimney pots gently rattled and the soot fell down in waves. He felt like an orchestral conductor in full power. The apprentice peeped through the window and stamped his boots to free them of the clinging snow as a hint to come within. When all was done and dusted the lady of the house returned. Once she had been indistinct in the smoke-filled parlour, but now she was all clarity and light.

Willie started. It was a friend, or rather the best friend of Ivy from years gone by. The good lady was delighted and three hot rums appeared and disappeared by magic. A second filling arrived equally quickly. The hot rum was liberally spiced and the lady chattered merrily and expansively.

Whether it was the soot (by disguise), or the rum, or the lapse of time (or all three) but William remained anonymous. He guided the conversation with political skill. Ivy, the love of his life, it transpired, was well and more than a little lonely; but still over thirty miles away.

The two men emptied the glasses and, with a graceful "thank you", left.

William laughed and tapped his top pocket. 'What an

address old son lies here. She didn't turn up at the old dance so I've never been anywhere near getting it, in the past. Not this new one. Mark my word! Now we've got it we'll be acalling on Ivy one of these days, won't we?' And with a loud and cheerful whistling they both went on their way.

Yet their good humour was short-lived. Passing the deep scree gully below Eel Crag, Willie gave a long deep whistle that made his companion look up with a start. Two low mounds of snow were clearly visible just below the towering, vertical rock face. They paused and raced forward - afraid of what they might find.

Chapter 26. The first snowflake of the storm.

Only a few days earlier than the sweep's arrival in Cranford Dale, the first snowflake of the storm had arrived and made the nine-year old girl laugh. To her young mind it had no hidden terrors, no nightmare qualities. Winnowing out of the blue the white spinning fleck seemed to appear from nowhere and in an unpredictable sweep stuck fast to her eyelashes. She laughed, gave a little hop of delight and went indoors.

Glenridden Farm stood in shelter of the storms, six miles up the valley, an isolated speck in the upland landscape between Compton Vale and Cranford Dale. The building had seen better days and the whitewashed stone cracked, crumbled and gaped to the elements. Draughts and damp played havoc with the timbers and walls, paint peeled from the rotten doors and ledges. But it was home to the seven members of the Emmerson family. They had known no other.

Alice closed the kitchen door behind her and sat down at a broad oak table. A large brown farm dog ambled slowly over; nuzzling the girl's hand, then it gazed into her face with rapture. ''Tis snowing, Father,' she said after kissing the dog, 'and looks dark in the hills'.

Old man Emmerson lifted his swarthy face. 'Snow, my beauty, did thou say "snowing?" We'd better mek haste to the sale then, thy mother and me. For we've a business to run and the money for the garments she's made will be fair welcome.'

The girl smiled and stroked the dog's broad head.

There was a small fire in the black grate and the logs were piled one on top of the other in the corner of the chimney breast. Eric wandered in, 'Did thou say thou was ganning t'Vale, Dad?' he asked without acknowledging his sister, 'can ah come?'

'Thou's too young lad for the eight mile walk.'

'No I'm not!' The seven year-old replied after a moment's consideration, 'ah've dun it a hundred times.'

'Maybe thou has, maybe thou hasn't!' continued the Father after a short pause to survey the boy's eager features. He reached over and ruffled his hair. 'Eric, my son, we need thee to stay with Alice for the day and watch the three young uns, Mother says she'll leave the little un but mek sure she gets some milk and bread slops afore she gans to bed, Alice!'

The eldest daughter looked up and stopped patting the dog. 'Thou knows it'll be fine, Father, for I've dun it afore'. The girl spoke in a voice which seemed mature for her age and shook her long blond curls that reached beyond her shoulders. Her dress, although old and too small, was a dark blue that enhanced the vivid colour of her eyes, and her grubby face broke into a slow smile.

'Little Edith'll be takin' me for her Mum right soon, the way am always anursing her.' The Father and son both laughed.

'You'll be a fine mother one day, our Alice, ther's niver bin no doubt on that,' replied the squat farmer getting up from the table. 'Let's see, 'tis eight of the clock and we'll mek the Vale by twelve or so and if the sale ends by four, with a drink or two - ah meyght be seeing Bert for a brief while, - we'll be back be nine tonight. With a fair moon could be that bit earlier.'

The other children played in the barn while Edith, the baby of eleven months, was dressed and cosseted by her mother.

Unlike Emmerson, who appeared old for his forty years, his wife was slim, with large nervously moving blue eyes and a thin mouth, both accentuated by a white skin. Life had never been easy and yet there was a graceful beauty in her bearing as she gently rocked and soothed the baby. 'You'll be a good girl for your mother, my love,' she cradled the child closely, 'and I'll be back soon with some money to buy my precious ones some fine things'. She reached forward to softly kiss the baby, holding her lips against the soft cheek for a few blissful moments. The child gurgled and smiled. Then she heard her husband's brusque call from the kitchen and sighed. At thirty-two she had rarely experienced a kind moment in the long arduous battle for existence on that harsh upland farm.

The moor, now dead of life, sloped slowly towards the horizon at first, but, after a mile or so, suddenly bent in steeper and less graceful curves, rising in dramatic boulders and crags, before twisting and contouring into deep ravines and sharply dropping rock-falls. While the brown heath coverings and peat dark gullies, the broken bracken and burnt heather, gave such a uniformity of tint that it would have seemed foreboding to anyone not used to such a desolate land. Yet to this family it was a world apart, and a world they loved in a strangely forgiving way.

Into the small peat stained, puddle-brown tarns flew the flaky whiteness, whirling over the still waters, and slowly dusting the rocky inclines into an early winter frosting.

The man and his wife waved a cheery goodbye. Both were well wrapped-up in thick black winter coats buttoned tightly, each with a stout leather belt to seal in the warmth. For the cold was 'biting' and without respite, even in the sunlight. The pair set off with bold steps on their journey along the ridge route towards Eel Crag, three miles away, knowing that they had a further five miles of descent beyond that rugged mountain.

Emmerson surveyed the darkening sky and cursed, then stepped forward with a rapid and resolute gait. But his wife paused and with sad eyes gave a long loving wave to the children who clustered in the doorway; Alice watched them cross the small stream, picking their way over the boulders arranged in a broad crossing-row, and then saw them slowly ascend the steep incline by the old sheep track. Her mother was five yards behind her father and continued in this way, but she did not look back although Jamie first called out loudly and then yelled in his disappointment.

'Whist, Jamie!' Eric took hold of the three-year-old hand, 'let's play hide and seek int' byre, we have them to ourselves, apart from the old cow. Fur the bullocks be still int' fields, until weather gets bad.' And off went the three boys with excited laughter and a bouncing ball, while

Alice sat on the doorstep until she had seen her parents become diminutive specks and vanish over the horizon. Then, suddenly remembering, she hurried indoors in her new role as 'mother' to check that the baby was well.

Farmer Emmerson walked on in thought, hardly glancing back at his wife. 'It be pickin' up soon,' he said looking at a patch of blue in the now overall blanket-grey sky. His dark hair hung in unpleasant clusters about his swarthy face, set firm against the elements. Rain, hail and twisting winds - he had lived with them since a boy; they held no fear. 'Tell me if I be gannin too fast,' he muttered, 'and if the strain be too great on thee.'

His wife did not reply but kept her head low, for the wind was beginning to pick up and sting her face once they had left the last culvert to start the two thousand feet climb to the ridge on Eel Crag. The ground was boggy and the slimy mud part-frozen, yet not sufficiently so to allow easy walking. Her old fell shoes leaked and squelched, 'She would buy new stout shoes that would be her priority,' she thought to relieve the monotony of staring at the ground, 'but only when the children had been seen to.'

She was pleased that they had carted all the produce to the Barrington Hall ten days before, when they had the chance of a horse and cart, so the walking was relatively easy now with nothing at all to carry. How she had slaved over the jams and bottled fruit, picking wild crab apples for jelly, straining the cores and rind, sometimes adding the crimsoned blue of the brambles or the pretty tinge of red currant; then the knitting and sewing, and all to sell. All to buy food and provisions for the farm... a farm that barely paid in a good year. Yet her husband was a proud man, content to battle on.

She stopped to gaze at the broad, short form that forged steadily ahead. She had been but a girl when he proposed, and from a family of fifteen what other future could she have had? She thought of her mother's guiltless words of encouragement. 'What future could she have?' And then her aunt saying, 'A swan can never sing so take all you can lass when the time is right.'

The woman hurried on as her husband crossed another rivulet by an angled rocky gable. He surveyed the sky, now blackening from the north. Clouds began to plump and then compress the hills, erasing all distinguishing features. In a world of silence she caught up, and briefly walked by his side.

But seeing no warmth or recognition other than a slight smile, she resumed her former position. 'It be looking threatening,' she said at length.

He stopped and put his hand on her shoulder. 'Divn't worry, Mother, it'll pass afore noon, there's bits of blue yonder', and he inclined his head to the west.

Only a raven's croak was heard as the snow began to smoke and swirl on the high ground. It started to fall in light, sudden flusters; then bitterly it whirled and spun, spraying the crags like icing. Finally it began to attack the low lying ground, inch-by-inch, so that the hurrying couple left deeper and deeper prints...prints that followed them higher and higher into the blackness of Eel Crag.

The farmer thought only of the need to get through to the sale, and strode on.

But the woman...her thoughts were of the children and when she would return.

She started to weep silently and unseen.

Chapter 27. The snow falls.

By the early afternoon the snow had fallen to a depth of six inches and the sky was brightening to a liquid blue, pushing back the grey clouds and casting their world into a crystal white. But the stark cold would not yield one inch, defying the sunlight's paler hues.

There was an edge to the silence until two of the children, shivering under the guidance of Eric, decided to push small balls of snow; but being powdery lumps they grew slowly then suddenly crumbled into a dozen smaller fragments to cries of dismay. But the game went on and amidst much laughter and rejoicing a snowman, of sorts, soon kept a watchful pebble-eye on the farmhouse and outbuildings. How the children loved the fun, in their shabby, holed clothes - which barely cut out the cold - as they tumbled and played, until the twilight started to fade, and the sky reddened the far crags and hills. Ice smoothed the small tarns into a tranquil uniformity, and the brown sedge and bulrushes bent in pointed fingers to the frosted ground.

Alice stayed indoors. She nursed the baby on her lap, fed and changed the little girl, and replenished the peat fire with logs. She looked at the small flames and glowing embers. She sang small rhymes to the watchful child.

The sun sank lower in the sky and the snow began in earnest. Large black clouds menaced the high grounds above Eel Crag and whipped the snow into the gullies once more. The ravens, that sheltered and nested there, were driven croaking to the lower reaches of Ullock Moor. Icicles clustered on the vertical rock faces, and the snow went on and on with a monotonous regularity that reduced the land to a featureless white.

More snow came and more; and a further five inches in an hour; and the peat fire smouldered and the small oil lamp flickered in the gloom of the farmhouse.

Now it was six o'clock.

Now it was seven.

The baby cried and Alice fed it the last milk, cold from the jug; and then Eric held the baby precariously. With a yawn the youngest child went to sleep.

Alice walked to the door and slowly opened it against the elements. There was a hush... no sound... no sight. Only a wall of falling flakes; silently gliding down, large obscuring flakes appearing from an ink-black sky.

Alice listened for a few moments.

Not the slightest sound broke the solitude..

She wondered whether to go outside; but there was no sound. She trembled with the cold and slowly she closed the door.

'Time for bed', she stated firmly. The two youngest boys protested and the girl gave way.

'Alright, ten minutes more! No bath, but straight into bed.'

Eventually two little figures clambered into the broad bed and pulled the dark navy blue goose-down covering up to their cold noses and after a few minutes of squirming and chattering, fell suddenly asleep and silence reigned in the small back room.

Alice returned to the baby who slept in the small cot in the warmth of the inglenook, while Eric lay on the clippy-rug floor stretched back before the smouldering glow.

'Where's father and mother, Alice? Shouldn't they be back afore now'

The girl shook her head. 'We mustn't worry, Eric,

136

they'll have had a good day and be eating in the 'Dog and Gun'. Father said he was takin' sup with Bert, and they'll soon be home.' But her voice shook slightly and she wrung her small hands together.

'I'm fair famished,' the boy stated firmly.

'Wait and I'll get you some bread and a bit of sliced ham.' The boy's face brightened in expectation as the girl left by the kitchen door.

The clock chimed the hour, eight hollow notes... then nine... and finally ten.

Eric was soon asleep on the floor and the sparks from the log blazed up the chimney. The warm firelight played on his contented face. Alice watched the flickering flames and waited; and still the snow fell and the darkness was absolute.

Came twelve and the little nine-year old hand turned off the oil light, and weary beyond belief she fell back on the old settee - and went to sleep.

Chapter 28. Time passes.

The next day the snow reached above head high, higher than the tallest of them; so a way out was impossible.

They could only wait... and wait some more.

****

Now it was the third day; snow crisp and white, a sun of palest pink and a low cloud that clung to the cliffs and shaded the land from the winter glare.

The children sat quietly by the warm ashes with only a small log blazing and the ice set fast in the back-kitchen stone sink. Their faces were resolutely set and devoid of life, only the baby whimpered in the girl's arms, but the cry was of a kitten not a child.

Eric and Alice decided to dig a trench to the barn to see what food was stored there, heaving and throwing the snow, carting it back along the thin deep line to the yard gate where there was some exposed ground, the snow having been swept away the day before by the gusts of wind. On that exposed, level patch the children stacked the snow, slowly, so slowly, layer upon layer, compressing it bit by bit with the shovel; then back and forth with another laborious and time-consuming layer.

They worked in silence. In turns they carried the snow in a large pail that made Eric stagger when even half full, and his mittened hand chafe and ooze. While Alice pushed slowly forward, shovelful by shovelful, towards her goal.

Now it was a race against time and weather.

Alice surveyed the trench, only thirty yards to the barn. But the gales howled again in fury after two long hours of toil and the snow swept back into the trench, wiping out all vestige of work and reducing Eric to tears of despair. Fearfully and dismayed they began the task all over again.

Three hours more and the sun slipped into darkness, and the clock struck four.

Alice dressed in an old black coat which her mother used on the farm - too long by far but warm - took up the digging with a hurried yet resigned air. By eight in the evening when the moon was bright and full, and with aching limbs and numb fingers, she reached the faded brown byre door. The sound of the bellowing cow within was music to her ears.

Yet here was another struggle. For the snow had splattered and ingratiated itself into the cross-bar and lock, so that neither would move an inch.

Alice sat down in despair and wiped her cold face with the back of a long black sleeve. She tried not to suffer the pangs of hunger and anxiety, but it was hard for her young mind to keep calm and she forced back the sobs time after time.

She got up and struck the metal cross-bar again and again, so that the beast bellowed in fear, while Eric raced down the trench in such enthusiasm that he fell headlong on a lump of ice, crashing against the wooden frame with a force to split his skull. Yet miraculously, and without tears, he simply shook his head wearily four or five times and said, 'Damn, blast' many times more, until his sister told him to 'whist' and 'be done, lest the wrath of the Lord will fall upon us.' So Eric tried to smile and look grown up, which was difficult for a seven year old boy to do under the circumstances.

The hammering went on and on for ten minutes until wearily the sat down in mute defeat.

But summoning up one final onslaught with a huge combined blow, the wood splintered and gave way around the lock. The door was free.

'Get the milking pail,' sang out Alice in her joy.

There was just enough from the hungry beast, just enough to feed the baby first and then the little ones. While Alice found an egg in the hay which she broke into the last jug - full, so that a golden hue was imparted to the froth and it was so enticing and so good that Tom sang out for more in his five year old voice, but was gently refused.

This was the pattern of the next day - an egg, some scraps of ham and bacon that had been hanging on the rafters, a little milk, eked out with melted water. But there was a cheerful, roasting fire, for the byre door was burned before they tried to dig a path to the wood pile, for Alice knew that this would be a tedious task when undertaken and would occupy nearly two whole days; for the old fir, which had been felled and sawn up, lay a hundred yards away. It could only be reached in the gully and there was a tortuous frozen burn and ice-packed swamp to cross.

There seemed to be no end to the bleached landscape. Only the ravens made large footsteps in the snow, croaking overhead in the search for any food, dead or alive. Theirs was a harsh blackness against the white, and to Alice's young mind, a threatening, raucous sound that she never forgot, even in the better years.

Chapter 29. The lantern light.

Almost a week and it was time to go.

But who was to look after the baby?

Eric, not Tom, for he was too young! But Eric? Yet there was no one else who could cope. For Alice knew there would be a small window in the day, between one and three, when the baby slept. That was the time to go.

The clock struck a quarter to one.

The baby gurgled and smiled and the girl sang a soft nursery song. 'See Eric, if she cries, sing it like this. Warm the milk, and keep her dry and clean. Mother will be back soon.' But the girl knew that this was a lie and crossed her fingers and then her heart without being seen. 'Keep her dry Eric and warm.'

Then the clock struck 'one', and then a quarter on. It was bluer now with a hazy sun drifting along the horizon - two and a half or three hours left, no longer. That she knew only too well.

But the baby hung on perversely until almost the half

140

hour. Then with a sigh little Edith fell asleep in the comfort of a makeshift crib. The remaining children and the dog hung about the front door as the girl, with her warmest black coat, Wellington boots that partly let in the damp, a bright red woollen hat and her precious, knitted blue mittens, strode purposively down the frozen trench and over the farm gate, heading for the far peaks beyond.

Eric first - then the two boys - had rushed forward to kiss and hold her for a moment; and with a few tears, they hurried back for the declining comforts within. For a second the dog hesitated, but with a slow wagging of the tail it slunk back into the building as if ashamed of deserting his mistress and did not give the girl a further glance.

After forty yards Alice paused for a second and turned to look at the front door. She was desperate to return, to stay with them forever, but in a curiously instinctive way she knew she had to go on. Slowly Alice climbed.

The silence of the snow was absolute unless she moved quickly; then there was a sharp crack of marsh ice which made her involuntarily jump as it splintered around her. Sometimes a fall of snow burst from a craggy outcrop, or a sharp icicle shattered down alarmingly from the rocks above. But she rarely looked up. She knew she had to walk on.

On and on she went; through flat lands with frozen rushes that snapped in unison with every step. Then, she scrambled up paths and gullies, regularly falling face down in the drifts, so that her skin burned and her eyes smarted. Yet she plodded steadily and solemnly forward - sometimes with the snow knee-high and all embracing.

She grunted and tugged her legs out of the white morass so that each step forward became a mammoth task. But on the fell-top the wind had whipped away the whiteness and thus turning back the covering cloth of snow had exposed a bare-table of a landscape with brown tufted grass, dead bracken, grey lichen rocks and the dangerously sloping, sliding scree that swept down to the valley floor in a nightmare incline.

Alice tried to cope with the scree, to take gentle steady steps with each foot of descent. But the loose flat stones slid icily one on top of the other, giving way with a sudden crunch or a sharp jerk so that she fell heavily time after time; and her knees bled down to her Wellington tops. But the wounds were numb with the cold and she watched the bleeding more out of childish curiosity than fear. Indeed she had no fear now - not even of falling - and the valley seemed so very far below.

But she had only made two miles in two hours. The sun's face halved and quartered on the horizon's edge. The rays levelled and were long. However, in four minutes it would be gone.

Alice looked in desperation at the sloping descent and the valley floor a mile or so away. Fear began to stir within her small, fragile form. It was such a lonely place. For a moment she thought of her mother and choked back the tears. She closed her eyes, screwing them up tightly and then opening them slowly towards the sky. There was no hope or inspiration, no guiding hand… nothing had changed in her darkening world.

She thought of praying but, as she bent forward on the incline, the drift and sway of snow on ice began. Then she started to slide and slide, and the frosted scree bumped and spilled, so that the young girl began a roller-coaster of a ride for two hundred feet or more. Then, with an abrupt jerk, she landed in a four-foot drift that soundlessly cushioned her fall as gently as any mattress she had ever known.

Alice felt winded but unhurt, although her best coat was ripped and covered in a muddy slush, and one mitten lost; while her chest ached and burned from the repeated blows. The daylight faded with its winter's abruptness.

Now Alice felt totally helpless in a world of pure stillness and gloom. She was lost and alone. She sat crouched in the hollow of a large rock to compose herself, but so hushed was the mountain blackness around her that her gentle sobbing became a strangely comforting sound.

She thought of her family. She thought of home; and the children's laughter seemed to echo in the solitude and she turned suddenly expecting them to be there. But there was only a huge cavern of rocks. Yet for a second Eric's face seemed to float past from the crag above like a raven's fall; it grinned and grinned, then waved her to go on.

But unsure and afraid Alice waited for a half hour more, patiently watching the dark on dark creep in and erase the surrounding white.

However, feeling colder with every second and shivering violently in her sodden clothes as the wind chilled her body and frosted her hair, the young girl knew that she had to strike out once more and risk all.

She slowly got up and with uncertain steps and stumbled on. Alice stuffed her hands deeply into the pockets as the air hardened about her. She had no idea of which way to go.

But for the first time in days luck was with her; for the moon, full and clear, suddenly broke out of a black cloud embrace and skimmed the top of High Crag, throwing a long band of magical light for the girl to follow. Down the steep snow-encrusted steps of the donkey track she went, slowly down and down, towards the valley floor.

Then came the welcoming snuffling-bark of an approaching dog,... and Russell's voice,... and a lantern light in a steady hand.

'We'll have you to the doctors soon, Alice Emmerson, and put matters to right.'

But the little girl said nothing and clung to a warm hand.

Chapter 30. Growing older.

The doctor sat by the fire and read. It was six o'clock on a bleak February day in Dr MacKenzie's house, the Old Keep; the Westminster chimes rang six, the doctor sighed, two minutes late by his repeater-watch and recently wound. 'Check the pendulum' he thought, 'check the weights.'

His grandson David looked up from the floor, lounged face down with chin on both hands and hair almost singeing hot. The picture book pushed by his side and edge-curling in the heat from the burning coals. 'How about a cat?'

The doctor looked up. 'What?'

'How about a dog, Grandad?'

'I thought you said a cat?'

The young boy pursed his lips. 'How about a dog and a cat?'

The doctor laughed, 'and a mule, six sheep and a goat. Mrs Bell can feed them and we'll get another helper.'

'She would have about twenty ears to wash,' chortled David back, 'unless the goat had one ear.'

'There's no such thing!'

'True! I saw one like that at Low Green Farm last summer. When I asked the old man what had happened he

144

said, "Goats are the darndest creatures on earth and eat just about anything". Then he pointed to the one next to it.'

'It would give him the old colic, David, if true. But nothing old man Bowes says is of much consequence although his animals are hungry enough to do it, I suppose.' They both laughed once more.

The fire blazed and crackled, and the light shone to the far corners of the room and cast long shadows on the ceiling. 'How old is Mrs Bell, Grandad?'

The doctor paused and lowered his book. 'Why do you ask?'

'Just wondering, she looks young for a gran, but old for a woman without a husband.'

'A man generally doesn't ask a woman her age, especially when she cooks and cleans for us, and a gentleman doesn't tell it. She's thirty two!' The doctor smiled, 'Which is older by far than six and younger than sixty, by my book.'

David paused and looked into the orange-warm glow once more.

The doctor said quietly, 'The years pass quickly; where do they go? God knows!'

'You could ask Reverend Clenham,' chirped up the boy.

The doctor rubbed his hands and took off his glasses. The grey hair, still fairly thick and curly for his age, was released onto the brow and seemed to decrease the years and accentuate the vivid blueness of his eyes in the same moment. He was just about to speak when there was a loud rap on the door followed by an even louder banging that sent the man scurrying out of the room with an angry waving of the arms. 'Whist man, why the noise?'

In the doorway stood Russell and Alice; and thus it came to pass (as the Good Book has it) that Alice and Eric Emmerson were domiciled for a few weeks at the Doctor's while the others were safely housed in the village, until further arrangements could be made. Their parents had been found by the sweeps at the foot of Eel Crag, having fallen a thousand feet some days before. They were buried in the graveyard of St Cuthbert's church and although the family was split up, the children were brought up lovingly by the inhabitants of the surrounding villages.

Chapter 31. Valentine's Day.

It was Valentine's Day.

Mary had no difficulty getting up early that morning and the snow had suddenly gone as the wind blew warm from the South. She had barely been to sleep. Her mind had gone round and round in a curious mixture of excitement, apprehension and regret. She had tried to remain calm but felt each second tick away with a slow, monotonous, boring regularity. The darkness and her emotions had been oppressive throughout the night. The silence of the Dale had been absolute. The old familiar barn owl had been curiously absent from his nightly haunts, the harsh barking of the deer suppressed.

As the first light of dawn broke through the cleft in the hills, Mary could hear the rooks. True to form they had returned to Darling Hill Plantation. She lay in bed listening to their calls, made more obvious and compelling in the crisp, cold air. Suddenly their calls had curious strangeness, a depressing quality that added to her regrets and uncertainties. There was still a feeling in the back of her mind that she should stay, a feeling tugging at her emotion that would not go away despite how often she reassured herself that all would be well, all would be for the better. Trying to dismiss these thoughts Mary sat up in bed and pulled back one of the curtains.

Looking into the half-light she mentally prepared herself for the long journey south. She had decided to travel by rail from York via Birmingham and then on to Oxford.

For weeks she had wondered how she would feel about leaving the farm. For years little had changed in her life, a daily routine which had almost become subliminal in nature. She would miss her life, this daily routine. However, as she lay contemplating her current situation she became more determined than ever to move on, to create something new. Any curiosity as to how others would feel suddenly evaporated.

She paused, but only for a few seconds, got up, and pulled back the remaining curtain for the last time. As she stood by her bed she stopped to take a last, lingering look across the valley. She did it slowly, as if to hold forever that final glimpse of the place she knew so well and the place she had loved all her life.

The familiar hills, trees and river were as present and as reliable as ever. She patiently scanned the village, roads and surrounding farms, searching for something new, something she had missed or taken for granted over the years. But all was as before.

She tried to absorb every detail. Yet strangely in those minutes she felt little regret and no remorse. She was not one to dwell on the past. She felt it difficult in rationalising her emotions at that moment, but it was not one of regret.

Excitedly, she washed, brushed her hair and put on her warmest clothes. She hurried downstairs. The rooms were peculiarly silent. She paused to gaze at the wedding picture of her parents, picked up the framed photograph, kissed the glass and then walked into the kitchen. No one was stirring upstairs.

After a short breakfast of tea and toast, Mary had a sudden urge to see the doves in the dovecote for the last time. The yard was dry and her shoes clipped the flagstones. She opened the door and the birds looked down from their ledges - five, ten and fifteen feet above.

Mary reached up and caught one, gently holding the passive white bird to her face and stroking her cheek with the side of its wing.

For the first time, a sudden feeling of intense unhappiness came over her like a gentle breath of air and she wept. Tears tumbled down the wing and onto the bird's back, like tiny rivulets, spreading as a miniature cascade along a delicate valley between shoulder and body, and onto the tail feathers with a final imperceptible drip to the floor.

Also up with the larks was John Bowes.

He had lain awake all night, searching for one approach after another; sometimes feeling he had the answer, on other occasions embarrassed by the plan. Which was the best approach, he was unable to fathom out. Overall he felt a firm approach was the best. But what would happen if she ignored him, or even worse, laughed at him. That was something too awful to contemplate, but his mind kept going back to this possibility, and he felt a deep dread. Unable to sleep any more and fearful of the future he rose early and sat for an hour studying the inky darkness outside his bedroom window.

The cold did not trouble his sombre, hesitant mood. He dressed and went quietly out, wandering around the field next to his house, clapping his hands intermittently, icy red in the dawn chill, as if applauding his own decisions; stamping footprints in the mud and patchy snow so that his fell boots were soaking and the damp penetrated to his stocking feet. He would, so he first thought, go to Mary directly, catch her before she set off and beg her to think again. Plead with her to think again. That was his best solution.

But within seconds, he felt that this idea was too brash. So he decided he would wait on the main road to the village until her carriage was passing and hail her to stop and make his point then. Then there was another change of plan. Perhaps it was better to just let her see him upset. Stand passively by the roadside; a quiet pleading which would bring about a change of heart. It was a gamble. It might not pay off, he reasoned, if her love was over, that she did not care for him at all.

John could not decide and round and round he flattened the crisp shoots of grass. It was not until the sun rose slowly over Compton Vale and the valley became bathed with a faint glow that he became finally reconciled with his course of action.

He crossed the fields from Low Green to South Hadley Farm and in fifteen minutes stood half-hidden by a wall and the slanting firs. The house was silent. Then suddenly he heard a noise and ducked down behind the wall, afraid to peer over.

Mary had not seen him as she hurried across the yard.

But as he crouched and listened, he heard the familiar footsteps, now he was even more uncertain than ever. John wrung his large hands in despair. Then, as Mary entered the dovecote, he quickly made up his mind. He had to see her again, to speak to her, to confront her, to persuade her to change her mind. He felt confident in this approach, - well thought out, totally rational - to his mind.

Taking a deep breath he quietly jumped over the wall onto the soft turf. He stealthily crossed towards the tall, cone-shaped building. He felt alien in the farm he knew so well, where he had helped out on so many occasions, a curious outcast now. He did not have time to stop and consider this sentiment for long, because two birds which were lingering on the domed roof suddenly scattered in fear, their wings clapping a sharp warning in the air. Had Mary heard anything? He stopped still and cautiously looked through the window.

But as he peered through the dusty glass he began to hesitate, - she did not appear to be there. The gloom fooled him for a second. As he peered into the darkness she was just visible, standing, head bent and weeping. In that brief moment all his determination flew away with the startled birds. He felt ashamed, an intruder especially in this moment of sorrow. He could not bring himself to intrude on her grief.

Poor John Bowes; he tiptoed back to the wall, paused to try and collect his thoughts, and finally succumbed to despair. He slowly climbed over the rough stones and as quietly as possible walked away; and that was the last time he saw Mary Norman.

By seven fifteen the carriage had arrived and been packed with her cases. The boys kissed Mary in turn, Russell holding her close for a few moments. June could barely contain her grief, trying to laugh though sobbing in turns. Grandma Wetherall seemed resigned. She gently smiled but her blue eyes signalled a deep and abiding

150

sadness that Mary was to remember forever - a look that haunted her for years.

Now the time had come to depart. She left the front door, pausing to gaze once more at the fields around her. The winter aconites were just visible as the golden heralds of spring, the plovers cried and tumbled overhead, the robin's thin plaintive call was high in the firs. She listened and looked for a few moments more, then walked firmly down the path to the carriage.

Soon the melodious clip-clop of the hooves lulled her into a false feeling of acceptance. As she reached the last bend in the Top Road, Mary turned and waved for the last time. She could hear their cries especially Russell's good luck call. Then South Hadley Farm disappeared from view.

Only once did she ask the driver to stop.

After a mile she decided she wanted to walk down a narrow path to the river, a spot where she had always picked primroses and violets for her mother as a child. The banks were bare now apart from the occasional early coltsfoot's powdered yellow bloom.

Mary looked across the valley to her farm on the opposite side. She thought of her father working long hours to support them. She thought of her mother's tender love and care. She thought of the warmth and the excitement of childhood, her family, her friends.

'Mother was right!' she said quietly, 'the farm had to go to Russell. It was Father's wish and he was such a good man, a lovable man. Poor Mother! Poor Mother! Martin would be happiest away from the dales. Mother always knew that!' She had no qualms about lying, or about what she had done

She reached into her coat pocket and produced a large envelope.

Not opening the package, Mary tore the letter and the new Will, her mother's Will, the missing Will, the Will that had been drawn up in secret to leave the farm to Martin, into a hundred tiny pieces and scattered them as a miniature blizzard into the running water. As each white flake rushed forward in the torrent and was sucked beneath the surface they carried away the hopes, despair and resolution of Agnes Norman in her quest for justice. Without the witness signature of the Reverend Clenham, the Will was invalid, although to the bitter end Agnes had hoped the Vicar would come. In a second each fragment had swirled away in a multitude of eddies and rills. They were never seen again; and the consequences.....

Mary hurried back to the carriage, the driver and horse waiting patiently by the long, white, wooden bridge. 'Drive on please,' she said softly, then added in the faintest of whispers, 'to my new and better life!'

As the morning sun rose over Compton Vale, the white-faced buildings of South Hadley Farm blushed, and by degrees composed themselves into darkening nooks and stately gable ends.

Here ends the first book.

Book 2. Home Before Christmas

On the fourth day of August 1914, the British stood out from the rest of Europe - they were the only country to declare war on Germany. So the bloodshed began.

Chapter 32. Martin writes in September 1914.

Dear June,

How are you? It is curious to be writing from an army barracks in the South, at Aldershot, where there is so little freedom and space. We sleep in rows, twenty to a hut. At first there was little pattern of rest at night and some of the men lay awake, talking softly or gently singing to themselves in a mixture of boredom, fear and loneliness. Then, when they did fall asleep, it was impossible to get them up at five-thirty. I must say, for me it is no hardship rising at that time, but some of the city types find it a nightmare.

The food is passable, but the training's not. I mean, we spend much of our time rushing forward in short, sharp attacks, spearing sacks of hay suspended like the dead on gallows, climbing walls, or crawling across deep mud on our elbows and knees, sometimes face down so that it's almost impossible to breathe in the slime. And then we scrape under obstacles usually decorated with loads of barbed wire. I wish we had as much on the farm. It was laughable at first, for there were so few guns and bayonets that we were given walking sticks for drill duties. Would you believe it? But it's right enough! The uniform fits none too badly and gun practice is easy, like grouse or pheasant shooting. Some of the men couldn't hit a barn, never mind the door. I think they'll get better.

A curious feature are the young boys, almost children to me although over sixteen, who have enlisted as trumpeters. Evidently in the heat of battle they stand next to the commanding officers and it's their responsibility to sound the bugle to indicate a unit's movement, quite a responsibility at their age. They're an innocent, cheerful bunch and seem happy. We're all volunteers, amazing all volunteers.

How is the farm? I bet the harvest was a bumper one this year, the weather's been so good. Old Vulcan would be a bit pushed, no doubt. We could do with him here instead of the decrepit old nags that hang around the stables and outhouses. Really, the cart shafts prop them up. Take them out and they'd sink to their knees in a minute. As well as the farm, the hills and everyone I love, I'm thinking about the dogs. And why? I'm just like one of them at times. Rushing forward, lying flat on the ground and crawling at command. Funny, I never gave it a thought in the past, I mean barking out orders and expecting an instant response. I tell you what, I'll never get annoyed with Sorrel and Sam again, and that's the truth.

I saw Mary for a few hours when I stopped off near Oxford. She looked very well and seemed very happy. I'm pleased! The family have a few good horses, including a Cleveland Bay, and the children ride around the estate a lot. They seemed very friendly and agreeable. Mary said all the school lessons were going well.

We are off to France soon. I'm looking forward to going, so are the rest of the men. They say it's not too bad out there and everyone jokes that the food and wine will be first class, if we can get near it! Still, tell Gran that I would rather have her meat pie and bilberry crumble. Also tell the boys I miss them, and you, so much of course.

All my love,

Martin.

P.S. They say it will be over soon, the rumour is 'Home before Christmas.'

Chapter 33. June writes in October 1914.

Dearest Martin,

Thank you for your letter, I have read it a dozen times. All is well on the farm. We miss you very much, so very much I can hardly say. It seems so quiet now. Russell and Joseph have worked the harvest well and the barns are full. Joseph has a wish to join up like you. He heard of some sixteen-year olds from the village and Cranford Dale who went to enlist and were refused. But they were told to come back in a week when they would be nineteen! So back they went! It seems everyone wants to join the army and fight. Millions have enlisted.

There are posters everywhere including the store and the Barrington Hall. They are very good! Have you seen them? One shows Lord Kitchener pointing a solid finger and stating 'Your country needs you!' and another which has two women and a curly-haired child which reads 'Women of Britain say 'Go!' - this poster brings tears to my eyes because you can see the soldiers marching off into the distance, and I think of you every time. I have enclosed a copy

I still think it was rash (although I must add very brave) to join up as quickly as you did. Grandma said the problems on the farm, about the inheritance and all that, would have worked out in time. But now you are going to France - take care! It is such a worry and no one knows what will happen. I told Dr MacKenzie that you said it would be all over before Christmas and he smiled and shook his head. He didn't comment and that worried me for several nights and I hardly slept, imagining all sorts of horrible things.

And the valley was so hushed, and the burn seemed to stop running - it was so quiet. Yet when I checked it one morning it was in full force with the trout sunning themselves in the deeper reaches by the overhanging banks. I do go on, don't I? I hope it's not too boring but the Rev. Clenham says that you will be starved of news and even trivial things will be entertaining. I do hope so! Tell me in your next letter if I'm boring, I will not mind a bit.

Dr Ashleigh has left the village to study in London. When he will return, no one knows. I must say that he was a marvellous doctor. I find it strange that he has gone...and Mother too! They seemed such a large part of our lives only a year ago.

By the way, the price of mutton and beef is soaring with the War, and wood is rising quickly in price also.

I have been promoted to financial adviser at South Hadley (my title and a joke) and I must admit I have some plans which I will tell you about in another letter. I have discussed them with the Rev Clenham, who has been really marvellous lately, and he thinks the plans have 'merit' (his word!). There is talk of profiteering already; at least George Havelock says so. I cannot imagine how anyone would want to make money out of suffering, can you? Still, it takes all sorts to make a world and looking at it dispassionately I suppose that to supply essential goods to the troops meets an honourable purpose.

We were approached by the Ministry to sell our horse; they have this plan compiled during the last three years in what is called the "War Book". There is a list of all available horses in Britain and, I am reliably told, they have even been commandeered in Scotland. They offer a flat rate of seventy five pounds which is tempting for many. But how we could farm without Vulcan is beyond belief. Anyway the scars on his back from that harvest day put them off, thank goodness.

Well, I hope you will write soon. The dogs have taken to Russell and he is out with them at the moment, probably bringing down the Swaledale ewes from Back Wythop to Ullock Moor. Both dogs missed you at first and Sorrel hung around the house for days, moping all the time. But they're as chirpy as grasshoppers at present, so don't worry, we will look after them so lovingly until you return, safe and sound.

Lots of love from us all, as always,

God bless you, Martin and may the good Lord look after you,

June.

Chapter 34. A friend and a friend.

The tall canvas tent was filled with fumes; almost twenty men were smoking, laughing and gambling. The canvas shook fitfully in the October wind, dispersing the blue smoke in gentle waves. Martin sat on one side of his makeshift bed and gazed by turn at the players and then into the Aldershot night air, heavy with autumnal bleakness and precipitant chill. The collar of his khaki shirt was open and the sleeves of his army uniform pulled half way up his forearms. He laughed with the others and looked over the shoulder of one of the players, a fat man of twenty five or so, called Jack Golightly, who shook visibly as he joined in the fun, causing more mirth to break out by example.

'OK Tubby, you flaming well win!' exclaimed a young private throwing down his hand in exasperation but still smiling.

'Flaming's the word, son, so I've won five matches more!' cried Tubby Golightly enthusiastically, 'and no pipe to fill! Where's the real money?'

'Search me, Tubs!' said another of the players, 'army pay is lean!'

Jack slapped his girth and laughed again, 'Even I'll be lean on the blinkin' swill they feed us if it goes on for more than a month. Give me French cooking any day! It'll make the old trip across the channel worth while, it will!'

'Bollocks! The speed we're going Tubby, it will be all bloody bratwurst and pumpernickel, because the fricking Germans will be everywhere,' replied the player laconically.

Tubby scratched his head and gently smoothed his clipped black moustache in a delicate movement.

'Ja!' cried another private in acknowledgement.

'Ja, to you, Bill,' responded Jack with another laugh, 'but if you keep shouting 'Ja!' in Paris they'll have you in clink before you can say 'Voulez vous!''

'Vooley voo? What's the Hell's that?' replied Bill.

'It depends who you're asking Bill,' said Tubby Golightly in a low voice by way of emphasis, and drumming his plump fingers in mock annoyance. 'To a barman, for example, 'voulez vous' means pull me a pint, numbskull!'

'And to a mademoiselle?' shouted another amongst renewed mirth.

'Now you're asking!' said Tubby gravely, 'but if you don't know by now Fred, it's too late, so say nowt!'

Martin laughed again and slapped Jack Golightly on his expansive back. 'Tubby I'm off into Aldershot, are you coming or not?'

'Certainly, and back by ten,' replied Jack with a gentle wave of his hand. 'Or it'll be kipping in the guard tent, extra fatigues and perhaps a couple of hours tied up as an example to all wrongdoers.' He chuckled and got up slowly, lightly brushed the remaining crumbs of a bun he had been eating from his trousers, and moved gracefully to the door with a mild swagger. Eighteen stones seemed little encumbrance to this genial giant who could not resist a mock trip on one of the guy ropes as he left, to the unbounded delight of the others. 'Where should we drink, Martin that is the question?'

'In the town, Jack, but where?'

'After today's training and those bloody boots that fit no one, the throbbing of my bunions tells me that the Duke of Wellington is the nearest watering-hole. The throbbing feels like a sort of Morse code; and I have the temerity to suggest that we obey their delicate signals and proceed there forthwith. Agreed?'

They both laughed.

'Agreed!' replied Martin with a further laugh. 'Anyway Jack, I'm pleased your feet are good for something...and I only hope they can spell!'

'Like a dictionary!' replied his friend earnestly with a look down at his shiny black boots. 'I call them Dr Johnson... and Mr Hyde! That's culture for you!' He laughed again and winked.

So in good humour, off they went. They crossed the main road by a narrow side street and headed for a lean building close to a large hotel.

From this building, the noise of two hundred soldiers cascaded into the darkness. While the gaslights outside flared erratically casting dark shadows on the pavements and accentuating the waiting carriage horses, whose long backs seemed to shimmer and steam in the gloom. Crisp leaves, withered and holed, swirled and crunched about their feet.

The room was lit by a series of lamps and the light just made it through the smoke. But the music and colour and general throng were welcoming. The sheer enjoyment of being away from barracks lifted their spirits. Jack pushed open the pub door, removed his cap, gave a polite bow and yelled, 'Attention!'

There was a momentary hush.

But in those seconds, Jack had hurried through the crowd of astonished soldiers who were waiting at the bar to be served. He called out his order.

Hoots of derision greeted the tomfoolery and finally gave way to laughter. 'A slight misunderstanding, ladies and gentlemen. Please accept Lord Kitchener's apologies!'

'Hey, you're not bloody Kitchener,' said a drunken soldier, 'you've not got a big enough 'tache!'

'There's more to a man than a moustache,' responded Jack.

'That's true,' replied the man slurring his speech, 'there is more to you than a moustache, much more if you don't mind me pointing it out!'

'I don't mind, my friend, for it's all latent muscle!' replied Tubby cheerfully. Picking up the two drinks he hurried back to Martin. 'A few more like him and the war's lost!' he said firmly after taking a long draught. 'The only way to succeed in war is to be brash, be firm, be resolute and above all... be sly!'

He paused to wink at two girls who sidled forward.

The one with bleached hair, dark roots and circles of rouge on the cheeks, linked Martin's arm while a plumper version smiled at Jack and said, 'Buy us a drink, love and I'll tell you how to get back to your original size!'

Tubby paused, considered the situation with a rueful gaze and gave a polite bow. 'My recently acquired and dehydrated friends,' he said with a slight hitch of the neck and a straightening of his back, 'my only wish is your command but....' he glanced wistfully aside, 'firstly the army wouldn't accept me if I shrunk back to eight pounds two ounces (Martin burst out laughing) and secondly, my current financial state is worse than Belgium's, without a spark of hope on the horizon'

Those around him burst out laughing and Tubby rounded off the proceedings with another guffaw which drowned them all.

A pretty blond girl with dark blue eyes and a matching coat smiled and her gaze fixed on Martin. 'I'm going home now,' she said addressing the two women but still looking at the shepherd, 'and since it's quite a walk, I was wondering if one of the soldiers would escort me home?' She smiled at Martin.

Jack gave him a nudge, 'Here's your chance!' he whispered.

Martin looked abashed for a moment, hesitated and then stepped forward and took hold of the girl's hand. With another accompanying wink from Jack and a brief conversation with the two women, they decided to leave.

The night air was fresh about them, and there was a cool, fitful wind. The sky was cloudy and threatening. While the gas in the street lamps rose and fell to the rhythm of the air currents. It caused their linked shadows to grow and contract at odd angles and intensities of blackness. These strange shadows followed the man and girl across and along the cobblestone streets, down thin, gloomy passageways until they were lost in the sombreness of a narrow alley. The houses were shabby there, made worse by the grime of the station nearby; where the trains shunted and chuntered in the night, puffing loud, rounded clouds of added darkness into the deep void of a seemingly eternal bleakness.

They entered a tall, terraced house and climbed up a long staircase past three floors, where the air was heavy and acrid with smoke and gas. Then they went into a large room, partially lit by a central lamp in a plaster ceiling which had seen better days. They sat down on a long brown settee and the girl took off her coat to reveal a pink dress, a shabby remnant of former summers.

She smiled. For a moment their eyes met and he looked away. Martin began to ask himself, 'What am I doing here'. They had walked largely in silence, although he was enjoying the change of company away from the heavy-humour of the soldiers.

She slid his arm around her shoulders and softly kissed his hand. She did not speak for a few moments and then said, 'You're a quiet one aren't you!'

The abruptness of the question took him by surprise. 'I suppose I am. It's part of my upbringing and occupation, I guess!' He paused. 'It's a curious life in the army, and we talk a lot and don't say much. But I suppose it's my life now, and for better or worse the war's my goal.' She did not reply. 'It's a strange goal really, for war is an allusion, I been thinking recently, and something non-tangible.' He paused, 'That's as about as pompous as I can get.' He laughed. 'Am I boring you?'

'Not at all!'

'Well, that's something!' Suddenly free from army constraint he continued in a more relaxed tone, 'The more you go through the tedium of basic training, the more you start asking, 'What on earth is this all about?' You don't get much news from France and if you do it's designed to brainwash. I have never really thought about fighting until now... they say it is for King and country, what ever that means!'

'And loved ones... and freedom!' she added.

'I suppose that's true also. But if you ask what might we die for? They tell us honour!' He gave a short, harsh laugh. 'Have you ever heard of such total rubbish as that? Who wants to die for bleeding honour, if you pardon the French.'

She rested her head against his chest and said nothing.

'In the first few days of the army life there's a sort of nervous excitement, very likely because everyone's fired up with ideals... and the unknown is always sort of exciting. You could call it patriotic fervour, I suppose,

164

whipped up by those that waves flags in your face and slap you on the back. And some minor military rank inducts you, with a "sign here" and a "bloody good show old chap."' Martin stopped short wondering if she was listening.

After a few moments of silence, she looked up and her reply was not what he expected. 'You know, a good few soldiers come here for one reason or another,' she paused, 'generally for one reason and it's not for honour or anything like it, I can tell you. But it's a necessary part of life, like fighting, I suppose. They're generally brash and try to appear manly in a swaggering way; although most of them are just kids and full of what they're going to do, which will not be much, in my opinion. Anyway, for the want of me boring you this time, I'll end by saying you're different... more difficult to fathom out!'

'Not that different I hope. If I am, perhaps it's a form of country shyness. Being alone on the fells with a flock of sheep for days doesn't make you the best talker in the world, least I don't think so.' They both laughed.

'I guess not! Anyway, at least you're natural - the sheep have taught you that, and not the type of person I usually bring back here!'

'And?'

'Whatever you mean by 'and'... what goes on here is without subtlety... a response-less charade. There's money in it, though.' Her voice went flat and unemotional. A small flame flickered on the gas mantle and hissed for a brief moment. He looked at the girl and despite her pale, careworn face she looked so very young that she reminded him of June.

Suddenly Martin felt uncomfortable and tried to hide it as best he could; but she was unaware of this alteration in mood.

'Are you afraid?' she asked abruptly, changing the subject. There was a moment of peace as the trains stopped shunting.

'Am I afraid?' he repeated the question with shrug of the shoulders. 'Of fighting or dying?'

'Yes, of dying?'

He looked at her for a second. 'I am, but can you tell me who isn't?'

'I have often thought - do soldiers have any remorse? I mean just putting a bullet through someone's brain and watching them die, does it affect you when you have to go into battle again.'

Martin thought for a moment.

'I wouldn't know and I can't say, and that's the truth of the matter. We have guns at home and although I've shot the odd game bird or pest, I cannot say I have enjoyed killing. So the short answer again is: yes, I'll have remorse. The thought of killing makes me feel physically sick. But war changes people's opinions and attitudes... it has throughout history... I may get to hate the enemy so that killing becomes a pleasure… we'll just have to wait and see. Do you have any remorse?'

She looked serious, 'When?'

'Taking soldiers money...'

She broke into his sentence by pressing her left forefinger against his lips, 'Anyway, we all need to earn money whatever way we can. But don't spoil the evening... although I expect you and your friends will all have a good laugh tomorrow.

He felt a faint blush of conscience. 'Why should I?'

'I have a miserable life in some ways, but it's better than others who are penniless. A few soldiers say they'll see me again but they never do.'

'Do you really care, about seeing them again?'

'Frankly no!' She wriggled in an unconcerned way and slipped her head onto his lap. 'It's different you know, I mean looking at your face from this direction. The lamp seems to bring out the best in your eyes and mouth and chin. You look very handsome from this angle.'

Martin laughed. 'Well, that's a comfort. I never feel that I look good from any direction.' He replied to hide his embarrassment.'

'You have nice eyes, bluish-grey and gentle!'

'I always thought they were bovine and bulging,' he said to make her laugh and trying to relieve his embarrassment. 'I wonder what war has in store for us all?' he said changing the subject. 'No one likes to talk about it...but it's on everyone's mind. Anyway, there's no point in worrying about the unknown and, for pity's sake, I'm not going to ruin the rest of the evening by discussing the damned war. We'll be home soon, and that's what keeps us going.'

Martin, so eager to talk at first, now felt a curious coldness, an indifference to the girl and the situation. He wondered what his family would think about him sitting there in such a shabby room with a girl he barely knew. This thought had suddenly cut through his conscience. He wanted to go; but out of politeness he stayed and they talked for half an hour; boring, inconsequential chatter. He kept away from any further physical contact and she did not seem to care.

Martin sat up. 'I must be going!'

'So soon, never mind!' she yawned. 'You couldn't lend me ten bob, could you?'

'Ten bob! Here's two half-crowns! It's the blood money of five men!'

She puzzled at the remark. He felt remorse at his brusqueness. 'Let me explain! We get a shilling a head - the King's shilling - for joining up. That's how much we're worth! So five bob's five recruits.'

The girl shook her head and he was just about to speak when she collected herself. She reached forward and placing her arms around his neck, simply asked, 'Kiss me! Kiss me at least once!'

Martin kissed her on the cheek and then on the lips and saw her eyes gently close, kitten-like, at the warmth and closeness of his body. She hung on to his embrace for a moment breathing quickly but softly. Then she raised her blue eyes and with a languid smile said, 'You're a rum one soldier, without doubt!' She shook her golden hair and it seemed to coil back with each movement like a taut spring. 'The bloody rummest yet! But the most manly, the most honest and the most loveable! '

Martin laughed and gave her the gentlest of hugs as if her body had, in an instant, become the most delicate porcelain.

'Please see me tomorrow,' she asked earnestly. 'You will, wont you?'

He laughed and gazed into her eyes, 'Okay, I will!'

But they never met.

For he sailed to France - on the following day.

Chapter 35. Leaving Home.

Martin stood transfixed in one of those curious, seemingly extended fractions of time and said a prayer. His Mother would have been proud that her eldest son is going to war. How he wished for a second that he could speak to her now. He would have asked for reassurance.

But it was not to be and he suddenly collected himself as the waves slapped against the jetty; and the shouts of men and the raucous screaming gulls, brought him back to reality. For a moment he let his left foot linger on the quay-side, his final tenuous link with home.

The fact that he was leaving his beloved country, the only one he had ever known, rushed through his mind in a confused amalgam of green fields, family, farm and friends. He paused once more to say a silent farewell, wished for luck, took a deep breath, collected himself and stepped forward onto the narrow gangway. Then he jostled his way up to the crowded deck.

Everywhere was laughter, shouting and noisy confusion. There were thousands of soldiers mobilised on board, mostly privates but with a few consciously strutting corporals, stern looking sergeants and languid officers scattered here and there. The latter looked like static interlopers amongst the heaving throng.

Around and above it all the seagulls heckled and screamed, perched high on the tiled shabby warehouse roofs at the harbour entrance. Their shrill cries, the red-tinged bills and arched backs added to the colour and clamour of the scene.

Meanwhile the assembled ships gently smoked from long chimneys, leaving a fine trail of black in the chill October air. Almost at peace with themselves, their compact frames rocked sedately at anchor in the murky waters; water which lapped to and fro in incessant rills against the jetty posts - now tarry and sticky in parts, untidy and encrusted with barnacles and green seaweed slime.

A misty haze brooded over the flatness of the shore, and the smoke condensed in sombre patches adding to the gloom. The dark sea and sky seemed to be as one, apart from the gentle swell of the ebbing tide. Despite all, there was serenity out at sea, away from the bustling noise. Slowly a small fishing boat, its sails fresh and white and small, crawled slowly against the horizon; an incongruous speck battling against a scalloped sea.

It had been a different scene a few weeks before. The cattle boats had been commandeered without a thought, and the troops had been so overcrowded that they could hardly move. The unwarranted optimism and humour had given way to silence as the lingering impregnated smell of the animals and the choppy sea had reduced a considerable number to sea-sickness. But their struggle to get to the ship's rail in time had produced a degree of ill-humour, only relieved by the warm and tumultuous welcome when they reached France.

The word had spread and the boats, which were due to sail that day, were filled with soldiers expecting a similar enthusiastic reception Men were everywhere, lining the decks, and it was with some relief when Martin heard a familiar voice; for he was feeling distinctly lonely and a little apprehensive.

'Martin!'

Jack Golightly waved from the crowd of faces already assembled together on an upper deck. 'Martin, over here!'

The young soldier pushed his way through the jostling troops, straightening his uniform and unloaded his pack as he arrived. 'Tubby, how was last night? I was asleep when you got back and missed you at breakfast'.

'How was yours, more likely,' asked Jack as he laughed deeply and slapped his friend on the back, 'but spare me the details, for I'm a gentleman - neither born nor bred but acquired - an attribute you'll find in most aspiring snobs!' He laughed once more. 'Anyway forget the blushes and let's find somewhere to sit. If I get up a full head of steam, which is more than this pathetic canal barge can possibly ever achieve, I'll cleave a path straight to those more than comfy benches over there.'

And he was true to his word. For Jack hardly paused, his bulky prow bursting through the mass of soldiers and sweeping all and sundry aside. 'Look sharp!' he bawled into a swirl of men, 'I require those there bench seats for officers and for gentlemen!'

Two young privates leapt to their feet in a reflex military action. But their startled faces quickly assumed an expression of mounting anger as Tubby, with a sigh of contentment, immediately flopped down onto both spaces. 'Squeeze in, Martin, there's just about room for two'.

'Heh! What about the officers?' exclaimed a thick set, freckled youth endeavouring to reclaim his seat. 'Punch me in the chops if there's not a bloomin' one around!'

'Well, what about them?' replied Tubby fiercely. 'They've room aplenty in their quarters, no doubt!'

'But you said....'

'I said... and gentlemen', boomed Tubby in the boy's face, 'and we're gentlemen,' he slightly bowed his head, 'not born...'

'Nor bred...' continued Martin smiling.

'...but acquired from the university of life,' said Tubby firmly.

'Sounds like a rotten place to me in a green and pleasant land if you're the best graduates,' stated a small man pushing his way through the crowd of soldiers and laying his pack on the deck. He had an innocent, child-like face astride his narrow five foot two frame, with large

171

brown eyes and a shock of sandy hair, cut short that seemed to point vertically upwards as if his body was imbued with an inherent electricity of its own.

'That, Sir, is a matter of opinion,' replied Tubby once more glancing towards Martin, 'and it's differences of opinions that make horses race,' he stated emphatically, 'as Huckleberry Finn once said'.

'Huckleberry Finn may be in your regiment,' argued the slight man pausing to take a deep breath from the exertion of carrying his heavy pack 'but, personally speaking, I'm not interested in what he thinks of horses ... or women!'

'And pray what have women to do with the situation?' inquired Jack.

'Nothing, but in this life you can't bet on either!'

Jack scratched his head for a moment, ruffling his black hair, while the smaller man beamed with the pleasure gained from a triumphant argument. 'You're a man after my own heart; - what's your name, my fine fellow,' said Tubby at length, while shaking the stranger's hand.

'Maurice Whinlow,' replied the other boldly returning the warmth of the greeting and shouting as the ship's hooter signalled the start of the voyage across the channel.

'Horace Minnow - a fine name,' yelled Tubby back with delight.

Maurice beamed again and nodded in the din; and thus inadvertently was born the curious nickname 'Minnow' that was to stick like glue to their cheerful companion throughout the whole of the First World War.

Meanwhile Martin had left his friend and walked across to the ship's rail. He watched the ropes being cast off and felt the boat slip away from the jetty, saw a few waving hands mainly from children and disinterested elderly couples who were loitering on the quayside and neighbouring steps. He marked the slow vibration of the water at the stern and the incessant foaming of the sea in the vessels wake. Vagrant gulls swooped and cried over the flecks of white churning spray. His thoughts were filled with both sadness and hope.

'We'll give the Germans something to tremble about', chorused the troops nearby, 'and after the Huns have had enough, we'll close shop and be home before Christmas!'

'I'm looking forward to that,' chirped the Minnow, 'I don't think I can support this sixty pound pack, as well as a wife and two children, much longer without developing some physical defect such as a hump in the back.'

Tubby stood up to gaze at the receding shoreline, his foot firmly planted, nonetheless, on the vacant bench. 'If you've got a problem, Horace, - sorry I mean Maurice - I'll take some ballast on board, it's all the same for me!' Both smiled and shook hands once more.

Martin continued to watch the gulls and to think of home.

The land declined and vanished so swiftly into the haze, the moment of final departure came and went so apparently quickly, that he wondered if he would ever see England again.

He closed his eyes and tried to visualise Compton Vale as it had always been. The valley, the morning mist hanging in serene stillness over the trees of Scarth Wood, and the sun in its imperceptible course around the distant fells burnishing the colours of the fields and glinting on the twisting burn as a liquid flame.

But a shaft of sunlight broke through the dark clouds and distracted his thoughts. Opening his eyes he beheld a small sparrow cheeping confidently on a narrow rail close to the funnels. 'Would it return to England, or in innocence stay on in France, perhaps...' and here Martin smiled to himself, 'becoming an aide de camp to a carrier pigeon in the Expeditionary Force.'

Meanwhile the ship churned steadily onwards, hour by hour, in a seemingly monotonous mission. The air became chill and dank, and the soldiers' spirits followed by degrees. Suddenly a grey line appeared indistinctly on the horizon, then a spike of a church tower; then the gauzy, seemingly delicate fabric of woods and trees on the rise behind the low coastal reaches. And finally, tiny ant-like dots that grew to resemble other soldiers hurrying around the shore and quay.

France was looming and what it held Martin could not even guess.

'If that's France,' exclaimed the Minnow trying to lighten the gloom, 'give me Clacton any day!'

A few of the listeners smiled, but a strange subdued hush had gathered over the ship like the prelude stillness of a threatening storm. Few talked, even fewer laughed. Most were brooding over their future.

They did not know, no one knew, that even fewer would return.

Chapter 36. Dear June. October 1914.

I have not been able to write for two weeks because of the incessant troop movements. The weather is holding in this Northern part of France and the trees are quite delightful, like the autumn days at home.

We steamed into Boulogne with an escort of boats – some fishing vessels, some yachts and a couple of cruisers that went back and forth in an imperious manner - with crowds lining the jetty. Most bizarre were the old soldiers in their red and blue uniforms stretched over paunchy frames, with grey whiskers and dimming vision. They had left off their spectacles for effect. They didn't look as fighting fit as I would have liked, or even imagined. But the warmth of their greeting was genuine enough, and perhaps I'm being overcritical.

Overall, there is a feeling of excitement amongst us and for the last week supply lines have been moving consistently towards the front.

We heard the guns in the distance the other day. Curiously, it sounds like hollow thunder and not at all frightening. Morale is high, thank goodness.

I have decided to return your letters after a while, so that I have them together in a bunch when I get back, it will be curious to read them once more in the comfort and security of the living room in front of the old chimney place. Such a small thing to dwell on, I suppose, but it gives a sense of reassurance and purpose to the days ahead.

Horses are everywhere in all shapes and sizes. They work unceasingly and are mainly well cared for. However, to our dismay, we learnt that the French cooks' tasty thick stew was mainly horse rump and they eat a lot of horsemeat out here. Some of the boys, even the tough ones, baulked a bit at this, although my friend (a plump chap called Jack) says he does not care a bit if he is eating the old nag that pulled his cart that morning as long as it's tender and the sauce piquant (you see we're learning some French) and anyway, he claims, the carts would move no slower without them. It is strange that the supplies arrive here so quickly and in such volume by train and then off they go so very slowly in small cartloads or wagons to the front.

Talking of arriving (by the way I'm not allowed to give our location or destination) we came by train, packed like sardines in cattle trucks! with only some damp straw and bales of hay to sit on. Mostly we sang or played cards when we could, but I was pleased to get out of the truck and have some fresh air.

On the brighter side I was invited to a meal by a French peasant family, their farms are much smaller than ours and they seem to have only a cow or two, a goat and a few poultry. I had carted some of his goods to a local market; their first horse having been taken by the French military (as is often the case!) and the other was lame. The result was a delicious meal. Don't ask me to explain what it was, but the fish dish had a creamy sauce and there were some fried frog's legs for the starter, believe it or not. What sort of frogs produce legs like small chickens I don't know! There are some in the ditch at the corner of our field but they wouldn't feed a mouse.

I was surprised to hear that John (*Bowes) had enlisted. I know from your letter that he has missed Mary since she left. He took that leaving very badly. Good old honest John, I would have told him to stay put, still when he comes (and if our paths cross) I'll be delighted to see him. I don't suppose he will have finished his basic training yet, but if you see one of his sisters pass on my message that he has got to find me, he knows the regiment.

The boys near the front are digging a great deal and they're very confident - so are the French troops we meet. But Christmas is fast approaching and there's little activity in our quarter at present. Keep your fingers crossed for a quick return.

All my love to everyone,

Martin.

P.S. I try not to think about the fells and the sheep and the dogs - it makes me homesick.

The other night I dreamed about Sorrel and Sam sitting high on the crag at sunset and the sky was aglow with every red, orange, gold and yellow in the book. I have made a resolution not to mention the dogs again, but to tell the truth, I'm dying to see them, just one pat or hug each would do!

Chapter 37. The first symphony of war.

The air near the French coast had a freshness, even a delicate perfume, heightened by the fine sea spray thrown up from the many outcrops of rocks and shale. The sea had a restlessness Martin had not experienced before, and the drift and roar from each wave soothed his sense; and the kittiwakes, herring gulls and petrels added an incessant cry to rival the crashing water beneath the cliffs. Martin enjoyed this communion with the sea, new to his world, and likened it to a flat expanse of a giant moor, gently undulating as it danced to the rhythm of the moon. The tangled seaweed floats looked like the shadows on the brackened valley, and the small swirls of white foaming wavelets could have been the distant flocking lambs. He would have liked to sit for hours near the cliff's edge but a new journey was beckoning.

And as they journeyed inland, first to the railway shunting yard for ammunition and provisions and then on towards Ypres by lorry, the atmosphere changed - initially a slight nasal unpleasantness, like an acrid itch, was just detectable, then gradually it merged into a faint burning stench as the front line grew nearer and nearer.

The lorries rattled and jolted along cobbled roads after they had left the yard, past peasant farmhouses - small shabby buildings with a cluster of dirty outhouses, barns and long, fermenting dung heaps. The cattle were sparse and lean; odd hens and geese were here and there; odd horses and goats, but no sheep. Their absence Martin observed in a languid way, hardly concentrating on the surroundings, pitching his thoughts into abstraction and away from wars, fields and the recent odd tangible effects of living. In effect, he tried to be preoccupied with nothing. Odd roads and cart tracks cut across the valley and at first the hedges were trim around the odd allotment or orchard.

As the stream of lorries turned through a scarred wood, the scene became one of contrasts. Just in front and beside them was fresh, vibrant greenery with birdsong; but the horizon was so blasted by war that the once smooth undulating edge had been whipped into a series of incongruous lumps. They paused and then halted as the driver checked the rough surface ahead. Martin took the time to stand and look around. He was curious as to what effects the shells had in sculpturing the adjoining fields. He saw the odd pig rutting in the fresh mud and goats grazing oblivious to the destruction; animals enjoying the scattered earth. While the gnats and flies had crept out of the decay and swarmed around them in profusion.

They set off again and the rear of his lorry bumped and lurched monotonously. The odd roar sent a pungent, half-ignited petrol smell their way which made a few feel sick. Maurice Whinlow and the young Geordie sat on either side of Martin. All three gripped the rail and braced themselves as best they could against the incessant jarring.

So the long column of foot soldiers, wagons and horse-drawn carts moved tediously on, a giant snake some ten miles in length. They seemed to progress vaguely and at random, Martin noted. Often he wondered what direction they were taking.

The good humour and song of the troops knew no bounds. It added to the rattling cacophony of the wheels on the rough rutted roads and the steady plodding, metallic sound of a myriad of horseshoes grinding slowly forward to an unseen, unknown destination.

Occasionally an engine would splutter and cough, alarming the sweating horses close by; but mostly it was a steady, workmanlike scene with little dissent.

Now the landscape appeared normal again and there was the usual discussion, that went round and round and never reached anywhere or formed any opinion, save that the war would be over quickly. The few who complained were sworn at, their bitterness and pessimism seemed alien.

One of the troops opposite Martin looked up, 'Hear that!' There was a muffled bang and then another followed by faint wisps of smoke. A hint of the acrid smell of cordite was carried on the breeze.

They listened. At first only an impression, distant, ethereal - a faint vibration in the air, a faint thrill within the ground as if the most minor upheaval had happened in a restless earth. And for most of the troops there was a feeling of tense excitement, coupled with an irrational exultation and the desire to fight.

Hollow and distant in the beginning were the sounds, comfortingly distant. Imperceptible sounds that aroused interest and curiosity, the first real taste of war. A symphonic sound; with guns of varying calibre, shells of varying size; a faint spluttering of machine gun bullets, and sometimes single shots almost lost in the overall volume of noise, but equally lethal. The songs of war that grew louder and louder by the mile, and less inviting by the yard.

A song that began to subdue the idle chatter and jesting by degrees, until only the odd serious comment broke forth, befriended by a forced, hollow laugh. What once beckoned as the imminent sound of thunder had now become the harsh reality of war.

The Geordie soldier stared fixedly towards the front, noticing the odd plume of smoke and the preceding flash and bang. Martin observed the paleness of his features, the slightly unkempt brown hair brushed flat to one side and the nervous twitching of his mouth and eyes, movements and expressions almost like a child who, while trying to comprehend the unknown, feels totally overwhelmed by the events around him. Tubby moved over and sat next to him. Taking pity on the eighteen year old, he asked, 'Geordie lad, how's it going? You afraid?'

The young private smiled back. 'A bit!'

Jack put his arms around the boy's shoulders. 'Only a bit, that's good!'

'Well, more than a bit Tubby. And you?'

'Even more than that son; more than that!'

The young soldier followed Jack's infectious guffaw with a shyer laugh. 'Stand behind me in battle bonnie lad, and you'll like the outsized man for the rest of your life.'

Martin looked away. Suddenly the boy seemed so very, very young to be facing such a war; and without warning Martin felt the tension in his own hands, the faint chill of sweat, as he gripped the rail on the lorry's side. But he was determined to remain calm - despite that oncoming crude symphony of war.

Chapter 38. Thoughts of the fells... and turnips.

The land had become bleak and cheerless. The land had a chill dread about it. Trees, fields, and farmhouses had been reduced to a shambles of destruction, exhausted of all life and greenery. Martin's attention was drawn to the destroyed pastures. No one spoke or needed to; all conversation had died for the moment. To them it was an unknown area of France, but it had been reduced to a sameness by war – anonymous to a degree he could never have imagined. Martin looked and listened. How could this countryside be so alien to what he had known and appreciated all his life? Most of the other soldiers simply surveyed the land; Martin felt for it, in a strange way, as if it was alive and being destroyed bit by bit with a thousand cuts. He thought of the training, that period of what he considered to be dull, empty waiting. He wondered once if he would be exhilarated by the challenge of war; now his feelings were mixed. The emotions were of self-preservation and uncertainty; self-awareness that he was doing the correct thing but for the wrong reason. Had he been too hasty to join up in his disappointment in losing the farm – a decision in truth, he felt he could never quite rationalise, and would never accept.

By late afternoon they had reached a small village, almost deserted, which was to serve as temporary headquarters. Captain Cranmer, young, brisk and efficient, with an upper-crust accent which slightly irritated Martin, ordered the convoy to stop and await others. Martin did not realise how their paths were to cross in the course of events.

Once they had seen to the lorries (there was no need to camouflage them with broken bushes), arranged the carts and fed the horses, the soldiers rested in their designated fields, enjoying the late sunshine and the luxury of lounging on soft grass.

They ate well, beans and stew being the order of the day, with slices of local bread and strong, strong tea in metal mugs that warmed the palms and occasioned a delicate fanning of the surface liquid by a shallow breath to cool it to a drinking temperature.

The horses munched a mixture of grass and hay, ripping at the food in their characteristic way.

Martin watched them as they stood in tethered groups, sometimes neighing softly. He liked the sound. It reminded him of home. It was a long way to home and he tried not to think of home, but to be positive and hope the War would bring some good against an evil oppression.

However, it was natural to think of home, and the valley and the farm. He longed to see his family once more, and the familiar rooms, and the villagers, and everything of old.

For the first time in weeks he felt homesick, and slightly afraid. The girl had asked him about fear, and dying, and where was she now? 'No doubt perfectly safe,' he thought, 'living as she had before. I wonder if she really expected to see me again. She will have got over it by now, if she had!' Martin shook his head. There seemed so much to war, such a curious turmoil; so many people here and there all jumbled together, all shaken around, by an incomprehensible event. He had met no one for the most part of his life, and now people came into his life by the hour and went by the day. No doubt more were to come and go.

He felt fed up and turned his thoughts to the distant fells, his beloved countryside. 'Why do I miss the hills and mountains so much?'

He puzzled for a while and gazed into the liquid blue of the sky where a few clouds seem to diminish one above the other like image on image in two mirrors, until they trailed as fine wisps into the heavens. He had watched such cloud patterns when resting on some outcrop with the dogs, surveyed the valley back home. 'What is the fascination of the hill tops, why do men walk the fells and feel so close to God?'

He pondered for a while. 'I suppose it's an escape from reality; to stand apart from other human beings for a brief period, in that exhilaration of an inner peace.'

He listened to animals moving and the subdued talk of the men fifty yards away. 'Three worlds, if you want to think of it', he surmised. 'We live in three worlds.'

The sky was darkening and two stars, the glare of Venus and the redness of Mars, were just visible against the star cluster of Virgo. They were comforting reminders

183

of Compton Vale and the tired journey home after a weary day on the fells; the evening star had been his chronometer, the impetus to return, and what was to follow…the hearty fried bacon and eggs, the apple pie with custard and a smiling grandmother beating and stirring in the kitchen.

Martin continued his deliberations. 'The first world is the inner world, be happy and contented there and the other worlds would follow in tune.' He nodded in agreement with himself. 'The second world is the one immediately around. That is the beauty of the high fells and mountains, they expand this world.' He remained motionless for a few seconds. 'While my third world is the one I only know from books, or have been told about. It's a world I will have to face in the next few weeks; a world that seems to be on the verge of destruction. Will my inner world survive? I hope so,' he reasoned with a sigh, 'or there's nothing to give me hope!'

A sergeant approached, 'Mind if I sit down?'

'Not at all, Harry.' Martin knew him from the next Dale, back home.

They sat in silence for a minute. The sergeant was an old campaigner from many wars and his exploits and tales were legendary. He had a natural affinity with Martin. 'The horses,' he began at length, 'will be a waste of time in this war, no bloody good!'

Martin did not reply but listened.

'They're too slow, the trains are fine and so are the other vehicles, but horses, well I ask you?' He sat silently watching the animals for a few moments. 'They say that a bit farther north the first attack by our lads was with a group from the cavalry. They were out reconnoitring and heard a handful of unsuspecting Germans trotting towards them. The Germans must have smelled a rat for they stopped and turned back. But our soldiers, true to idealism, did a cavalry charge. They got one with the sword; a satisfying, if archaic way, to start this War, don't you think?'

'I suppose so,' said Martin ruefully, thinking of the horror of being impaled at speed, 'I would have thought a gun would be better.'

'It would at that!' There was a long silence. 'It doesn't matter how you die, Martin, it's all the same in the end. I've seen enough dead and dying to know it's all useless; but at my age I'm good for nothing else and have five children and a wife to feed.'

Martin said nothing.

'When the lads went to Mons in August, a pal told me, it was cheering all the way with women sighing and waving handkerchiefs and the men offering almost anything they wanted, even their wives, if the truth be out. However, a battle or two later, then the lads took to the road in a different direction and different bloody frame of mind. The women and children were howling the place down while the men-folk plodded along in a daze with whatever they could salvage. Troops and civilians pushing around in each other's way' Harry reflected for a moment. 'There were loads of food dumped by the wayside, enough to feed a battalion. But there was no stopping, no respite, and our soldiers were forced to march on. Some of the lads almost fell out of their saddles or off the carts, they were so tired in the end; dazed and numb from lack of sleep. It was a rum business, it was!'

Martin said blandly, 'I don't know what to expect from war. But nothing can surprise me now.'

Harry was not to be deflected from the thread of his

185

conversation. 'Some things will, Martin! It's a hell of a mess, the attack is, you know; it's bad enough avoiding the bullets and craters, you mark my word. But there's the tangle of barbed wire, and the horses…well, they get caught in the wire, running every bloody where, kicking and struggling like demons and sooner or later they break a leg and all hell is let loose.'

Because he was not getting much of a response from Martin, who was weary and his feet were chaffed and swollen, the Sergeant got up, wished him luck and moved on to another group.

The oncoming darkness was cleft by a shell as it burst in a blaze of colour, some three miles away. 'The blasted front is getting nearer by the day', he heard a familiar voice followed by a laugh. Martin looked up. He was surprised by the sudden appearance of Tubby and the Minnow as their respective heads shot over the hedge in front of him. Maurice's spiky hair appeared first and then Jack's affable smile shone like the rising sun.

'Quel chance!' laughed Tubby. 'Here's nature's bounty, Martin lad. If I had to ask you to make a wish - only for food Martin, only for food - I reckon I'd know what you would say.'

'What?' replied Martin whose spirits had been revived and was laughing heartily with his companions, as usual.

'Turnips!'

'Turnips!'

'Yes, turnips,' said Maurice with glee, 'and fresh apples...' (produce cascaded forth from their jackets), while Jack interjected ...'plus cheese!'

'Cheese?' asked Martin in amazement.

'Martin you're in danger of becoming repetitive and

monosyllabic', continued Tubby beaming, 'it wouldn't be so bad if you were learning French but you should have mastered such simple English nouns at your age!' They all laughed.

'Where's the knife?' asked Minnow in his practical way. 'And the Royal Worcester plates,' he added.

'I've left them behind, Maurice, with the wine glasses, they're too delicate for the army, you know,' responded Jack, 'and the best I can do is this old pen-knife which worked when my grandfather had it.'

It worked, and within minutes they had peeled the apples and turnips; the cheese was split into thick, crumbling white slices. Jack looked up and waved to a few of the men nearby to join them.

'This countryside can support us for ages,' said Maurice during a pause in the eating.

'Like a week,' said Tubby, 'the way we're gobbling it up. Anyway, the foods fresh and wholesome, thanks to Monsieur le Fermier and his neglected orchard and fields. His farm was sad sight though; the Germans had wrecked the place, clocks, furniture, tables all smashed to bits, and clothes burned in the fire-grate. Some other village buildings were also wrecked - windows and doors chopped to pieces. So the French peasants have done a bunk.'

'Can't say I blame them,' said Martin cleaning the knife and handing back to Maurice. 'Talking of farms....'

'Not the old reminiscences again, lonely sheep, coughing heifers, pining ducks,' joked Jack, slapping Martin on the back.

Martin felt crest-fallen for a second; while Maurice removed a fragment of turnip from between his back molars with the point of the knife. 'Please the Lord that I won't want any dental work out here,' he said reflectively, 'or chip a front tooth.'

'Chip a front tooth, be damned if that's all...' muttered Jack.

Martin looked up. 'I was only going to say Tubby, before you interrupted me for the second time tonight, 'that we get more like farm animals everyday - eating turnips like ewes, packed in trucks like cattle and crawling around like dogs!'

Jack stroked his clipped black moustache reflectively, 'I reckon you're right, Martin, we are like our four-legged friends. That's why Maurice keeps his mouth shut. For any army horse-doctor looking at the rings on his teeth would make him out to be thirty-one and destined to be dumped by the military and put out to grass - turnips or not!'

They laughed again. Maurice had the most perfect set of all and showed them proudly like a mating stallion. 'It is funny,' he suddenly said, 'how your brain is the servant of the stomach.'

Jack groaned in mock appreciation and said, 'Go on!' in a disparaging voice.

'When you've eaten, it says go to sleep and most likely you do,' Maurice stated gravely, 'a substantial meal would make me feel fairly benevolent even to Fritz and...'

'Do shut up for heaven's sake,' said Tubby 'your philosophical drivel about the Germans is driving me mad. We're here to fight the Hun not to dine with them.'

'I still think that they're not a bad bunch at heart, only led on by idiot politicians and their stupid Kaiser. Anyway, Jack, if you'd just eaten six buttered muffins I bet that you'd be all benevolence and light. Muffins worked on us a treat at bedtime when I was a tot,' continued Maurice gazing into the night air, 'with Ovaltine!'

Jack tugged at a corner of his moustache in exasperation. 'Perhaps you're right, Maurice. Muffins always lay heavy but warming, and cheaper than brandy too! Maybe we are too soft, too gullible, and too benevolent. For it's a difficult argument to persuade a man to give up his skin for his country; but our politicians seemed to have managed it, and here we are - muffins for brains or not!'

'Never mind bloody muffins, mates, we'll be more like mutton chops if those damned shells hit us,' said Bill, a Cumbrian private, in a chilling response.

For as they settled back, a huge flash with falling debris lit up the horizon. In the distance a small farmhouse burst into flames. Martin noticed the leaping tongues of red and orange licking and swirling through the windows, doors and roof; while miniature explosions shook the stone fabric. Black plumed smoke spiralled upward into the night air. No one rushed out. 'Was it deserted?' He hoped so! 'Did the food come from there? If so it was probably deserted.' That thought consoled him. How safe were his family at this time, protected by the British Fleet, the best in the World. He tried to focus his attention on South Hadley but another terrific explosion scattered the blackness in an overwhelming cascade of hot, glowing fragments that seemed to light up the sky for minutes. The darkness was under attack as Very lights, shell tracks and scorching yellow columns of tracer bullets bisected the night air into a weird series of abstract geometric shapes.

'See that,' said the Cumbrian. 'That's what war is about - the bloody butchering of people, not bloody games and idle bloody chat. We'll all be dead one day, you mark my word. What does it matter, one way or the other?'

189

His sombreness was infectious. No one replied. A great struggle of ideals was going on within each soldier. Except Bill, 'I'm not a great thinker, a far-seeing bloke. But this mess could go on and on. Strikes me the politicians are hiding something. Officialdom has pleasure in keeping the public ignorant. That's a big rule in life!'

Maurice disagreed but his comments broke no ice with Bill who stroked his oily hair and lit another pipe.

A long pause followed.

Jack had wandered over to speak to some soldiers and having returned sat next to Martin, their backs propped against an old tree trunk.

'Jack,' said Martin quietly, 'I have to tell you that your kindness and humour has been a consolation and a moral-booster not only for me, but for all the rest of the troops. I just wanted to tell you, in case… anyway, how you manage to keep so cheerful all the time, beats me.'

Jack paused, 'Beats me sometimes, Martin. I have always been a joker, even at school because I decided it was better to smile at myself and all about me; so that others could laugh with me, rather than at me, and the habit's stuck; although I must confess I get down at times like the rest. But I can't spend my days, and they could be my last days I suppose, being miserable. There's no point, is there?'

'I suppose not! But thanks a thousand fold both to you and to Maurice, who's the perfect foil,' Martin replied.

'Aye, Maurice… he's special with his chirpy ways…like a canary, I suppose.' They both laughed in the warmth of their mutual friendship.

Suddenly the distant sounds of the guns - sometimes baying, sometimes murmuring - the universal movement and mayhem at the Front, intensified. Someone said, 'There's going to be one hell of a bombardment tonight.' No one replied. Lights sparkled and sprayed everywhere as the night became electric and alive.

Glowing embers appeared like a million falling stars, crackling and hissing. The earth seemed to pour down from the sky in a mysterious aberration of nature, a fearsome attempt at the annihilation of mankind. They watched more out of curiosity than fear.

And thus began their first night of war.

Chapter 39. Friends for a moment.

'It will be the battle of shavers, not Wipers,' said Maurice Whinlow the next morning, 'because the shaving waters cold and I can't wipe the stubble off my chin.'

'Humour as heavy as the cannon' observed Tubby in a quiet voice as he strolled past Martin in the crisp, morning air. It was just after seven am. The sun was up and shining, albeit with some remorse; and the dew had polished the grass and hedgerows. No birds sang. There was still that faint chemical smell in the air of spent ammunition and shells - and decay.

'It was one-hell-of-a-night, it was,' said the Minnow shaking his head and admiring his teeth in the cracked glass which served as a mirror; 'one-hell-of-a-night!'

'The noise!' exclaimed Martin, still stripped to the waist and with a towel around his broad shoulders. 'The noise!'

'Worst I've ever heard,' said Maurice shaking his head gravely.

'You can't expect shells to be silent, you numbskull,' rejoined Tubby to the Minnow.

'Who said shells?' Maurice bawled, 'it was bloody snoring, Jack, snoring! In the midst of one of the most divine moments in army life there's a noise like thunder. Will the storm pass? No, you realised that half a dozen mouths are wide open at this point. Use tact! You get up and shake 'em hard, they answer "Sorry" in the meekest voice, and within a minute it's blowing and bellowing all over again. On the way back to your bed, for the pan's outside, you stubs your toe and give a dignified squeak. Then what! Half of the snorers leap up astonished and say 'Keep quiet idiot, can't you! And it's useless protesting, because the blinkin' din's as bad as before in a flash. I'd rather have Wagner!'

Tubby stopped clipping his moustache and stared straight ahead. 'He's another blasted German; you'll be bringing in the whole country next.'

'Well, Puccini, then,' hurriedly added Maurice, 'it's a name I always fancied for a horse.'

'Anyway,' continued Tubby giving a short snort and not looking up, 'You don't mean to impugn... for when I snore I'm as quiet as a spider, as that eminently rotund figure... I forget his name...used to say...'

'Oscar Wilde,' added Martin.

But Maurice was warming to his theme, 'Not you, Jack, some of the men! I can put up with the guns, it's the blinkin' snoring I detest. Have done since we were six to a bed, when I was a nipper.' Maurice beamed at the family anecdote, while Martin swiped him with the wet towel, causing the hair to spike ever upwards.

'It's time to water down all this philosophy, Jack,' said the smiling Martin. 'Let's go for a dip in the river'. He also called to Geordie who was strolling towards them whistling the Blaydon Races shrilly but jauntily, 'Hey,

Geordie, come and join us.'

The four soldiers ran down the field, passed through a gap in the hedge, crossed a further two hundred yards of meadow still alive with buttercups and daisies; and throwing off their clothes plunged into the grey fast-flowing river with a series of bellowing cascades. The water was chilly, but crystal clear as if it had just emerged from a spring. The sandy bottom and smoothly worn rocks - from a million rills - were seen through its shimmering transparency. The men splashed and swam in the deeper part, the bodies three-quarters submerged.

'Any trout?' yelled Martin as Geordie appeared from beneath the rippling surface.

'None.'

'Pity, caught many a dozen when I was a lad.' With a deep breath and a gentle glide beneath the surface Martin's browned body shimmered through the water and trawled the bank. Several speckled trout darted off in all directions. Once he managed to grab a tail, only to feel the smooth scales slide through his fingers. He came up spluttering.

'I'm not any good at it now,' he said laughing and shaking large droplets from his wet hair. 'Anyway, that's some of the Army dust washed off; and I'm getting hungry.'

'The army grub's not too bad, Martin, is it?' asked the young soldier, waiting for approval, 'and I'm also famished.'

'The army can sharpen both bayonets and appetites,' sang out Jack, splashing around like a miniature whale, 'a good polishing for the first, a long march and the mess room swill for the second are the secrets, my friend.'

'Don't listen to Tubby.' Martin strode out of the river

avoiding some large, grey stones that framed one corner of the bank; and two others who had been scrubbing assiduously in the shallows, plodded out with much splashing and throwing of water. Soon they were all frictioned into dryness by the rough army towels. Slightly shivering, they donned their uniforms as quickly as they could and strode briskly back across the lower field.

Martin was the last to dress and was thus a few paces behind when he noticed a farmhouse, just visible to the left. It was partly hidden along a short road. The tall trees and the glancing sunlight between the shadows gave the rough furrowed track a marbled appearance. The scene spoke of an untouched serenity that seemed to beckon.

Curious, he diverted towards the building.

The smell of grass and the dampness of the earth vividly recalled home and brought back a feeling of security. It was the first time that such an emotion had afflicted him since he arrived in France. He looked around with an irrational feeling of being in Compton Vale. Suddenly he hated the mud and stench which filled his world day by day, his body soggy and chilled hour by hour; here was warmth and security, or so Martin thought.

The house he approached was a typical peasant dwelling with cracked white plaster-covered walls, modest in size and sheltering only three small rooms. It was adorned by four narrow windows and a faded oak door.

The door was open and he knocked; gently the first time; then louder. There was a sharp rustling movement from within. It was followed by a loud bang; then a sudden suppressed whine of pain.

Martin froze.

He drew his pistol. Tense and straining every sinew,

he paused for a moment; then he braced himself and, with a deep breath, raced in.

He started, stopped and he was down on his knees in a second.

Trussed and tangled on the floor, entwined in the rope that was designed to restrain it, was a dog - a hound of the variety favoured in that part of France. Its white and brown body was emaciated with starvation and dehydration.

The distraught animal raised two sad eyes, and a dry tongue reached out to lick the soldier's hands as he cut the rope free. Martin massaged the thin limbs for a second hoping to restore their circulation and warmth. 'Poor boy, easy now, easy.' He hugged the broad head.

On the bare top of a wooden table there was a large, round metal saucepan. Quickly, Martin filled it with water from a tap by the back door. He placed it in front of the dog and it drank and drank, the broad head jerking to and fro, pausing between gulps to look at its saviour. Twice Martin called out. But there was no answer; his voice echoed around the deserted house.

He cautiously inspected the two other rooms.

In the larger room a clock ticked on one wall and an old pair of wooden clogs rested on the brown stone floor, close to an abandoned bed still covered by a dirty sheet hiding the criss-cross metal springs of the base mattress.

In the second and smaller room, a straw-bottomed chair was angled against the shabby wall, overshadowed by an imposing walnut cabinet. On it were arranged some provisions left behind; perhaps in haste, perhaps because they were too bulky to be carried. A large ham, smoked and brown, attracted his attention. He immediately cut a thick wedge of meat and threw it to the dog who was shakily pattering behind.

Crusty farmhouse bread, a stone flagon of dry white wine, a small pile of hazel-nuts freshly cropped and a selection of hard cheeses were also present.

Martin paused, 'Well, chien, should we eat or should we not? It's your master's food.'

The dog's strength was returning in an almost miraculous fashion now that it had drunk its fill, and the answer (Martin swore later) was a distinct 'Woof' which sounded like a 'Oui!'

After he had eaten and finished about a third of the wine, Martin lay back on the rough, tumble-down bed and waited for the protesting springs to settle; and contemplated life in a dreamy haze.

He could see the images of the trees outside, gently stirring and waving in the greenish glass of an old mirror. The whole scene was framed like an old master by the antique copper fittings. 'From one farmhouse to the next, dog, wherever will it end?'

He smiled and stroked the animal's broad head. 'Prosperity is an illusion, without doubt, but I feel rich today on bread and cheese, with wine of course.' The dog, despite the linguistic barrier, enjoyed the warm tones of friendship and nuzzled for more. But Martin ignored it after a while and, putting all thoughts out of his mind for ten minutes, he lay in the luxury of being alone.

The smell of leaves once scorched and cracked by the summer sun and now in ill-assorted heaps by the corner walls, gave the room a distinctive autumnal odour that disguised the stuffiness, the mouldy smell of decay.

He spoke to the dog again. 'I'm a man who makes no decisions until after breakfast, I seriously over-react when hungry.' He chuckled slightly inanely. 'Thus a soupcon more is needed, if the flagon's not empty.'

He gazed at the faded panelled walls and the small grey curtains, so thin that they would never totally cut out the rising sunlight. Suddenly he collected his thoughts.

'What shall I do with the dog?'

After a few seconds of earnest contemplation, he decided to leave the dog free - with the ham shank, plenty of water and the door open. As he got up the animal wagged its tail, and pawed and nuzzled the soldier's arm in pleasure. Martin stroked its head. 'Well, time to go old boy, time to wander on.'

He paused to look out of the window and down the narrow avenue of trees which gently rose up the sloping road. The converging lines pointed to the clouds puffing and slowly foaming in the south, gently swirled by a hastening breeze. But overall the sky was brightening into a liquid blue.

As Martin slowly walked up the lane, the dog trotted ahead. It proceeded quite jauntily until they had half-crossed the large meadow. Then pausing, it surveyed the new-found friend. Suddenly the animal made up its mind, stopped, wagged its tail and whined.

With this final note of gratitude, it turned round and ran back to the house.

In later weeks Martin often thought of that dog.

In his heart of hearts, he hoped it would be well.

Chapter 40. A letter from Ypres (Belgium) October 1914.

Dear June,

We have arrived at our destination (where I cannot reveal) after an arduous trek, and being diverted first towards the front and then north-east again to here.

197

Evidently plans had changed! So relatively flat is the countryside that from the higher hills we can see the English Channel glinting as a line in the distance.

For some reason it is reassuring to know the sea is there and that home is not too far away. On the other hand we can witness the dense clouds of smoke from the German trains as they haul to and fro with troops and armaments.

The town has moat ramparts and is all intricate buildings, domes and spires, with rows of houses of unequal height and appearance - some being plain fronted, others festooned with sculptures. But basically it is a flat land with little raised above the common level, except the windmills and how they swirl their wings like giant birds of prey.

The headman - a Burgomeister - met us all and, accompanied by other leading citizens, made a great ceremony and gave grave exhortations for us to fight and fight until liberation and victory were achieved. He then retired with the rest of the senior officers and politicians, who had been looking on with severe faces, to a hearty meal - at least that's what one of our cooks said! The French were already here and observed the pomp of our arrival with some amusement and perhaps a little envy. There was a stir when a Highland regiment, in kilts, broke out with their bagpipes. That took the Frenchies by surprise! But this din overshadowed the fact that there was little room for both us and the horses; the town being full. It suddenly started to pour down. The army in its wisdom decided that the animals had priority. A local deputation ordered the men to stick them in what appeared to be part of the town hall, although later we heard it was another ancient and valuable building, the Cloth Hall. Anyway, imagine the horses' shod feet on the shiny marble floors, it was confusion everywhere. The animals were slipping and making a mess all over the place. When the downpour stopped, the orders were reversed and we ended up tethering the beasts outside, where they were at the beginning! Three of us had to go and commandeer extra rooms - Jack Golightly, a Welshman named (you guessed) Taffy whose real name is Dai and myself.........

*****

Martin and the two men crossed the main street of Ypres and headed towards the bridge.

'Where are we going?' sang Dai Llewellyn.

'182, St Julien Street', replied Tubby scratching his head. 'It would be easier if half of these bloomin' signs hadn't been damaged or taken down.'

'That's true, one house looks like the next in this street,' said Martin looking down a long line of uniform buildings. 'Let's see... that's 155 something…'

'And the something is nothing to me', moaned Tubby 'and what is worse we'll miss our evening grub at this rate, never mind a decent night's kip in a real, genuine, honest-to-goodness clean room. The first for months!'

'In that case it must be on the other side,' continued Martin ignoring his friend, 'about there.' Dai swept across the almost deserted road. 'You're right, boy-o,' he called out, 'and here it is!'

They crossed over and stood looking up at the frontage of a neat Belgian hotel. There were six steps leading to the front door. The house was three storeys high, capped by a large attic rarely used. Two large windows framed each floor, those at ground level being barred with an iron grille. The door was painted a glossy black and decorated with a rounded brass knocker that became the focus of attention.

It was rapped professionally by Tubby (having spent some part of his life in lodgings) and who volunteered the information 'that some landladies were uncommonly deaf especially when they had already surveyed the impending lodger from behind the front room curtains. In fact,' said Tubby, 'I only met one old woman who, after peering out for some considerable time, decided to let me in. And she talked for fifteen minutes about her bad back as she hobbled around the rooms and went on to enliven me as to how arthritis can spread so mightily quickly that I left in a hurry before it had completely taken over her body.'

Eventually the door was opened by a girl of twenty-five or thereabouts. She stood framed in the wooden arch like a Dutch painting, with heavy features and brown hair pulled back in a bun. 'Goeien middag, wat wilt uw hebben aub?' she asked slowly.

A further discouraging slamming of doors emanated from within.

'Your mistress around?' enquired a perplexed Tubby with a slight bow.

'No!' said the girl abruptly, finding her English tongue.

Tubby paused. 'Not in?'

'No!'

'Definitely not in!'

'No', continued the girl emphatically.

'Nor your mother,' stated Tubby suddenly wondering if she was not a servant after all.

'No, but my aunt is!'

Jack rolled his eyes, one moment heavenwards and then sideways at his friends.

The last thing the girl was expecting at that moment was heavy humour. She looked indignant and attempted to slam the door. Tubby's generous boot got in the way.

They patiently explained their mission. Eventually, and with an unconcealed annoyance, the girl led them into a large hall from which she conducted them to the second floor via a broad staircase; it had carved wooden banisters that seemed to angle inwards by a strange slight of perspective. The second floor was festooned with vases from which sprouted tall prickly plants surmounting a variety of intertwining tendrils that also seemed to come tumbling down towards them. A barometer hung on the wall in vertical precision, while a brass-inlaid clock struck the three quarters with echoing chimes.

A prim elderly lady with a starched outfit, pinched face and wiry grey and brown hair was sitting in a large velvet chair. She stood up. She was holding a piece of needlework and laid it on a chest of drawers as the men approached.

She walked slowly, and all three glanced at her back. 'No arthritis,' whispered Martin.'

She stopped. Looked them up an down with obvious disgust and moved sedately forward as if she was treading on eggs (as Tubby remarked later).

'We have been asked to obtain extra rooms for the night, - the town quarters are overflowing - and we have a request or really an order from the Burgomeister's office.' Martin spoke slowly rounding his vowels. He paused, noticing the look of distrust, 'Please, how many rooms have you vacant?'

'Eight.'

'That's four to a room less the one we share, Martin, making thirty soldiers in all,' reasoned Tubby in a flash.

The prim woman showed no emotion, set her thin lips, and prepared to hurry off with the girl to her down-stair's quarters. 'You see the mess this family is put into by war,' she said to the girl in a stage whisper that was designed to carry round the room. The girl, noting her aunt's tone of displeasure, glared at the men who stared back not certain of what course to pursue next.

There was a short burst of conversation between them in their native tongue.

'God bless the woman!' sighed Dai, talking with a sense of injury, 'Pretty soon we'll have stood here all night.'

Martin gave a rapid glance towards his friends and then took a pace forward and interjected. Their gabbling stopped. 'Of course we will pay you a fair amount,' he said firmly, determined to press his mission.

The prim woman shrugged her shoulders, 'It'll hardly bear the cost of laundering the linen. But what can I do in these difficult times?' She spoke with a rising inflection, suggestive of more rancour to come.

'You have no other rooms,' asked Dai seemingly oblivious to the trend, 'for there seems to be five doors on this landing?'

The elder woman hesitated and said suddenly, 'As the Lord is my witness, our lot is cast amongst fools!' And the hissing ferocity of this remark almost made the soldiers step back with surprise.

But the young girl quickly looked from Martin's face and down to the floor.

She linked her aunt's arm.

'Only one you have not seen,' said the aunt archly.

She motioned to a door at the far end of the corridor and Tubby, striding ahead, pushed it open without ceremony. It was a large, airy room with a welcoming four-poster bed, washbasin and stand, and a large gilt-edged mirror. Two portraits in pastel hung above the washbasin, with a brightly coloured tapestry chair beside.

'If I never say a truer word, this one's for me,' Jack whispered drumming his plump fingers in pleasure.

The girl continued to look down and Martin noticed her pale sad expression.

She hesitated and then said softly, 'We were hoping to keep this room as it always has been, to respect the memories.' She paused and her lips trembled slightly. 'You see it was my parents' room and my mother only died a month ago.'

Some time later Martin remarked 'If the worst comes to the worst, you and I will sleep in the stables Tubby, I didn't like that large room much anyway'. They had settled the negotiations and were strolling down the street.

Jack said life was often curious, 'The room was gloomy, the woman was gloomy and he was...well guess?' But Martin yelled out, 'Hungry' and cut him short. This remark forced the genial mouth to broaden into a lingering grin. While Dai said he thought the place felt creepy, possibly haunted and rolled his eyes in several diverse directions to raise another laugh.

However, before leaving the street they did pause to give a warm and considerate smile in the direction of the waving girl.

She responded with, 'Dag!' blew a kiss and then closed the door.

Chapter 41. The attack!

The Western Front was a parallel line of deep trenches that spawned lesser trenches and dug outs behind. At Ypres conditions were no different, no less appalling.

They were long pits in the earth and they were deep and they were usually filled with stagnant water or inhospitable slush or mud.

In these conditions an hour seemed a week and a month became a grinding eternity.

A year was unthinkable.

There were sandbags and more sandbags piled here and there along the hostile perimeter. Some leaked sand from bullet holes and shrapnel cuts, and like the ancient sand or arena of Rome, it soaked up the surplus blood and excreta.

Also like miniature Roman outposts the corrugated shelters were spotted here and there, usually in the lowest reaches of the trenches where the soaking water lay longest. These were the places of rest and safety, the refuge of the weary but giving no refuge from the incessant guns, flashes and ammunition patter that did not seem to cease.

Water drizzled from the sky.

Water seeped from the rock faces and vertical mud.

And water hung round the ankles and lower leg as a constant squelching companion to the leather of the boots and the woollen socks within. Martin had always hated mud, even back home he hated mud; cleaning his fell-boots was a priority. He hated the world about him.

It was a visual world of intermittent brightness; an audible world of jarring sounds; a palpable world of unremitting benumbing dampness.

The dampness was just as bad. Cold, penetrating to the bone; he used to think that he could not get any colder. But he had; and now he did not care.

In that world rode death, almost as an afterthought to disease, and almost welcome.

Soon the deadly army of lice and rats began their havoc with typhus and rat bite fever. Soldiers shivered in the cold of the trenches, then heated up with fever, then became dehydrated with dysentery, so that their flesh shrivelled and the skin of their tongues cracked and parched in a perverse world of abundant water, and not the brine the Ancient Mariner feared; an unremitting thirst in the grey, slimy, stagnant ooze of the trenches.

And the rats!

They revelled in the death and destruction. If any creature gained from war, this animal was the victor. Theirs was a snuffling, squeaking, body to the ground, slinking feast without end, a bounty of slops and more flesh and more bones.

While in front of the main trench ran the barbed wire, a snare for the unwary as it twisted, gnarled, looped and straddled across No-Man's-Land. It was the mutual enemy of all, to be encountered during attack or retreat; a deadly trap for animals and men.

And finally there were the shell holes; a moonscape of varying shapes and sizes according to their metal sculptors. Ragged holes, jagged edges with hedge and trees uprooted, broken boughs spiking upwards like a thousand Viking spears, huge boulders flung hither and thither as if a giant reaper had passed by; scorched wood, metal and earth fused into an unholy alliance.

The shells would rain down in waves. He had learned their sequence, the preceding palpable vibration, the increasing whine that suddenly deepened to baritone like an on-rushing train. The anticipated explosion, the cloud of dust, the shell hole formed from other shell holes. The troops knew that when they heard the bang clearly it was too near and too late. While the pungent smell of cordite added to the smell of death and decay.

There would be the odd muttering and cursing; the odd prayer which had become less frequent of late. Nobody said they were afraid now; if anything war had tempered them with hate and apathy, or was it resignation? Martin did not know. They were in the hands of fate, chance cards of imminent eternity.

He had given up trying to appraise the situation. He had reached the Front at noon. The rain had deferred council to a steady drizzle. Wisps of grey mist, thickened with sulphurous fumes, drifted on irregular breezes, moving slowly and wantonly across the land.

He had jumped down into the trench with a hollow feeling bordering on despair, and had immediately felt the dismal wetness soaking to his knees. The mud sucked at his boots; he stamped to keep warm. 'My God, I'll never run in this,' he said to Dai who was standing next to him, 'and swimming is out!' He gave a hollow laugh.

But the other soldiers paid no heed to the remark, shivering in the cold, mesmerized by the despondent bleakness of this November day.

The guns suddenly began in earnest on both sides. A sergeant shouted for them to fan out along the trenches, to fill in the gaps left by previous casualties, to position themselves alongside some hardened troopers.

This they did as quickly as the conditions would allow.

Then came the shout, the stand-by for orders; a period of resignation, a period of waiting. 'How long is this damned delay going to last?' Martin thought, standing propped against a wooden post which had been blown from the No-Mans-Land into the pit.

The hours dragged, amidst an intermittent hail of shells and bullets and explosions.

The early darkness of the late afternoon arrived and was immediately challenged by the flares and Very lights. Martin still watched with some degree of fascination as the colours spun and twirled in the sky adding an extra dimension of beauty to the overriding terrifying greyness.

There was a steady drip, drip, drip from the trench wall, like the pendulum clock back home; drip, drip, drip - steadily beating out the moments towards the attack. Not quite a second, he believed; slightly longer... slightly longer... but equally pedantic.

Some warm tea and biscuits were served and the troops, their tension heightened by the delay, tried to joke amongst themselves, tried to feign relaxation for a short period.

Martin felt no thrill, no fear - just a bluntness of emotions - an emptiness! The steady eroding of self and spirit over the last two months was beginning to take its toll.

Towards midnight the noise began to reach a crescendo. So loud that the troops clasped cold hands over their ears or plugged them with strips of cloth from torn handkerchiefs.

The shells began to find their bearings, landing closer and more menacing. Fine wisps of pungent smoke and small fragments of earth drifted their way on a strengthening breeze.

The noise from both sides became overwhelming, horrendous. For a moment the explosions were everywhere. And then there was a lull – a strange period of quiet that made ashen faces glance round in bewilderment.

As they looked at each other, the tension was plain to see. Some had faces drawn with apprehension, some were marked with fear. But most had countenances etched with resolution, some with anger suffused around tightly clenched mouths, some with clammy palms or coalescing beads of sweat on brows or noses. All clasped their bayonets and rifles in readiness; some sat, some chewed on an unlit cigarette, some stood and a few vomited quietly in fear.

At first the Captain, Thomas Cranmer, was just visible running along the trench. Martin smiled when their eyes met, but in his apprehension it was forced and quickly faded.

'Well soldiers,' began the Captain, 'now it's our turn to soften up the enemy. So we start with a steady bombardment.' He rubbed his numb hands to revive them, 'then comes the attack, sometime in the next few hours. So rest well,' he spoke softly, 'for it's over the top at dawn. And when I yell "Get down!" - keep down. For the German machine guns, they'll be spraying mayhem in all directions.' He looked into the faces of his men close by. 'I have every confidence in you; but remember for God's sake keep low at all times, get swiftly through the wire, move quickly and go straight for their lines. Expect no mercy. But, by God, we'll not give them any. Let me say finally, I will not sacrifice a single man.'

No one stirred; no one showed any expression or gesture. All felt an unearthly dread coupled with a curious helplessness. However, the fighting words conveyed an underlying feeling of confidence and concern. So they collected themselves, with a shrug of resignation, a general murmur of appreciation and a few handshakes. They were determined, they were still alive, that was the overwhelming emotion – they had survived the first onslaught with no more than sore eyes and streaming noses.

'Sooner or later there will be a lull and when the signal's given, we move as one,' he continued in a matter-of-fact way. He stood up straight and saluted. 'Good luck men and may God be with you at all times.'

Martin watched him leave. His frame silhouetted against the flashing lights showed up as a crouching form running; and in the intermittent light it reminded him of the flickering figures in his toy-lanterns of his childhood. He watched and he waited. He thought of childhood, but the images chopped by the distraction of the background din and he gave up. He could not decide if he was afraid. There was a subtle confusion in his mind, yet he did not feel afraid – at least not as afraid as he thought he would. He did not think of home, the family, the dogs, the animals either. He always felt he would when the moment to die came – but the past was erased. Nor did he feel panic, he felt curiously cool and collected. He was determined to remain in control, come what may. It was an ice cold sensation, as if all fear had drained out of his body.

He looked up. There was no moon. The night dragged slowly forward straining against the elements; the sky was alive with a million lights and crescendos. The ethereal beauty continued, especially when the tracer lights fell in cascading showers through low lying cloud, abruptly appearing from its inner greyness.

A rum-ration was handed round.

The men were to find out later that it was the prelude to an attack; a final bribe some called it, others saw it as the final holy communion. Saving this ration was forbidden. All gulped the sharp burning liquid which suffused some life into aching limbs; while cold hands and feet glowed for at least a minute.

Down the line Martin could make out the young Geordie, Dai, Maurice Whinlow, and far to the left the unmistakable form of Jack Golightly - only seen however when the lights glared fiercely in that quarter; then he would disappear suddenly into the darkness, like another silhouetted marionette in his lantern show.

Martin had his tin helmet pushed back for ease of

running; because when it was worn bent forwards the strap seemed to catch his throat. He kept readjusting it. It was nervous habit but he felt that it disguised the trembling of his hands. He thought he had barely dozed, yet to his surprise it was four in the morning. The light was fitful now and he could just make out the pointers on his watch. He looked again, he had not made a mistake - it was four in the morning.

Suddenly the barrage of shells began again and in minutes it crept closer and closer as the enemy tried to erase all living things.

And then there was a lull; just a brief lull.

A moment when his nerves were taut to breaking.

Then a glow from the Allied front, a cascade of Very lights like the resurrection.

Then came the command and the attack began.

Martin felt a surge of pent up energy rushing through his body. He vaulted out of the trench. His heart raced; for a few yards his breath was laboured.

Ahead nothing seemed to be happening.

His second wind came quickly which added power to his legs.

The barbed wire was crossed with only minor scratches; the open, rocky, pitted, waste of No-Man's-Land was reached at running speed. He was hardly conscious of the rutted surface, the numerous unseen snares and holes.

He simply forged forwards with bayonet at the ready; his gaze fixed on the enemy lines ahead.

Then the rattle of the German machine guns began; then the single shots in harmony.

The scene changed in a second.

Fit, eager soldiers slumped forward like rag dolls, some twisted or turned as they fell; many screamed but most were silent, with only a dull thud or thump to sweep them down like corn before the blade. A man in front of him twirled violently and dropped dead, the flesh ripped from his neck. Running as fast as he could Martin glanced to the side, Maurice was moving swiftly on his short legs, head crouched low but Geordie was outpacing him to the front and his gun rang out. So Martin thought! But the young soldier seemed to stop and look round as one dazed. Maurice swerved towards him and then remembering orders ran on. Geordie raised his arm to call him back, then sank to the ground, first on his knees in a praying position, then on his side with his right hand aloft, a hand in the mud that seemed to point to nowhere. Slowly it slumped to the ground. The young soldier had feared the war. For him it lasted less than sixty seconds.

Explosions came, first one side, then another, then in front, then behind. One blast shook him, and he stumbled to the left. Instinctively he regained his balance; he felt he was living in a strange, terrible nightmare – a nightmare that was real. For a second or two he began to imagine that he was strangely invincible, as if it was all a harmless game, when a bullet stopped the man in front. Martin leapt over the falling form. He glanced back; the face was unknown but the spurting blood was real enough. Despite the overwhelming din, everyone appeared to be moving as if in some agile, obscure dance. Another bullet whined past, and the movement of the air rammed his helmet against his head. He felt pain but in a moment his attention was distracted by loud shrieks; he could not determine from whom or where, the cries lost in the volley of bullets and the fury of the mortar.

Martin did not feel afraid or in danger. He was strangely aware but detached. He saw people falling on all sides with a curious rationalisation. Wisps of smoke, grey and black and pungent, choked the breath out of him. But he was through the fumes in seconds and the freshness of the clear air sucked into his throat and lungs.

Men were vainly looking for somewhere to hide, somewhere to find refuge; but there was none, other than the pock-marked-earth's meagre holes. Flesh and bones, recent and old, were displayed in a bizarre pageant in their depths. All the while, Martin was running, feeling more and more out of breath; around him were the endless screams - sounds that burnt into the machine gun rattle, a horrific cacophony of war.

He heard an ominous whine and tried to duck. Suddenly there was another flash of light - a million volts, and night was day. He swerved past a deep shell hole and leapt three large rocks instinctively. Then a wobbling black object spinning over and over reared up in front and raced towards him. Martin dived. A huge explosion, and slush and mud showered his body and small stones cut his face and hands. A hundred droplets of blood appeared as tiny instant freckles. He was up in a flash. But the Allied line was broken and the onrushing machine gun bullets whipped past his face so closely at times that he felt their searing heat and shrill vibrations. They spattered to and fro, sweeping across the advancing soldiers like hail on a corrugated roof.

Yes! The advancing British line was broken.

Bodies piled on bodies, rivulets of red appeared from their chests and backs. Most lay face down in the earth. Some choked on water, some on mud, some on blood; some without jaws, faces, and throats died slowly while fighting for air; some without heads took an instant road to eternity; and others with no eyes stumbled blindly on, dropping their guns to flounder into a merciful machine gun blast. Those injured that could rise, did so quickly and seemingly without pain, driven on by that primitive urge of fight or flight; an instinct which allows men with one arm to discount pain and men with only a stump of a leg to hobble on regardless of the protruding bones. So the crippled fought on, in the mayhem they call war.

More shells and more shells rained down. Craters appeared in scores, bullets whistled and pinged. Martin dived into a crater as a shock of earth and stones cleared his head by a fraction. A private twenty yards away, and still running, glanced round and was gone in an instant, blown into a thousand fragments. A corporal collapsed with a short grunt as a huge stone swept down from the sky. His face suddenly assumed the blueness of the dawn, while his lips blackened alarmingly. In another moment, Martin was up again and running. Dai fell bleeding profusely from his thigh and called out in anguish and pain. Martin was conscious of his voice as he flew on, but not the words; it passed in a second, the feeling of despair, the longing to stop and help.

The enemy line grew closer and closer. The guns pounded and pounded. Wire cutters chattered like sheep shears, wooden planks were hurled forward by support troops. The enemy's barbed wire was breached. The soldiers swarmed into the gap. Martin swerved to the left as a hail of machine gun bullets scythed through the amassing troops. Bodies tangled and flailed in the barbed threads like fish on trawling hooks. Another flash from a gun and the whine of bullets from the left. Martin spurted closer and closer, the hand-grenade spinning from his hand with more accuracy than he dreamed possible. It quivered in flight and then disappeared into the enemy trench next to the pillbox. He dived down. For once the wet mud was welcome. Only a second, then the blast ripped across the earth turning night into day, bleaching his vision for a minute so that the world was a red and white canvas with black shapes etched around the periphery. A cloud of flames hovered around him for a few seconds. There seemed no escape. Then the debris and dust settled. Suddenly the gun was silent. Metal fragments littered the ground. He opened his eyes and looked around. Other German soldiers appeared; miraculously with arms aloft in surrender. But in the confusion no one seemed to notice.

Captain Cranmer arrived, running and firing his revolver to the side. He motioned to the enemy troops but there was a dull thud and a bullet caught him in the shoulder, splintering his collar bone. The gun flopped from his hand and waves of pain swept over his ashen face. He groaned, and tried to run on; while the surrendering Germans scattered as other British soldiers appeared. There flight was in vain; two were shot and the rest were quickly rounded up.

Martin watched the Captain fall, not ten yards away. His face was white and bathed in sweat, his features twisted in agony. A second bullet slopped in the thick mud nearby. Martin grabbed the fallen officer and pulled him, without ceremony, back to a shallow crater. He waited for a few minutes. Then as the noise and confusion subsided, he picked up the injured man and carried him across his right shoulder towards the welcoming British trench. The Captain's blood spurted onto Martin's chest then abruptly stopped. Martin thought he was dead, but he did not have the time to glance round. On he ran, ploughing through a gap in the wire towards safety. Bullets whistled and whined. He heard another groan. Martin dived into the bowels of the earth. And they landed in the soft, slimy earth of their own dug-out.

Breathless, they both lay back, exhausted.

Martin furtively looked over the top of the trench to see if the enemy were attacking; then looked at the Captain. The bleeding from the wounds had stopped and he was just conscious.

Martin sat and watched the weary soldiers returning - some limping, some crawling, some with broken limbs or gaping flesh wounds, some supported by caring comrades, some coughing blood, some staggering, some dying on the very edge of safety. Hell reigned on Earth.

Then there was a period of solitude, a short lull, a short peace.

A pale sun began to make inroads into the lingering dust that hung densely in the air, while a paler moon still visible in the lightening sky looked down in disbelief on the fifteen thousand dead or dying; in every yard of land - a body.

Martin drank from his flask; the water ran down his chin. It was a heady feeling. He felt exhausted, but calm in the enormous relief that he had survived.

Then, with his back against the comforting earth wall, he fell asleep.

And for the first time in weeks he slept, and it was the sleep of the just.

Chapter 42. The butcher.

Martin was to experience another form of sleep the next night and this is how it happened.

There was a wire cutting detail.

Into the vast cratered space they went, over sodden earth and on towards the tangle of wire. Ahead at times on hands and knees; at other times crawling forwards, yard by yard, hardly daring to draw breath least the smallest sound would betray them.

Martin was in a small platoon which had been moved a half a mile or so to the east of the salient in order to weaken the defending line there. Troops could then spill round the hill and behind the enemy's line, it was reasoned.

The plan was the brain child of the Field Commander, standing in his acquired chateau set back from the Front and secure; a man of stern mind and strong will. But his movements showed he was getting old. A veteran from the Indian campaigns; solid, not brilliant; shrewd but indecisive. He puffed on his cigar. 'The Hun could be broken at that point,' he had reasoned the night before. 'There was a danger.' The loyal subordinates agreed. 'But there was always danger!' Everyone looked solemn. 'War was a dangerous game, that's why the real men were there!' The officers liked his reasoning, after all he was high-ranking, and powerful men never make mistakes. 'But the prize was great and worth taking.' Everyone cheered up. 'Grasp the nettle.' All murmured in appreciation. 'There's no better life than the Army,' he continued slowly, 'so let's have a bit of pride and bravery and finish the job!'

'There was...' he said in a laboured way, searching for more clarity of thought as he swirled his cognac, '...a natural preference to wear the enemy down, but that took time. And time was becoming expensive. Damned expensive! The men should realise that!'

Thus the Field Commander made up his plan accordingly. The others in the room concurred.

So within twenty-four hours Martin, hardly having had time to meet up with his comrades, was sent off into the darkness, with Brewis, to play his part. Thirty other small groups were to creep forward too, at different points, on that sector of the front.

More cigar-glows and heavy drinking, 'Splendid, the troops were already in action and the whole damned thing should be in position for tomorrow.' The Commander did little to conceal his delight other than to hide his plethoric face behind another large brandy glass.

By coincidence there was other alcohol around that evening.

Martin had his tot of rum; and so had Brewis. They sat opposite each other behind a large boulder on the edge of a small crater breathing heavily. The ground was dry and his elbows and knees ached from crawling with a heavy shovel, wire cutters and a gun on his back. Brewis said little.

He was the one Corporal that Martin despised, indeed hated, and he had groaned inwardly at the detail. With the Butcher… Butcher Brewis; but Brewis liked his nickname – it made him smile and grind his fist.

The others had laughed when Martin told them who would be his companion; but in a considerate way. The Butcher was a man whose brutality was written in every line of his face, unbroken by smiles, by the broad swaths of acne, by the bristly beard and the long brow that served to highlight the menacing expression. To his sensitivity, death was a matter-of-fact part of war. He had no conscience, no fear and no regard for anyone but himself. Death, everyone said, was the part he enjoyed. Ignorance and indifference combined to make Brewis the most hated of men. 'Well, it may as well be me and you Norman, as anyone else.' He laughed when they first met and had said nothing else since.

Martin looked grimly ahead over the parched and pitted earth. In one of the hollows lay a dead animal, charred so that it had lost all identity. They rested half reclined and cautious. After a few minutes Martin said quietly, 'Are we ready to go now?'

Brewis, crouched on the ground, raised his head a few inches and considered the remark with a slow smile that showed his discoloured teeth, 'Bloody hell, do you want to end up rotting like that bloody animal stuffed by gas, in that crater over there! I'd like to pop it with a bullet though, it'll hiss for hours. Anyway, son, sit down and relax.' Content with his own humour he took out a plug of tobacco, spat, and began chewing. 'I'll give you the all-clear, when the time comes and that'll be after a chew or two.'

Occasionally there was a single shot that distracted him, but generally Martin watched Brewis intently, as a man watches a snake. The Butcher, he knew, had a knack of avoiding danger that gave him an aura of immortality with the troops. That was his strength; he worked by instinct, like a predator. Suddenly his large fist clenched hold of Martin's wrist.

After a few moments he turned his head slowly. 'You afraid son?' He gave a coarse laugh that annoyed Martin. 'Bet you are!' He looked him full in the face as if searching for the hidden fear. 'You'll be scared witless, I'll be thinkin'.'

All pretence of friendship was impossible, even detail–camaraderie. 'No, I'm not. Are you?' replied Martin sarcastically.

'I have the balls for anything, son. We'll soon see if you have.' And he laughed again. Brewis surveyed the scorched earth. 'Make for that bloody 'ole.' He nodded towards a deep pit some fifty yards on. 'You see it? Next to those dead uns. Germans they were once, but they're harmless enough now, and all the better for it, I'll be bound.' Once more he enjoyed his own humour, and spat by way of recognition.

Although the Very lights had become subdued Martin could easily make out the pit. The bullets still hissed and rattled past like swarming bees. They came in a rush and Brewis knew their rhythm. The machine guns would pause and by instinct they both were off again, scrambling side by side, crouching as low as they possibly could.

Unusually the shooting has ceased for while, and Martin began to appreciate the Butcher's diabolical luck. They reached the hole unscathed. Martin cowered down for a moment, then straightened up and peered anxiously over the rim. All was silent. They sat and regained their breath. It was only as their breathing settled that Martin was conscious of a rustling movement about thirty yards away. Brewis also looked up.

In the night brightness, Martin could see the softly breathing body of a dying horse, shot through the hind leg on the day before. There was a diminishing rhythm to animals breathing and that picture of the innocent animal dying seemed to strike through to the very sinews of his heart. His natural feeling was to dispatch it cleanly. But the sound would have given their position. Martin looked away. He could not understand why this animal's suffering, considering all the dead soldiers of the previous months, seemed to typify the utter hopelessness and futility of it all. He was shocked by this sudden realisation; but a firm nudge by Brewis brought him to his senses.

The Corporal pointed to the barbed wire that lay twenty yards ahead.

Martin felt a relief to be moving again and away from the dying animal. They both slowly eased themselves forward and began the regular snipping. Metal wool, Martin called it, sheep-shearing with a difference; something that was part of his nature.

Brewis grunted with his effort; his heavy body squirming across the hard earth. He would stop, give a staccato series of grunts and occasionally pick at a large sore behind his ear; scratching it viscously and uncontrollably until it oozed serum, pus and blood. They reached a shallow hole and lay face-down in the soft mud, pleased with the added security it gave. They listened for that fine whining, that token of an approaching bullet or the shivering, soft fluttering of air that spoke of an approaching shell. All was still. They breathed a sigh of relief. It was time to move on again. Brewis crouched taut and animal-like, as if he scented the air for danger.

Martin had felt chilled when they set off but his body was curiously warm and he could not decide, in that brief moment, if it was fear or anticipation. He concentrated on the man ahead, knowing that one false move could mean a sudden death; so sudden, he thought, that there could be no anticipation

Now there was a mellow light from the moon but, once more, the battle illuminations had subsided. Martin could just see him gently easing forward; then pausing to chew – first on a bit of old, dried bread he produced from his pocket, and then on more tobacco.

Brewis looked so unconcerned about it all, Martin gave him credit for that. He slid sideways and turned to whisper, 'All this's bloody laborious son, 'tho' I'm not concerned, there's a feeling of security meanderin' about 'mongst all these corpses, none o'them can do owt about anything. They're a stiff as boards…it's as safe as houses. See that pointing hand, what's that about? You can crack those fingers like rotten twigs… if you had too.' He laughed, 'You think that funny?' Brewis did not wait for an answer but chuckled to himself.

In single file they worked slowly and hesitantly around a small undulation at the side of the hill; sometimes so bunched together that Martin could smell the stench of stale sweat on the Butcher's bulky figure as he crawled before him. Occasionally Martin went ahead which he found more agreeable, although the grunts and cursing were a downside but better than the smell.

A shot rang out and struck a piece of discarded metal and the sound chimed like the tolling of a bell. Martin wondered if they had been seen and, if so, where the next bullet would come from. But Brewis went crawling forward, muttering and cursing everything German.

Suddenly they both froze.

A German helmet was just visible to the immediate right of a small clump of rocks. Martin feared it was the sniper, but Brewis said 'Look at the head, man! It's dangling like a rat in a trap.'

Martin cautiously drew his weapon. But Brewis laughed in contempt.

Hearing the noise, the stricken soldier attempted to raise his head. His mouth flickered and the lips rounded with effort. He did not utter a sound; but the eyes filled with relief. It was obvious that the chest was deeply gashed; and through the red and yellow flesh, three ribs showed white and incongruous. The ribs barely moved and blood dripped slowly, congealing on the black uniform.

Martin held his gun to the German's head. 'Quiet!'

There was a deathly silence. The Butcher surveyed the injured man with contempt. 'Bloody Fritz', he hissed. 'Well I never! This is a bit of luck! Bloody Fritz! Well I never!' He pressed his thickset features against the man's face and showed his fangs. Then he stepped back for a further appraisal with the expression like an angel of doom.

Martin tried to work out the age of the German soldier. 'Perhaps eighteen or nineteen,' he thought. The bewildered soldier reached out in a slow, trembling, pleading gesture; and made a supreme effort to stand. But the fragile weakness from his injuries sapped all strength and he slid back to the ground.

Martin whispered, 'Get his gun, Corporal'.

Brewis slowly reached to the ground where it lay, and turned it over in his hands two or three times, as if savouring the moment.

'Let's move on and finish the detail. But we'd better gag and rope him although he looks far gone to me,' whispered Martin, still crouching and glancing around.

'So that's your solution, is it son? Truss him up like belly pork and leave him to die. But there's a quicker bloody way, at least to my mind'. The Butcher waved the butt of the gun and rolled it in his hand once more. But the German was intently gazing at his gaping chest and did not look up.

Martin shook his head. The sight of the gun, the imminence of death, appalled him. 'The gun…the noise man, for God's sake.'

Brewis smiled. 'I'm the bloody Corporal, in case you've forgotten. The decisions are all mine. And there's a few ways to skin a cat even with a gun.'

Martin bit his lip. 'I know, but we can keep him quiet with the gag and the rope. Anyway, he's not got much left in him; he'll be no trouble, Corporal. Forget the gun! Let's tie him up and get out of here.'

Once more the Butcher's pale features broke into an unpleasant smile, made even more unpleasant by the night-shadows. He was unaware that Martin's fury was mounting. 'Brewis, leave the boy alive!' He said it so angrily that the Butcher was, for once, stopped in his tracks. 'If not, it will be reported when I get back.'

Brewis did not say a word. He just looked. 'You're going to report me, are you?'

'I will, that I'll promise you!' Martin caught hold of the Corporal's shoulder and attempted to spin the half-crouching figure towards him. Such was Brewis' strength that the thick neck barely moved.

'Okay! No gun, son. I'll give you that!'

The German was desperate. Although the sounds

swirled around him, the anger in the voices was self-evident. He began to fear for his life. Weak and unsure, he began to slither slowly away; his head close to the ground, a faint film of blood marking his trail like a giant snail track.

Martin, still crouching, made a sudden grab at the boy's foot. But as he did so, the flat metal of the Corporal's shovel flew down twice, each time with the faintest of vibrations and the power to fell an ox.

With the second vibration, Martin felt a searing pain in his head, a sudden wetness above his right ear and a gushing film of red over his right eye.

The Butcher vanished into the night.

Martin began to crawl back. The young German's skull had been crushed to a crimson pulp. He was beyond salvation; Martin could just make that out.

As he tried to stand Martin was overcome with a mixture of nausea and faintness; blood poured from a jagged head wound. Suddenly he slid to the ground. Confused and vomiting, he began to creep towards the trenches, with a pounding headache, and a hundred rolling thunders all at once.

He knew to survive, he had to get back.

Chapter 43. A visitor.

When Martin awoke it was in a period of confused thoughts and voices, a blur around him, a hazy echo. At first he was conscious of keeping low, in a crouching run to the stone wall and his byre. Then there was a lark singing, then a hollow explosion that reverberated around his head like a clash of giant cymbals, then a girl's laughter -indistinct- more laughter and a familiar voice saying, 'I've found you at last squire,' and a nodding red face which beamed with enjoyment and relief.

It was John Bowes.

Martin reached out and grasped his half-cousin's hands, holding them tightly for a moment. A pretty dark haired girl of twenty-four, with unusual violet-blue eyes, smiled down. The roof of the hospital tent flapped. An aroma of carbolic filled the air. The white and red of her uniform caught his eye, and then the sweet smile.

He instinctively reached for his legs as so many soldiers did when they came round.

He moved his toes and laughed. 'John, where did you come from and how did you find me? In fact where am I? I can't remember what happened to me!'

'All's well Martin, you're in hospital with a bit of concussion from the blast. But nowt else!'

John grasped Martin's right arm in his burly hands and wrung it gently. 'Nowt else!' he continued by way of emphasis and reassurance, chiefly to himself. 'They say you'll be fighting fit in a day or two.'

Martin lay back on the pillow and gazed at the scene around him. There were about thirty injured troops on beds or makeshift beds. Some were bandaged, some with stumps, others groaning and moaning with a mixture of pain and the delirium which goes with infection and gangrene. The men with lesser fractures of the ankle, shin and arm smiled with the reassurance that they were going home to England. These lesser injuries became known as a "Blighty" for their ability to send the wounded homeward bound, back to dear old blighty.

'War's a rum business, John.' Martin shook his head but noticing the slightly crestfallen gaze on the farmer's face, cheered him up by saying, 'but we gave them hell the other night, and the rest should be easy! Anyway, how's the family, thine and mine?'

'Champion! Everyone's fine. Dad and Mum are in fine fettle and the two girls, well, they're not courting much as yet but the outlook's better for Vera. She's tain up with the shepherd Simpson's brother from Cranford Dale.' John paused to smile at the convalescing soldier. 'And your brothers are working the farm a treat. Do you know there's niver been a better harvest and back end of the year as this'n. The grass was almost waist high, it fair nearly broke the old horse's back, Old Vulcan. But he's strong! And June, she's smarter and prettier by the day. Fair running the farm, selling the mutton direct to the front by the ministry men. Divn't doubt that we could even get a piece here!'

Martin burst out laughing and John looked perplexed at his own humour for a minute and then laughed too. 'Chance would be a fine thing!' Martin said. 'How about a horse or a donkey or a goat, instead?' They both laughed again and the pretty nurse smiled as she hurried by with a dressing for one of the soldiers in a corner bed; his stump of a thigh was beginning to ooze.

'And Mary?' asked Martin, 'any news, John?'

The farmer smiled slowly and paused with a deep, almost longing gaze. 'I had a letter Martin, soon after she left, about the time you decided to jack in the farming...' he paused, 'but little else. I expect she's fair busy in that posh place, but she'll be back one day, probably when this war's over, I wouldn't doubt. Would you?'

Martin propped himself up to watch the dark haired nurse at work. How sweetly she smiled and how considerate and unaffected was her manner with the suffering man.

John waited for the reply.

Martin saw him glance towards the nurse then back again. 'Oh! Yes! I've little doubt you'll be together again when this mess is over. Let's look to the future and the wedding.'

John appeared relieved and then perplexed. He was about to confide in Martin that all was not well on that front when there was a deep, familiar rumble of laughter from a man standing next to a bed at the tent entrance. It arrested his attention. The unmistakable figure of Jack Golightly ambled towards them. He beamed with pleasure expressed in every line of his face, every fold of flesh re-echoed the mood. 'Martin, I knew that early cold dip the other morning would be the weakening of you. You need extra beef to survive, although hang it all there's little on Maurice.'

Martin could not hide his delight at seeing his old friend, for a second it produced a few tears. 'Tubby, is Maurice well?'

'Too skinny to hit!' Jack strode forward and shook John's hand.

'My half-cousin from the next farm, Tubby, this is John Bowes, and a better horseman never drew breath.'

'Anyone who can handle these old mules out here deserves all our admiration. Half of them lie dead in the ditches. But like Falstaff, another lightweight (he slapped his waist), they're probably feigning death. Anyway John, delighted to meet you!' And in his characteristic fashion Jack shook hands again, then tugged at his clipped moustache. 'You will see some horrible sights round here, John,' said Jack slyly nudging the soldier, 'such as my friend Maurice with a half-grown beard or Martin crunching turnips.' Both farmers laughed.

'There's a rum beggar over there,' said Tubby stroking his moustache reflectively… 'asked him where he'd got it, at the salient or on the hill and he said "No! In the backside!" Bankside, say I, never heard of it. "No, bum" says he. 'Shrapnel?' says I hopefully, "No mule bite" says the idiot with a stupid grin.'

They all laughed once more.

'But good news Martin, old boy! We're allowed a few days behind lines, and we're taking them right now, so I've spoken to the doctor and it's agreed that you can come out tomorrow.' Tubby clapped his hands with pleasure.

'We'll find a drink somehow,' exclaimed Martin 'and not in the Duke of Wellington. That was a strange night!'

'Spare John the blushes Martin or you'll be the talk of the Dales when you get back, which according to the return ticket they promised me when I enlisted, should be pretty soon; unless the war trains are late, as usual'.

Martin watched the pretty nurse gently sponging a soldier's brow, now damp with sweat; the right eye swollen with a jagged cut which had transected the eyebrow and cheekbone. The spreading infection produced the characteristic weal of St Anthony's fire (*erysipelas), and the vascular communications with the brain had already assured a septic meningitis - always lethal. The soldier in confusion called her "Mother" and held her hand tightly complaining about the throbbing, excruciating headache and asking for relief. Martin reasoned that the wounded man was about twenty and from Worcestershire, but knew little else. The constant crying of "Mother, Mother!" unsettled him.

Tubby and John Bowes had also turned to follow Martin's gaze. The plump, genial soldier shook his head for a moment and then changed the subject. 'She's not as pretty as you think, Martin, you are still confused,' he chided with a sly wink at John.

Martin looked serious. 'For goodness sake Jack, if she's not pretty who is?'

'Oh! mostly any nurse. They get all the proposals, you know.' He winked at John again. 'The first thing the men do when they come round is to propose. Don't ask me why? But then I've never been wounded.' He smiled at Martin's serious expression.

'Propose… is that so?'

'Why everyone knows that! It's probably in the manual our old Sergeant left.'

Martin looked up, 'He left - you mean Harry!'

Jack stroked his black hair solemnly. 'No, not him… old Veharckles, as we called him: "Bring up the ve-harck-les men." He would order, day in, day out. Sadly he caught it in the chest and neck he did, and Dai and young Geordie and...'

'Good God!' In despair and horror, Martin motioned him to stop by pressing his finger against his mouth as he had been stopped by the young girl in the past. 'It's too much to take at present, Jack.' He went silent. 'I'll think about them most the time when I get back on the fells, Jack; yes, most of the time.' His voice trailed away in anguish.

There was a pause and John said hurriedly, 'I'm pleased I've found you at last, Martin. We'll be seeing a lot of each other, this is my regiment,' and he wrote down the name on a piece of paper, borrowing a stubby pencil from Jack. 'There! In case you forget it as you're ill; although you seem in fine shape to me! And I'm pleased; so very pleased.' John looked overwhelmed for a moment.

'Martin, it must be purgatory to be left in the company of that pretty nurse – they're all beautiful you know, but she's an extra exception.' Jack beamed, 'And I've got to put up with Minnow and his lice for another few weeks at the least. Come to think of it, John, have you any disinfecting soap with you, Durback or anything like that? The lice, they're the German's secret weapon. They're doing more damage than the shells as far as shaking morale goes.' He laughed. 'I'm serious! Wait and see!'

Martin waved them goodbye as they paused at the tent entrance.

It was the best day he had had since he left England; warmth, good food, good friends, good company, and a pretty girl - albeit at a distance.

Chapter 44. The Sister.

As the chill November air bathed the upper reaches of the tent, there was warmth within - the warmth of blankets, soft beds, gentle attention and loving care.

It was a comfort to be resting in bed in a secure and warm environment, away from the endless mud. The injured soldiers were arranged in long parallel rows, their beds being only three feet apart; enough room to allow the nurses to pass between. Sometimes a bed was wheeled or pulled out with a victim, pale and sallow with shock; or others sun-red with fever. Surgery was in another tent, near enough for transportation but far enough to drown the screams when the anaesthetic wore off or did not take effect.

When he looked at the soldiers about him, Martin felt a sense of relief. His injuries were so mild in comparison. He wanted to be out of the place as soon as possible.

Sleeping as roughly as they had in the trenches, at least he was amongst friends, with a different sort of noise. Although he had been so exhausted and ill that the groans, sobs, incoherent muttering and shouting and the occasional screams did not disturb him; Martin was not embarrassed by his indifference. After all it was only war.

The pretty sister was more than compensation, or so he felt, for the period of his confinement in such a stale almost putrid atmosphere. He had managed to say a few words on one or two occasions and she would smile. 'What's the worst thing about this job, other than the Matron?'

She laughed, 'I will have you know she's a wonderful nurse and organiser and behind that disciplined and sometimes half-contemptuous stare, there lies a heart of gold.'

Martin waited and he was about to repeat the question, when the Sister continued, 'The worse thing is washing feet,' she laughed and Martin did not know if she was kidding him, 'some hate the cold water, others are ticklish and to some it's totally new even in war.' She paused and looked at a pale-faced man as he lay face-down and cautiously tried to turn to one side. His face was pinched and erased of all emotion. Martin knew that part of his back had been blown away and even the slightest movement was agony. She simply said, 'His nights are even more hellish than his days, for no drugs can touch the pain, you know.' She hurried off.

He watched her feverishly attending the new batch of wounded, the younger nurses gazing in horror at the mutilated bodies and partially amputated limbs. The facial injuries, with the grotesque masks of torn flesh and bare bones, repulsed them the most; but they remained cheerful and caring, trying to revitalise life into confused, fearful, hurt eyes.

The sister pointed to a boy in the corner and directed a nurse to remove a tube from his arm. The boy shook with fear and began to scream long before the tube draining the pus had been pulled out. The sister walked over and gave a deft pull which so mesmerised the soldier with its speed that he stared blankly at them both without a murmur. 'Get the new one in place before the round,' she said quietly to the nurse.

Everything had to be correct for the grand round or inspection which occurred three times a day. Then Matron in charge arrived. She had to organise the care of the new batch of wounded as quickly and efficiently as she could; as well as preparing the lucky few for discharge. She was a bustling lady who was not stout but heavy in flesh - that made its presence felt through every fold and fastening in her uniform - disciplined in manner and firm in direction. The younger nurses waited for her arrival with some anguish, for they had to memorise the patients and their treatments as much as they could, and under taxing circumstances (for they were not allowed to consult their notes during the ward round). In addition they had to make the place as spick and span as they possibly could prior to her arrival.

The stove glowed warmly in the centre of the tent, and a golden colour suffused through the gloom from the piled embers.

In this delicate light, Martin was aware of the beam of a sister's lamp; slowly cutting through darkness towards the evening round.

It was his last night and he sat up in bed feeling more than pleased. On his left was the canvas wall at the opposite end to the entrance and on his right a man of about twenty four from Edinburgh. Two weeks earlier this soldier's right leg had been amputated below the knee; he talked confidently of home and the new life he planned ahead. From his cheerful reminiscences, Martin had learnt of Princes Street, the imposing castle overlooking the great park and this beautiful thoroughfare, the Royal Mile and Greyfriars Bobby. This story intrigued Martin as the man spun out the tale of the little dog that gained everlasting fame by standing over his master's grave for years and years in all weathers. 'He was made a freeman of the city, ye ken. Quite an honour, laddie!' Martin chuckled with pleasure while the Scotsman's earnest lilting voice expounded his vision and events of the city he loved.

As the lamplight grew brighter and the beam entered the tent, Martin waited to see which nurse would attend with the Matron. He wished for the pretty sister but secretly felt that she would be off that evening, having toiled for most of the day.

But luck was with him as the two figures emerged from the darkness, the Matron with the lamp and the young pretty girl a step behind. He saw that the Matron was taller than expected with grey hair and brusque in manner. She wore a dark uniform, embellished by the ribbons of the South African campaign. The young sister had a long white uniform neatly starched, with a red cross and graceful flowing cap over her black hair which was just visible at the back. The arch of the white headband across her forehead accentuated the loveliness of her eyes, at least Martin thought so. And he was in no mood to argue with himself. The unceasing devotion of the nurses had impressed him from the start, they were truly the

234

angels of care and contentment in most of the soldiers minds. To him she was the best and he was delighted to see her again.

About a third of the men were seriously injured, many in the slow progression to death; their thick dressings concealing cotton wool and gauze soaked in blood and pus and abdominal contents - if the stomach wall had been ripped away. The nurses glanced at the men, mostly lethargic and silently suffering. But some of the troops had an expression of adoring gratitude, gazing fixedly and bashfully in the girl's faces as they checked the tubes and temperature charts, repositioning blankets and pillows then moving swiftly on past gently pleading eyes and the pale fingers of clutching hands.

He heard the Matron say quietly, 'There have been thirty-six operations in the last forty-eight hours and over half of them have been amputations. The surgical tent is overflowing. If there are any more casualties tonight sleep the fittest men on the floor.'

The Sister nodded in acknowledgement.

They had just reached the confused soldier with the jagged cut on his face and the spreading infection.

Martin heard them discussing the case in a low voice, so low that he could not make out the words but was more than content with the soft voice of the young nurse, when the soldier called out, 'Don't let me die here, ladies, not without my mother. In a sacred place, please God, but not without my mother.' He muttered incoherently to himself for a few seconds, and then lay back on the stained pillow.

The young sister reached slowly forward and put her hand so gently on his fevered brow.

'Not 'ere in this scout hut! Or is it a circus tent? I've got it, it's not a church, it's a bloody circus tent, in't it?'

He waved a fixed finger in a loop above his good eye, which stared in terror and bewilderment.

'Rest! Lie back and rest and I'll be with you again in a minute.' The sister spoke so reassuringly that the bewildered soldier looked towards her face for a few seconds, searching for identity, love and consolation before staring blankly towards the roof. Then he struggled to reach up and press his dry lips against the fold of her uniform's sleeve. Her fingers closed round his swollen wrist for a moment as she coaxed the stricken man to lie back.

The Matron paused to read the temperature chart. The graph swung wildly up and down, a certain indication that the toxic infection had entered the bloodstream and it was only a matter of time. She shook her head and reached forward to gently pull back the bedclothes.

What happened next was so unexpected that Martin could hardly understand it for a moment. In a flash he was out of his bed as the confused soldier cried, 'Leave off my legs, let them be! They're not for him!' He pointed round vaguely, 'nor him!' But as he spoke there was the sharp glint of steel, a lethal bayonet tip that swept towards the Matron's neck.

The onrushing Martin flung himself forwards, unaware of the pain, instantly colliding with the pretty nurse and then crashing into the Matron, knocking her to the ground. He had barely had time to scream, 'Look out!' before the bayonet spike dug deeply into the mattress.

He grasped the man's forearm, but it was to no avail. His fixed, white face showed that he had left his city, forever.

The Matron never wavered.

Rising briskly to her feet, she brushed her dark

uniform, picked up the lamp which had miraculously survived, calmed the pretty sister and other nurses with a few gentle remarks and then said to the few fit soldiers who had struggled out, 'Back to your bed soldiers, the round is not finished.'

The men, although used to iron discipline, were so impressed that they quickly resumed their places; and the Matron and the Sister moved systematically on.

Martin smiled to himself. He had learnt not to expect praise or gratitude in war - and he did not get it then.

Still, he was happy. He felt a new contentment - in his inner world.

Chapter 45. A return to the Front.

When Martin returned to the front it was mid-November 1914. It was a scene of change. He had said goodbye to the Menin Road only a few days before; now it ran past shelled and smouldering towns.

The Earth had disintegrated at this point in Belgium and Ypres was struggling to exist.

The Cloth Hall, the ancient buildings were reduced to charred rubble, its long, narrow canal afloat with debris and the bodies of mules and men, drifting aimlessly in bloated lumps, side by side. The French and British forces were also struggling to exist; almost ninety per cent of the troops had been killed or seriously wounded.

An uneasy calm was present as a prelude to the threatening German offensive. The battleground was living in a respite of uncertainty and suspense. The Germans had every intention of fighting their way to Ypres and taking possession. By degrees they had crept forward, an insidious threat that was unnoticed by the British and French forces. The Kaiser's troops were determined to make one final attack, to drive back and crush the enemy had been the order.

But such intentions were unknown to Martin; he was simply preoccupied with the dismal and depressing scene he encountered. For when he arrived at the Front, he saw Battalions shrivelled to the strength of companies, and the latter little more than the platoons he had previously led.

There were gaps here and gaps there, wide open spaces in the trenches where the dead bodies lounged almost life-like against the side walls, as if taking a moment out for a well-earned rest.

The rats had long since lost all fear and gnawed at exposed parts, squeaking and tugging unashamedly, scattering digits, pieces of flesh and garments like so much superfluous confetti. And they were unafraid of the vast, crater-ridden belt of No-Man's-Land; a tangle of wire, a tangle of bodies, a tangle of the grotesque and the putrefying.

The remaining troops were in good spirits despite the stench, soaking mud and water-filled trenches, lazily stepping over dead comrades as if they were languishing asleep. Even the odd German body seemed to be in repose with his enemy, occasionally with hands outstretched across an English face or chest in a mute and final token of eternal friendship.

Bob said, 'It's quiet here now. But it was hell two nights back! The cook was killed to add insult to injury.'

Martin put down his rifle and pack. 'Good to see you Bob! How's the rest of the boys?' and without waiting, 'Hell, eh!' Abruptly he sat down and lounged back against a stone wall that had miraculously survived. He watched a small butterfly flutter around looking for some semblance of normality.

'Sheer hell!' continued Bob after a quiet and studied reflection. 'Got into the wood at the salient with two of the lads - Brian and Dennis - and we're making good progress towards a German outpost when we heard a noise. It was a Hun with a shrapnel leg. I'm for shooting, but not Brian. He creeps across and what happens. Gets it in the chest; point blank! Dennis fires and takes half of Fritz's head away. But the wrong half! Bits of his mouth and jaw are gaping and flapping everywhere, and he whispers "Bitte, bitte, wasser, bitte." We're a bitte stuck, if you don't mind the pun. Well, I got my gun out to finish him off but he looks already done for, so we pour in the water and he said "Wielen danks", gurgles for a minute and dies. We check him out and guess what? His wallet showed that he was just married a week before he left, poor bastard. Just a week!'

Martin was trying to find a dry wooden plank on which to rest because the earth felt dank and putrid. 'And the attack?' he said unconcerned.

'Bloody good,' replied Bob, laughing. 'Dennis lobbed

in a grenade and bits came flying out in all directions. 'That spoilt a few Christmases, and a good thing too!'

Martin studied the surrounds and his gaze went back to the butterfly. 'There are not many men around on this side of the line, Bob.'

The hardened soldier shook his head. 'Don't know exactly but they say that our lot, the ones I came out with, have shrunk from a battalion of over a thousand to forty or fifty. The great Army's gone, Martin, like snow on a spring day. There's no bloody troops, no officers, nobody at all.'

'And we've got tonight and the next night and the next and the next to come!' said Martin.

'Yes. Bloody true! The generals and politicians have gone stark raving bonkers. There are two solutions. Put the Huns and our officers and political jokers in a large field and let them fight it out while the rest of us go home; or make the high command work the latrines for a week, as Dans. That'll dampen their ardour for war!' Bob laughed and so did Martin.

'What a gulf there is between home and war,' said Martin at length. 'People back home know nothing about war, and being here, I understand even less. Still, there's no point in being dejected. It can only end one way or the other.'

Bob agreed. 'I never thought about war much before I joined up and it's not bloody-well worth thinking about now. If I'm going to die, I want it to be with something pleasant on my mind - like good grub, or soft blankets and a beautiful girl. See this dead rat,' he picked up the swollen creature by its long coarse tail, 'I bet it enjoyed his bit of the war without a thought for its future.' He lobbed the animal towards No-Mans-Land.

They were joined by a taciturn man from Berkshire. 'Hello, Charlie,' sang out Bob. The approaching soldier shook his head slowly.

'Seen everything!'

'What's up Charlie?' said Martin.

'They'll be bringing in the cooks and cleaners next,' stated Charlie calmly while settling on the dry plank.

'What do you mean?' asked Bob looking up and offering a chew of tobacco.

'Thanks, Bob! Seen everything lads. They're bringing up the Territorials to the front line. There's so few of us fighting men left! It's bloody well come to that!'

Both soldiers looked surprised and Martin whistled. 'May the Good Lord help us now! It's just lambs to the slaughter these days, until we're all wiped out, one by one.'

But the other two soldiers, hardened by war, showed no other emotion and both returned to their tobacco and pipes.

'Brought them by a London omnibus they did, straight to the front,' continued Charlie after a few moments of gently sucking at the clay stem. This made a whistling sound like a toy shell. Strangely at that moment few guns were firing, although this fact was not noticed. For the soldiers had come to subconsciously shut out the noise unless one of the shells flew perilously close by.

There was a patter of military boots on the wooden plank, a couple of rats squeaked in fear. Martin looked up and smiled. 'Afternoon, sir,' he said rising sharply to his feet. The two others followed.

'At ease men!' It was Cranmer. He flopped down beside them. 'I'll share a pipe if there's any spare,' he said laughing as he took hold of Martin's arm in a show of affection. 'Nice to see you fit and well Norman and such is the shortage of officers that they have rushed me back to the front despite the scars'. He laughed again. 'I should not laugh, it jabs the wounds, but what the heck.'

They all sat and contemplated life for a few minutes. Martin had no feelings of home now, it seemed to be erased from his consciousness by the stark horror of war. He had a capacity to think in blankness and he did this while the others smoked or chewed. 'This mud is so wholesome and friendly, it will stick with me for life,' he said at length, almost to himself such was the quiet tone of his voice. 'To think I used to spend hours cleaning my boots when I worked. They haven't had a shine for weeks.'

The others continued reflecting on their situation. 'For me,' said Bob slowly, 'for me it's a hot bath and plenty of bubbles and soap when I get back. That's a priority!'

Charlie shook his head and growled. 'Doubt if I'll get back to anything, but if it happens, heaven help us, it'll be a pair of clean sheets or a decent toilet seat. That's what I've missed the most.'

They all laughed.

'Without wishing to spoil the fun,' said the Captain in a good natured way, 'I'm here with some news. We have to prepare for an assault. A German offensive is feared in the next few days, hence the lull. Reinforcements are expected but don't build up your hopes. I'm here to tell you that we're so damned short of troops that we are being moved towards Polygon Wood. He paused and the soldiers listened intently. 'I must admit you're next to what I consider some of the poorest bloody fighting men on the line - the blasted French Zouaves, lent to Haig, God bless him, to bolster up our numbers. If those bastards fail, we have only got the territorials and then anyone we can muster - servants, cooks and the like. By the grace of God - thus it has come to pass!'

The Captain gently wrung his hands in bitterness. He closed his eyes in quiet contemplation. After a few minutes he took a deep breath, 'It's annoying, it's exasperating... it's bloody unfair.'

Someone grunted and there was an uneasy silence. 'Lambs, more lambs, more to the slaughter, Sir'. Martin repeated abstractly after another pause. 'When do we move?'

'As soon as we have finished this break, I suppose,' he spoke resignedly 'but only after you have eaten. There's no point in rushing anything now. No point!'

'That's very considerate, Sir,' continued Bob looking round, 'but we can get some food, pack it up and go at any minute, if you like!'

The others agreed.

The Captain shrugged his shoulders and said slowly, 'So be it, if you wish,' without much enthusiasm.

Thus the small platoon of men, some eighty in number, were quickly organised by the Captain and Martin. They left in half an hour. There were no stretcher-bearers and Martin wondered what would happen to the injured that night. Slowly they pulled back from the trenches and by a detour of a mile and a half reached the area of Polygon Wood.

The flat fields stretched pock-marked and scorched towards the Menin Road - the road that led from Belgium to the French border at the frontier post of Menin. The fields were part of the great Flanders plain surrounded by a series of gentle undulations that formed the ridges around the wooded areas. The destroyed ruins of Ypres were a mile or so to the west; isolated fires smoked into the afternoon sky and the verges were littered with the burnt out shells of lorries, charred and angular on broken wheels. Within its walls the remaining inhabitants tried to conduct their business and daily lives as best possible. But most knew that an attack was imminent.

Martin settled down behind a series of fallen tree stumps with Bob on his right and the Captain a hundred yards away. He had drunk some cold tea and eaten a dozen oatmeal biscuits with, as a luxury, a slice of dark Belgian chocolate. It had been given to him two days before and he had kept the last piece as a luxury.

The night was quiet and cold. At midnight a hush fell over the salient. Martin could smell the musty pine leaves, musty without the freshness of the pines back home. Naturally his thoughts wandered to the farm and his family and friends. He had never understood war at the beginning, and could not understand it now. The killing was useless, the suffering pointless. But there was no retreat from the dilemma, and he never thought of shirking his duty. Some soldiers had deserted, especially on the French side, and they had been court-martialled and shot. But it was not this fear that kept him rooted to the spot, simply a sense of responsibility to the family he loved, and to his friends for that matter. He had always imagined facing death to be worse than death itself, but once again he had no fear.

A quick burst of rain fell sharply and slanted through the trees, but the boughs caught most of it. The night was darkening and the grey clouds were in absolute possession of the sky. He wrapped up in his damp coat and stamped his feet. At least the ground was dry on the edge of the wood and the fallen pines gave shelter from the night breeze. In fact he felt more comfortable than usual on the Western Front. In the far distance a house was burning, but the plumes of smoke ebbed and flowed seemingly without enthusiasm in the grey, uncertain light. Occasionally a small burst of flames raced skyward but without reason fell back into the spiral of smoke. Martin

245

watched with a halting curiosity, two dozen men lay on the ground wrapped in their own thoughts of home and immortality. One said, 'Where the bloody hell are we?' but his voice lacked enthusiasm and no one deigned to reply. Martin had an inner calmness born of constant suffering, the fear he had experienced once was only a memory, a thread to the past he did not acknowledge. He wondered if the others felt the same.

He wandered off to be alone for a short while and no one looked his way. He found a small clump of green pine needles, untainted by war. The fallen bough was within easy reach and he pulled a few and rolled them round in his hand. The delicate aroma reminded him of the firs near the farm. 'Those sighing firs! Eternally sighing and whispering!' he mused. 'How the doves liked the firs, always cooing and flapping in them on a warm summer's day. And the hawks! Forever watchful, like the men in the trenches; an eternal battle at his back door he had never thought of before. Strange when men fight - it's in such numbers; but animals kill continually, one by one, almost surreptitiously, but equally devastating.'

He sighed and smiled at his own musings; 'Not worth much really,' he thought. He waited for the moon but it did not come. But the night was not so dark for although the grey clouds drifted slowly across the sky from south to north, there seemed a luminescence from above. Bob was lounged forty yards away and breathing regularly, although not asleep.

On and on crept the night, so slowly; at one stage it seemed to move so impossibly slowly and his mind wandered and thoughts accumulated and came and went like the clouds. Martin did not speak to anyone. Nor did anyone address him. The best thoughts were about his mother. How she encouraged him with his studies at first, and when his father died everything was different. He did not blame his mother. She had relied upon him from the first. He wondered what his future might have been had his father lived. Then with a look around, he felt the futility of such thoughts. Still his mother's image was a reassuring presence. At least if the worst happened she would not have to mourn, like thousands of families on all sides.

Then imperceptibly the morning star began to appear in the East, just visible through the lessening cloud canopy, and the cold night air began to remit. How often he had watched this star, so familiar a beacon on those cold early mornings when he had to get up early and the lambs came with the dawn and breathed new life into the spring countryside.

At about six thirty in the morning the bombardment began.

Some were as flashes, lights that lit up the sky and erased the stars, others as shattering bangs that shook the earth into a thousand pieces with each devastating explosion. The shells went on and on, more and more, louder and louder, until they reached a crescendo that no soldier had ever heard before. The excruciating noise reverberated into every ditch, shell hole and trench. There was no shelter. The inferno grew and grew. To Martin the bombs seemed to concentrate towards him, an accumulation of hatred; yet still he felt no fear. He would see it out and to do so he pushed small pieces of cloth into his ears and crouched behind the fallen trunk. The hollowness of the shells and the muffled whine and splatter of the bullets cascaded around him. Occasionally an explosion ripped the boughs off a tree and lurched it sideways; sometime he felt the judder run through him.

The German guns, massed and ranged to rain down shells on the British front, suddenly ceased firing. Some of the soldiers to the side of him cautiously looked up, unsure. In front of Polygon Wood the British and French forces stood braced for the attack. They had no idea that no reserves existed to help them, they stood alone.

He knew in the next minutes the enemy would appear; and he held his breath and said a silent prayer.

He could only lie and wait.

There was an uneasy short silence, and Martin stared straight ahead.

A subdued silence!

Followed by a strange thrill of expectation!

And then it came.

Nine miles wide and ferocious; the explosions were everywhere; shells and more shells, like a raging storm, uprooting, earth-shattering; a convulsion from above. Martin watched the countryside burst in all directions.

Suddenly he saw the German troops coming up the hill, as almost in slow motion, wave upon wave. He had no time to look round, to see the grim faces of his friends, the harsh reality of impending death written in every feature.

As the sulphurous fumes poured in, the rats scattered with squeals of fear. And the machine guns sang and the rifles cracked amongst the scrambling men. And the uniforms flew in lumpy black-clothed pieces of flesh. Martin was oblivious to the screams and the tumult of the guns. The fighting veered in waves from side to side and back and forth; a burst of fire from the right, a cry of anguish from the left or simply a dull thud as bullet met flesh head on.

It was a man to man – a face to face - confrontation,

248

of medieval intensity and bloodshed. Almost twenty thousand of the Kaiser's army, including many of the crack divisions, poured down from their line. The bullets pinged and hissed and flew. Men met in single combat and killed breathing into each other's faces and bathed in enemy blood. The bayonet and knife reigned supreme. The land around had become one giant graveyard seeped in red.

Martin felt a slight exhilaration in being spared for the moment, a strange ethereal triumph over disaster. 'Better use the gun,' he thought, for he had heard tales of the bayonet blade being stuck fast in the chest, so that a hard kick on the enemy's thighs was needed to pull it out; and then it often broke. Even a sharpened shovel was useful,- more weighty, - more likely to cleave through to the lungs.

He lay flat, his head low behind the large fallen tree, rifle in hand.

He still felt little emotion, a detachment from the horrific scene about him. For a second, and only a second, he wondered what death would be like and who would kill him, someone he neither knew nor hated would be his executioner.

He had a strange feeling that it was no more than a grouse-shoot back home.

He held his breath and waited.

The birds were getting closer, with thudding boots - a covey of eight, flying straight.

He raised his rifle and picked them off one by one.
Cleanly and with no feathers! They fell cleanly too!

Some crawled forward for a few yards.

Some shook for a moment.

Better watch!

But there were no flapping birds, no finishing off

249

required. Within a minute they had all flattened to the earth with hardly a grunt.

He reloaded and waited, the barrel of his gun wet with the palm-sweat of concentration. A few shots whistled over his head. Bob was firing with great accuracy and violence to the right. Then the soldier spun round and the volleys stopped. He did not even cry out as his head disintegrated.

Cranmer went down also; hardly firing a shot with his injured arm, hardly giving an order. He fell in a pool of blood. Martin could not see where he was hit and if he was dead.

Then a series of explosions! And the line gave. The French troops folded, and thus the line gave. It was the weak point in the salient.

The Germans began to pour through, to sense victory. But Martin raced to his left, head low, for a further clump of trees. Bullets whistled around him. He flung himself on the ground. Then he was up in a lull, sprinting back two hundred yards or more. Breathless he was down again, lying flat on the chilled earth. Some English troops, partly marooned, fired at random from a nearby hillock, crouching behind stones for as much shelter as they could get.

A grenade whirled into their midst. There was a sudden explosion. Martin rushed forward and shot the thrower between the shoulder blades. The German just hung suspended for a moment; sighed and seemed to concertina to the ground with blood spurting out of the hole between his ribs in a fine crimson fountain.

Martin reached the small hillock. Five British men were dead and one was dying - his arms severed at the shoulders, a mass of shredded muscle, sinew and bone.

The gravely wounded soldier looked up.

It was John Bowes.

Martin was crouching beside him in an instant. 'John, John! Oh, My God, John!' he exclaimed in anguish.

The farmer looked into the soldier's face, his large eyes even more pronounced. 'It's no use Martin No use! But I'm fair glad to see you. Fair glad.' He spoke slowly and tried to ease himself off his broken chest. The stumps flapped as miniature wings spraying droplets of red onto his friends face and uniform.

'Here, drink this!' Martin produced a small flask and gently poured water into the stricken soldier's mouth whose face was pale, his brow bathed in fine beads of sweat.

'I'm right dry at present Martin, what would I give to be in t'old Plough now'. He tried to smile.

'We'll get you back, John, somehow.' There was a sudden screaming of shells and bullets and Martin held the farmer's head low, cradling it in his arms.

'I'm a spent force, Martin' John said very slowly licking his lips and choking back the emotion. 'A wounded bird... without hope!'

Martin did not reply but stared towards some firing coming from an area about two hundred yards to his left.

'Martin... if I was a pheasant... or any other damned beast... in this predicament... what would you do?'

Martin looked down at the reddening ground on either side as the stricken man flapped his stumps briefly to emphasise the point. 'Not... much... pain, Martin... see... just a... bloody mess... no use... to me... the farm… or anyone.' Martin did not reply. He was lost in thought. 'If... you... could tell them... all back home...' Martin gently rolled the farmer onto his less injured left side, so that he faced away. 'Give… them... my love… I'd be grateful, Martin... truly grateful... and most of all to my darling Mary...'

A shell burst in the sky with a deafening explosion. It hid the single shot to the head. No one knew. No one ever suspected.

Martin stared at his gun for a moment and slowly put it away. He kissed his friend from home, softly and lovingly on the cheek, and said a silent prayer. He held the body for a few seconds of comfort and then laid it gently on the ground.

Rising quickly he began running towards the ridge and the bullets. He fired twice. Then suddenly there was a flash of orange, white and red. And the world went into the blackness of infinity.

****

On the day that Joseph Norman left for France, June received the news that John was dead and Martin missing. His body had not been found.

Too shocked to weep, she looked silently across the valley at the rising sun. 'Whatever will happen next?' She could think of nothing else, but 'Whatever will happen next?'

The British and French soldiers could have been excused for thinking the same. Not one German soldier reached Polygon Wood, and the British counter attack beat the Germans back and out of the copse nearby, called Nunn's Wood. This was the last devastating attack in what was later called the First Battle of Ypres. The Germans had come within a whisker of breaking through. Only a determined, almost supreme, effort had held them at bay.

Little did the Germans know that behind the ill-assorted but brave line of fire, nothing remained but the barely manned headquarters. But the advancing enemy troops retreated. It was one the most eventful days in British History.

Luckily for the British defence, the railroads were to pour in troops faster than the advancing enemy could muster. Thus the British Expeditionary Force survived. So day by day and month by month, more and more men were fed into the voracious war machine. This mutual pounding of wills and battering of bodies set the pattern. Attack was no longer the key word as both sides settled down into a war of attrition. The Western Front solidified for four years. At the time, it was something no one could have foreseen. The soldiers still longed for a quick victory. It did not occur. And Christmas day? In many quarters firing stopped. The troops of both sides met, exchanged small gifts such as tobacco and cigarettes, gossiped and played football. Who won these matches? History never recalled. The following day; the shots sang out again and mayhem ruled once more. While at home, the Christmas bells rang out in town and country. Prayers were offered for victory - and for the men who never came home.

Here ends the second book.

Book 3. In August 1916
-a period of disillusionment.

Chapter 46. Great Battles.

In August 1916 one of the most notorious battles mankind had ever unleashed was at its height. It was called 'The Battle of the Somme'.

In December of the previous year the decision had been made to succeed by attack, despite the stalemate of the preceding two years. The Commander-in-Chief of the British forces Sir Douglas Haig's reservations evaporated as Joffre pointed to the Somme, the spot where the British and French lines joined. It had no other value - no great prize could be gained, no important centre destroyed.

Then came the German offensive at Verdun on the 21st of February 1916. The prize an ancient fortress at the head of an awkward and useless salient on the French line. The mincing machine began its grisly toll, by the end of June the French army had been decimated, a loss of 315,000 men.

The German casualties were not so far behind. So the British were left with the Somme. These were the men who had answered Kitchener's call, 'Your Country Needs You.' Hastily trained, reckless, instructed to go forward in straight lines, lacking in initiative, inaccurate with the gun, they were the rigid, cannon fodder that struggled against the deep trenches and strong fortifications of the German lines. The bullets sprayed to and fro from the enemy's machine guns as the British soldiers stumbled blindly on and on.

July the first and the Battle of the Somme begins - by early afternoon there are 60,000 British casualties, over a third of them killed. These were to be the heaviest losses in a single day by any army in the First World War, and yet by a miracle Joseph Norman was to survive his injuries and escape from the battlefield of death.

Chapter 47. A long run for freedom.

Joseph sank down on the hay.

His first impression was of a soothing, soft dryness; a contrast to the squelching mud that had haunted him during the past two years.

The second sensation was one of inner peace. The solitude was so welcoming. The inner confusion, the unremitting inner turmoil had subsided for the moment.

He did not mind the trampling horse in the next byre, or the steady drip from the broken gutter outside the barn, pattering coarse droplets onto the cobblestone yard. The thunder shower had abruptly ceased.

He had no formed plan of escape, just the vaguest of ideas. And he was content just to be alone. The whole thing was a gamble and that was hope enough.

The mood of exhilaration had gone. He had seen his chance and seized it. He was too exhausted, too battle weary to fear death now.

But how his side ached and the livid foot long wound pulsed with the recent exertion. It stretched tight and red, half-healed, from the right lower ribs to the navel. The bleeding had stopped and the bandage was dry inside, but curled and wet on the outside. The shrapnel had been close, but not close enough and that made him smile. Yes, he had seen his chance and gone, as if by magic; out of the hospital tent with the fussy, fat matron and into the night. There would be no ward round for twelve hours and that was time enough, and he had flown. Taken a zigzag course to freedom; the odour of cordite and phosphorous could hang in the air forever as far as he was concerned – he had left them behind, far behind. A few gnats whined in the air outside the barn afraid to venture within; that was the only sound. The artillery had ceased and now seemed so far away that he felt the pent-up terror drain from his body. He felt strangely calm and at peace in this familiar farm setting. How he wished to be home.

It was the first light of morning and his eyelids drooped with drowsy fatigue. The vague smell of mould and cut hay mingled with the August scents on the dew.

The first rooster called. The Somme valley seemed a thousand miles away in spirit, although he knew he would soon hear the guns. An outburst of death! That he knew and used to dread!

But now there was a contented feeling, as a man experiences when he watches others work from a resting bank. He always tried to sit back and contemplate the scene in the trenches, to be alone amongst the slime and mud.

He had always enjoyed others working, and now he would reflect on their fighting; but not with an inner joy, but with a feeling of curiosity. How many would fall in the next few hours? How many saw the sun as a herald of death? Thousands, as yet unselected.

What fools this war had produced! What fools - eager to suffer and even die for a cause that now seemed utterly useless. The war would drag on forever. Yes forever! And he was out of it - one way or another. On the run! The thought made him wince for a moment.

Then he laughed. How Russell would approve of his sharpness. After all he had done his bit, raid after raid, counting the seconds to dying; watching the bullets and shells whirr past But it was all luck; pure chance; like cards or dominoes with Bert and the boys.

Fate dealt good hands and bad ones. He had aces; stopped nothing but a lump of metal and that in his side. No worse than a deep tear.

He had no scruples now. The dismal army could go to hell for all he cared, a route it was probably taking day by day.

He had to move on to the sea or another country, but his knowledge of the land was sparse, although he had not undertaken his escape lightly. He had found a few old maps and learnt them as best he could.

Maps were never his strong point at school but fear and hope had been an inspiration. With skill and luck.

He could have caught his lot that morning, perhaps this dawn would have beckoned his last day. If so, the

army would have been without him anyway, and spared the pitiful expense of a burial.

His brown eyes stared forward with a simple contempt. He brushed his wet hair with some dry hay, releasing long dark waves. His features were hollowed with two years of deprivation, and covered in a coarse beard that aged him beyond twenty. He had scraped his hands and feet, a few bleeding cuts caked in mud; and his clothes were shredded at the elbow and knees and dark where the water had soaked during his many crawls to freedom. 'Don't take chances in the open,' he kept repeating, 'crouch and keep low, that's what I've been told.' And that is what he had done, crouched when afraid, listening to his own heartbeat and rapid breathing in the darkness. But he had seen no one other than a few peasants in the fields or walking aimlessly along the village roads.

He reached for his prize possession - a small bottle of rum, his illegally stored ration. He put it gently on the ground, parting the six inches of hay, scrubbing the dust and chaff aside to form a small table oasis. The bottle held his gaze for a few seconds. How he wished the boys were there, like old times. Poor Martin! Poor John, for that matter! He would drink to their memory.

The liquid was harsh and hot on his tongue and throat. But he enjoyed the sensation and awaited that feeling of complete relaxation. That crude directness the alcohol had on his spirits.

He contemplated the horse. The animal stared back.

'Too scrawny to ride', he thought, placing the neck of the bottle in his mouth once more and letting the burning liquid pool on his tongue. Then a warm feeling suffused his body. 'What was the time?' he spoke to himself with such ferocity that the horse stepped back from the partition with a sudden jerk of the head and flapping of the mane. But it was the flat, weary sound of his voice that startled him.

Then he did not care but stretched back on the crisp dryness and crossed his legs and folded his arms behind his neck to serve as a makeshift pillow. He didn't curse his luck now. He watched a returning moth flitting in the gloom amongst the rafters as it settled on a broad wooden beam. This structure excited him. He looked at the side wall of the barn. It was so easy to climb.

Up he went onto the broad, double beam and looked down. 'Perfect camouflage,' he laughed. He could only be seen from the far wall of the barn and there the hay was piled twelve feet high.

He was thus suspended, thirty feet from the ground and safe; security he had not felt for months. He had no pack, no burden now, nothing to leave on the floor. Joseph smiled at his luck.

The morning sun crept over the horizon. A few rays lit up the barn dust in thin shafts of light that peered through the wooden planks of the long walls. The dust hovered in these beams, then swirled on the gentlest of gust; hardly a breeze. The day would be warm and sticky. It had been for a week; apart from that thunder shower the night before.

As he lay and contemplated life he was startled by the sudden cry of "Attack! Attack!" But there was no one near. 'My minds playing tricks,' he repeated the words, 'Attack! Attack!... yes... with a body drenched by fear, and tongues dry with fear, lips parched with fear... no one knows the fear of an attack better than me. But I did it, time and time again, no one could doubt that!'

Joseph felt his injured side. It was so sore. He peered at the cut, nervously pulling back his hospital shirt and curling down the rim of the encrusted dressing. It was red, but not bursting. My God! How he feared that it would burst. He had seen it so often. Men carrying their innards like women hold groceries in a pinafore. Cautiously returning to the trench; bemused by the absence of much pain, mesmerised by the long squirming mass of red and fat. And the gurgling made him physically sick. Not the sight, but the sound.

No one put that on the posters. No politician or officers waxed eloquent about this! Total sham, the bloody lot of them! And what else could be shown? Men who were hobbling on shattered feet or running back with their wrist between their lips. Pressing as hard as pain would allow; men trying to stop the short, sharp fountains of blood from the spurting arteries. No way! It was always delectable women waving goodbye, but not goodbye really; home soon, and a kiss for a conquering hero.

He eased off his back and looked down; a scratching

sound. Was it human? No, not anybody - only a cat, shabby and hungry like himself; creeping into the straw with an almost silent grace - suddenly pouncing with the only sound but the shriek of a mouse - another casualty of the day. A mouse!

He was about to climb down. There was a sound of thunder in the distance as the British guns opened up. He knew the time then. It was six twenty-five, it always was when the guns opened up, like clockwork. Go on until seven forty-five.

There was an echoing sound as the Germans guns responded in kind. 'Over the top boys', keep down, under the wire, lie flat - run, run, for your life… jump, duck and run.' For one short, black, solitary moment he was afraid; and then the feeling of cleverness returned. Pride was a load he had abandoned like his pack.

He felt for the men. Saw their scared expressions in his mind's eye. And his first attack... he would always remember it so clearly. It was imprinted in his mind, with a vivid intensity forever; the Somme - how the name stuck in his throat after all else. The heaving ground, with the earth moving sideways. It was uncanny - unreal. No one knew what was happening.

A huge mine tunnelled into the German lines had been blown up and it went off with an ear-splitting roar. The guns were drowned out for a few moments.

Then the earth column rose to four thousand feet or more, like a giant cypress tree, before falling away into a cone of thick dust; someone called out, 'It's a walkover, men, a bloody walkover.' Then someone else, bless his soul, kicked a football straight towards the enemy line. It was their signal to advance. But mainly the whistles blew and the barrage of guns began and the battle began and mayhem began.

The first off were in No-Mans-Land. Down they went; rat-a-tat-tat; spinning tops, not men. Then the firm line to attack, well rehearsed and at a steady pace out of the trenches. No shouting, no rushing; and the officers began running along the parapet yelling instructions and encouragements. Over the top went more men, wave upon wave like the sea; platoon leaders up the ladders first, followed by soldiers, line after line and into the fresh air; and the bugle - it still echoed in his ears.

He tapped his forefinger in its rhythm on the wooden beam; the German bugle. While our men struggled through the fine paths cut in the barbed wire mass, while they climbed out of the trenches, it sounded the death knell. It signalled the machine gun onslaught; bullets smacking everywhere. The curious sound when metal met flesh. Dead before they left the trenches they were, or happy to slip through the wire only to catch it all as they broke free. Men were falling right and left, screaming above the sound of the shells.

Joseph clasped his hands over his ears and looked down at the ground which seemed to spin and wobble precariously for a moment. Suddenly, his side began to throb.

He had seen five thousand or more at the dog trials. But in that first hour of the Somme at least six times that number must have got it one way or another. When he looked across the couple of miles of attack there were bodies everywhere. And all in an hour - one red, bloody hour. Probably the worst hour man had ever known. He shuddered.

Still what did he care now? That was weeks ago and it was still going on… in an eternal August. How would the hay be back home? He hadn't written for over a year, other than a postcard at Christmas. Perhaps home - for Christmas. He lay back on the beam and let a small shaft of sunlight sparkle on the eyelashes of his half closed eyes producing miniature rainbow colours; and there was the cat scratching around below. He slowly rolled onto his good side, and held his breath.

A young girl of sixteen or thereabouts stood with her hands on her hips looking at the hay and then towards the horse. Joseph continued to hold his breath until his lungs feared to burst. But she did not hear him, or see him. He gently eased himself forward and with effort peered cautiously through a small knot-hole in the crossbeam. The girl tossed her head of fine black hair. It flowed down her back just beyond her shoulders. The barn was gloomy but the brightest rays picked out her skin. It was gently tanned, her nose fine but the rest of her features were partly hidden as she looked down.

He had an urge to descend and speak to her, ask for help. Would it work? Would she understand English? Probably bring in the family and they'd guess he was a deserter. No! Better to wait and move off silently into the night. He heard a faint rustling of her green dress. When he looked down again she was gone.

The day was long. The horse shifted idly around its stall, munched hay and flicked at the flies with its tail. The heat grew oppressive. Joseph drained sweat onto the hard beam which became harder by the minute. Finally, about noon, when the shelling sound had softened in the distance he climbed down and collapsed back onto the pile of hay. What to do next?

He waited for a half hour. The bees hummed outside and the faint smell of the meadow drifted into the stagnant air of the barn. Then thirst began to torment him; then a slight nausea. He had to drink.

He walked slowly to the stall. The horse had gnawed at the top rails. The wood spiked and undulated and he scratched his hand. There was water and he climbed in and the horse stood back with a quizzical air. The boy rubbed its neck for a minute and then bending over drank from the brownish liquid in the trough. It was tepid and stale, but he drank it all the same, gulping like a dog. Then he washed his face and chest, splashing the water to cool his sweating body. As warm as it was, it felt cool by comparison.

What to eat? Some oats, scrubbed by the horse's coarse lips, lay damp and flaked in the bottom of a pail. But there was no option. Moistened into a grey paste it was eaten without relish. Then more water. How he perspired. How his wound ached.

It took a few hours before Joseph felt sufficiently secure to venture to the barn door. Cautiously he opened the upper section. It gave a loud squealing sound that had him stop instantly and crouch. Slowly he raised himself and looked out. There was a large cobblestone yard, a disused water pump (brown and rusty), a large dung heap; and fragments of an old hay cart littered one corner. Swallows swooped the yard and the young birds gave demanding squeaks from the mud cupped nest, against the wooden eaves.

He opened the lower section and slowly moved into the sun and heat. The cobblestones felt burning to the touch. He found no one; he paused and held his breath. There was no one. Crossing the yard he lay against a tall hedge, revelling in the dark shade. The grass felt so soft and cool and he was soon asleep.

At first he was conscious of a bee buzzing near his head. Then, as he looked up, a pair of brown eyes stared nervously down, but there was no fear and amazement.

It was the girl.

Joseph's first instinct was to make a run for it. But he suppressed his fear and tried to smile. For a few seconds she did not respond. She noticed the hopelessness in his face. Then she slowly smiled. He sat up so that his legs stretched on the grass and she settled beside him, holding his hands. Then she kissed him. It was a compassionate gesture.

Joseph felt in a dream.

'Un moment!' She inspected his side and saw the red gash partly exposed by the slipping bandage. In an instant she was on her feet. 'Attendez! Attendez!'

Swiftly turning, she ran down the meadow, scattering the red petals as crimson snow. How gracefully she moved. The flies wheeled in tiny arcs about his head and abdomen. The sweat ran to the tip of his nose and down his back and chest. He covered the wound with his shirt, ripping off the old bandage hardened with dried blood.

There was a total stillness in the afternoon air. Even the guns seemed sullenly drowsy on the few occasions they fired.

Joseph felt at peace. The fells came back, those distant fells and the sound of the church bell summoning across the valley. Compton Vale seemed to breathe life into his tired mind. His pulse quickened and he thought of one thing - going home, going home!

He could not put it into words but could visualise the scene - the fresh hay being raked, the cotton dresses pressed by the wind, the bluff lads from the village singing in tune, sturdy hands on the wagon rails and Old Vulcan contemplating the world with a switching tail; and the dogs dashing the pump water over their heads in unbound delight, spraying the air with a shaking coat, cooling long tongues in the blazing weather. And having drunk their fill how they would let the ducks rush forward to take their chance.

The soldier smiled and closed his eyes, hoping to awaken and see the girl again. But the hours crept on and the air began to chill. The guns began again in earnest.

So the night came with the first silent winging of the bats. He went indoors and lay down on the hay. At least he was dry and safe. What horrors that day had brought only a few miles away he could only surmise. But he was safe - and content in that fact he slept fitfully with hunger as his companion.

Now and then a rat or mouse would scratch and scamper across the beams. Once he saw the cat stealthily creeping, and suddenly disappear with a scuffling noise into a small pile of hay. An owl seemed to appear like a giant moth and ghostlike vanish in the gloom.

The dusk was strangely dark yet cloudless. The low hills looked like crests of purple and black in the August gloom. There was no wind.

Suddenly he was awake and sitting bolt upright.

Hurrying clogs on the cobblestones.

It was the girl clutching two small loaves and a bottle of water. She did not speak for a moment, then thrusting the bread into his hands she pulled him onto his feet by his shirtsleeve.

'Allez! Allez! Vite! Vite!' Her hushed tone conveyed the meaning.

Joseph listened with dismay. The horse whinnied loudly and he heard galloping feet in the distance. With shaking limbs the young soldier had left in an instant; and so had the girl. Both flattened the meadow grass into long furrows. The furrows diverged at the bottom of the field.

She waved and was gone.

Joseph headed to the woods about a half a mile away. Three British soldiers arrived, their horses stamped impatiently at the barn door as the men disappeared inside with guns raised. Joseph could only see their disturbing shapes in the gloom, as they wandered round and round the building, gliding in and out of the shadows, shouting for surrender. He lay motionless, flat on the ground behind a small thorn bush. Although he strained his weary eyes and ears he had little fear. As soon be shot by your own men as the Hun, perhaps even better, cleaner.

He could hear their racing footsteps, the occasional kicking over of a barrel or pail; the splintering of wood being smashed in.

Suddenly the men mounted and quickly rode in the direction of the farmhouse. There was a sound of raised voices, some angry. Joseph listened. At one stage they seemed to be arguing fiercely. The girl must have told her father of the injuries, and the stupid man had unsuspectingly informed the military police. Tough! He was going to the one place they wouldn't look for him in the next few hours.

In five minutes he was back in the barn, and eating the loaves on the broad beam. Perhaps the girl would come again tomorrow and the whole process could begin once more. He laughed and almost choked on the water. War could have its amusing side.

Then descending to the floor as the last flicker of light faded he curled up in the hay and fell asleep; and dawn came at four and the rooster was up bright and cheerful.

Joseph decided to take no more chances. It occurred to him that the military could come back or the farmer could arrive unexpectedly. So he climbed up to the beam and waited. The horse looked on once more.

Another day, with slanting sunbeams through the barn timbers. Smooth meadows in the distance, lime trees on the horizon. He felt exhausted; so weary and stiff.

A fleeting mist had crept out of the low valley leaving the permanence of dawn. He used to watch it drift out of the craters. A mobile diaphanous shroud pulled back to show the havoc of the previous day. He hated the morning mist and what it would reveal. Now he felt weaker and how his stomach rumbled. He felt his abdomen. It was fuller.

He thought of Martin and, for the first time in years, he felt like weeping. Suddenly his heart seemed to cry out. Nothing seemed to go right; Martin had lost the farm and then his life. How the rest of the family were taking it worried him, but what could he do? Poor Martin and he thought of the dog trials and the celebrations and the betting money they made in minutes. Life was good then. He had to get back to it. Was it right to go off - to desert - like he had achieved. 'Faced with water,' Russell used to say 'would a duck swim?

He had seen so little of life in the sheltered dale. Curious, he now knew more of sorrow and death now than life; and only twenty.

He waited all morning for the girl but she did not come. The water had not been changed in the trough, and needed replacing again. He waited another hour and then had to drink. But there was a green slime to it that snagged in his teeth and furred the tongue. The horse did not mind. The day dragged on and on. It was hot but he dared not go outside. Best to see the day pass and give the military police time to abandon the hunt.

And on and on, and thus the day dragged on.

Night came drowsily with the same flitting bat; almost imperceptible in the mysterious light, sweeping overhead in long slants and turns. Then the cat arrived – but not the girl. 'Where on earth is she?' he thought over and over again – and the minutes slowly passed - each one longer than the last.

Joseph lay in a waking dream, overwhelmed by recent horrors, thinking of the fragile band between life and death. The fate over which he had no control - until now! He did not consider the Germans or recapture even by his own troops. He tried to smile despite the danger. He found himself discussing the situation as if Martin or Russell were there. It was eerie but comforting, they seemed to stand before him, Martin with the dogs and Russ lounging on a hay-fork. He shook his head and tried to concentrate in the increasing confusion as a terrible yearning came over him to 'Go home'. To forget forever the dripping timbers of the trench huts, the wet and weary men, the smell of death. 'Go home Joe', they clearly said and he said, 'that's what I think brothers, that's what it's all about. We'll go to the old Plough for a pint, wont we?' But there was no reply. They had vanished and he decided he could not linger any longer - it was time to leave. Travel in the dark. Avoid the crowds, avoid the blazing weather.

He drank from the stagnant water and it made him feel sick, so he spat most of it out. Better find a stream. His thirst dominated his mind. Better find a stream!

He affectionately scrubbed the horse's neck with the flat of his hand before leaving. It had been a strange companion of the last two days. Then he was alone in the night air - fresh and cool. The guns bayed in the distance. He walked away from them feeling happy.

At first he was ultra-cautious fearing each bend or twist in the road; keeping low behind the hedgerows, waiting in the deep grass for distant voices or footsteps to fade. For a mile or more he followed a small valley, the bank surging up around him, but he arrived at a small coppice and the route fizzled out. He sat down and waited for five minutes, resting in the deep grass to ease his aching side. A small breeze ruffled the trees and a pond's waters lapped on the pebble stones adding to the desolation.

He thought that he must get rid of the clothes; but how? He got up and walked slowly on, drinking from the pond until he almost choked. No one was around.

Cautiously he crossed a broad road and there diagonally in the distance was a small house, with a village beyond on the crest of the hill. He must be sensible, proceed cautiously. And he did!

He watched a tiny speck appear like a star on the horizon, but it moved closer. He began to run. He was half way along the road to the house when the bright lights suddenly became closer and there was a roar of a motorcycle as it reached the outskirts of the village. He ran as fast as his weak state allowed. But the roar got nearer.

He felt trapped. The hedge was high and impenetrable on both sides of the road. He attempted to dart into the low branches but the thorns cut his arms and face. They caught at his trousers, ensnaring him like a rabbit. The light was approaching at speed. A military outrider. For the first time Joseph felt the terror of being hunted. There was nothing in the landscape to offer cover. But fate stepped in with both hands.

In fact it was a pothole.

The light skewed viciously right and left and then travelled forty yards at an odd angle before the driver slewed sideways across the road. He struck a fence post. Joseph's natural instinct was to rush up and help. But he waited. No one appeared from the nearby house. He waited a few seconds more. The engine cut out and the bike lay on its side. Joseph ran to the soldier, his French uniform torn but his body intact apart from a blow on the forehead, and mild concussion.

Quietly as possible Joseph wheeled the motorcycle to the bend. With one kick the engine roared and the night air whistled in his hair and it did so for a further thirty miles. He sang as he travelled along, the gamble appeared to be paying off. Then there was a sudden splutter and the engine cut out. Now he was alone in the darkness and in nowhere, totally isolated in the depths of the French countryside. Leaving the bike at the side of the road he wondered which way to go.

He had hardly eaten in three days and the hunger made his whole stomach ache. Now his one instinct, his one thought was to find food. Onward for a further mile and he reasoned it was past two in the morning. There was no church clock to help him, and the villages were few and far between. Life was suddenly scarce and that made him smile.

He cut across a meadow towards a farmhouse but a barking dog scared him off. He ran quickly for two hundred yards and then panting collapsed on the ground to see what damage had been done. The silence remained and he composed himself.

But the pangs of hunger groaned through his stomach. He could think of little else than food. Joseph Norman had many faults but lack of optimism was not one of them.

So cutting across a broad plain with scrub bushes and thistles, he reached the outskirts of another hamlet. The odd goose squawked and hissed as he passed in the darkness.

He reached a small group of houses and stealthily climbed onto a low garden wall of the first. By candlelight an old woman sat and read in a rocking chair. She wheezed from a shortness of breath and her ankles looked swollen over her shoes. The young soldier was amazed at her being awake. He did not know of the problems of lying down with a defective heart; the choking sensation of cardiac failure.

Suddenly, and to Joseph's horror a stone clattered down onto the gravel path and bounced off into the shrubbery. He held his breath. But she did not look up.

'Is she deaf?' he wondered.

For a few moments he froze, then to test his theory he picked up a large rock and threw it against the ground. She did not pause and look up. Next he coughed loudly. Still there was no movement, her eyes remained fixedly down, scanning the printed page through a magnifying glass. Thus Joseph made up his mind. Sliding stealthily to the partly open window of the bedroom he pushed up the lower half.

With a screech a black cat leapt down and hissed as it disappeared into the darkness. He started in fear. A black cat, Joseph's instincts spoke of luck. Superstition became his guide. But it was a hard decision.

Robbing an old woman? What would his Grandma say? In an instant he turned and slid out of the garden. 'There must be a change of luck sooner than later'; and then it happened at the next house he passed.

A dry brown shirt and grey woollen stockings hung from a small washing line close to the outhouse. Slowly and deliberately, he reached up and took them down. He paused, everywhere was silent. How good it would feel to wear clean clothes. But he needed a bath; he had not itched for days. With luck he was louse-free from the hospital scrubbing.

Joseph hesitated for a moment as a dog barked in the distance. He paused and after a few moments headed for the sound of a running brook. There he scrambled down the short steep bank in the blackness, tearing his leg on a briar. Naked he slid into the shallow water. He drank and bathed alternately, content in the gloom for ten minutes, cold but content in the blackness.

It was time to take stock of his precarious position, bruised, shaken and frightened. He contemplated his future as he sat in the cool water, it felt fresh and luxurious compared to the army bath. He realised that he had to steer north and east towards safety. He would rest by day and travel by night. Stick to his original plan. There was no feeling of helplessness, no pessimism just an anxiety to get on with events and make his full escape. Joseph clambered out and dressed. He sat with his back against a tree on some soft grass, feeling his injured side. He began to climb a short hill, crossed under cover of a low wall, and sat on the earth beneath it for a few moments and looked about. Ahead was a broad field which seemed to stretch to infinity in the gloom. But the clouds swept back and moonlight, pale and comforting sectioned through the trees.

'Only the army trousers and boots to get rid of,' he mused as he sauntered along. It was now nearly three thirty and he felt sleepy. He crossed four more fields, the grass grew long and the lower parts were damp with dew. He made rambling progress, keeping under the shadow of the horizon. Once, however, he stood on the crest of a small hill. The Western Front action was sporadic and just visible in the distance, but fainter than he had known it for two long years. He laughed out loud, and luck was with him still - and more was to follow.

There was a groaning cry in the next field, long deep groans interspersed with a heavy breath. He knew the sound so well, it was a cow in calf. And a meal was only a half hour away.

The large white and black beast slowly clambered to its feet, the placenta still cloaking the wobbling calf's back. She tugged it off and stood looking slightly bemused. Joseph grabbed the flattened jelly mass and considered eating it raw. Then stopping himself he dropped it to the ground.

He waited patiently for the first milk to come. Thick, rich and brown! The cow was relieved. The breasts congested and the calf not yet sucking. Joseph held the calf back letting it rasp wet-lipped on his free fingers until he had squirted handful upon handful into his mouth. How curious life was! How many times he had milked in the byres without such frantic haste and enjoyment?

Then he released the little frightened animal and it tottered to its mother with rasping tongue; nuzzling along the flanks until it reached a teat. Joseph laughed again, and went on his way. He had to guard against recklessness - war had taught him that harsh fact.

But after half a mile a deep drowsiness began to envelop him - wave upon wave. At first he tried to shake it off and staggered on. He kept thinking 'Not tired, not tired' He tried to run but it was a stumbling, shambling gait.

'Where's a wood?' he thought, 'damn it there must be a wood somewhere!' In five minutes he stumbled across a dry ditch once filled with moss, now lined with cracked earth, but with gorse bush cover. 'How curious everything is!' he repeated to himself in his confusion, 'How curious!' He collapsed forward as he sat down and instantly fell into a profound sleep until late in the following morning.

It was another sunny day. The sun was forever brilliant in a clear blue sky as it bent towards the west. There were a myriad of insect sounds, an endless chirping hum, as he became conscious of the world outside the spiking branches. A dog barked, and then another.
They were enjoying a hunt. Rabbits! He thought of the times he'd done that; millions of the beggars to be run down. That thought made him hungry. He must eat soon. That was the number one priority. Then new boots, not the regulation give-away army size.

But his back ached and his right leg felt sore. Numb and sore. He wiggled his toes. They were okay. But his thigh felt weak. It did not bend as quickly as it should. The hip felt weak also. He rubbed the areas with his hand to try and bring some warmth and sensation. Funny, the day was hot but the leg felt so cold.

The dogs barked again, this time much nearer. He lay flat and thought' Pray to Heaven they don't barge in here!' Suddenly he was unsure and crawled forward to look around. A small coppice of poplar trees blocked his view to one side, but the rest of the flat meadow seemed at peace. He scrutinized it as best he could. A few cows grazed in the distance, many with calves.

He crawled back to the ditch. How strange was his leg. How weak, all of a sudden. How dizzy he felt and the sun made the dizziness worse as it beat upon his back. He would wait and his luck would see him through. Every hour and every day increased his chances. Unlike the Front - where time sliced away to death.

He lay flat in the ditch and gazed at a small rectangle of blue between the uppermost gorse branches. The few yellow flowers stood out in contrast to the dazzling background blue. There were a million shades of blue and the sun, at first uncertain in the twisting branches, moved into view, glared inquisitively into his sanctuary. It bleaching out the colour this beaming sun. He closed his eyes. The sun was warm and comforting on his face.

Suddenly the sunlight shimmered and glinted on the barrel of two guns. He was caught in a trap and the French police said, 'Levez vous, vite! Vite!'

For a moment Joseph was confused. 'Get up, get up, British soldier.' There was nowhere to run and the dogs were jubilant, running around and whining with pleasure.

They were ignored. For the handcuffs took priority. The soldiers shouted to some others but their voice seemed a jumbled echo and he could hardly stand on his weak leg. But they bundled him along like a lame nag; dragging him by his shoulders. He felt too dispirited to offer any resistance.

In an hour he faced the French military police. They were hesitant at first. Joseph protested his innocence. But the French officers gabbled so quickly and dispassionately that he gave up all hope of convincing them. But it was an impasse through the lack of understanding between each other. By comparison the two English soldiers when they arrived said little, other than 'Desertion and attacking a French dispatch rider', there's a penalty to pay for all this, you know!' There was a pause. 'You fit the description given by three villagers. The shirt's different but the rest fits. Anything to say?'

277

Joseph began to speak but was interrupted.

'You will be court-martialled. There's far too much of this sort of thing going on'.

One said, 'It was becoming a bit of an epidemic on both sides'. While one of the French police replied with an oath and shook his head.

'There's too many volunteers who have no will to fight, no guts,' said an English voice.

The other English officer agreed. 'There had to be examples' was the reply.

Joseph looked blankly and asked for food. He was given a cup of black coffee and a thin slice of brown bread, dry at the edges. He sat in silence and contemplated his future. 'Better to be killed by your own side than the Huns, if it came to that,' he thought. And he repeated his own philosophy, rolling the phrase over and over in his tired, confused mind - and said nothing more.

That night he slept in a cell. He had been driven forty miles towards the Front. He thought he recognised the barn as he passed. There was a horse in the field but it was indistinct. He looked for the girl. There was no sign: just an indistinct horse cropping on the shallow bank.

The cell bed was hard; hard on his wound. Still he was warm and had soup which was pretty thin with a few peas and beans, but better than nothing. His one wish, 'An apple sponge, Mother's best'. Fresh Bramley seedlings picked when rosy in early November, just before the first frost. Mother was a good cook. He missed her now; hadn't thought much about her in the last two years. But he missed her tonight. That was one consolation seeing Mother, Dad and Martin. And a good consolation, what would they all say? He smiled and turned to try and ease his side.

His cell was to one side at the end of a short corridor. The main block of cages was also full.

The air was chilly and at midnight the guard changed; a heavy soldier with a short black beard and ponderous step. The guard sat down on a wooden chair and gazed at the wall for a short while and turned to the boy. He put a large bunch of keys, embraced by a stout ring, onto a small table. Joseph wondered if he could in some way get his hands on the keys or perhaps persuade the guard to come over with them.

Would his luck change?

No doubt each dispirited prisoner felt the same.

Someone was snoring loudly and the guard was annoyed and rapped on the bars of the cell. The snoring stopped. He wandered over to the boy and gazed through the bars.

'What are you in for son? Desertion?'

Joseph did not reply at once but looked doggedly at the ground. 'So they say!'

The guard plodded back to his chair.

He sighed and reached out to light a small oil lamp. He had a blue book in his hand. 'What's your name son?' He arched his neck to relieve an imaginary crick and tugged at his beard and moustache in turn.

'Norman, - Joseph Norman.'

The guard did not look up but tugged at his beard again and looked solemnly into his book. He sat staring at the wall for a further five minutes without speaking.

Slowly he arose and walked over to the cell clasping the keys. Joseph watched him with apprehension. 'I've orders to shower each prisoner as they come in, so come on!'

Joseph wondered if it was some ploy before execution. Until that moment he had not feared death.

Then his legs trembled and he broke out in a cold, clammy sweat.

The cell door swung open and the huge guard peered ferociously into his face marking each feature in turn. He only said 'Little to compare' in a quiet voice and led the boy through the narrow door adjacent to his cell.

They crossed a small room - shabby, brown and musty smelling - to an outer side door. Joseph still trembled and the guard clutched his gun with a stern gaze.

'They could not execute him like this, could they?' he thought. He had heard of all sorts of atrocities on both sides, especially to deserters. He felt like screaming out, but said haltingly, 'Oh Mother of Mercy help me!' And the guard looked round and whispered brusquely 'Keep quiet, will you!'

The shaking boy waited to see what would happen next.

The side door was slowly opened and the night air was cool. A crescent moon was in the ascendancy with a scattering of stars.

The guard stood still in the doorway and peering out - slowly looked to the left and right.

The main barracks was a hundred yards to the right and a sentry stood quietly at the gate watching that section.

'Stay here!' the guard whispered.

The patrolling sentry crouched down and furtively lit a cigarette. The red glowed in the darkness.

'What did you say you were called?'

'Joseph Norman.'

'Of South Hadley Farm, in Compton Vale?'

Joseph looked startled.

The soldier displayed no emotion.

'Yes.'

'Listen son, it's up to you. Strike left and head for that long meadow you can just see past the village.'

'But why..?'

'Ask no questions and you'll get no answers.'

Joseph stood still as the sentry coughed, extinguished the glow, and rested his head on his arm for a moment. The guard had put a warning hand on the prisoner's shoulder. He now released his grasp. 'Get going son, and God be with you.'

The grateful boy disappeared into the night.

The guard smiled and shook his head. 'It would be a pity to lose both lads, what would happen to those lonely sheep and coughing heifers?' With a wry smile and a smoothing of his moustache…Jack Golightly went swiftly indoors.

******

The Somme had been chosen solely as a joint venture, a firm partnership so that the French and English could fight side by side. The Germans dug themselves in and the operation became a fiasco. The Generals had boasted of success, and none was forthcoming. Over a million people died or were seriously injured. It was an unmitigated disaster. Idealism perished on the Somme as well as the troops. After this battle the soldiers decided that the war would go on forever. For Joseph Norman it ended soon. The large abscess in his side invaded the spinal tissues and he died sleeping in a small barn, the main artery of the abdomen rupturing. He was not the only person to be classed as a deserter. Desertion occurred by the thousand, especially in the French army, and executions were carried out in a random manner. He escaped that fate.

In August 1916 Western Civilization reached its lowest ebb, but the tide was to turn - especially for one woman.

Here ends the third book.

Book Four. An Extraordinary Woman - a question of temperament.

Chapter 48. A price of victory.

The Reverend Clenham said, 'She is an extraordinary woman!'

So the word spread round Compton Vale and pretty soon it had travelled to the adjacent valleys, but that was in 1916. At the beginning of the War, the Vicar had simply asked about the likelihood of keeping a goat.

'No point,' she had replied without a minute's hesitation. 'I'll sell you a young heifer and you can have milk and calves enough during these lean years.'

She had smiled as she said it and looked so like her mother that the Minister had held his breath in a sort of joyous admiration and a suppressed longing for the times past.

June Norman had come of age. The Minister saw all her mother's beauty and strong will blossom again - day by day and month by month. Soon he became a frequent visitor to South Hadley Farm, especially when his first calf was due to be born.

To him it was a momentous occasion, a turning point in his life; and, for some odd reason, he could not fathom it out. But he was tied inexorably to June's future fortunes. She asked Russell to deliver the calf and the Minister watched the rowan coloured tottering form being licked by its mother amongst the dry straw. The farmer stepped back, laughed in the satisfaction of a job well done, while June clapped her hands with pleasure, 'See, what did I tell you! Now you have two animals and pretty soon they'll be a herd and you'll have to vacate the vicarage or turn the tithe cottage into a byre.'

The Vicar began to admire her more and more. Especially when she tried to look serious and a frown hid those clear brown eyes and the long dark eyelashes. Suddenly her even teeth and dimpled smile would break out, as the sun through furrowed clouds.

'You know what, Vicar, there's money in the War,' she had exclaimed one day as they met in the top meadow, 'although I hate to say it, real money!' She had looked so earnestly into his face for encouragement, 'A price in peace... and a price in war.'

The Reverend Clenham had appeared composed. 'I think best with a cup of tea,' he said as an excuse to deliberate on this remark.

Grandma Wetherall obliged. She had been soaking some clothes in a large bucket, and pounding away at them with a possing stick, throwing a hundred small rainbow bubbles into the kitchen beams.

'I love Earl Grey, June, on a summer's day. Don't you?' He had sipped from the fine china cup. 'And war is not to be exploited, but... the men need food, ammunition and supplies and the horses need hay.' He had laughed with this remark, laughed really excitedly, 'and we shall provide, shall we not? Listen to this!'

The Matriarch had strained her ears in the kitchen and stopped scrubbing.

'June, this war may go on for years, I don't believe the optimism of the politicians; and who knows how many men may be taken to enlist and even be killed. So it is quite possible that women may have to run the country, make more and more key decisions especially at local business level, and of course,' he paused, 'even in farming; something that would have been considered ridiculous a few years ago.'

June had listened with profound interest.

'Yes, the War will change many things and a woman's place in society will be first. The suffragettes have a noble cause, but even they do not, as yet, comprehend the fundamental change.' He had sipped from his cup and the Matriarch in the kitchen had said, 'Stuff and nonsense!' to herself very quietly but firmly. 'My advice June is to be first; and the "first" I am talking about is "big" farming business.'

The young girl had laughed once more and swept up a meandering kitten, as she spun round on her feet before kissing it.

'I have been around here many years, and there are some things many have forgotten, about common land, grazing rights and all that. But I do recall that the Darling Hill forest was only a lease, and the man who planted it, I buried three years ago. God rest his soul but not his Will, for he didn't make one. And he had no dependents!'

June had stopped playing with the kitten and looked into the Minister's face. She examined his features and the rapidly darting blue eyes, but they showed no avarice. He paused for a few more moments that taxed the Matriarch's curiosity. 'Go on, please! Please go on'.

'So I looked up the facts in the local council office just a few days ago. The lease was included in a whole plot of land that once was part of South Hadley and relinquished by Low Green Farm. In fact, what I'm saying (if my research has proved correct) is that the wood's yours, or rightly your family's - from almost a century ago.'

He had spoken triumphantly and held out his cup for a refill. 'Only a small drop of milk, if you don't mind'.

Grandma Wetherall who had ventured in from the kitchen now stood with the milk jug suspended in her hands and had not been able to resist chiming in. 'If that'd been the case, I'd have been the first to have heard of it!'

'I do not doubt your memory or its veracity,' was the Minister's reply, 'but that is the case as I found it.'

The Matriarch waited for a moment as if expecting some response, but he went on sipping his tea. 'Some men aren't such fools after all,' the old lady had muttered, half-smiling as walking back into the kitchen. 'But funny how the old mind forgets.'

At the time June could hardly contain her excitement. 'The price of wood is rising sharply with the war, why we could get at least ten pounds an acre and there are over one hundred acres on Darling Hill.'

'A thousand pounds, June, and with it we will buy more grain, - horses and men need grain - and ship it to the channel ports' he had replied. And that was how it began in early 1915, the Vicar recalled with satisfaction, as he sat one night while playing the piano and eating dried fruit.

The first thousand! Morgan and Peters whistled up the contracts and the plump bank manager smiled in anticipation of more to come – as it did. June was built with an iron will.

'Beauty and drive, an unstoppable combination,' the Minister maintained; so men smiled condescendingly into her pretty face, marked the warmth of expression, immediately felt strong and confident; but in the end walked away with a bad bargain, - gullible and still remarking on the girl's naivety.

So the grain transactions grew. Farmers in Compton Vale and the surrounds were quick to grab the chance of a few extra pounds, even at times recklessly, to the cost of their own livestock the following winter.

But if June cared, she did not show it; there was not a hint of remorse as she returned along the Top Road, idly looking at the oak trees with their branches bleached by the sun 'I will hire more lorries to speed things up,' and they were hired, the largest available in the district.

But it was at a bargain price, even though the owners tried to hang out for more in those lean times. When they expected a favourable reply, they did not get one. June told them quietly and simply that if they did not agree with her figures she would go out of the district to get her transport. 'We mustn't make hasty decisions, must we young lady.' Many had decided that the possibility of a long delay would be the decisive breaking point in her iron will. But she waited and ignored any further communications. So that after a week or two's procrastination and dithering, they gave in; some with insults and oaths, others submissively and resigned. She discounted all they said, the foul oaths and innuendos, giving them a look of contempt. When June returned to renegotiate later she made some of them pay for their coarseness. 'It's a pity,' she would say, with a withering look, 'but that's the final offer.'

'Shipping… where do I get the ships?' was the next dilemma. At first the ships were not forthcoming. June tried the nearest available port on two occasions without success. Thus, in desperation, the grain was trucked farther away, and the extra expense was annoying, for it ate into the profits. So one day she returned to the nearest port, spoke her mind and gave a slightly increased offer. Finally, worn down by her persistence, money and charm, the ship owners saw sense. A few were obdurate, but a compromise was eventually reached.

'Why are men so condescending, it makes me sick and even more determined.'

The Vicar laughed, and said it was probably the male constitution, and June laughed to mollify her irritation and agreed.

Next came the purchase of hay. She gave the matter some thought and even briefly asked Russell for his advice, which she promptly ignored. 'It's tough, but if hay's cheaper in the surrounding Dales, so be it. I'll buy it there.'

'June, think twice,' was his comment, 'nobody will thank you for it.'

A reproach was on the tip of her tongue, but she hesitated and said in a low voice, 'What will be - will be. Getting provisions to the army is my priority.'

Russell wondered if there were other factors but did not reply. So load upon load was bought as June toured the adjacent countryside. For Nineteen Fourteen with its long hot summer stretching into September was a bumper year. Russell continued to help not question her judgements or motives and sweated under the strain of moving cartload upon cartload from the surrounding farms. The farmers helped willingly in the satisfaction that they were aiding the war effort; and all reasoned that the War would be over soon.

June watched them with interest as they worked in the burning sun, thinking at times of the ridiculous poster – 'Women of Britain Say Go.' If all the men went, who would work the fields, the old and the children? She marvelled at the stupidity of politicians, the strange patriotism and gullibility of man; and wished the War would soon be over for all sides.

As June visited all the farms in Compton Vale and adjacent dales she was not always kindly greeted. Some said, 'You're only welcome for the money and not for yer'sel, the way you're acting doesn't seem right.' While the more amenable said, 'Young lady hang on a bit, thou's going too fast, and a bit hasty like.'

'Do you think so?' she asked blandly.

'Maybe'.

'So the money's not good then?' They hesitated in their reply but did not dare argue after they saw the indifferent toss of the head and the feint to walk away. Thus the men from the Ministry were well-pleased and paid this beautiful agent more and more. And there was a general discussion in the 'Frozen Plough'. 'Damn me, she's good for a pound or two.'

Some remarked that June drove a hard bargain that would bring the locals down. But most replied, 'Bloody rubbish!' or 'speak for y'rsel, fur we've never been better off in our lives.' And the muttering, disquiet and rancour spilled over into the corn halls, markets and bars. There they would gaze at their ale pensively as if seeking a glimmer of enlightenment in the barley-clouded depths; while a few searched for consolation and explanation as to what was happening in what they considered to be a man's world. 'Aye, she's a rum one fur a lass!'

But one observation ran through their thoughts as a common, unifying thread. They all recognised 'her toughness'.

June, if not totally oblivious as to what people said and thought about her, had the strength of character and self-will to ignore it. She spent not a penny on herself, got the Matriarch to crop her hair even shorter, and weekly counted the money going into the bank.

'That was generous,' said the Reverend Clenham when he saw the large, white-embossed, five pound note deposited in the collection box. 'That is positively the first in my stipendiary.'

They both laughed.

While the plethoric bank manager twirled his fingers over the notes, 'Another two thousand pounds, you will need expert financial advice before long.'

She replied, 'I get it,' so sweetly that the man was not in the least disarmed when she continued, 'from my cats'.

'I never thought I could make nine thousand pounds so quickly,' she thought as she walked along the Top Road marking the long ribbon of houses along Iris Force Burn. 'In such a short time, only two years, what ever will happen next? But I've said that before!'

Never one for the future, she strolled on reflectively, whistling to the dogs she saw in the distance.

Then the Minister appeared and broke the sad news of Joseph's death.

It was 1916 and June shed tears, left the room and broke down alone. Over the ensuing months she became even more determined to make amends. 'Perhaps the Vicar was right; perhaps it would be a woman's world if things went on like this.'

Chapter 49. A soldier returns (i).

'That was a blinkin' lucky escape,' said Willie Pearson mopping his long brow with anxiety and replacing the strands of hair in their regular manner. 'Least some good came out of the barrel of a gun. That's more than we can say about the War!'

There was a subdued atmosphere in 'The Frozen

Plough'. Mabel, the landlord's wife cleaned the bar top with a circular motion of her hand, and pursed her lips.

Russell Norman looked at the dogs - Sam and Sorrel - beneath the long settle. He grimly set his teeth. 'You're telling me!' He stated emphatically putting down the pint glass, half-empty.

It was January 1919 and the late afternoon air was pleasantly warm for that time of year. The bar had opened at six, afternoon closing hours being one legacy of the Great War that was to remain for generations. 'Go on,' said Mabel stopping the cleaning and waiting with mouth half-open. Willie concurred.

'To recap for George here, I'd just taken the dogs across Ullock Moor and thought it was better to pop off some rabbits for a pie (Willie nodded in agreement). We were close to Low Green when I heard the screams. It was Vera Bowes, yelling at the top of her voice ('And some voice', ventured George Havelock adjusting his stool so that he faced the fire.) Well, we were down that bank in a flash. There was a roarin' and a hollerin' like all hell had broken loose.'

The young farmer stopped and smoothed his waving brown hair. 'All hell! Then Vera yells "In the byre" "Help" and in goes Sam barking like mad. Well, the Ayrshire bull looks up but goes to work again - battering old man Bowes about the arms and chest, him rolling half dazed on the floor like a giant bale of hay. There was nothing else to be done. I fired the gun into the rafters and the bull lets out one almighty roar and bounds out of that byre in an instant.'

The farmer paused and drank again.

'Go on, for goodness sake Russell,' said Mabel impatiently her face flushed with excitement.

'I will, Mabel, but give me time. Where was I? Oh! Yes! Out goes the mad beast and into the pen at the end of the yard. So I've got him. I still had the gun but when I pushed it up against his square brow, and you know what strong foreheads those beasts have, his brown eyes bulged and rolled so fearfully that I thought, pity to kill the beast in these lean times - so he's in South Hadley Farm. And when I left he was as gentle as a baby at the breast!'

'And Old Bowes?' sang out all three.

'Not too injured. Dr MacKenzie says it's bad bruising and a cracked rib or two but nowt else.'

'Thank the Lord for that!' said Mabel with a sigh. They all smiled, and the round of drinks was replenished. The fire crackled and hissed as the dead holly leaves blazed.

'Three years is best,' said George, who looked sadder and older following the death of his eldest son in the Paschendale encounter. 'Wood should lie three years when chopped, and the logs'll blaze like that!'

Willie thanked him in a kindly, considerate way and smiled at his old friend. He turned the subject to June. 'That's some sister, Russell, if you don't mind me saying?'

'I don't,' replied the farmer, laughing.

'She's got some wood at her disposal, now that she has Darling Hill and a big block out of Scarth Wood'.

'Well, the farm's mine, t'is only fair and right that June should have the plantation, it rightly belonged to our land,' continued Russell.

'June is getting to own every darned thing that grows in this dale and beyond,' said George with a slow shaking of the head.

'Do you think you'll cope?' asked Mabel.

Russell puzzled over her remark. 'Cope?'

'With the bull?'

'Oh! You're still on that track, Mabel. Yes, we've had one before and he was penned in the small byre and paddock field. We'll cope.'

'I don't want you being injured like that,' she said looking at the blaze so that the red glow added to her ruddy features. 'We've lost enough customers already, wonderful boys, so take care!'

George Havelock nodded. 'A lot went, but only a few came back; doesn't seem fair to lose a whole generation of fine boys with so much to offer.' His voice trembled a little as he spoke.

'Life's not fair George', said Willie grasping his friend's hand, 'we all know that. But there's little we can do about it. That's democracy. We vote the politicians in on false promises or downright lies, then throw them out after suffering their incompetence, and vote in another lot equally bad. It's unending but it's democracy!'

'There'll be changes in the years to come,' said Russell, 'mark my word. I don't want Martin and Joseph (his voice also wavered for a moment) to have died in vain. Nor John and your boy, George,' he continued sadly.

'And the rest!' said Mabel.

'Aye, and the rest.' They all agreed in silence. The fire continued to blaze and Willie added another log.

George spoke. 'Speaking of soldiers, I was mending a wall, by the Top Road when I saw a soldier in the distance; looked a bit down at heel. A biggish fellow, but my eyesight's not so good these days. Had on khaki trousers and carried the old regulation pack. He was a soldier all right.'

'Where was he heading, George?' asked Russell.

'Don't rightly know, didn't seem to be heading your way, but then that old wooden sign of yours is down. He did look up the path though for more than half a minute'.

The young farmer scratched his head and studied the wall opposite for a moment.

Outside the night darkened and a heavy roll of thunder preceded a short burst of hail.

It was surprising weather, but not so surprising as the events which lay in store - for June.

Chapter 50. A soldier returns (ii).

There was an inherent snugness about the front room of South Hadley Farm, warmth written into the rafters for generation after generation. The fire glowed and hissed, a cricket chirped occasionally and a kitten romped with a small ball of wool. One of Katy's kittens had not been drowned and had been kept to replace an older cat who had succumbed to some type of jaundice.

The 'old' June would have joined in the frolicking, but the mature girl, although young in years, had her lips pursed and was pouring over a ledger which rested on the table. 'We need more land to expand with the price of hay and grain going to fly through the roof. Never mind the poultry market!' She rubbed the side of her face reflectively leaving a faint blushing circle. 'We can either move, perhaps south, or expand here!'

She paused again. The clock struck and with the first sound the kitten scampered in mock alarm towards the far corner. 'Oh! Baby don't be so afraid,' sang out the girl cheerfully. She picked up the tiny form as it rushed back towards her and rubbed its small warm head against her cheek.

Grandma Wetherall had retired to bed. Then came a faint roll of thunder. 'Like distant guns,' Martin had written. June looked in sadness around the room and for a moment heard the laughter of the two departed boys as it used to be. Then the faint echo died in her brain, and she shed a silent tear.

'Still, got to get these accounts done; the present was now so important, the past beyond recall. That is what she believed once, and that is what she believed now.' 'Five years since I saw him! How young and impressionable I once was.' Her mind turned to Julian for the first time in months. She had thought of him every waking minute for the first year, and almost as much the second. But by degrees that feeling of loneliness, at first a deep longing and then an emptiness - had slowly ebbed away, leaving her with a faint hollow sensation, when she considered the past. She tried to think of him positively, what she considered pleasant thoughts, but usually bitterness crept into the recollections and which moved onto self-recrimination. 'Well, I've got on without him, and that's one consolation.' She shrugged her shoulders in resignation and stared into the darkness.

The thunder disturbed her train of thoughts, and she returned to her calculations. She looked up. 'Was that footsteps in the yard?'

She turned her head with some alarm and a quickening of her heart. 'If it was Russell why had the dogs not barked their usual greeting?'

For no apparent reason she trembled slightly; felt stupid and put down her pen. There were no more sounds. She strained her hearing and satisfied that nothing was amiss resumed her writing. The old cat was peacefully sleeping on her side and the kitten played at her feet. Still there was an uneasy feeling that made her skin tingle and her heart beat even faster. The cat went on sleeping and the clock ticked. There was no other sound but the hail beating on the rooftops.

The ticking seemed to get louder, but it was only an illusion of her heightened mental state, an aberration of her anxiety. Then the downpour ceased as abruptly as it began. There was silence. Yet, the kitten ran to the far corner and began to tremble. But the clock did not strike and the half hour was five minutes away; 'How the kitten hates the chimes,' she thought, 'why is the little dear so nervous.' June took a deep breath, looked at the clock for another moment and then into the night.

The oil lamp's yellow glow smudged as a reflection on the mistiness of the glass. She could see nothing of the world outside, just the hazy comforts of within. 'Probably a fox disturbing the hens'. Once more she felt reassured and her pulse settled.

Then came a creaking sound, the sound of stealthy footsteps. That was not her imagination; the cat raised her head and looked to the door.

June quickly rose for the gun by the corner cupboard.

It was not there.

Russell must have been cleaning it somewhere. But where? Suddenly she felt helpless, but only for a second. Then her resolution returned.

It was broken as a face peered through the glass window. Startled her colour drained from her skin.

It was a large whiskered face, indistinct. She called out firmly, 'Who's there?' and ran to the door.

But it slowly opened.

Imperceptibly at first; and then with a confident rush; 'It's only me, Ma'am, a soldier from the war, an old soldier down on his luck who knew your brother. Only me, Ma'am, wanting a bit of food and shelter on this stormy night.'

June relaxed and even managed a slight smile. 'What's your name?' she enquired politely, opening the door a little wider to try and discern the speaker in the blackness.

'Dan,' said the stranger still reluctantly standing back in the shadows but grasping the side of the door with a huge fist. 'Dan Brewis, Ma'am, at your service!'

Chapter 51. The Ayrshire.

He placed a huge boot in the door. It was filthy and worn down at the heel.

The Butcher of old had lost none of his coarse ugliness. For a second June recoiled, but said, 'Which brother?'

'The fair one, Martin,' came an indifferent reply which the young girl in her excitement missed.

'Martin,' she said softly. And then was silent while she saw his face suddenly light up in her mind. 'Please tell me about him.' Her voiced quavered. 'Was he brave? Did he suffer?'

'Not on your life Ma'am. I mean the sufferin'. And as brave as a lion, he was. Come with me on a detail wire cuttin' and was the best. Told me, "Dan lad, if you ever needs help just ask at the farm and he writes it down". So I've come'. The ex-soldier rubbed his rough hands and smiled. The sore on his neck began to itch and he scratched so violently that it began trickling blood towards the rough collar.

'Is that a wound?' said June rushing towards a cabinet where they kept dressings and bandages. 'Let me get something for it.'

'Shrapnel', lied Brewis about his chronic fungal sore with its curled and weeping edges. 'But before you 'elp in that manner, Ma'am or should I call you Miss, for you're a young 'un all things considered. A drop of brandy and some food would do, us old soldiers don't demand much you might say.'

June apologised and hurried to the kitchen. To her discomfort he followed. She watched him out of the corner of her eyes. His long forehead and shaggy eyebrows added to the sinister expression. Suddenly she felt uneasy and tried to hide her shaking hands. 'Surely Russell will be here soon,' she thought. But there was no sound of the dogs.

She played for time, slowly cutting three rashers of smoked ham and placed them on the sliced bread. For a second she held onto the long bladed knife, undecided, then quickly reasoned that it was best to hide it at the back of the drawer. It dropped over the back onto the shelf below with a sharp crack and June held her breath, but the soldier's gaze did not alter.

'You alone, Miss? No husband or anything about?' he asked in a non-committal way.

298

June steadied her voice. 'My brother's out the back and my Grandmother is upstairs dressing for bed.'

'With the dogs, Miss? The brother is with the dogs?'

'Yes with our dogs!'

'Happen'd I've seen 'im wandering to the village, least 'e came down the path! Must 'ave forgotten to tell 'ee, Miss'. He pointed towards a brandy bottle on the corner shelves. 'A drop would be most welcome with the chill and damp in me bones, Miss. Been there since the trenches, the chill and the damp. But you'd know naught about that, living here all snug and comfort like, wud ye, while us brave men suffered. So you wudn't deny a man a bit of pleasure?' He rubbed his rough hands in an expansive gesture.

June remained silent and listened for her brother. She reached up for the brandy bottle.

In a flash it had vanished from her hand. She was startled, then angry. 'I expect manners. Mr Brewis, when you are in this house.' Her temper flared momentarily. 'So if you can't oblige, take your food and get out!'

'Same old spirit as the boy, although he was not half so pretty,' he said with a coarse laugh putting down the bottle after a prolonged swig, so that minute droplets of brandy sprayed from his mouth. 'A bit of a limp squid I used to call him.'

June reacted in a flash.

'Get out now! You disgusting man! Do you hear!' And then quietening her voice so as not to alarm the old woman upstairs, said as calmly as possible, 'Just go please!'

He pressed his face close to hers and she could smell the drink on his stale, foetid breath. His head was thick on a short neck and it stood bolt upright in anger.

299

He grabbed her hair and aimed his fist at her face. The kitten and cat scattered.

June felt a sharp pain in her scalp as her short hair broke free, but she managed to dodge under the blow and swiftly put the table between herself and the man.

There was an uneasy silence only broken by the kitchen pans trembling on the dresser. She held her breath and tried to think.

Feigning to the right, she tried to throw the attacker off guard. He moved with overpowering, outstretched arms to stop her exit into the front room. Standing there menacingly, like a huge bird of prey.

Not a word was spoken. Only the pans continued to tinkle against each other. While his eyes never left her face.

But she whipped round so suddenly and then darted to the side that for a moment he was left astonished. In a flash she was through the side door, the one that looked like a cupboard, and into the dairy. She almost slipped in her haste, then steadied herself in an instant. She ran down a short passage and into the byre.

June bolted the second door behind her, the one at the end of the passage. For a moment she felt safe and waited, hands on hips, to collect her breath. Where were the dogs – she listened intently hoping to hear Russell returning. But there were no sound of the dogs.

Suddenly she thought 'What to do next?' Into the fields; or up on to a high beam with a pitchfork in hand?'

As she darted forward, she struck the cheese-press so that it jangled into the gloom, startling her for a moment before a roll of thunder drowned its noise. She puzzled, but did not have long to make up her mind.

There was a faint scratching at the dusty byre window.

Through the cobwebs grinned the Butcher, his face bleached by brightness of the lightening flash.

She rushed to the main door and flung across the bolts. 'How stupid not to have thought of this straight away.'

But the respite was short lived because there followed a blow from the huge fists and the bolts gave.

Suddenly the Butcher was in the byre, barely visible in the darkness. But the girl heard his heavy boots scraping the floor as he slowly approached, thick army belt in hand, breathing excitedly; and Corporal Brewis prepared to attack.

June looked wildly round. There was no escape, the door behind her she had just bolted. The door ahead was barred by the grinning man.

She thought at once of the long pen at the end of the byre and escaping into the field.

While she rapidly assessed the situation, he swung the belt and it whistled over her head by a fraction. June had no option to protect her face other than grabbing hold. The belt coiled like a snake round her wrist. She pulled as hard as she could but his grip was too powerful. She was almost spun off balance. But as she turned the leather uncoiled and she was free.

Brewis laughed loudly; a deep throaty laugh as he bounded forward and ripped at her pink cotton blouse. It broke from her back as she tried to sprint away. For a moment he held her captive again. Then it tore to the waist.

But he was too strong and fast and June suddenly felt an overwhelming fear, which sapped her strength; as if paralysed. She trembled in desperation. In a second he held her by the waist, and his huge arms plucked her into the air.

Brewis had gained his objective. He forcibly flung her over the four horizontal bars and into the pen; and she landed at a sharp angle on the deep straw, striking her head and her right hand against the side wall. A searing pain shot through her wrist.

She felt concussed and her right hand refused to move. In a daze she tried to push herself up with her left hand.

In a flash he was over the five-foot tall bars, roaring and laughing. 'Worth the bloody war this'll be, worth every stinking minute.'

June was still half on her side and in pain. However, summoning up every ounce of strength, she kicked his right groin as hard as she could.

He roared with rage. And the roar brought a rustling sound from darkness of the field; a sound that slowly closed on the open paddock door.

Brewis did not seem to hear. June, summoning all her will-power, hurled herself through the bottom two bars.

Then Brewis spun round in surprise. 'So another bloody Norman's arrived, cocky and good cannon-fodder like the other fool.'

But there was no reply.

The only sound was a sickening crunch.

The sound of compressed ribs bursting one by one. The Butcher stood back to the wall.

The bull stood head to the wall and it was no contest.

The khaki trousers kicked wildly for a short while as the torso was transfixed by the broad brow with the horns rested on each side.

And as quickly and as silently as it began, the legs went limp.

June tried to be composed although she shook

violently in every limb. She ran behind the back of the pen and with a pitchfork chased the Ayrshire bull into the field where it roared defiantly in the blackness.

Dragging the attacker into the paddock she dropped him on the ground. She let the animal playfully roll the huge, lumpy rag-doll of a man around for a few minutes.

There was surprisingly little blood. The stained top straw was pitch-forked onto the heap.

When Russell returned he sat down by the fire and asked about the bull. Wondered whether to keep it or not. Perhaps the attack on the old farmer was a one-off thing. 'Doesn't look like a rogue to me.'

June said she had decided to defer judgement until the next day. She was sitting at her desk trying to look as if she was doing her accounts although still shaking. 'You know Russell, always when things go right, something else has to balance it up by going wrong. Why? I'll never know. True happiness is only possible in an ideal world. The War was an ideal, and that failed.'

Russell was too tired to think deeply but asked about his cocoa.

'Make it yourself', replied June still trembling, 'it's been one hellish night.'

The unknown man had no papers and was classed as 'being of no-fixed-abode' by the Coroner. 'Probably a deserter seeking shelter in the byre or going to rob the house! Unlucky! The bull had to be put down.' Everyone else in court agreed.

June said nothing but prayed fervently in the church. The Reverend Clenham prayed at the same time. He held her clasped hands while he said a special prayer; and he never mentioned the matter again.

Chapter 52. Another bargain.

The old man, half blind with age and considerably deaf reached for the half-boiled kettle and tentatively placed it back on the side of the range. 'No tea! I was hoping you would stay a bit.' He held out a thin hand in a sudden gesture of goodwill and then withdrew it abruptly.

'No tea thanks. I'll be on my way.'

'No tea,' said the man in a thin voice, 'and no sale.'

'You're correct Mr Chivers. I am afraid, "No sale!"'

The old man shook his head. 'Your father and me were school pals those seventy odd years back. My dad taught him to ride. It was a bay gelding about...'

'Mr Chivers, I love to hear about my family but business is business in this new competitive age and it is "No Sale!".'

The old man with an arched back looked at the girl with a curious sorrowful expression and sighed. 'You used to bring the eggs as a little un June, you did. What a picture you were and right proud was James Norman.'

'Mr Chivers, I have always enjoyed coming here, rain or shine, apart from that old ram who tried to head-butt everyone and everything, and who gave a bit of spice to crossing the low fields. But the ground is too damp for my use. All right I could put hill cattle and a few ewes on it but I am after bigger things.' The old man sat silent for a short while.

The room was damp in the February air and the small scattering of snow remained on the dyke backs. Winter had not yet passed. He looked around at the old byres with their faded red tiles, part broken in some areas where the timbers showed through. A few firs patrolled a narrow horse-pond and the dip was topped by a crumbling stone wall. He collected his thoughts. 'I was hoping…'

'I know you were hoping for a sale. I fully realised that when you sent for me. But…'

'You gave me hope June,' he interjected, 'for a sale in these hard times, money's scarce and the animals have almost gone. I can only feed a few now.'

'Mr Chivers, please understand. I came partly out of politeness. George Havelock said you wanted to sell to me and I said I was a bit interested. But I knew the land was too damp. Still, I came and that's my answer.'

'No sale June?'

'No sale! Except the shorthorn heifer! Not the one in calf. That can be yours. I have a friend who would give you two pounds, but I'll make it five for old time's sake. And do not ask for another penny!'

The old man gave a slow smile. 'And tea?'

'At that price a full cup will suit me nicely. And, I tell you what, I will do my best! Do not doubt it! I'll try to find a way to help.'

Twenty minutes later June had left feeling pleased that she had got this encounter over. She crossed the lower fields down to the burn. It was a three mile walk and in the solitude her mind wandered back to the days she used to deliver the eggs.

Those were her first errands for the farm.

Her father did not mind, he even encouraged her, proud of his daughter he used to say; and how mother smiled when she completed the first task. She had held the basket of eggs like gold. Afraid some might spill out. What relief she had experienced when she returned, money clenched tightly. How Grandma had been stern with her admonitions about safety as she left and how she hugged her when she got back.

There was sweetness in the few pennies she had earned then, more sweetness than the thousands that rolled in now. She crossed the burn and strolled along the damp rushes by its side. 'Curious how the land changes month by month,' she thought, 'it should have permanence about it, but it hadn't the brownness of the bracken, decayed and slumped - the dead fingers of hogweed, brittle and bent by the harsh winter's wind. She looked up to the distant fells. Still desolate and depressed; it often seemed that summer would never come.

She tossed a pebble in the water and watched the ripples fade one by one. 'Julian had that childish trait; forever throwing small pebbles into the brook and scattering the trout and heron.' It was the first time for weeks she had thought of Julian. Strange how that tiny inconsequential gesture of throwing a stone, in that briefest of moments, suddenly caused a pang of regret, a glimmer of missing him! 'He said he would return, only a few letters and that was all. No news for years and the dales had almost forgotten him, until harvest time. Then he was on everybody's mind and lauded to the skies'.

As she climbed the steep hill she saw the church ahead, half-hidden by the trees, some of which were trimmed and cut into shape. As she approached there was a sudden compulsion to relive the past. She hesitated for a few seconds almost afraid to confront her past. Collecting herself June pushed open the large oak door with the brass handle, surprising chill in her grasp. It groaned and creaked within.

The church was cold and still as death.

She shivered and wrapped her long black coat around her body. The grey February light was strong enough to appear as a myriad of colours as it shone through the stained glass windows. 'Suffer the little children to come unto me.' The immobile Christ and his small gathering seemed to arrest her gaze. The simplicity of the message; the love in the craftsmanship within and around, the smoothness of the pews, the arched grandeur of the carved stone; there was nothing so beautiful in her Wesleyan Chapel, a place she had ignored for the last six years. She felt a slight twinge of conscience.

She gazed along the nave and slowly walked down the aisle where she had the last meaningful meeting with Julian. She looked round, half-expecting him to be there. After a short pause she sat down on a wooden pew in the middle close to the aisle. More and more her mind turned to that encounter. She thought of his anger which had completely taken aback; his harsh voice which somehow seemed to still echo in the nave, each outburst getting fainter and more hollow... 'Where have you been, for God's sake? This is absolutely indefensible! Every time later than the time before! Could you ever be a doctor's wife?' And the forced laugh. 'In a dress, looking like that! Have you had no regard for my work? If you think I'm the next best thing to a farmer, forget it. Some people, you know, have a busy schedule, which you obviously haven't'. His tirade had gone on and on, initially shocking, then distressing and finally she went as cold as now... and as indifferent.

In her mind his voice swept round the building, swirling down the aisle, and crashing round the nave. She clasped her hands on her ears and held on tightly. In a few moments silence and stillness returned, and she felt as if she had just suffered a terrible dream. Yet it had only shaken her temporarily and she felt calm as she contemplated the colours playing on the alter cloth; in some respects fortified by the experience. 'I would never have asked him to stay. I never wanted any favours really.'

This aberrant thought gave her consolation. The incident seemed small and pale now. She knelt down, the roughness of the hassock contrasting with the softness of her skin. She prayed to forget not for forgiveness, to harbour no resentment.

June arose and left the church to its solitude. 'Yet he had been so wonderful for most of the time,' she argued with herself, 'so wonderful.'

With that conflicting emotion she descended the hill and crossed the Waggoner's Bridge and headed for Low Green Farm.

Vera saw her coming and had already opened the door. In her late thirties, with her hair pulled back, she was a brunette who was adorning herself prematurely with flecks of wiry grey and a jealous spinster manner. Her thin mouth did little to relieve the hard impression she gave on first meetings, her features were gargoyle-set like stone. It was a curt, 'Hallo'.

June was generally unaware of her beauty. Many other women, including Vera were very aware of June's charm, and found it a subconscious, insufferable barrier.

June hesitated before she walked in. 'Your father has improved?' she inquired politely without sitting down.

'Greatly, but it has left him frail,' Vera replied sharply and without feeling.

'I am sorry to hear that,' said June with a serious expression, 'but I have come to see him if I can?'

'No reason why you can't,' stated Vera without feeling. 'Barbara has just slipped down to the village with Mother in the horse and trap. But make it sharp!'

'Oh!' June hesitated. 'I wanted to talk to all four.'

'Whatever for, June?' said Vera her voice rising in amazement.

'On business,' replied June becoming impatient with the waspish sister.

'Father does the business, fit or ill!'

'Well I never', answered June sarcastically, 'I thought it was you and Barbara. But no matter I will be sharp.'

They walked into the back room and old farmer Bowes sat idly on a large wooden chair with a faded shawl around his legs. The room was quite plain apart from a broad, brightly coloured clippy-rug and a heavily carved walnut chest and drawers.

He looked round and smiled. Unlike the girls he always enjoyed June's visits. 'Sit down dear and have some tea. That's a good chair next to me, best Windsor you know, but of course you do… it was your grandfather's. Did I ask about the tea?'

'Yes, you did, 'replied June laughing and settling back. But no thanks Uncle Arthur! I have already had some.' She paused. 'Tell me, have you ever thought of selling the farm,' she added quickly, anxious to get to the point of her visit; feeling uncomfortable nonetheless.

Vera stepped back in amazement.

The farmer rubbed his chin ruefully, 'Often in the last three years. Few people make a living on the land these days, except you.' He reached out and took her hand firmly. 'Speak out June and have thy say.'

Vera stepped forward but was waved back by the old farmer. 'Whist woman!' was all he said.

'Uncle Arthur! You have good land, that's not in doubt. But who is to farm it, now you are not as strong,' she spoke slowly choosing her words carefully, 'as you were. Now, I'm not throwing you out!'

Vera snorted but held her peace.

June ignored her. 'Mr Chivers is frail and wishes to move from Christmas Common back into his younger sister's place in Cranford Dale.'

She stopped to allow the farmer to study her words. He straightened up in the chair but did not reply until he had pursed his lips a few times.

'Go on,' and he waved his hand once more.

June looked up and smiled. 'There are three good bedrooms.'

'Yes, but the lands damp!'

'I know it's damp,' said June firmly, 'and I don't want to offend, but you'll not need to farm it. You're going to retire there and rest. The views are amongst the best in the land, never mind the Vale.'

Vera's bitterness mounted.

The farmer looked out of the window and rubbed his chin ruefully. 'That's true!' He said nothing for a minute; nodded and then, 'How much?'

'A fair price!'

'To you no doubt,' yelled Vera.

'Quiet woman or leave the room, you're first cousin to a banshee, I'll be bound,' snapped the farmer, 'How much?'

'A thousand!'

He threw the rug onto the floor kissed the girl and said 'Done!'

Chapter 53. Going home, once more.

'Just think, Grandma, going home once more.' June clapped her hands in glee and hugged the Matriarch, who looked slightly bemused with the excitement.

'To Low Green where I was born! True child, t'is true. And a merry day this is! I expected it would be my spiritual home when I passed on, but we're going back to that old easy comfort of my youth. No more of those westerly gales that make these old walls wail and shudder. No more winter's rage or the old hail battering the windows. It be more sheltered up there, 'least that's how` I recall it so.'

'I have loved it here Grandma, but there are so many memories, and too many are sad. Mother would have been so pleased. I bet she never thought the day would dawn when I would own half the land on one side of Compton Vale, that's if you include the woods, and before twenty five!'

Grandma Wetherall hugged the girl. 'Who says beauty and brains don't mix. If he does, the man's a fool!'

'You know Grandma, I never think of myself other than what I am. There are faults enough in my face, heaven knows.'

'God bless the child for her modesty and talking nonsense at the same time. June there must be a man for you, and he doesn't know how lucky he is!'

June smiled and whisked up the kitten as it entered the room. 'Martin wrote of a man called Taffy once and I think we will change it a bit and call her Toffee because she's a cinder colour'. She kissed the cat, and put it down despite the feeble entreaties for more.

'You and your cats, June; you'll be getting more selfish and demanding like them everyday if you're not careful.' But the Matriarch laughed as she said it.

Meanwhile Russell was out on the top fields mending a gate. The light was good although the sun was often hidden by wind-driven scudding clouds. So the morning gloom was capricious, one moment grey, followed by a period of brilliance

It was in one of these February blue sky moments that he heard the familiar sound of the postman's whistling as he came cycling along.

'Any news, Harry?'

'Only a letter from Oxford. Couldn't read it cos it was sealed,' he said honestly. 'Probably from Mary, though. She's not written for a fair while, I can't recall seeing that frank, well… not since I got my new bike anyway, which is a few years, now let me see..'

But Russell waved him on with a long laugh, 'You're not often wrong Harry, I'll say that!' The dogs watched the postman cycle into the distance, anxious to give chase, especially intrigued by the whistle. 'Aye, probably from Mary, no doubt,' he thought.

But for once they were both wrong.

June open the letter and gave the postman a drink of warm milk. He hung around inquisitively, but she shooed him off the premises when the glass was empty.

She quickly read and then re-read it. She put it in her pocket and picking up some washing climbed the stairs to the chest on the landing.

Compton Vale stretched out as usual below and a few rooks had returned. But only a few since the plantation had been felled. They hung in the half-light in twos and threes, swirling, tumbling and flapping long wings. But the valley seemed much quieter now. The first yellow of the daffodils cut a line through the snow still gently heaped against the cobblestone yard wall. A few ducks and hens scratched around. It was becoming a serene winter day as the arctic blue of the sky developed as the last clouds dispersed.

June went into the bedroom and lay on the bed. The sky was reflected in a large oval mirror with prism shaped edges that sparkled the light as a fine halo around the plainer glass. She looked at herself, first full face and then profile. Was she so pretty? Men stared. Had done for years. But so what? There was always that awakening period in every woman's life when men took extra notice, extra attention. And when they tried too hard... that curious, male self-conscious preening like strutting dogs or mating stallions, it amused her. How gawkish some men were, how domineering or condescending they could be! Was a woman so inferior in God's sight? But she provided the rib in the first place. Perhaps Eve should have stamped on the apple! So why should it be a man's world. Or was it! What did the Vicar say, 'Times would change, the men had gone! A generation was lost.'

She slipped off the bed and looked into the glass. She saw no lines. No coarsening of the features. No puffiness around the lower eyes from lack of sleep, strain or overwork. 'Perhaps I have good features. But what about my inner self! Did anyone notice the person within, the person who lived and thought behind the looks?

Fed up with such contemplation June looked in the wardrobe and pulled out a crimson silk dress with a softly gathered skirt flowing to a ruffled hem, holding it in front of herself for effect. She could not resist pulling on the dress, flicking her short hair to surround the outline of her face and setting her expression into a superior smile. She stood back from the mirror so that the half-light of the room seemed to shimmer around her as it slanted from the window.

June Norman felt beautiful and a woman in control of her power and her destiny. Suddenly she remembered the letter lay on the top of the blanket chest on the landing.

She read it for the third time.

At first she had presumed it was from Mary. She had paused before she opened it. 'Why had she not returned to visit them?' June could not guess. And her correspondence had been so irregular during the last few years. She shook her head both in sorrow and annoyance.

But how strange; a friend of Martin's!

She had heard that before! She shuddered slightly and clenched her teeth; a friend wishing to live in the country for the summer, to escape to tranquillity after the ravages of war.

His letter was brief and courteous. He had heard that some rooms at South Hadley Farm might be available; had met Mary at a point-to-point near Woodstock; been given the address and awaited a reply.

June put down the letter and changed back to her everyday clothes and went downstairs. Settling on a stool by the fire she then read it out loud to the Matriarch who nodded at salient points.

'What do you think Grandma?'

'Too much eye make-up gilds the lily,' she replied with a shaking of the head, 'there's no need....'

'Oh! Grandma Wetherall. Away with you! Weren't you listening? I mean, what about the man wishing to rent the farmhouse for four months with a view to extending?'

'It's a capital plan.'

June smiled. 'We will charge what I consider a fair rent, but only after I've doubled it. He is a man of means. A Captain of the Guards! But a strange name, if history serves me right. Thomas Cranmer! Captain Cranmer, we mustn't make him a martyr, must we?'

The old lady laughed and said nothing. She had seen it all before.

314

Chapter 54. The new thatch.

The little boy, still young for ten, stared fixedly at the man, an unflinching, innocent gaze in his large brown eyes. June stroked the top of his brown waving hair, some spilling about his face, and asked him what he was about? 'Just watching', he replied quietly and with a childish honesty, 'just watching Tom thatch.'

Those eyes of yours are forever peeping out, David MacKenzie, what they take in is another matter.'

'Most things,' added the boy laughing after a short pause to study the question, having glanced up into the girl's smiling face.

June knew that he had a lonely life after the death of his mother. 'You're not for feeding the hens or the ducks today?' she asked sweetly.

The boy was puzzled and rubbed his hands. 'Would you mind if I watched Mr Wallthwaite for a minute or two, June?'

'Not a bit, David, but you'll be wanting to become a thatcher next, you mark my words, and I was keeping you for the farming.'

The thatcher laughed. 'Sometimes we're up in the world and at other times were down, but we're always atwistin' and aturnin'.' He picked up a bundle of long soft straw. The heafty yealm (*a bundle of straw arranged in a long row) was laid precisely in position on the farmhouse roof and, with a twisting hand, expertly and firmly tied to the battens next to the eave. Many of the layers of long straw were already secured with hazel rods.

'You see this straw,' asked Tom looking down from the roof at the small boy who seemed even more diminished in size by the perspective. 'It'll last for twenty five years'.

The boy responded quickly, 'I'll be almost thirty six then Tom and married.'

'How do you know you'll be tain?' queried Tom with a slapping of the straw to finalise its position.

'Aren't most people?' replied the boy.

'Well June's not and she's pretty enough, 'argued the thatcher at length.

'She could be soon,' the boy called up, 'and anyway you're tain and, if you don't mind me saying you're not half so good looking.'

'Okay, young David you have a point. I'll concede that! See this, it's a leggat for smoothing out the straw.' He held up a rectangular wooden block on a short handle with deep grooves in its facing. 'This is a bit too big to comb that tousled mop of yours, but it'll fair beautify t'old thatch. Then we rake her down and finally... see these shears... we fashion it off into good clean edges.'

'Have you ever clipped sheep,' asked the boy looking at the shears, 'Russell promised me a go this summer, so that's three months to go.'

'You're a keen one for the figures, David, but mathematics and me sort of went our different ways when I was seven and we've never become acquainted again… other than at the dartboard and I subtract sort of subconsciously for some reason.'

The boy stood silently for a few minutes while the thatcher toiled. David returned to a former subject. 'I suppose not all farmers' daughters get married, the two, Vera and Barbara, who have moved into farmer Chiver's old house are not wedded as yet.'

The thatcher looked down and laughed. 'Some people lead lonely lives, others full and happy ones, depending on the constitution. Some like old Angus gets wed almost weekly! For my mind June'll marry when the time's ripe.'

'Could be soon,' said the boy earnestly once more.

'You seem to be aprophesying like old Ezekiel, David. But why I don't know.'

'Well', said the boy slowly, 'there's a Captain coming to this house tomorrow, if you're done, and that would be a fine match. One of my books has a soldier hero marrying a rich and lovely squire's daughter and she wasn't half as beautiful as June.'

'I heard that young man,' said June wagging a strict finger but laughing as she came out of the farmhouse, 'and I will have a small wager with you that if I marry this Captain you can have South Hadley Farm, thatch and all.' All three burst into laughter for a good while.

The boy looked into the smiling face of the girl and shouted 'Tom!'

'What!'

'You had better make a good job of that thatching because I could be the owner and around here for the next few years.' Then he ran off to feed the hens while the ducks splashed under the tap in the cobblestone yard.

Chapter 55. A new arrival.

Grandma Wetherall looked with suspicion, her expression darkening, her grey eyebrows pulled canopy low over her blue eyes.

'I don't like the thought of it much,' she said to herself, crisping the bacon in the hot pan and filling the spacious kitchen of Low Green Farm with a delicious aroma. 'No! And I don't like the look either!'

'What are you muttering about Grandma,' sang out June from the kitchen doorway as she entered with a brisk step.

'That new fangled thing on the wall.'

'That new fangled thing, Grandma dear, is called a telephone. It rings and you speak into the mouthpiece suspended there (she pointed half way up the wall, in the direction of the front room) slowly and clearly.'

'What if I can't speak slowly or clearly, it's not in my nature. Anyway, what's that ear-trumpet bit, dangling on the fancy cord! How can anyone hear a bloomin' word through some string, it's like the toys we had as a child with two tins and a bit of rope,' she added emphatically.

'Say what you will, but it works and,' said June solemnly, 'it will make us our fortune.'

'You've gold enough, honey,' replied the Matriarch spilling the bacon onto the bread cut thickly, letting the fat soak into the brown slice.

'Not quite enough! The two tractors and three wood-wagons are proving expensive to buy, never mind the new trailer.'

'Lord bless us! What with a tractor rattlin' about the place and the telephone aringing every minute it'll be like Bedlam, and that's for sure!' She sat down and ground the bacon between her teeth in exasperation.

'Stuff and nonsense, Grandma, 'it's progress.'

'If that's progress… well stop the world I want to get off. Progress… progress at a price, ask Vulcan. He's retired now. Soon the dales will look at a horse with awe as if it came from another planet, you mark my words.' The Matriarch tapped her fork on the plate side and rocked in the old Windsor chair.

June smiled and walked back into the front room. She sat down and surveyed her books. The Reverend Clenham was expected shortly before eight and since it was a sunny March day, she felt he might be early. She stared at the pages turning them slowly one by one and noting the change in her fortunes. 'Almost ten thousand pounds once,' she thought, 'but a slight decline recently.'

She looked out the window and across the fields towards South Hadley Farm. She had no regrets on leaving it, the excitement of her new life was compensation enough without the good fortune and riches. She stared into the large mirror above the long sideboard. The grey glass did not flatter her. She felt anxious for her hair was untidy and her face slightly pale from a long night's bookkeeping. She had not dozed off until two in the morning.

She definitely did not look her best. 'Anyway, it's only the Reverend Clenham who is coming,' she mused.

There was his familiar knock. The vicar was punctual as usual. June ran to the door, scattering the kitten.

She stepped back in surprise.

The Captain gave a slight military bow and smiled pleasantly. 'Miss Norman? I'm Thomas Cranmer, Tom to my friends. I am pleased to meet you in person, especially after all I have heard from Martin.'

For a second June forgot herself, caught unaware by the handsome face, kind expression and military bearing. In her confusion she was in danger of keeping the Captain waiting on the doorstep forever. Then the Matriarch's call of 'Who is it?' defused the situation. 'Oh! Please come in and have some coffee and breakfast if you have not eaten.' There was slight nervousness in her voice. He looked attentively at her, himself slightly abashed.

He also collected himself. 'That is most kind', he said instinctively looking away. His brown eyes sparkled with good humour and his affable smile put the girl at her ease.

'Who is it, honey?' repeated Grandma Wetherall between mouthfuls, noting the unfamiliar voice and pronounced accent.

'A friend of Martin's, Grandma,' she paused, 'the gentleman who is renting the farmhouse.'

'Well, don't let him hang about outside, bring him in,' shouted the old lady quite unconcerned and instantly putting the stranger at ease, 'and he can have the last of the bacon, with a couple of eggs - fresh laid tell him,' she added by way of explanation.

The Captain strode into the kitchen, warmly greeted the Matriarch, who after surveying him intently for twenty seconds as if he was a prize ram, was on her feet and frying the eggs within the minute. 'We do them lightly here, Tom,' said the old woman without turning her head, 'keeps the yellow soft and running and the white firm. No crinkling the bottom either, it spoils the feel of it in your mouth.'

The Captain agreed and glanced round at June who was looking out of the drawing room window for the Vicar.

'You from Hampshire, Tom? That's where that boy used to eat live bees, 'least the Reverend White recorded it so. How they didn't fettle his throat is beyond my comprehension. We'd better stick to bacon and eggs. We're more predictable in the North but no less interesting.' And they both laughed heartily for several seconds.

Their enlightened discussion was interrupted by another knock on the door. This time it was the Reverend Clenham. He greeted the soldier warmly too. 'I am so glad to meet you. I will be most interested to hear your views and experiences about the War, one evening when you have time,' he said politely. 'You must come to the Vicarage. The events have been so momentous it is almost

320

difficult to take them all in.' He paused and stared ahead for a short while.

The Captain said he would be only too pleased to visit whenever it was convenient for the Minister. But he spoke stiffly and with some reserve on the matter which the Matriarch noted, but she let pass in her preoccupation with the eggs, one of them getting slightly overdone in the delay.

June and the Vicar sat down in the front room. They heard the Captain laughing heartily from time to time at the Matriarch's anecdotes and her familiar fork-tapping for effect. She returned to the olden days of tenant farming, with its free sheep-stray or right to graze the blackfaced on the moors, the quantity of peat allowed for fuel and the amount of ling which could be cut for kindling; matters that were discussed at length; while the problems that ensued were embellished with more laughter. To the Matriarch such former times seemed by far the best, and the most bountiful.

June tried to ignore their laughter, concentrating on an explanation of the financial situation, her mind composed and business-like. 'This is the vexing situation. Almost three thousand spent on wagons and equipment, and a thousand on land purchase, but I still need the offices; probably at the bottom of Cranford Dale where they would be close, within twenty miles of the City. That would be at least another thousand and a half. Can we afford it all?'

The Reverend Clenham put his head in his hands for a minute and cleared his throat a few times. Then he tugged at his large ears and gazed out of the window with the sun illuminating every feature into light and shade. 'We must be cautious June and not overstretch ourselves,' he said firmly. 'Is it extravagance or not? Let me think!'

There was another pause and he stood up and paced around the room. He rested his broad hands and bent over the window-sill, his tall body stooping, his head close to the glass. He gazed at the patch of moors behind. 'Well, that is good news!' he laughed, 'the first migrant, a wheatear (*a black, grey and white small moorland bird) bobbing on the wall. Summer will be here soon.'

'And the swallows,' June added happily.

'And the bills; work bills, I mean,' he corrected himself with a laugh. 'But we must press on. That tiny bird can make thousands of miles against the odds, desert, ocean, gales and hawks, so we can overcome all obstacles in our path as well. A sign from nature's store.' He sank back into the chair. But only for a moment!

There was another period of pacing round the room. June needed some inspiration and she watched the Minister intently. The soldier's existence was forgotten.

'Everybody is after the woods now. There's hardly an acre without someone measuring up,' he said decisively.

She nodded and instinctively screwed up her mouth and ruffled one side of her dark hair.

'I know,' replied June gloomily having paused to reconsider the situation, 'except... except the three thousand acre spread by Sprawling Hills Lake in that long, sheltered valley behind Christmas Common. But it's too bleak up there and steep. But most of all, there is no road. To build one for the lorries would cost a fortune, we would have to blast out part of the ravine to get to the lake, the bit with the waterfall, as well as work though masses of large boulders. I cannot see any profit in that wood, nor can anyone else. But it's some prize and going cheaply from an estate that is selling up because all the sons were killed in the fighting.'

Suddenly the Minister paced with a livelier step. 'You have got it June,' he said almost shouting with pleasure, 'we will blast out the narrow part of the ravine, just a short forty yard stretch.'

'And then...?'

'Then we can partly dam the river back and float the trunks down to where the road begins, it is markedly shallower there and it will act as a natural break on the floating logs. They do it in Canada all the time, so why not here!' He rubbed his hands with joy. 'We do not need much depth of water, three to four feet will do, and that's easily achieved even without the floods.'

'That's true enough,' said June jauntily, 'a log at a time, guided down for just under a mile, picked up at the reach and hey presto... we're in clover!'

They heard the Captain depart by the kitchen door, not wanting to disturb the meeting, and he left his best wishes and hoped to see Miss Norman and Mrs Wetherall again soon.

Then the young boy arrived from the village to feed the poultry. But June was too busy to see him. She was on the telephone once the Minister had gone and speaking normally, to the amazement of the Matriarch who took a cautious peep into the front office room. 'Pity you can't hear the reply,' she thought shaking her head, 'still half a loaf is better than none at all.'

She winced when she heard the figure of eight hundred pounds mentioned, even more when it rose to thirteen hundred. But June seemed very pleased when she put down the telephone to the agents.

She ruffled her tousled hair and her large eyes looked even larger. 'With luck, Katy,' she said kissing the cat, 'we are going to multiply that figure four times, let's say in round numbers… five thousand pounds. At this rate we will own this valley and the next one, bye and bye. And you, 'she gave the cat another kiss, 'can dine on caviar, with the Captain, if you'd like to. He seems quite nice. But with me in this state,' she looked in the mirror, 'Goodness knows what he thought.'

The Captain was still chuckling as he crossed the upper fields. He had not enjoyed himself so much and felt so relaxed for years. Thus, at least, one woman had impressed him... in the confines of Low Green Farm.

Chapter 56. The first signs of spring.

Most of the village was against it. Russell had heard the disquiet when he was helping the blacksmith John Turner who had damaged his wrist earlier that morning; and the farmer said he would help.

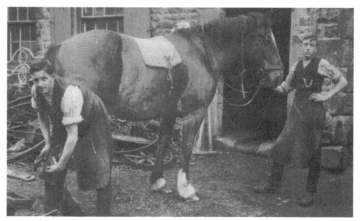

'Mind where thou's puttin' the nails, Russ; the shoes must fit perfectly, there's no two ways about it.' His forge was cut off by a narrow stretch of the river, which served for cooling the iron and watering the horses.

'You've never said a truer word, John,' replied Russ in a careless manner as he picked up the back leg. 'For the Lord's sake, why do these animals always have to lean all their weight against you?'

The blacksmith smiled and went to have a pipe sitting on a discarded anvil while his boy held the horse. 'Used to shoe ten horses a day,' the blacksmith said at length contemplating the scene to his satisfaction, 'the ministry's taken' a fair number and it's barely four or five now.' He sighed. 'The materials also gone with the war and I have to make do at times with old cart wheel iron and horse collars. We've got the old reapers, chain-harrows and the like to repair, though; so all's not doom and gloom.'

Russell was getting the shoe hot enough to burn an imprint on the hoof. John had wandered over to check. 'Mind, that sister of yours is doing well, so I hear.'

'Aye, that's about right,' said Russell examining the mark on the hoof. 'When she makes up her mind there's nothing in heaven and earth that can shake it!'

And that is exactly what Grandma Wetherall had said to George Havelock when he arrived at the farm the same morning and had voiced his opposition in no uncertain terms.

But June responded by saying that his criticism and lack of tact had cost him a lucrative job; for she had promised the stone to the village that morning, and the school was to be expanded with an extra room and the church porch was to be elongated for the stormier days. The contract for the stone work went to a firm fifteen miles away; and she brooked no contradiction.

Young David said that his Grandfather was against it, but that he didn't mind, and hoped that this was some sort of consolation.

June smiled and went on with her plans; and the waterfall went away. The blasts rocked the village. The birds took flight and the cows leapt up from the cud-chewing; and the rocks whirled in the air and tumbled with a crash.

So the ravine opened up like a chasm in the ground, and within weeks the stripped pine logs rolled through; and the bank manager smiled and rubbed his hands.

The sawyers toiled and the horses lugged great chains, and the ground was bared for the first time in a hundred years or more.

Crash!

Down came another tree.

Roll and splash!

Down the water gully it went to the waiting wagons.

In all this commotion June had one feeling of anger but none of remorse. The village could hate her if they so wished. There would be no regrets. Why couldn't the tractors reach the wood? That maddened her. She puzzled over various ways, making a huge raft to ferry them across, scraping a temporary road from the other side of the hill. But they lay idle and cost money, and that hurt her more and more; and so the work went on.

It was late April, and the blossoms were fulfilling the early pledges of the spring, each delicate perfume lingering to merge into the other. The higher-rising sun had beckoned and the first swallows chittered overhead at its command as she surveyed the week's work on the plantation. By the beck side she spied the early primroses, violets and stiff petalled daisies. Once she would have spent time and picked them, but time was money and anyway she had the financial strength to buy as many bouquets as she liked.

She checked with the foreman, a shuffling, round backed man with a hollow face but an honest expression. The work was proceeding well and the thirty or so labourers were content in the knowledge of a steady income for at least two years ahead.

Few workers doubted the wisdom of destroying the burn, even if their families felt it was a shame.

June returned to the Vicarage. Checked that the heifer was in calf and took the Top Road, using her pony and trap. Being so busy she had seen little of the Captain other than an occasional 'Hello' although he had visited Grandma Wetherall frequently for afternoon tea and on two occasions collecting the old lady to take her back to South Hadley Farm..

'Keen on poetry and such nonsense,' the Matriarch had told her, not unkindly but with a puzzled air. 'Said he wanted to paint. She suggested he whitewash the farm, to spruce it up. But he said it was too broad a canvas and wondered if her granddaughter would sit for a portrait.'

'What nonsense,' exclaimed June impetuously.

'Don't be too hasty June, 'they have those oil paintings in all the grand manors, you know'.

'Well, if I decide he can, then he has to come here. I want to be near the telephone and work and not fiddling around in the old farmhouse.'

A few weeks went by but he had not replied. So June put it out of her mind.

One day, standing at the yard gate, she watched the sun dash in and out of the clouds in some giant game of hide and seek; while the bouncing lambs with their stiff little gait bounded behind the dyke backs occasionally making a fortress from some protruding stones. Just before she opened the gate a voiced called, 'Miss Norman'.

To her surprise it was the Captain carrying an easel and stand. 'For goodness sake call me June, I feel so ancient being addressed like that!' She tried to speak warmly but there was a slight irritation in her voice.

For a moment he looked discomforted, then brightening up, 'I have come to paint!'

'Not now I hope, not in this outfit!'

''No indeed! The farm from this perspective! I thought you might like it as a gift for Grandma.'

June paused and surveyed the Captain's not unpleasing features and easy smile. Their eyes met and lingered, fixed on each other for a few seconds. He did not feel flustered. She smoothed her dress; then they both looked away. June smiled, 'I think she would like that! She's fickle enough but such a gift would delight her.' June lapsed into dialect. 'Aye, it would at that! What a grand idea.'

He had reached her side and quickly hurried forward to open the wooden gate. 'I felt that you might like your portrait painting.' There was a pause as she brushed passed through the angle of the kissing gate. 'But young David, my only advisor in the matter, said that unless I could almost have it done in Low Green farmhouse, and with the cats on your knee, he emphasised, that I was to forget it, because you were too busy,' the Captain replied.

'That's his interpretation, not mine, it's certainly was not the impression I wanted to give.' June turned and looked at him for a moment and then continued ahead. She suddenly stopped and turned. 'On second thoughts, I will find time to come to South Hadley and you can paint my cats with me. At least they'll look good.'

They both laughed and the horse stamped its feet impatiently. 'Well, that's settled then.' He replied.

'It is!'

'Is there any way you could tell me when…'

'Not at present.' June did not like being tied down by his preoccupation with her portrait and hated being fussed. 'I must be going.' Before he had time to collect himself she turned and cut across the meadow away from the path, flattening a small furrow in the grass with her hurried steps. He had wanted to ask more, but she seemed to vanish almost in an instant, leaving the Captain more in love than ever.

Chapter 57. A short walk, but a happy one.

Although the Matriarch of Low Green Farm had vision that was failing with age she could, in fact, see more than June in one respect. Namely that Thomas Cranmer was in love. 'There's none so blind as those that will not see,' she mused to herself as she watched the young man scanning the fields for the girl's arrival.

In the earlier days he had often taken his leave just before she returned; an abrupt, somewhat nervous farewell. He was excessively careful not to refer to the girl too often or with too much enthusiasm, in spite of his love which swung like a barometer with each visit and departure. His affection was spontaneous but furtive, embracing but concealed, at least he believed so.

This day he was sitting patiently watching the low fire and stroking one of the cats. He was no animal lover, but its proximity spoke of June, and that counterbalanced his natural antipathy.

'June's a pretty girl,' began Grandma Wetherall testing the water, 'but not so fine as her sister Mary.'

She awaited the reaction.

The Captain who had been growing inwardly impatient in his desire to see June looked up suddenly and stopped stroking the cat. He did not reply for a few seconds but gazed at the old woman. He was about to say, 'I find that hard to believe,' when he corrected himself and replied, 'Her sister must be beautiful indeed,' then gazed at the fire ruefully.

'But June's the more wilful, don't doubt it, Tom. She used to lead our boys a merry dance when she was young, always organising the games and such like, and she's just as strong willed now. Like Agnes to a 't'!'

The Captain smiled. He saw the girl approaching and his face suffused with a faint glow not hidden to the watching hawk.

'I must be going and make the necessary preparations, because June is coming to sit this afternoon and it is nearly one o'clock already. There's a chance I will meet her on the way back,' he continued reflectively gazing around the room. 'I will say, 'Hello' to her in the fields.' Although an inconsequential and obvious remark he spoke with sincerity and some feeling. 'She seems so busy these days!'

Grandma Wetherall did not reply but watched the cat leap down from his knee and hop up onto the broad window ledge, chattering at a robin which had settled outside. The scraping of the chair on the stone floor as he got up drew her wandering attention to the present.

'I must be on my way.'

'Come whenever you like,' but her attention was centred on the cat and a glass vase next to it.

'Thank you, most kind,' was his reply which seemed mechanical in his preoccupation of scanning the fields to see if June was coming in.

The old woman watched him depart. She felt sympathy for the ex-soldier, occasioned by the loss of the boys. He had survived and that thrilled her. At least some had survived the dreadful, ruthless war. The recollection of the past time brought a lump to her throat for a moment. She collected herself and smoothed her pinafore. She thought about the past, and the futility of the last few years. Yet he rarely spoke about the war, in a curious way keeping the whole spring of events bottled up inside.

When she had, on occasions, probed him quietly and gently about the trenches, he said little; sometimes he would reply 'that some wounds would never heal, some scars would never fade.' And then go quiet and reflective. In a rare moment he would remark that the peace of the valley was so wonderful after an inferno of guns and bombs. Once, and only once, he had told her that he had a fear of heights, a nightmare from the time when he'd been thrown by an enormous explosion; a blast that spun him down a steep embankment and into a crater. It had given him a fearful sensation of falling forever into the very centre of the earth.

She remembered the look on his face and the long pause. 'I still have nightmares about that fall, you know, years have come and gone but the nightmare keeps haunting me, real and recurring. A horrible sensation of falling and being buried alive in the cascading earth, of dying alone amongst a million men running and walking above, oblivious of my fate, with no breath to call out; just lying there alone.' Suddenly he had collected himself and said more calmly, 'I don't know if they will ever go.'

The Matriarch sat thinking deeply when there was a clash of the heavy oak door and the cats scampering across the room to welcome June.

'Oh bother and blast the drizzle this morning! Look at my hair.' She entered the kitchen shaking her dampness out of it. 'The sooner that car is delivered the better, I'm fed up with a pony and trap.' She did not pause to acknowledge the old woman's reply. 'Damn this weather. I'm due to sit for the portrait again this afternoon, looking like this.' She kicked the back of a wooden stool. 'The Captain saw me and flew off into the distance; probably shocked by the dismal appearance of his subject. Well! I don't blame him!'

The Matriarch waved a lean hand. 'I've been thinking honey.' The girl sat down on the chair by the fire in a defiant mood and warmed her hands. 'Thinking about the Captain.'

June looked curious, and pursed her pretty lips. 'And what have you surmised in that wise old head of yours,' she said laughing.

'More than you would care to hear!'

'More than I.... oh! fiddle sticks. I'm hungry!'

'More than you would care to imagine.' The old woman paused. 'Stop pouting June and listen.'

The girl knew from childhood that the Matriarch was warming up to something good. She listened.

'I have just found out that the Captain's in love!'

June let out a cry of amazement, 'Who with Grandma?' She could hardly control her curiosity.

'Do you really want to know?'

'Oh, don't be so obtuse, Gran, and spare me the suspense.'

'Look in the mirror honey!' stated Grandma Wetherall emphatically. Noting June's expression she thought, 'Obviously she had no suspicions. But a young man of sense and ambition couldn't get a better catch, with her money and the land. I hope that's not his intention.'

June sat quietly, at first appraising the situation, eating her food in silence. But she chewed over the facts one by one. The old woman had related past conversations word for word; and June was irritated; his vagueness, his nervousness, his attentiveness all irritated her now! If he had decided that Compton Vale was to become his refuge from the world and all its problems past and present, she was definitely not going to become the support for his future life? She looked up, caught the eyes of her grandmother for an instant and whispered to herself, 'Never!' She now finished her meal in silence.

After lunch June crossed the fields with a measured tread, her mood anything but generous. Her opinion and attitude of the captain had suddenly taken a turn for the worse. Oddly enough she did not begrudge him her company until then. The coming and goings, the stiff politeness had amused her in a strange, endearing way. Being with him had an ambience of Martin and that pleased her a lot.

The drizzle had stopped and the sun was hesitant in its moods, patchily yellow and diffuse. She yelled at Russell who was checking the new born lambs, his arms covered in a fine, bloodstained slime from a recent delivery. By his feet the tiny, fleecy-form was being lovingly lick-nibbled by its mother.

Sorrel raced across the fields towards her in a mad dash and bounded about her waist with delight. 'Get down Sorrel...get down! You'll muddy my dress and that's the last thing I need!'

Seeing the dog's crest-fallen gaze she patted it on its black and white brow. 'So you don't know that I'm his intended Sorrel, at least that's what he thinks, or you wouldn't try to make me a muddy mess.'

333

The collie paused for a few seconds looking into the girl's face, then turned and raced off to join Sam and his master, alarming a few ewes as he crossed obliquely through the flock. Russell looked up, waved and the girl waved back. She hesitated for a few moments as she reached the old, familiar farmyard, now devoid of poultry and cats. The yard had a curious emptiness that made June suddenly realise for the first time the enormity of her move and the disruption on her family's life. She crossed the cobblestones to the door of South Hadley Farm and politely knocked before entering into the lounge.

He had made a preliminary sketch and the portrait was beginning to take shape, with a background paler shade of blue accentuating the embroidered whiteness of her dress. The outline of the cats was just visible on either side of her lap.

Thomas greeted her stiffly but warmly, trying to conceal his affection but tending to be obviously over-zealous at the same time. June watched him carefully. As she gazed she thought, 'I'm a fool not to have noticed before.' Suddenly the whole situation felt ludicrous and she tried not to laugh but could not stop chuckling to herself. 'I cannot sit today, I'm afraid.'

He seemed taken aback but tried to conceal his anxiety by a forced smile, 'Why not?' There was a hint of desperation in his voice.

'Oh… to tell the truth I'm not happy with it so far,' she said walking away from the painting towards the window and surveying the valley as she used to see it.

'Not happy.' he said in astonishment. 'I have hardly begun.'

'Well, that's a lie, Thomas. But there is a reason.' She continued looking at the hills in the distance.

'What?'

'To be brutally frank, I do not want you to be in love with me.'

The Captain almost fell back with astonishment. But in a second he composed himself. He slowly walked up to the girl and stood behind her. He was about to say, 'Suit yourself' but quickly changed it to 'And why not?' He spoke in the firm, clipped military voice of old.

'For a start and as an end discussion, let me tell you I'm too happy being what I am, and how I am, to require any other emotional burdens, such as love.' She only glanced his way for a second but did not turn round.

'Wordsworth said...'

But June shut him up with a frown. Her brown eyes scrutinized his face without embarrassment. 'Is that all you can say, quote someone who's been dead for two hundred years. Really, Thomas!' She turned to face him. 'There's no need for some eloquent lecture for an explanation, most men around here speak for themselves.' June watched how the last barbs stung.

There was an uneasy silence and June, still feeling firmly in control, laughed. 'If you want to discuss love let us do it in a more agreeable way. There was that feline glint in her eyes that the Matriarch knew only too well but the Captain, perplexed and taken by sudden alteration of expression in her fell into the trap,

'I am willing to discuss the matter... in the church, if you are not afraid to!' The eyes narrowed for a moment, before assuming their full roundness.

'The church, June - For God's sake, why in the church?'

'Well, let me see... it will be the true test of your love, at least getting there will be!' She spoke abruptly, then

335

smiled and stroked the side of his face in a brief gesture of encouragement; and laughed. 'If my reasoning is correct.'

The soldier looked astonished and shook his head. 'If you so wish, to the church, rain or shine. I frankly have no idea what you are taking about, so…'

So…,' June was purring with delight, 'It's fun getting there, just you wait and see!'

They both left the house in a light drizzle. June was not concerned about her appearance, or the portrait, any more. For a moment he tried to take her hand at the stile, but she brushed it aside. Then they crossed the upper fields largely in silence, Thomas Cranmer wondering what other idiosyncrasies the girl would reveal next. He was perplexed, but still fascinated by her brisk purposeful manner and the mischievous glint in her eyes.

He had only to wait a further twenty minutes for the explanation. They climbed the hillside, the drizzle intermittent and punctuated by bursts of cloying rain, the mountain peaks shrouded in a background of overwhelming grey and at times invisible. The Captain walked slightly behind her, occasionally surveying what he could see through the gloom, but generally head down and pre-occupied. The weather made him unsure of the directions but the girl strode on in what seemed to him an endless and pointless journey, and in the increasing gloom a surreal experience.

June paused, slightly breathless. 'There's the church,' she said pointing to the sturdy white outline just visible in the shrouding mist that played about its walls, undetermined whether the true shape of the building would be released at all, 'and there's the path.'

It was the Captain who blanched.

Purposively, June had led him to the side of the

narrow dangerous rake, the path over the cliff-face she had used before, the last time in her haste to see Julian. Thomas stopped and considered his position, he was determined not to lose face but the inherent fear of falling dominated, so that every step took him towards the path. There was a confusion of light and dark as the wind picked up on the rock-face, a confusion that made the situation unreal, but June remained cheerful.

'Come on, Thomas. I've done this a hundred times.' She waited for his nervous expression to change, hoping it would settle, but his features had assumed all the hallmarks of fear. 'Just follow me Thomas, 'she laughed, 'you're not afraid are you? Anyway, we will be in the church in a few minutes, you'll see and all the better for it.' 'She turned towards him still smiling, 'Then we can talk about your love, if you have a mind.'

Stepping onto the narrow ledge June edged forwards, slowly feeling with her feet as she had done before. The wind and drizzle added to the drama, and that amused her more as she looked at the Captain, nervous and tentative. She urged him on with a quick gesture of the hands. The elements swept round her dazzling white dress. Against a back-cloth of black rock, June looked an angel suspended in the mist; as tendrils of spray flew towards them from the long, narrow waterfall that plunged in its enjoyment through a cleft of stone.

Then trees took up their cue, creaking anxiously and erratically beneath her as the burn roared into full spate with the hollow, fading echo of below.

The Captain stood transfixed on the first few yards of the ledge. He watched the girl as she stopped half-way across. Her carefree laugh confused him. For a moment he closed his eyes; then a strange compulsion overwhelmed him. He tried to go but seemed paralysed by fear. She called out, 'Come on, Tom, it's nothing!'

The fear that had manifested itself in every pore by thin beads of sweat, the rapidly beating heart suddenly settled. In an instant he forgot his morbid dread of heights, that eternal falling of his darkest dreams, that spinning into oblivion, with the sickening thud as the bombs exploded around him as he struck the hard earth below.

He heard June encouraging him and quite how he did it, he did not know. But the Captain was suddenly moving forward, purposeful and afraid. He did not look down, nor attempt to look down, but slowly forward towards her. He grasped the vertical rocky face, attempting to find a finger-hold. But none existed in the moisture and slime. He did not even hear the river roaring and racing below. He was just conscious of the wind which seemed to tug at his suspended body, intermittently jerking it away from the narrow path, into a void of destruction.

The Captain halted for a second but as he was aware of a spinning sensation that unexpectedly started to take over and a strange buzzing in his ears. He knew he was about to fall. But a hand grasped his wrist. 'No you don't! You wont fall.'

The Captain's head cleared. He straightened up. He saw June's brown eyes and lips so invitingly close, so very close, that he put his arms round her and kissed her in an impulse.

But June stepped back and without another thought or comment led him across the rake, more determined than ever and they slipped into the church, the scene of her former downfall.

Chapter 58. Another perspective.

With the lovely song of linnet, warbler, finch and cuckoo hidden in the hedgerow, May entered that appointed year of 1919. The countryside was a marvel of brightness and colour. June had never been happier. She lay in her old bedroom at South Hadley Farm and scanned the valley.

Compton Vale had that joyous mood of early summer and the light and shade of the land reflected the rambling clouds overhead. Buttercup yellow were the fields and June pointed to the small pasture, fringed by hawthorn, where her father had first taught her to ride. 'The sweetest Shetland pony and not a bit stubborn or temperamental'; how she loved it so much and how she shed bitter tears when it was sold as she grew older and she became too big to ride it.

The Captain was lying beside her and gently smoothed her dark hair. It had a texture and perfume of its own. He found himself only half-listening in a contented, drowsy sort of way. June laughed as she finished her tale; she suddenly realised how tritely serious she sounded. She reached over and kissed him on impulse and felt the tension in his firm fingers. Then she laughed again and his hand became warm and relaxed, not the least bit like the day on the Rake.

They lay silent and unmoving; June contemplating her life, looking into his smiling, contented face, feeling pleasantly happy while the Captain gazed at her oblivious of her mood; and as he looked he tried to analyse his own emotions. It was, he concluded, a strange feeling of almost helplessness in her presence, as if paralysed by the beauty. But June, he puzzled, could remain so placid, and almost detached in his company. That always bewildered him. 'Was her love more mature than his... less emotional', he found himself thinking and forgetting the present. 'Perhaps she did not love him at all?' He felt a tinge of humiliation, and then a slight panic – the feeling he had just before the attack. The summer light gave a spectral halo to the mirror high on the wall and he stared at the broken colours and listened to the voices of the birds in the trees, the only sound in the room.

June saw him gazing at the mirror and scrutinized his features. 'Do I really love him?' she thought. 'It's not like I imagined, not like before!' Thinking about Julian hardly seemed fair at that moment and she suddenly felt ashamed of herself for doing so. Suddenly she was analysing her emotions. 'Maybe he has fallen in love due to loneliness with no one else around, a sort of inevitable happening. Perhaps, for my part it is only possible to fall deeply in love once in a lifetime.' June paused and looked away. 'What do I really want in this life? '

She pursed her lips as she reached this conclusion. 'Life's funny! There's a chance he'll go away like Julian and in the years to come he would forget.'

June felt uneasy in the once familiar surroundings, her old bedroom. She refrained from imagining how the room used to be, the childish fun she had with Mary. 'If he asks me to marry him, my God, what will I say?' It was a terrifying conclusion, as she felt his arm slide round her waist. Her heart sank. 'That is the last thing I want at the present time, a committal for life. I will have to refuse.'

She was about to say, 'Thomas, I've got to speak to you about something before I go'; then changed her mind.

Thomas was still oblivious to her emotions, concerned solely with his own, watching her, deep in thought. He had given hours of contemplation to the problems, some days it absorbed most of his day, forever at the forefront of his mind. 'She must love me,' he pondered, 'we are so close, and yet there's nothing given in return. I feel each time we meet, but she smiles and sort of acknowledges it. She's an enigma all right. I should not doubt her love, but it isn't very flattering to be ignored. She's always herself and a bit distant but surely one day she'll respond with that final token of her love, her committal to marry, something that still eludes me.'

As the Captain had reached this final conclusion he made up his mind once and for all. He would do everything to persuade her to marry him.

The sunlight struck impulsive and warm across the valley, beamed low across the fields and was tossed heavenward once more by the thousand dancing cups of yellow. He started to speak in a measured voice and June, somewhat lost in thought, looked out of the window. It was a curious vision she had of a white stallion in the distance. The more she pondered the more apprehensive she became. Instinctively she had a feeling that something was wrong. She stood up and as the stallion grew closer she observed a tall figure, turning before the path to South Hadley Farm.

It was instinct alone, but June knew it must be Julian. What made her feel that way after such a long time - she did not know. She was ready in a minute, however, and did not look round, whispering a curt, 'Goodbye'. She left the room and the Captain, perplexed, shrugged his shoulders and sat thinking for a few minutes. Within five minutes there was a loud knocking on the door, and hurried downstairs.

Chapter 59. The dovecote revisited.

June's first instinct was to hide. She made straight for the dovecote and positioned herself at the back of the building, outside but totally hidden from the yard and house. She heard the brief conversation and recognised Julian's voice. Strangely they both sounded very similar - she had not noticed that fact before. More talk, but indistinct, and she strained to hear it but the horse's trampling feet on the cobblestones distorted and drowned the words.

Then there was a click as the farmhouse door closed and followed by more trampling of horse's hooves as the animal spun round before being mounted.

She waited. All would be well in a moment. But she faced a dilemma. Should she return to this farm or go straight home? She pondered the question and looked to the sky for inspiration. Her natural desire was to return to Tom and find out what had been said. Her knowledge of Julian suggested she had to return home because he would probably go straight to Low Green when he found out she had moved. She knew him only too well; he would not be dissuaded from finding her, even if he suspected the worst.

But she was wrong. There was a further staccato movement of the horse's shoes as they turned on the cobblestones. Julian had not mounted, she had been mistaken, and he was leading the animal across the yard; and soon she would be in view.

June looked wildly round. There was no option but to hide in the dovecote. But here she encountered a problem. Over recent months the door hinges had become rusty. She pushed as hard as she could but the door did not move. She pushed again, once more the door stuck.

She perspired, pressed against the wooden frame and cursed her luck. There was nothing else she could do, she had to confront him. She paused and waited, still out of view.

In that instant June felt slightly at a loss, slightly ashamed for some obscure reason; probably because she had tried to run away from him on the spur of the moment.

Then mysteriously, almost ethereally the door creaked in the wind. Small wisps of dust furrowed on the stones. She cautiously pushed again and the hinges relented. Through the small crack she saw that all the birds had gone. There was not a sound inside the tall, hollow building.

June held her breath and listened. The door had not opened sufficiently to let her in; once more she was trapped. However, there were no sounds of approaching footsteps, only the slurp of the horse as it drank at the trough, a regular slurping sound of enjoyment.

She listened intently, had the animal moved a few paces away or to the side? She could not determine. Then to her horror the footsteps moved slowly towards the dovecote door; June became increasingly incensed by her predicament. Self inflicted. What a fool! How stupid could she be!

Again she made up her mind to confront him. She smoothed her hair and looked at her dishevelled dress, with dust and straw about the hem. In desperation she pushed one more time, and the door opened by degrees, the hinges groaning with each jerk. Had he heard it, that iron screech? The horse had stopped drinking, he must have heard it.

June took a deep breath and prepared to face the man

343

she once loved almost to distraction. It was a curious sensation as if he had suddenly hit a raw nerve.

Suddenly a voice rang out. 'Dr Ashleigh.'

It was David MacKenzie. June cowered behind the half-open door and listened.

'Dr Ashleigh.'

There was a laugh. 'Why, it is David, my once-partner's grandson! Well, I never! What a man you have become young Davy. I hardly recognised you.'

The boy rushed up to his old friend. 'But I haven't forgotten you, Dr Ashleigh. I thought it was you on that fine stallion, so I raced over the fields. I was feeding the hens,' he added proudly as an afterthought.

'Come here and let me look at you. I must say you have grown.' He clasped the boy round the shoulders and held him to his side for a moment and laughed. 'How could I forget my companion and playmate of old? How's everyone?'

The boy looked up at the beaming handsome face, with its fair curls still accentuating the fine features. He grinned, lost for a reply in the happiness of the moment. 'The horse is not mine. I hired it from a friend in Cranford. It cuts a dash does it not?'

The boy continued to beam and look at the doctor with admiration.

'Yes sir! I was on my way to your Grandfather's house, but... and here's a little secret like we used to share some time back... I am looking for June. In fact,' he laughed merrily, 'I could say in a round-about way that I am looking for a wife, or,' he lowered his voice, 'I'm hoping for a wife. But, and this is the problem, she may have forgotten me, and then it is no use, is it? So that's my secret!'

June strained and listened, with her anxiety and desperation mounting.

But David was not to be subdued. 'She should be here Dr Ashleigh. I saw her going in, about an hour back. She having her portrait painted, you know, by the Captain and he's putting in the cats.' He was proud of this detailed observation and grinned broadly.

The Doctor laughed. But to June's finer perception it appeared strained.

There was a brief silence. For a few seconds the doctor stood with his back to the horse and glanced round the farm, from the house, to the outbuildings and to the dovecote. He portrayed no emotion.

June leaned forward to hear more, almost appearing for an instant in the shadow of the half-open doorway

There was another silence.

Slowly footsteps moved towards the half-open door. June pressed her body between the back of the door and the dirty wall.

The doctor gave the handle a wrench. But the door jammed. It would not move backwards or forward and the gap was too narrow for him. He kicked the wood hard in exasperation; the door nearly compressed her against the wall. But he did not look in.

With an almighty tug the Doctor attempted to pull it shut, but once more it jammed and the loud bang echoed in the gloom, cascading dust and dead insects onto her hair and forming fine speckles over her clothes.

'If you would like a ride,' she heard Julian say in a composed manner, 'up we go!' A moment later the horse and riders had cleared the farm and when June slowly came out the dovecote, there was no one to be seen either in the fields or in the house.

She was now in a quandary from two points of view.

Her dress was filthy and her hair a mess with dust, straw and dead flies. She did not seek a rebuff from the Captain, as she had experienced in the past with Julian. Perhaps Tom was different, perhaps not! She was taking no chances. She remembered the former irritation, the uncalled for rebukes.

She would head home and, if necessary, accept the consequences of another such meeting with the doctor. Was history repeating itself? She looked down and folded her arms. 'Wasn't it time she buried old grievances? – the humiliation and the bitterness. Yet somehow such things were difficult to forget.'

She clenched her teeth. 'It's ridiculous! Can't they both be my friends? Could she make the effort, forget those silly moments, forget the anger and despair, and remember the loving, the endearing times with Julian. Surely we can be friends?'

That seemed to be the simple solution to her first problem with the Doctor.

But the second threw June into the turmoil of despair. The voice, the kindness, just seeing him again, had ignited the emotional flame she had felt totally extinguished. Suddenly she was overcome with regrets.

Now she had a faint but steady longing to see Julian again. He had not returned as a stranger. Deep inside she knew that she had only to see his smiling face to regain the warmth, her confidence and his love; and it was a long time since she had felt so inwardly excited.

She stamped her feet for a few seconds on the hard ground to clear her head; cursed her luck and her predicament; argued that she had more money and power than either; had more willpower than both, then broke down on the grassy hillock in a flood of tears.

Annoyed by the sudden weakness she decided the one solution was to marry neither of them.

So with a resolute step she crossed the upper fields towards home.

Chapter 60. A messenger in short trousers.

Matters do not always proceed in the selected course of events. Human nature is fickle and prone to irrational change.

June would tell Dr Ashleigh exactly how she felt. Her mind was made up. The matter was irrevocable. They could only be friends. Still she mused upon his constant love after all this time. How had it survived with so many fine ladies around him in London? That thought pleased her vanity and she went over it and over it repeatedly as she got dressed. She had, so she believed, retained her hold over him despite the many challenges which must have come his way.

Nothing had ever given her such an intense feeling of absolute joy as the recent knowing that he was her possession; and with a strange reasoning, she felt she could possess and reject at will, as a cat plays with its supplicant quarry. She smiled, and as she did so, she glanced in the mirror.

Her humour merged imperceptibly into a frown.

Perhaps it was time to lose that boyish look and grow her hair longer. To be more sophisticated, groomed and elegant. But it did wave uncontrollably when it was long and it seemed to take its own course whatever style she chose. That recollection peeved her for an instant. Generally she was disinterested in glamour, looks and fashion, short hair was a practical style when farming; and as for fashion June felt it was simply a way to waste her new found wealth. People in 'society' could throw their money away, but definitely she was not going to; like seed she planted in the spring it had to multiply and grow.

Picking up Katy and placing her on her lap, she surveyed the valley knowing that within a few miles two men were completely dominated by her charms. She was content in the knowledge that she could mould them to her will if she so desired. But she knew that her resolution would mean disappointment for both of them.

If she was confident of her beauty, they could not be confident of her love. Wealth had added other dimensions to her character and in that dimension was a toughness of spirit subjugating the previous innocent and naivety. She was definitely not a country farmhouse girl any more, something they had to understand.

As she walked round the room her eyes sparkled with a new found confidence. But there was to be a surprise and it was not long in coming.

For the hens had to be fed; and it was two days since she had seen David in the presence of Julian. She surmised that he was loath to leave his old friend but would appear after a day or so, perhaps a week, when the novelty had worn off.

But no!

There was the usual shrill, jaunty whistle, commonly out of tune, and the small figure arrived hands in the pockets of his short grey trousers that flapped baggily just below his knees. The hair was tousled and spiky as usual, and he wore a blue Fair Isle pullover with a few obvious clicks from the barbed wire fence. 'Use the stile Davy,' she used to say, 'and save your Gran's darning.'

There was a polite knock at the door. He slowly came in, stroked the cat for a minute and sat down.

'Well, what's news my fickle friend,' June spoke in mock reproach.

The boy looked slightly abashed. He finished stroking the cat and Katy meowed for more. 'I have something to tell you, what Dr Ashleigh said,' he continued after a pause.

June waited, slightly blushing.

'What is it Davy?' She took a deep breath. The boy was in no hurry but stared at the cat. 'Has someone been cutting Katy's whiskers at one side? They look mighty peculiar to me.'

June hastily reassured him that nothing so untoward had happened. (How she wished that "that" was the only problem in her life).

The boy gave a nervous cough. 'Dr Ashleigh said I had to tell you,' he paused again and June could have shaken him at that moment out of excitement and frustration, 'that you should let me keep pigeons in that dovecote.'

June inwardly groaned in disappointment. 'Is that all?' she said brusquely, turning away to hide her face.

'Yes, that was the main gist of what he said. I'll pay for the corn and oats of course, not take it out of the hen feed or anything like that,' he added honestly.

June smiled and reached over and kissed him on the brow. 'Davy with that lovely smile, perhaps I'll wait for you.'

They both burst out laughing.

June went to the kitchen and returned with some lemonade, freshly made by the Matriarch. He sipped the drink in pleasure. 'It might not be a bad thing June, if I'm

349

a top thatcher with a steady income.'

'There's little chance of thatching in your curriculum David, Dr MacKenzie will see to that!'

The boy looked sad for a minute. 'Grandfather says I've got to go away to school next autumn.' He shook his head. 'I do like this school and I was looking forward to that extension you're making,' his voice brightened. 'They say there's going to be a woodwork area and more.'

June laughed again.' I wonder if you'll come back as a doctor, be the second Dr MacKenzie in the dales. What a proud moment that would be!'

David smiled and wriggled in the chair just managing to avoid spilling some of the sticky drink, a potential calamity which almost threw him into alarm. Dr Ashleigh said just that this morning. He said, 'Davy boy, since I'm never going to return, work hard and in ten years or so you'll be the Dr MacKenzie of the valley.'

June bit her trembling lip.

The boy fed the hens, innocent of the inner turmoil he had evoked. Happy to have two friends, probably the nicest in the world!

Chapter 61. A rose by any other name.

Agnes Norman had one favourite child above all others and that was her second son - Russell. Handsome, affable, reliable and kind - he was universally popular with the folk in the dales, and the women were no exception.

But he eschewed a steady courting, content to flit the field like a wayward butterfly, forever seeking new conquests. That May evening found him in the 'Frozen Plough'. Mabel lounged over the bar, smiling in a coquettish sort of way. Russell drank shandy beer from a long glass, for the days had been full of toil and the nights too. He felt exhausted; for the lambs had arrived in fits and starts that year and the darkness seemed to encourage problem births, or so it appeared to him.

Mabel sliced a fresh onion and laid it in his cheese sandwich, firming the bread together.

'Thanks Mabel, you're the best,' he exclaimed with a broad smile before taking a generous bite. Willie Pearson chuckled on entering the room, 'if you're speaking of me that's definitely true; a pint of old Tangle-foot, Mabel at your leisure.'

The men exchanged a cordial greeting.

'How's things William.'

'Mostly high notes but some low.'

'Tell us about the low ones then,' continued the farmer not looking up and still chewing, savouring the bitter bite of the cheese.

'To tell you the truth, George is thinking of leaving the band.'

'If that's a roundabout way of getting me to join with my harmonica, forget it! You'd be better off with a pair of spoons.'

'Or a singer,' suggested Mabel.

'Like Ivy,' the farmer laughed but Willie frowned and sighed.

'I wasted my life on that girl... I have, some forty years. Funny, once I got her address about six years back I seemed to lose interest, as if I'd completed my mission in life, so to speak.' He paused and took a long gulp at the frothy beer.

'Once the unobtainable is obtainable, William, it loses its shine,' replied Russell.

Mabel nodded and wiped the bar top with a circular motion of the cloth, as she always did. She laughed, 'at least this top won't, while I'm about to polish it up.'

Russell shrugged his broad shoulders and ate on.

'But I loved her once; missed out though, to an undertaker. Can't have been a cheerful match, cos mainly they're a gloomy breed, although a gin or two tickles their humour after the funeral.' Willie surveyed the wall. 'Loved her at first sight. Knew at the beginning. Sometimes a quick glance means a whole load more than the most careful scrutiny. So it is in life and so it is in love.'

The others concurred.

'Often I said, especially when she were a widow, George do you think she'll marry a musical man, a fiddle's a poor substitute for a wife? There's little to be gained for forever practising and playing, even at the most cheerful gatherin's. And it takes up the spare time something seriously.'

Russell slapped him on the back. 'The time is right, William esquire for a trip to the homestead beyond Cranford Dale. I'm marketing some bullocks that way in a week, so stand by for action. Just give me that address and I'll sort it out!'

Mabel watched Willie laboriously write it down on a piece of paper, mouthing each word as he progressed along the line. 'There!' he said with some satisfaction. ''Tis done and to hell with it.'

Mabel took up the conversation. Her voice was so suddenly solemn that Willie started. 'There be less than six hundred odd souls in this village at the best of times', she began.

'True,' replied Willie waiting.

'Yet seven dead, Lord have mercy upon them.'

Russell looked up. 'Aye! George Havelock's lad, the Lowry twins Bobby and Billy, Don Pattinson and,' he paused for a second, 'and our John, Martin and Joseph. Such fine men, what a waste, what a waste!'

Willie continued, 'Don't forget the eighteen wounded from these parts as well; two boys lost a leg a piece. Doomed for farmin' forever, they be.'

'What I am driving at,' said Mabel shaking her head, 'me and my man have agreed to change the name.'

'You're not going to be Braithwaite any more?' exclaimed Willie putting down his beer with a thump that spilled froth onto the bar top to the landlady's annoyance.

'No stupid, the pub!'

Such a major happening took the two drinkers by surprise.

'The pub! What to?' asked Russell.

'The Local Heroes,' responded Mabel triumphantly.

'We'll drink to that!' was uttered simultaneously.

'And on the house,' said Mabel smiling. After she had pulled the drinks she continued. 'And what is more, we have commissioned a statue of a soldier, with gun aloft standing remorselessly defiant. It can go in the square outside this pub. We'll ask George to carve the names at the base.'

'There's enough men to bring a marble block from Cranford Dale. I'll get one of June's wagons. While the figure can be a hard rock, not sandstone, and I know just the man to carve it,' said Russell as he smoothed back his long dark hair which had fallen across his brow in the excitement. 'And I also know just the man to advise us on the uniform and bearing.'

'The Captain', said Mabel in advance of the farmer's

remarks and thus cutting him out of the conversation.

'If he can give up painting June's portrait,' said Russell innocently and in a weary tone.

Mabel looked into the farmer's face but gleaned nothing more. However, she secretly stored that information in her mind.

'What worries me,' said Russell, 'is that he seems mighty slow about his contract. I've a feeling he means to be there for some while; and what if I should fancy taking a wife.'

Mabel shrieked with laughter and Willie said that remark was worth a free pint. Mabel agreed it was 'good', but not 'that good'. 'And anyway at this rate she'd be bankrupt for life and moving in as a housekeeper to the Captain pretty soon.'

'Well,' said Willie in good humour, 'if you're takin' up in that line, Mabel, how about looking after me, a lonely bachelor with my mother two years gone.'

Russell laughed, William, the Captain's a better bet for any woman, with his money and all that.'

To which Mabel concurred, and day-dreamed for a minute as to what might have been if she had been a single woman, smiling constantly. But at what, she did not tell.

The clock struck the hour and Russell yawned and stretched his arms. Sorrel pushed herself forward from under the settle.

'Home James, and don't spare the horses,' joked Willie brandishing his glass in a fond farewell to his friend.

Mabel watched them go as another customer opened the door. She did not look up for a second lost in her thoughts. 'Airs and graces, now! And a portrait! No one knows better than me that's there's no smoke without fire!' Then she looked at the chimney breast for inspiration.

Chapter 62. A moonlit night.

June was in bed, thinking; and the night had a surprise in store. She watched the last lingering light of sunset, an insipid hue as it reached the dome of the sky from behind the farm. A brooding moon appeared, hazy in the fine clouds that hung about its fleeting face, clouds that were more a wash of steam than heavenly forms. The cows were as silhouettes in the sunburnt intake of the clumps of trees, where the ground was firm and dry, and the night shadows cool and free of fretful flies.

She heard the ponderous step of Vulcan in the paddock field, shuffling his hooves at times and softly chuntering in his loneliness.

It was almost the only valley sound.

She lay in total silence for a while, looking at the sky. Occasionally a fitful wisp of air would creak the byre door, and the sound would spill in small vibrations round the stable yard and echo though her open window; the window that surveyed her wealth and power.

How suddenly she yearned for her childhood again; to experience that inner longing, so suppressed. She felt her small hands grasping the coins so tightly that it almost hurt, afraid to let them fall. And the hens, sitting in long rows, reluctant to reveal the concealed egg. Squawking birds, and flapping roosters. How that old bantam cock ruled the cobblestone yard at South Hadley. Better than any flock of geese, he made that rectangle his own with strident call and strutting pomp.

She gazed wistfully at the moon as its face broadened

from behind the outhouse roof. 'The moon's fixed gaze, so clear and unremitting,' she muttered to herself. But she felt restless, sensing a feeling of loneliness she had never experienced before. For a few moments it made her ache inside. She wished she could feel as placid and sweet like Mary always used to appear. But her life seemed to have an inner turmoil with so many unexpected reverberations. 'Still it was an exciting existence, not dull and.... definitely not boring.' she told herself.

She arose and sat on the broad window-sill, her light nightgown pulled tightly around her bent knees as she reclined with her head against the side wall. The gentleness of the air from the open window dispelled sleep and freshened her senses. She smoothed back her hair from her brow and the occasional sudden chillness of the breeze across her face made her frame tingle and become alive. Outside the summer air was humid, but the cool rushing vapour held the smell of pine needles and fresh cut hay. It beckoned her outside towards the purple mountains.

She listened to the silence and looked. She wished for Julian to return. She held her breath for a brief moment.

She suddenly became aware that she had to see him, even if it meant leaving the business for a week, and travelling to London; and she could see Mary in Oxford at the same time... and perhaps seek her advice.

The matter seemed to resolve itself in a second's thought. A worry of weeks had suddenly gone. She would head to London, the solution was simple. Except what would she say? She paused and closed her eyes. What could she say?

She took a deep breath. Tell the truth, her mother would remark, and you will have to remember nothing else. She looked at the moon's primrose haze and marked its gentle movement against the long outline of the roof, and listened to the faint call of a nightjar in the wood, and felt so lonely.

Her restlessness increased. The agitated breeze continued to flutter her hair and whisper across her cheeks. The restlessness overwhelmed her emotions.

Now she had to get dressed. She had to go out. Quickly pulling on an old blue jumper and a black skirt so that they brushed directly against the folds of her soft skin, she surveyed herself. 'Bizarre,' she thought, 'going out like this, I look like a potato-picker'. And she laughed again, ruffled her hair and strode positively into the night.

Sorrel slipped out of the door, unbidden and unnoticed. She trotted by June's side, scenting a vixen on the wind but with restraint keeping protectively close to the girl.

June wandered down the long meadow, past the startled cows which paused in their cud chewing to sniff and snort at the dog. Sorrel was oblivious to their moods, winding her way through the grass studded with buttercups and pignut.

A night moth wheeled above them both and was lost in the endless shadow of Scarth Wood. The half-shadow gloom gave the river and forest glade the sheen of coloured glass, with hesitant shafts of light reflected from the still pools emphasising the beauty and stillness around her. Clear, pure and distinct was the valley before below.

June reached the stile by the Top Road and sat down. She instinctively pulled back the coping stone of old.

And there was the message; a square of folded paper as before. 'It has probably been there for ages,' was her first consoling thought, although she had a nervous energy as she opened it.

But the hesitant light of the moon made it difficult to read. So she screwed up her eyes with both effort and vexation. "Dearest June, I pray you will look in our old secret place. If you do, well... I suppose you will be surprised to find this note and even more surprised to find that I still love you so much." She read on in the gloom. "I have agonised about meeting you after all these years. I have missed you, but the War has so interrupted my studies, although my knowledge of treating infections after major injuries gave me the chance to continue in London, working with the injured troops who had been shipped home. Darling June, do not forget how it used to be. I suddenly felt so alien and so unwanted when I recently returned to the Vale and that is why I did not see you. Later I realised how foolish I had been. I really regret that it has been so long since we saw each other, but I do hope we can start again - that is my one hope. Please believe me! Love, as always. Julian."

Then came his address and the telephone number of the hospital.

Why had she not thought of this before? She could ring him. Yes! Speak to him. It might be awkward at first, but after a few seconds of hearing each other's voice, all would be fine. Instinctively June was apprehensive. She consoled herself with the final conclusion. 'All would be well!' But she frowned in exasperation, 'Is this the best way to handle the situation? It's got to be!'

So in a few hesitant moments June managed to persuade herself on her best course of action and as she pondered the future began to take shape in her imagination.

Once more she gazed at the note in disbelief. Sorrel whimpered and sat down, the pure white patches on her face and legs were accentuated, almost ghost-like, in the darkness. Her ears swivelled and pointed towards the Top Road.

June put down the paper to think.

But in a second it had gone. There was no wind, only the firm hand of Thomas Cranmer. He pulled her off the stile and into his arms.

Sorrel wagged her tail, and suppressed the growl as the soldier kissed her mistress not once but a dozen times and more.

The wind picked up the half-read message from the wall. It held it stiffly in the moonlight. Then without further ado it swirled the note away.

The paper flitted like a moth and into the endless darkness of Scarth Wood.

Chapter 63. The snare.

The non-breeding vixen slunk through the shadows avoiding the pale moonlight whenever it could. The five cubs were now in the process of change. Just over six weeks old, their blue eyes were altering to a permanent brown and their dark colour was assuming the reddish over-hue.

And they were hungry.

Their mother was with them in the den under the old oak tree roots just at the outreach of Scarth Wood. The farms had offered so little that night, not even a hedge bird or mouse. She paused and sniffed the gentle breeze, her coat now bedraggled by the summer moult. She smelt the dog-smell in the air and the human presence nearby.

Out of caution she took the long way round the fields, waiting at the Top Road until another human shape had hurried past. Then with a short snuff and a swinging of the tail she scampered over, slinking swiftly to her customary entrance in the thicket, but shedding some tufts of hair as she passed. She left the man and the girl to their lives. Hurrying in a loping run her instinct led her on, to where the food must surely be. The moon was in its fullest face, but she did not need a guiding light.

Straight to the trap! At first hiding in the grassy depressions closeby, where a small burn ran in uncertain loops and rushes. The vixen heard the distant cascading roar of the waterfall as it left the narrow reaches on the high rock with its bluff of heather and fern. Her senses worked beyond that sound, her ears flickered in several directions and then became still and pointing. She moved forward, slowly creeping to the briar thicket, dark and protective where the man-smell was strong and repugnant.

Above her head dangled a dead hare, caught by its neck in a wire snare. The vixen gave a bound, tugging with a powerful jerking motion of her body. The noose gave and the prize was hers.

The waterfall continued its rushing course, and a summer's night stillness overwhelmed the wood.

Very early next morning there was a rasp of boots to

break the silence, a shuffling gait in the dew. The footsteps crossed towards the trees just behind the falling water.

A man, somewhere between the ages of sixty five and eighty, such had the years erased his features, growled in disappointment, and Wexham Tanner spat with despair. His coarse – woven poacher's jacket with its voluminous pockets was still empty. The black flat-topped cap sat angled back from his brow. He pushed it back a shade further. 'Blast it if it were a fox or a stoat, or a crow come to that! Those beggars are t'worst poachers amongst us! Dang me if I'm not an 'onest un by comparison, and that's furest estimate th' can get!'

He looked around for a minute, 'I'll soon tell which un it were.'

Now had the fox hunted elsewhere that night, all would have been well. But the poacher as he strode around the far end of the thicket and with his usual sharp eye said, 'Fox' and 'What the devil's this?' almost as one.

Caught on the thorns of a bramble fluttered the paper; the message from the night before.

Wexham gingerly took it down and scrutinised it intently for a few seconds. 'A note eh! Written by someone!' Having reached that startling conclusion the old man put it in his pocket, neatly folded, and shuffled off to another trap. 'Pity when a man can't read,' he muttered to himself as he swished through the undergrowth. 'But no odds! I'll have a rabbit or two for Mabel before the sun gets high, and she can tell us what it be about.'

Content with this conclusion, the poacher went on his way.

Chapter 64. The message goes on its way.

The first day of June 1919 - her birthday month and the sun was excluded by long curtains pulled close, creating an oppressive warmth; and a girl in bed at eight in the morning. The golden light of a friendly sun that tried its best to force a way into the large bedroom, but in vain.

June had just awakened.

Russell had loaded the beef cattle on to one of their newly acquired lorries and was on his way to the town at the head of a nearby dale; a small expanding industrial conurbation, ill-formed by heavy industry and quick profit. June had not heard him go. She was still exhausted and turned over in bed, pulling the pillow in a close crook to her head. She was filled with an innate happiness that seemed to hang about her like that misty breath-cloud on a frosty day. She opened her eyes as widely as she could, focussed on the blue folds of the velvet curtains, rubbed them for a second or two and then smiled to herself.

'She was in love!'

'She wasn't in love!'

She was undecided. She was suddenly wide-awake, and knew she could doze no more.

'Julian or Tom?' The same old enigma! 'Julian or Tom?' She suppressed another smile. 'Could she love two men at once? Was it possible?' She pondered these questions. And then another sprang into her mind. 'Do I love them both without being in love? There is a difference,' she concluded with a sigh.

Her first reaction was 'to pray to instinct'. She gazed at the bright lights refracting from the mirror where the cut-glass edges touched the wall. 'One was purely an idolised image from the past, but such an intense image; the other was a tangible, physical reality of the present'. For a moment she saw them both so clearly, but the visions faded. 'Perhaps it would be better to throw a coin and let fate decide, but what a way to give up the future.' June said to herself with a gentle laugh.

She continued watching the clouds scud over the distant fells. 'Perhaps it would be even better,' she decided, 'to forget them both, at least, for a while, and get a few luxurious minutes of rest.' She settled back on the pillows.

At one moment she was exhilarated; the next moment she was calm. 'Perhaps neither loves me really,' she reasoned in a subdued moment, perhaps they find something lacking in my personality, my demeanour or even my education.' Briefly saddened by these conclusions she turned over once again, and her thoughts returned to the exhilaration of the early hours that morning.

The sun moved across the curtains, and broke through the join. As she gazed at the more defined shafts of light June felt that she had rediscovered life. Why she felt like that, she did not fully understand. But for the first time she considered herself an adult, with all of life's complexities and emotions, and that her childhood and youth had vanished into the past forever. Now she craved more power, more control of her future, and if that meant more wealth, so be it.

But as she lay contemplating her future the bright shafts struck the old leather bible left on the dresser, her Mother's bible. It was as if she had returned to council and to warn. Thus June came to another decision. She could not endure more than a certain amount of affection. She would have to break free from their cloying love, any feeling of possessiveness.

Content with the sudden change of emotion, she pressed her warm body firmly against the mattress and pushed her face against the soft pillow and tried to close her eyes. She laughed again, in an impulsive way. 'It was great to be young in this new woman's world. Women had never had such freedom and power. She had a thousand things to do, and all could wait for a few more luxurious minutes of contemplation... and rest.'

Grandma Wetherall called loudly from downstairs. But June ignored her. How calm the sunshine made her room as it toyed with the curtains. How calm the retaining hand of summer's heat, how compact it made the lying cows by Scarth Wood. She could see them in her mind's eye - stirring, grazing with heads down, and trampling the grass where she had lain that very morning. 'And Tom, what was he thinking now?'

She did not pause to consider a possible answer, but lay for a further five minutes before she got up, stretch-ing slowly.

She had never felt so optimistic or so happy. She sang

softly, life had never been better, 'Another summer's day to enjoy!'

But nothing is quite so simple. For unknown to June the message slowly shuffled up the valley. The poacher stopped to watch a travelling group of Gypsies raising a dusty cloud, obscuring the wild roses that lined the highway; the fell ponies plodded past, with rattling caravans and grinning occupants with deep brown faces.

The poacher nodded, knowing some. He hit out at the odd slinking lurcher that sniffed inquisitively at his bulging pockets. 'Four rabbits and good uns too,' he muttered, 'that's all those damned dogs'll get from me.' He stick whistled through the air then suddenly stopped short. The poacher peered through the dust; for as it began to settle a Gypsy boy stepped out of the haze, all smiles.

The old poacher stopped shuffling and surveyed the child from head to foot. But his eyes had deceived him. It was young David MacKenzie homeward bound.

'Tis you, young Davy lad,' Wexham said at length, 'and what be you about on this roastin' morn?'

'Very little Mr Tanner,' replied David earnestly, 'considering I should be at school. But my throat's been bad and Grandfather has given me the day off.'

'Has it now! Well, it's probably tonsils, Davy, but you grandfa'ther'll know best. Suffered a bit mysel' when I was about your age.'

'Really,' replied the young boy, amused by the reference to the old man's youth, which by his rapid calculations must have been a long while ago. 'Did you have them out, Mr Tanner?'

'Couldn't afford it, me Dad being only a quarry blaster, in Dr Ashleigh's grandfather's day. Never had a real quinsy tho.'

The young boy mused on this fact for a second or so. 'Do they ever hurt now, Mr Tanner?'

'No son, they don't, praise be the Lord.'

The boy continued thinking. 'Pity in one way, Mr Tanner, for it's not too bad having a sore throat, and with a day off now and then.' The old man nodded and walked on in his slow, ambling, heavy-footed way. The boy easily strode by his side. 'Caught much today?' David asked at length.

The poacher nodded again and gave a sly wink. 'Four! Four beauties. Mabel'll knock up a pie or two and I'll get a couple at least'. He gave another wink.

The boy winked back. Not very professionally like the poacher, but with both eyes moving in unison.

'Here, look at this pair!' He pulled out the dead animals and stretched them in his hands.

David surveyed the catch. Then said, 'What's this', very quickly as he stooped to pick up the folded paper that had fluttered down and onto the road. 'Here's your letter Mr Tanner,' he said politely handing back the message. The old poacher looked at it upside down.

'Thanks David lad,' and proceeded to place it back into his side pocket.

'I wouldn't put it there, Mr Tanner,' continued the boy, 'it'll get all bloody.'

'Well, bless my soul, it be already!' exclaimed the old man.

David looked at the crimson stains across the page.

'Who is it for?'

'Mabel.'

'A recipe?'

'Don't rightly know,' replied the poacher in an awkward voice, still shuffling along the highway and peering at the note in all directions.

'I tell you what! I will write it out again if you wish.'

The old man stopped and contemplated the stained paper. 'The same, mark you!'

'Of course the same, Mr Tanner! Or would you like me to read it to you?'

The poacher laughed. 'Writing will be fine me lad, cos Mabel will tell me all about it. It might be grown up stuff, you never can tell!'

David was away in an instant, home and back again before the old man had covered a half-mile.

The young boy ran up panting, pencil in hand, with a piece of official looking notepaper, a remnant from a visit to his grandfather's surgery.

He waited.

The poacher scrolled through his pocket having taken out and deposited the message at least half a dozen times before finally, with a shrug, handing over the piece of paper.

David wrote out the new message as neatly as he could. 'There Mr Tanner, it's not marked and the better for it.'

The poacher smiled. 'The next night line I set, Davy, and the sea-trout's yours.' He rubbed his gnarled hands.

'I'll throw away this old scrap of paper,' said the boy laughing, 'but don't forget about the fish Mr Tanner, I won't.'

The old man rubbed his chin thoughtfully. 'I bet he won't, if he's like the old grandfa'ther, for he rarely missed a bill in his life!'

Mabel was delighted. She made four pies, two with carrots and peas, two plain.

Mr Tanner was pleased with his two. He had waited

expectantly while she read the note, with a fixed smile on his face and a craning forward in anticipation.

'It's only some kiddies' homework, Wexham, declining a few verbs and the like.' She handed back the paper with a shrug of the shoulders.

'Seems a rum job, declining a few words in t' wood when there's game about,' declared the poacher. 'Better no education for some,' he added ruefully, 'and a happier life.'

Mabel laughed and gave him a gooseberry tart for luck. So he shuffled off home content in the certain knowledge that for him, at least, ignorance was bliss.

Chapter 65. A lonely night.

David MacKenzie, being pleased with his luck, had no reason to doubt, in his innocent view on life, that anything else could go wrong.

In that fact, he was sadly mistaken.

Still, as the mid-afternoon approached and having helped his father to wash the pots and pans, the youngster made for the open country, on what was a perfect summer's day; there was not a cloud to embarrass the sky; and the wheeling swifts, martins and swallows had the unbroken blue all to themselves.

But David's behaviour would have aroused interest in all but the casual observer. First he stood stiffly on the riverbank. Then he bent on hands and knees surveying the lie of Iris Force Burn intently. Satisfied as to the lack of impediments over the next quarter of a mile he stood stiffly once more with one hand outstretched. Then with a quick flick of the wrist up went three small pieces of wood, each accurately measured to four inches in length and coloured with a spot of red, yellow and blue respectively. Into the fast flowing water they went, swirling and disappearing into the many small waves that leapt and chopped over the array of rocks.

The red one led, with that he was well pleased.

The blue vanished beneath a particularly generous wave and was not seen again for five minutes. The yellow one stuck in the rushes. Off darted the red. The boy ran along the bank, tripping once in his haste and grazing his right hand.

He was up in a flash. Fifty yards to go and the red boat had won.

But alas, the red spot spun round and round in a swirl of foam, near the overhanging bank. On came the yellow; straight as an arrow. It swept past the final marker, a large fallen willow that straddled the burn.

David accepted defeat by throwing a small brick at the red wood to give it a new lease of life and went on his way to Low Green Farm. Reaching the paddock field next to the house he took the message out of his pocket, looked at it for a short while, and walked towards the door.

He knocked; he would give it to June in secret and depart. He heard Grandma Wetherall's, 'Come in!' And in he went, with jaunty step.

Then he stopped short, undecided. For June was not there, only Russell and the Captain sat in lounge. They turned, smiled and said, 'Hello!'

Russell ruffled the boy's short hair. David sat down slightly discomfited, still clutching the folded paper. The Matriarch was the first to notice. 'Heaven's child, what have you done to your hand. There's even blood on that letter.'

David looked down in alarm; then laughed. 'It's only

a graze Mrs Wetherall. It happened when I was racing my stick-boats in the burn. The best one lost!' he added in a factual way.

The Captain reached forward and took hold of the boy's right hand and looked at it closely. 'Well, I'm sorry to hear that!' he said chuckling, 'but it is only a small wound you've got Davy, and a little antiseptic will do it no harm.'

But Russell did not speak. He was reading the note he had taken from the boy's hand; and the Captain glanced at it also.

Nothing more was said about the letter and Russell put it in his jacket pocket. David regained his jauntiness and humour.

However, that night he lay in bed thinking. 'Have I let down Dr Ashleigh?' kept going round his mind in an unbroken wheel. 'I hope not! I really hope not!' He tried to console himself as best he could.

But it was a worrying night - and a lonely one too.

Chapter 66. The sound of breaking glass.

June's exasperation knew no bounds; she had successfully negotiated the land purchase and architectural details of the new offices, and the Town Council had eagerly agreed. Her new maroon Daimler with a black roof was the admiration of the Dales. The tree-felling was proceeding apace.

And here, to spoil it all, was a rumour.

She would confront Mabel Braithwaite. For three days June had not seen her young helper. She thought she would call on David in the village and show him the car; a demonstration ride with the driver, who was giving her instructions. 'How new fangled everything seemed after a pony and trap'. She sighed. But for old time's sake she thought she would walk to the village and get some exercise.

The midsummer weather continued hot and the hay was ready to come down, early for that part of England. She looked towards South Hadley Farm but there was no sign of Thomas, he too had been missing for the last three days. She would call on him later that afternoon, business permitting.'

The Front Street was unduly quiet for eleven thirty. She paused at the Co-operative Store, greeted Mr Penruddock the manager, handed in her order, and walked briskly to 'The Local Heroes' as the new sign proclaimed. She paused for a second to collect her breath and walked in.

It was a strange experience. She had often wondered what the inside of a public house would look like, but the dinginess and stale odours slightly repelled, and the horrid dark curtains made the room dingy, despite the overall spit and polish of the place. She noticed how the horse-brasses gleamed, and she gazed at them for a short while before reaching to ring the small hand-bell on the shiny bar top.

'I just knew it,' the voice paused (belonging to the unseen face and figure of Vera Bowes), 'that woman would have the effrontery to do it, the jumped-up trollop.' There was a pause while Vera moved some crockery in the kitchen.

'Over there Vera', said Mabel, also hidden from view, 'near those rabbit pies.'

There was further movement of pots and chinking utensils. For a while there was a murmur of conversation, constant and companionable like a steady drone of bees. She heard a poker rattling in the fire and a hissing of steam and the chattering of a pan lid dancing in tune.

'Such airs and graces, I've not seen before. Flashing the money around as if it had just come into fashion.' The words were barely audible against the background noise and June strained her senses.

She began to take a deep interest in the conversation and put down the bell as gently as possible. It tinkled for a brief moment.

'I'll be through in a second,' sang out the landlady.

June dodged behind the half open door to the back yard. Mabel's shadow appeared in the kitchen doorway, but only for an instant and then disappeared back in. June heard her say "My mind's playing me tricks" before a whipping of batter drowned the conversation once again.

June paused, undecided what to do. Then she quickly moved closer but could only hear fragments against the beating and rattling, until the rapid stirring stopped with the comment from Mabel, 'Mind you, Vera, she's been carrying on somewhat shamefully with the Captain. Painting her picture, fiddle-de-sticks!' They both laughed. 'I'd be up to more than that,' continued the landlady laughing, 'and I'm twice her age.'

Vera shrieked with amusement then added, 'She can stop the chasing, for you've got more passion,' said the waspish sister, her voice becoming shriller with each vowel, 'in your little finger than she has...'

But she did not finish. For a large pint glass hurtled into the kitchen and crashed on the wall. Half a dozen pans cascaded down in an unrehearsed crescendo.

They both stopped laughing, struck dumb by amazement and fear.

June called in, 'For God's sake shut up and mind your own business,' but feeling that was not enough rapidly continued, 'if you were to run after Captain Cranmer, Vera Bowes you wouldn't get far, with legs like tree trunks, they're better served for kindling wood than speed'. She paused to take a deep breath. 'And you, Mabel Braithwaite, can pull your hair out with jealousy if you like, but don't forget to add some Brasso blacking polish from the grate, it will hide the roots when they grow back in, or you'll pass as a badger, and that's the worst thing I've said about an animal in years!'

With that closing remark she slammed the door, left the inn in high dudgeon and strode across the village square. The more she fumed the more she felt dissatisfied with her own behaviour. 'Why haven't I been ladylike, elegant, and supercilious, as an important, rich businesswoman should be? Perhaps its my lack of education and the refinement that goes with it. At least I shouldn't be yelling like a fishwife,' then she consoled herself, 'to those jealous old crones.'

Hurrying up the hill to the Top Road she saw the white blur of the church. How she wished she had Julian's telephone number. She told herself, 'How stupid of me to throw it away.' She stamped in annoyance scattering small clouds of dust over her shoes.

Then looking at the peaceful ribbon of houses in the valley below her, the pastel shade of green, the ever compact woods, and the darting swallows, she smiled and said, 'Stuff them all', three times. 'People can stomach everything but success, as my mother used to say, but they always make a meal out of failure!'

June laughed and wandered home - altogether in a better mood than when she began.

Chapter 67. New resolutions.

'Reverend Clenham,' began June, the Minister having stayed for lunch on the same day as the incident in the public house, 'do you think, at first impression, that I am anything more than (she hesitated and the Vicar put down his coffee cup)... than pretty. If that's the right word.'

'June, you are in the eyes of the Lord - beautiful, sometimes wilful, very kind and considerate, intelligent and a woman of great character, in fact for your age, an extraordinary woman. Beyond that I can say no more!' He smiled and sat back in the chair.

June had not expected that reply and felt slightly abashed.

But Grandma Wetherall, listening from the kitchen as usual, looked extremely pleased, wandered in and offered him a piece of Wensleydale cheese. 'Always the finest after a good meal, it'll aid in the digestion,' she stated firmly, her blue eyes twinkling, her grey hair pulled back in a tight bun as usual, 'finish on cheese Vicar and you've dined well.'

June was deep in thought for the moment as she half-listened to the clock beating away in sonorous tones. 'I mean... well I lack refinement through a lack of education, I mean your sort of university learning.' She wrung her hands and the Matriarch interjected. 'There's more to life than forever nosing about in books, 'least that's what Francis Bacon said!' The old lady looked very regal and superior after this statement.

'True Mrs Wetherall, you are perfectly correct,' replied the Minister. 'There is an ignorance of the learned.'

June still looked pensive. 'I behaved in a foolish,

boorish manner this morning and, having flown into a rage, called Mabel Braithwaite and Vera Bowes some unkind things, made personal remarks and...'

'Heaven help us honey if you said anything that'll sting those crabby old wasps,' laughed the Matriarch clapping her hands and showering crumbs from a ginger biscuit on the floor. Instantly the two cats disappeared under the settee, thinking that it was an unexpected peal of thunder. 'There's more to life than worrying about what you've said or haven't said. Forget it!'

The Reverend Clenham burst out laughing. 'We all have our moments of weakness. Each Sunday I recite "We have erred and strayed like lost sheep and followed too much the devices and desires of our own heart." He stopped for a second and cleared his throat in his characteristic preaching way. 'Perhaps I have erred the most.'

The two women looked at him in surprise, as he gently sipped his coffee.

'It is so long ago now that I think it must be forever buried, sadly like the person involved.'

He produced such a slight but deeply emotional tremor in his features that the Matriarch and June looked away.

'You have been so kind to me, in every way... kindness personified.' And the young girl reached forward and clasped the Minister's hands, giving one a gentle kiss, 'I do not know what I would have done without you?'

Grandma Wetherall echoed the sentiment. 'Agnes always held you in high regard, Vicar', said the old lady slowly and with affection to the memory of her departed daughter.

The Minister smiled, 'She was an extraordinary woman also, Mrs Wetherall. Not part of my flock,' he stopped for a second, 'but a woman any man would have been proud to marry.'

June looked slightly puzzled but the Matriarch laughed, 'Well, if she'd been in your church you would have married her, but the Wesleyan minister was James Norman's choice at the time.'

The Vicar, pausing for a moment, laughed, 'and a good choice too!'

June still surveyed the smiling face. But there was no trace of any deeper meaning and she let it slip from her mind. 'I mean to educate myself, and with your advice I am willing to purchase a place at a University... providing I can have an initial grounding in the classics. And that is where, - my dearest Vicar -, you can help; paid of course!'

'Unpaid, June, of course! Or there is no agreement. So I do have a slight objection, don't I?'

The Matriarch waited for the answer knowing June's volatile temperament could swing in either direction. But the young girl simply smiled showing her face lighting up, 'You do! But I might ignore it. I will agree, on the condition that one day you will officiate at my wedding.'

The Reverend Clenham had not expected this reply. 'Hardly a penance June,' said the Minister now clapping his hands in mirth after the initial surprise.

'Whatever next?' muttered the Matriarch, also flabbergasted, as she scratched her head by way of inspiration, 'it must be the Captain, lucky man, and a fine fellow he be too!' she thought.

However, at that moment Thomas Cranmer was unaware of such delightful thoughts. His preoccupation was the eventual meeting with June. His one thought was about the note. He went over it and over it again; sometimes he felt profound anger, at other times deep despair. 'How can she do this to me? How can she be so bloody deceitful? She has obviously been told by Russell that I have seen the note, that I know everything. Now she is avoiding me avoiding the dreaded confrontation'. That was the Captain's firm conclusion as he sat gazing out of the window and across the fields, half-hoping she would come. Then, out of the blue, came more moments of anguish and black torment.

Thus his mind raced from one scenario to another; initially almost exploding with rage, to the docile approach of forgiveness. But he was undecided and his weakness gnawed at his very soul. 'Why does June puzzle me so? On the surface she is a very ordinary country girl, isn't she? Perhaps not! Perhaps not!' His voice tailed away and he felt a sudden depression that seemed to compress his thoughts and produce a jumble of emotions. Slightly shaking he sat down in an armchair and rubbed his chin. 'If I married her, I will be rich beyond all expectation, and we can live in a fashionable city. Or would we continue in the relative solitude of the country with, perhaps, a town house? Or am I charging ahead.' He rested his chin in his hands. 'How can I think like this,' he muttered in despair, 'it's irrational, almost bloody obscene.'

There was a brief interlude as he gazed into the valley, 'Yes! How will she react when they next meet? That is the burning question. Probably with remorse! Yet, what if she doesn't have any, ridicules me, and walks away forever.' There was another period of contemplation. 'For God's sake, I must be reasonable, not too angry or severe. Make my point in a firm but gentle way. If all goes well I will propose, sometime soon.'

This thought gave him a sudden thrill of exultation. 'But what if she laughs in his face? My God! No woman has ever done that! But June's so headstrong, and rich! And money brings power and independence. She might be impossible to convince; and what did he have to offer?'

Suddenly the Captain stood up and began pacing round the room as the soldier of old. Round and to the right, forward and back, quick time, halt!

He stopped in front of the walnut corner cupboard. He reached for the bottle of rum on the top shelf, unscrewed the top and gazed at it for a moment. He took a long drink. 'It's just like the bloody good old days, those good old days in the trenches, when everyone faced death and disaster, the blasts and shrapnel and whine of bullets, the encore before the battle begun, that good old time when everyone collapsed in a bloody fountain and bits of flesh flew everywhere' He tried to laugh but it was a fearful, hollow sound. Now, for a heady second, Thomas felt the pent up pounding of his heart, racing in fear before the surge of excitement as the attack began.

He had another drink, a long gulp that burned the back of his throat. Then by a weird aberration of thought, the blast of guns and the roar of shells took over his mind. Suddenly the room began to spin.

He had to steady his nerves. He took a long gulp and then another. Then he began to tremble uncontrollably and sweat poured from his face. The battle was alive and real and for a moment the room vanished and was replaced by the dead and dying, and the cries and groans of screaming men, the terrified leaping into the shell holes for protection. Just as suddenly the battle ended, the sounds receded, leaving a strange echoing vibration, and finally an unreal calmness in his mind.

He felt foolish and collapsed on a chair next to the table, still shaking. Thomas suddenly noticed the unfinished portrait. The face stared back mutely, with a smile. Was it a condescending smile or not? He tried to fathom it out but the more he stared, the more it became enigmatic.

He became vexed. He had to have another long drink. Suddenly his nerves felt steadier. Impulsively he picked up the brush and squeezed out the oil paints, methodically, so methodically, one at a time. How the ribbons of colour waved as his hands trembled.

He started to paint. Slowly, and seeming of its own free-will, the brush moved back and forth. He watched it in mute astonishment, slurring to and fro on the canvas, blurring the beautiful features one by one, - first, the smile, - next, the outstandingly fine cheek bones, - and finally, the eyes, those beautiful eyes, the first features to strike home.

Thomas tried to stop the brush by grasping his wrist but it continued to work with its own volition. There was no other course but to throw it down; it clattered on the stone floor and bounced against the wall. In anger he hurled the paints after it.

Imperceptibly the red paint trickled towards him, it looked like blood; and there was more blood on his hands – another shrapnel wound! In fear he squeezed the sticky red though his fingers and let it drip down his palm and onto his wrist in patterns that fascinated him.

My God! How the shells hissed and screamed in his mind. How tight his chest felt, how his shoulder ached.

Another long drink, and the bottle was finished. He smashed it against the wall, then felt remorse and knelt down collecting the pieces, mopping the liquid with his shirt cuff, scratching and scraping his hands as he went, so that tiny droplets of blood melted into the crimsoned skin.

Thomas looked up from his praying position; the painting leered back, a weird vision of buried loveliness. But the eyes followed him as he crawled around the room, remarkable eyes that seemed to smile at him through half-shut lids, full of pity and condescension.

He felt trapped by the beauty. 'Looks that will not last,' he repeated. Thomas saw the future in a strange hallucinatory sensation. 'Looks that will ensnare me for some part of my life, until they begin to fade; and what will remain? Only her wealth; and I'll be dependant on this because there's nothing to interest me up here. What can I do? He scanned the canvas once more. "A woman's face, with nature's own hand painted"... yet... "among the wastes of time must go". Shakespeare's sonnets had spoken the truth. He kept repeating, "Mine eye hath play'd the painter", and his hands still trembled and the portrait seemed to tremble also as he grasped the frame, and the scarred features shimmered to and fro.

Ashamed, the Captain looked away. He had to burn the painting - that would be his release from the torments that plagued him; and he needed time to think. To collect himself again! He had to leave Compton Vale. Why? Thomas could not exactly determine. His mind raced in a confusion of images - some bewildering, some cruel... but he had to leave the Dales.

And leave he did. Within three hours he was packed, after tidying and cleaning the house as best he could. He found a penny dated from the year of his birth and pushed it into a small crack in one of the wooden beams, a permanent token of his occupation and an emblem of luck, or so he hoped.

He wrote a hurried note for June and left the money he felt he owed. Then he was gone, down the narrow path from the farm, staggering under the two cases, and the waning influence of the rum. The sheep cropping in the main fields did not look up.

The sky was reddening and he saw the two border collies slowly winding their way up the cliff-side to the meeting line of the reds and greens and blues.

He paused on the Top Road and put down the cases. There was a moment of regret. He said, 'Goodbye Darling,' in a quiet voice, almost nervously and reluctantly. Then he decided to hurry on to the house where he could order his taxi, and quickly return for the bags. They would be safe.

But as he surveyed the quiet valley below he knew, in his heart of hearts, that he would not come back.

And the portrait was gone, burnt in the barn with some of his sketches, poetry and notebooks.

Old Baty's taxi, the first in the Dales, rattled along the valley roads to York station. He was a kindly old man and he swore faithfully he would deliver the note, when he got back. Although it would probably be the next day, by his reckoning, since he was busy that evening.

It was a tedious drive in the warmth of the summer's night. Captain Thomas Cranmer felt both dejected and resolute, although he did wonder what emotions June would feel the following morning when she found he had gone.

However, June was to find he had left sooner than the Captain thought - but not in the way he envisaged, or ever knew.

Chapter 68. Sam goes missing.

On the same afternoon, as Captain Thomas Cranmer made resolute plans to depart, June sat pensive but happy, wading through the half-year accounts. If she was happy in the morning, she was even happier now! She had expected a small profit in view of the recent capital expenditure, but the logging had gone so well and the sale of land in Cranford Dale for building had been such a success (for the parish council had waived all building regulations in the return for the much needed cheaper homes) that she surveyed the balance sheet with a mixture of pleasure and satisfaction.

There was another two thousand pounds to be banked. As she gazed at the valley, peaceful in the shafts of afternoon sun that broke free from the clouds, she made her plans for the future. There would be a full time manager and several clerks to oversee the business. Then she could finish her education and, she hoped, act and appear more refined.

'One snag,' she said quietly, 'where should I live?' The incident at 'The Local Heroes' had upset her in more ways than one, as she had expressed to the Minister. And unknown to her, Mabel and Vera had decided to remain silent, money and power being a subjugating influence in their case, June was firmly fixed on a move to a mansion or hall, no less.

She now had the money. Russell would continue in the farm and Grandma could choose where she wanted to live.

Lost in these thoughts the warm summer's night grew slowly inward.

The two dogs left for their nightly wander up the local fells, as the sky coloured behind the purplish silhouette of the crags. Sam wandered along somewhat less exuberantly due to the increasing stiffness in his legs, while his deafness and failing vision made him less adept at negotiating the winding paths and boulders on the inclines. Sorrel charged ahead as playfully as ever.

June's meditations were broken for a second as she looked at the telephone hanging on the wall. She heard Russell enter and he shouted through from the hall. 'We've fair cut some fields today, June! The tractors are the best thing since rabbit pie. Old Vulcan could never have charged on at such a pace.'

June laughed in agreement. 'We can hire them out, Russell, after we have done and it will help offset the cost.'

Russell sat down on the settee. June's business sense always impressed him and he was learning quickly too. 'By the way June, I hardly dare mention it but I have a present for you, delivered by young David MacKenzie.'

June waited.

'A letter from an admirer, he brought it a day or two back and I've clean forgotten about it...' the farmer reached into his jacket pocket on the coat hook... 'here it is!'

June looked at the lost letter with astonishment. 'From David?'

'Yes, he must have found it somewhere or other.' Russell paused. 'It has little business with me or Grandma, but the Captain...'

'Thomas, what on earth has he to do with it?' exclaimed the girl fiercely.

Russell stopped short for a second. 'Nothing I suppose.'

'Thomas didn't see it by any chance?'

'He was here and may have glanced at it while I read it, but what the odds, it had nought to do with him as you've said!' said Russell cagily and he looked away for a second or two.

June pursed her lips and frowned. 'So what if he did!'

Russell smiled. 'Yes, so what!' His voice conveyed a feeling of tenderness and slight remorse.

'I will see him tomorrow and no doubt he will have something to say if he's seen it, if not...' tis best forgotten,' she said quickly lapsing into the northern dialect. 'Either way, I don't care!'

Russell walked into the kitchen where Grandma was cooking roast lamb with new potatoes packed round the meat and steadily browning.

'Come and get it!' sang out the Matriarch with a clatter of plates and pans. She strained the cabbage through an old colander. 'Russell be a honey and chop up the mint for the vinegar sauce.'

Russell obliged.

The meal was eaten with much chatting and laughter, the harvest was going well, the lambs never more plentiful since Teesdale breeding had been introduced into the stock, and a handsome profit was assured for the half-year. But despite the joviality there were to be mixed fortunes before that night had fallen.

June sat in an old rocking chair and smiled. She thought of Julian and looked at the wall where the telephone hung. The letter gave her new hope. She would speak to him directly.

Julian's telephone number was smudged but legible. She asked the exchange for the London number. There was a long delay as the request was relayed from operator to operator, like a dozen faint echoes along the wire.

Another wait; the hospital answered curtly. 'Please try his office'. He was not due in the hospital for a further two days. June sighed to herself with disappointment and a feeling of anti-climax, as she wrote the office number down with a slightly shaking hand. She paused as if to make up her mind, and returned to her task.

Another maze of wires and requests! Then a telephone rang. Somewhat indistinct at first; and June felt nervous as she clutched the earpiece.

It was a woman's voice, 'Dr Ashleigh's office, his personal secretary speaking. He is out of the office for an hour, can I take a message?'

June's face went from shock to anger in a instant. She could not speak with astonishment.

The woman repeated the words distinctly, 'Dr Ashleigh's office, his...' But June slammed down the telephone and stood shaking in anger. She pressed her brow against the wall to recover her composure. She paused for a moment, her mind in turmoil from past events and emotions.

She had not spoken to her sister Mary for six years and she refused to speak to her now; and a strange foreboding came over her like a chill breeze, and she thought of the Minister and his concerned face, saying 'There was another Will and a letter to prove it. That I know! That I know!' And the events and calamities tumbled into place. And June stared at the ground for a moment, then looked up - indifferent to that voice forever.

So she took stock of the situation and the people in her life. She could manage alone, if she had to. If that was what life decreed, she would just make it on her own.

Then another apparent calamity to disrupt her mood, for about nine-thirty as darkness began to fall, Sorrel arrived home, her coat muddy, paws wet and her tongue lolling with happiness and fatigue.

She drank copiously as Russell patted her head. But where was Sam? Concerned, the farmer walked to the door and looked across the fields. He whistled but he knew it was no use if the old dog was far off, and being partially deaf.

June hurried to the door. 'What's wrong?' she asked anxiously noticing Russell's serious expression.

'It's Sam! I've never known him not be the first home before. Do you think he has had an accident?'

June became even more fearful and ran to the high stile at the back of the house. There she shouted and scanned the moors in the fading light. She called again and again, her voice more anxious with each call.

'I'm on my way!' Russell had his fell boots on in a minute. 'Sorrel will find him, I don't doubt it,' he tried to sound confident as he climbed over the farm gate.

June watched them disappear over the rise of the hill to Ullock Moor, then reappear for a brief minute as man and dog wound around the side of Dancing Gill. She could here the shrill shepherd-whistle echoing in the quiet summer air.

For it was a warm and tranquil night with an incipient chill on the awakening breeze.

She watched for ten minutes and prepared to go indoors. She had decided that she could do little other than sit and wait.

But the breeze had its own plan. It gathered momentum as it channelled down the Gill towards South Hadley Farm, sweeping across the fields and gently ruffling the new mown hay. Circling around the farmhouse it seemed to disperse, but as it entered the barn door it burst into life again; and so did the grey ash of the afternoon's fire, the remnants of the burnt canvas.

A few embers glowed and died back.

Another short gust more which was more forceful than before; then a further spray of red sparks. Then a more vindictive burst and the sparks spun merrily upwards and around. Most fizzled into oblivion but there was a recalcitrant cloud.

On it swept, upwards and upwards to the newly thatched roof of the house where the straw was tinder dry. The crisp overhang seemed to embrace the sparks for a second.

Then came the glow and smoke almost as one. Up and up curled the fine column of grey and blue, redder and redder glowed the eave above the window, yellow and golden flared the roof. Soon it was a sea of flames.

Meanwhile, although nearly deaf and blind, Sam had a mission.

Lingering on the gully side and unable to cross at the stones so easily jumped by Sorrel, the old dog had sought an alternative route by the lower reaches.

The path took him close to the young vixen's trail and he digressed for a further half mile.

Now he was close to the Church; and that is where he picked up the scent. Not of the fox but a scent he knew better, one he could recall from long ago.

Head down, he was off as quickly as his old limbs would allow; for the smell gave him a new vigour and he barked excitedly.

A stranger, crossing the lower fell, paused to listen, and stood with hands on the stone wall. He looked in amazement. There were flames on the horizon, orange and red tongues pouring out of the windows and roof.

It was a scene he had seen so often before. He leapt the wall and was running towards the lower field in a minute. They had said that no one lived there now but a retired soldier.

'Could anything be done?'

Over the upper fields from Low Green Farm a girl was seen to be racing; he knew it was June. While Russell was visible in the distance; he was scrambling down from the crags, and yelling at the top of his voice.

South Hadley Farm was in flames and the thatch gone although the outbuildings seemingly saved.

But it was Sam, most of all, who summed up the situation. He took a giant bound and for a moment he was the sheepdog of old, landing straight into the outstretched arms of the stranger, almost knocking him to the ground.

For the old dog knew

- he really knew-

- that Martin Norman had come home.

Chapter 69. A Postscript.

This is a story of many sources and beginnings, but of even more endings.

Grandma Wetherall remains as hale and hearty in Low Green Farm, as indomitable a Matriarch as ever, and Russell soon married to a quiet girl from Cranford Dale and moved into Low Green Farm. The old lady was determined to continue as before. Some villagers pitied the poor girl.

Dr Julian Ashleigh works in London; he never returned and Mary works as his secretary but they never got married, although no one cares.

It was believed that Captain Thomas Cranmer did marry and move to Kenya to farm. Little else was ever heard about him again.

Martin is an enigma. He was diagnosed by a variety of specialists as having suffered brain concussion and a fractured skull; with a long period of amnesia, complicated by a form of shell-shock. Initially he was held by the Germans, but why he remained in France is not known – whether through guilt in having to return home as the only survivor or his hand in the fate of John Bowes.

He always considers himself lucky to have come home at all. He regularly visits the war memorial to tend the small garden there, and on the Remembrance Sundays he often gives a dignified address. For in those November misty mornings as the minute's silence ended and the guns broke the gloom of chill autumnal days, all eyes turned to the stone monument in the village square.

Martin rarely speaks of the war, and never met any of his former comrades. He returned to the solitary life he loved, as a shepherd on the moors.

As for June, she never changes from a dynamic, beautiful and vivacious woman. She lives in a fine manor sixteen miles from Compton Vale and as years went by she sold the business to teach and open a centre to help the wounded and their families to find employment. She always says, when asked, that she had moved to kindle new memories and start a new life, but can never forget the past. 'Time protects the images of youth', she often quoted.

The Reverend Clenham lived beyond his three-score years and ten; and is helped by a new curate who dwells in the tithe cottage.

George Havelock died three years after the war ended

- a bitter, broken man. Sadly the war never ended for him.

However, his friend, the violinist Willie Pearson finally married the one he had always loved, his Ivy. One day, as a favour, he was checking the cowling with Russell on a faulty chimney in one of the offices belonging to June. They had begun work at dawn before anyone else had arrived. He had clambered on to the office roof for the fourth time, when the upper rungs of the ladder snapped. He was poised for a second in space and wildly grasped the nearest object, a thick telephone wire. Ivy had just arrived in the office to seek a job as a receptionist. Suddenly a dangling figure was seen through the half-open window, swinging to and fro. She almost collapsed with astonishment. There, to her amazement, was William Pearson slowly spinning in mid-air. But in an unrehearsed display of chivalry he paused to raise his cap as he slipped slowly past, valiantly smiling and trying to look so totally unconcerned, as if such a descent was a natural feature of his trade.

****

As was said at the beginning of this story, to understand the remoteness and appreciate the beauty of Compton Vale requires a walk along the Top Road to the village. One hundred years on and the houses remain unscathed by the Great War, compact and as beautiful as before. But the people changed after that time – they were humbled and saddened by the unnecessary sacrifice and carnage. While they lived, they never forgot the good old times before the War; times that they knew could never return, but were worth savouring, worth reminiscing by the fire-side and in the inns… and life went on and gradually these tales faded as memories gone.

Today there is no case of rights or wrongs for the villagers who sit by the gnarled oak on a summer day; only the realisation that so many lives were lost, "those heroic dead who fed the guns". No one now, who sits in its shade, can recall the boyish laughter, the fun, and the love as it used to be; or those remarkable sacrifices so unselfishly given.

And for those men, with packs and guns and hope, who stumbled on in the needless years when nights were long and days were weary endless hours, they rest now, as one alone... forever.

Dr David Sutherland.

DSc. MB BS.FRCS.Eng. MS. MD. FRCS.Ed. has an international reputation in science and orthopaedic surgery. Honorary surgeon to The FA and England team, UEFA and FIFA, he has written books and articles since 1966. His first book was serialised by the Sunday Times; and his second was published consecutively for eighteen years in five languages. Two others (the first in their genre) on Football Injuries and Femoral Neck Fractures were international best sellers. Awards include the first recipient of the British Orthopaedic Association Research Society Gold Medal (1970), Euro'92 and Euro'96 Final Medals – the first person to receive consecutive medals; and the Press Association Children of Courage (Child Surgery) (1986 & 1993). He was awarded the higher doctorate in science (2010) for his work at Oxford and Durham Universities on the discovery of the use of anti-inflammatory agents in trauma. He is currently a visiting academic to the School of Science and Engineering at Teesside University; and has been a visiting professor to many universities worldwide.